*...edgy novel...ground breaking...without ~~~~~~~~~~~ ~ated by Devorah. ...read this fas~~*

**Richard ~**

*This treatment of the life of ~ ~~~~~~~~~~~~~~~~~~~~~ ical age, bringing new life to old ~*

**Rabbi** ~~~~~~ ~udea

*A must read for anyone seeking to live a life "in spirit."*
**Roselyn Smith**, Ph.D., Clinical Psychology, Florida Licensed Psychologist, author and voice over of "5 Minutes to a Stress Free You"

*"Masterful use of words and imagery, fleshing out the lives of Biblical characters. A must read for anyone interested in Old Testament history!"*
**Beth Gaudio**, Realtor, Coconut Grove, FL

*...wonderful! Steve uses the historical context and the characters, such as Devorah, to impart deep spiritual ideas in a very palatable way. His characters are highly believable and leap off the page.*
**Ilene L. Dillon**, M.S.W., Coach, Parent Educator, Radio Host
Full Power Living, www.emotionalpro.com

# Devorah

## *The Covenant and the Scrolls*
## *Book One*

## Steven Liebowitz, Ed.D.

HARMONY-QUEST PUBLICATIONS

Published by

**Harmony-Quest Publications**
7825 SW 103 Pl
Miami, FL
www.HQPubs.com
sliebowitz@aol.com

**Copyright © 2013 Steven Liebowitz, Ed.D.**
All rights reserved.

No part of this book may be reproduced, stored in a retrieval system, or transmitted by any means, electronic, mechanical, photocopying, recording, or otherwise, without written permission from the author.

ISBN: 978-0-9884755-0-2

This book is printed on acid free paper.

Printed in the USA

# Dedication

"To my wonderful wife, Tanya, without whose support this book would never have been written."

"To my Life Coach, line and content editor, Deki Fox, without whom this book would have been written, but not as well as it is."

# A Note from the Author

*This is a work of historical fiction, based on biblical, scholarly and archeological data. Some characters as well as names for places and things are made up to support the story and are not intended to be correct, accurate or factual. The relevant Old Testament portions are Judges, First Samuel and Second Samuel.*

*The book's inspiration came from a trip to Israel six years ago. We visited the tel at Meggido. A tel is an archeological term for a site that has numerous civilizations one on top of the other. The one at Megido had 35 civilizations going back perhaps 5,000 years! Struck by the multitude of civilizations represented there about which I knew nothing, I resolved to learn more at least about my own Jewish heritage. This book represents some of what I have learned.*

*One of my favorite references was given to me by my brother, Sandy-Joe Liebowitz:* Chronicles News of the Past Volume 1 in the Days of the Bible (From Abraham to Ezra, 1726-444 BCE), *(Reubeni Foundation, 1968). The book is actually printed on newsprint broad sheets to add authenticity, and describes biblical events as a modern contemporary newspaper would.*

# Important Characters and Places in Order of Appearance

**Devorah:** Judge over Israel: spiritual and secular leader

**Lappodoth:** Devorah's husband

**Sar:** Honorific for President

**Haibru:** the Canaanite word for "Hebrew"

**Shiloh:** Small village in central Canaan, north of Jerusalem and Jericoh; home of the High Priest, Malachizer and the Ark of the Covenant

**Moab:** Another Kingdom east of the Dead Sea

**King Jabin:** Leader of the Canaanite Federation

**Hazor:** King Jabin's capital city in what is now Lebanon

**Jezreel Valley:** Much prized fertile land west of Jerusalem, under Canaanite control

**Sisera:** General and Chief of all Canaanite armies

**Charoshet:** Canaanite regional capital, west of Bethlehem, Sisera's headquarters

**Yael:** 'Average' Haibru woman, cousin of Jereboam, wife of Haber, becoming a great Israelite leader

**Haber:** Yael's husband, Kenite – a non-Haibru tribe, artisan, and tinsmith

**Kenites:** a non-Haibru tribe, cooperating with the Haibrus

**Jereboam:** Yael's cousin, a warrior captured and tortured by the Canaanites

**Betheena:** A Canaanite royal princes; Sisera's mother

**Melka:** Betheena's body slave

**Atrim:** Canaanite King before Jabin

**Zeber** and **Sostrum:** Sisera's two adjutants

**majlise:** a town hall public forum community meeting

**Barak:** Haibru General and Commander in Chief

**Hakim Saul:** Doctor Saul, a healer and physician

**Asmara:** powerful Priestess of Astarte in Charoshet

**Elkanta:** body slave to Asmara

**Malachizer:** High Priest in Shiloh; keeper of the Scrolls and the Ark of the Covenant

**Tzevah:** Honorific for Captain

**Abimelech:** Devorah's newborn son

**Janina:** Mother of King Saul and his sister, Abadantha, 137 years after Devorah

**Abadantha, Dantha for short:** Sister of King Saul and daughter of Janina

**The Teaching:** Established by Devorah and passed matrilinealy--the explanation of the Covenant as an alternative to the Scrolls

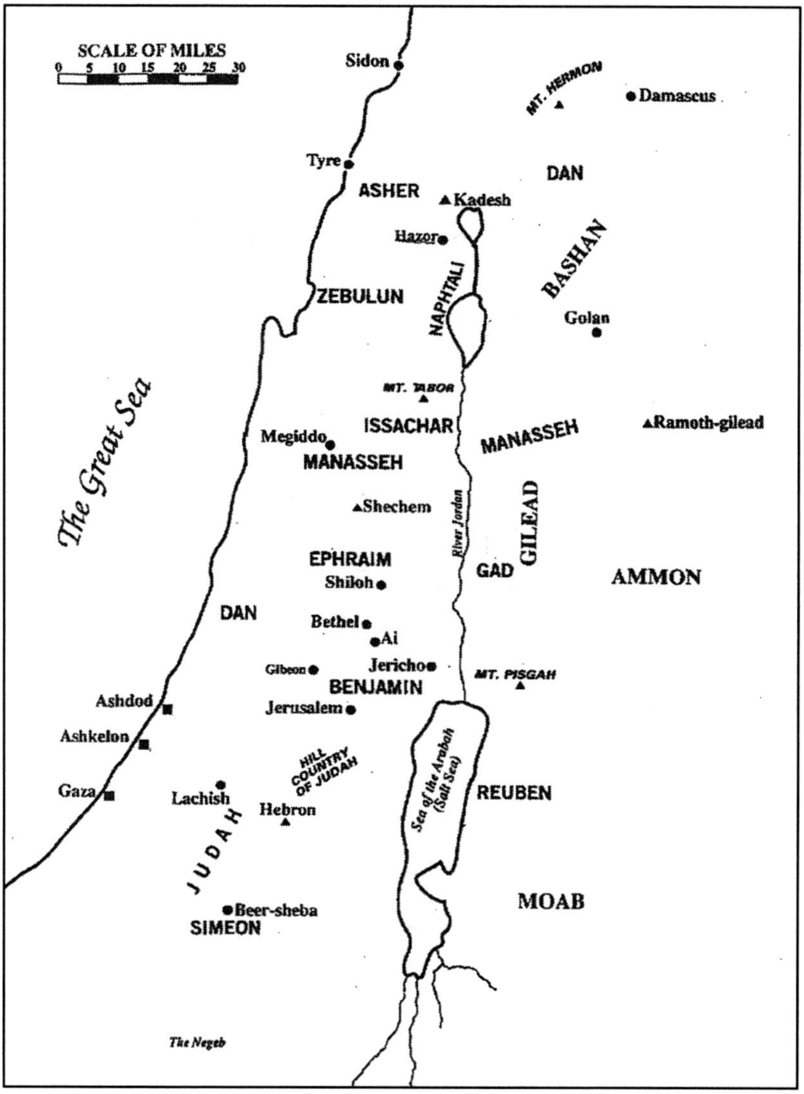
SCALE OF MILES
0 5 10 15 20 25 30
Sidon
MT. HERMON
Damascus
Tyre
ASHER
Kadesh
DAN
Hazor
BASHAN
ZEBULUN
NAPHTALI
Golan
The Great Sea
MT. TABOR
ISSACHAR
MANASSEH
Ramoth-gilead
Megiddo
MANASSEH
Shechem
River Jordan
GILEAD
EPHRAIM
GAD
AMMON
Shiloh
DAN
Bethel
Ai
Gibeon
Jericho
MT. PISGAH
BENJAMIN
Ashdod
Jerusalem
Ashkelon
HILL COUNTRY OF JUDAH
Sea of the Arabah (Salt Sea)
Gaza
Lachish
Hebron
REUBEN
JUDAH
MOAB
Beer-sheba
SIMEON
The Negeb

*The Bible tells us that 175 years after Moses led the Children of Israel out of Egypt, there arose a woman, Devorah, a daughter of Ephraim, to be a Judge over her people, a prophetess and a righteous example unto them. The Bible also tells us of Devorah's husband, Lappodoth; Barak, the great Haibru General; Sisera the Canaanite General; Yael the Kenite, slayer of Sisera; and of Sisera's mother, Betheena. The Bible touches only the high points of their lives. What follows is a more complete story.*

# Part One
# The Covenant

"Devorah! Devorah! It is time."

The young woman turned from contemplating the blossoming olive trees to face the climber intruding upon her sacred space. *So soon,* she thought. *I would spend more time with You, Abba.*

Dry wind lifted Devorah's flowing black hair, spilling it across her forehead and into her large green eyes. Arising from the soft grassy place on the rock strewn hill, Devorah adjusted the robes billowing around her. Lappodoth, the man violating her sanctuary, had only a few cubits before reaching her. She sighed, warmth suffusing her chest, heart still aching with devotion.

*I am always with you, daughter.*

She nodded, and whispered, "I know. I am deeply grateful! I rely on you so...." This place nourished and nurtured her; gave her strength. It wasn't the grassy knoll on the rock-strewn hill per se, it was the hill *within* her: a place of deep peace she carried everywhere she went. And, if she chose - remembered she *could* choose - she was able to experience it anytime, anywhere. Here on the hill, with the crystal blue sky and windswept, puffy white clouds, choice was unnecessary as she simply experienced that exhilarating contradictory sensation of empty fullness.

Not vacant unconsciousness, oh, no, but a fully-aware alertness, sensitive to the potential in each moment. In this place, she was without identity, not Devorah, not a woman, nor lover, nor Sar—a Judge over Israel, but just a being: a pure, effortless *being* and energy incarnate. It was the place God dwelled; *was* God. In this place, when she thought, felt and acted from this place, all was well. Outside it, life was more difficult. "Thank You, thank You, thank You!' she whispered. Gratitude was cause, not effect.

Devorah brushed the hair from her face and smiled down at Lappodoth, admiring his vigor and sure-footedness as he drew near. Her teeth, even and unstained, gleamed in the bright noon day sun. Raising a hand to shield her eyes and perfect oval of her face from the harsh light, she realized she enjoyed the sun and wind, but preferred experiencing them from the shade of her great palm tree.

She felt Lappodoth's eyes on her and blushed. He'd barely looked away from her the entire time he'd been navigating the boulder strewn slope. After eighteen months of marriage, Devorah was still not used to her husband's carnal appreciation of her.  He especially admired the evenness and symmetry of her features and her skin - more white and creamy than olive-tinted, as was normal for her tribe, Ephraim. He was a Judean and they were more fair.  She was a great catch - all four limbs intact, and the great bride price her father Eli had given, and she knew that in spite of her sudden mood shifts, trance-like episodes [which were becoming more frequent] and an assertive directness, bordering on the demanding, Lappodoth considered her a great prize.

Now, panting from his exertions, Lappodoth opened his arms to her as he reached the summit. Devorah stepped into them, hugging him. He smelled of sheep. Not an unpleasant odor, but distinctive. His body was firm and well-muscled beneath his robes. She felt her nipples grow taught, broke the embrace and stepped back, holding him at arms length to admire him.

"The children are assembled, my Queen." Lappodoth had taken to calling her that early in their relationship. At first, it bothered her. Now she enjoyed it, especially when he paid homage to her with his tongue and mouth. *Oh, what joy*, she thought. *I am blessed! Thank you, Father.*

Devorah nodded and lowered her arms. "What news, husband?"

The playfulness disappeared from Lappodoth's eyes. "Sisera may be on the move." His voice was low and tinged with anger.

*At last!* Devorah thought. *Thank you, Abba!* Now, Barak. "You know this…how?" Devorah's green eyes stared intently into his brown ones. If this were true….

"Daniel told me. He was taking a flock of our father's sheep to Charoshet."

"If Sisera goes west…." Devorah saw the plain of Sharon stretched out in her mind's eye, from the Great Sea to the Jordan.

# Devorah

Lappodoth completed her thought. "He will cut us in two."

"And we will have to fight!" Devorah's chin jutted, her eyes narrowed, and Lappodoth thought he saw sparks of green fire fly from them. A truly magnificent woman!

Devorah blinked, breathed deeply. The children were waiting and after that, the majlise. The majlise... If they were to fight, the assembly would have to agree, as would the twelve tribes. The wind whipped her hair. *The Canaanites have chariots, many chariots, we....*

"I must be a clear channel," she said.

"What?" Lappodoth asked.

"I must be a clear channel, husband." She smiled up at him. She was only 5' 1" and he, 5' 6". "For the Lord," Devorah added, wanting to be clearly understood.

Lappodoth nodded slowly. His eyes searched Devorah's. "What is it like, when God speaks through you?" His eyes shone and his voice was filled with compassionate curiosity.

Devorah knew he'd wanted to ask her that question from before they'd been formally introduced or ever spoken - from when he'd sat before her in the majlise beneath the palm tree that was in the hill country of Ephraim, between Ramath and Bethel. She'd been attracted by this same sensitive curiosity in his eyes and his strong handsomeness. More intelligent than most of those she judged in majlise, and Lappodoth accepted her authority less grudgingly than did other males, even though she was 20 and he 25.

"God does not speak through me, my husband. I hear something. Words or sometimes see visions, then tell what I understand." She reached out and caressed his bearded cheek. "Sometimes it is easy and I merely repeat exactly what I hear. More often I must think about what He means. It is for these times that I pray to be a clear channel, to get my own self out of the way of the Presence, and give the message as He intends, not as I intend..."

"You get yourself out of the way very nicely," Lappodoth said, reaching around to squeeze her buttocks, "for such a lusty maiden."

She stepped closer and hugged him back, allowing his hands to linger, enjoying their soft caresses. "I have had much practice," Devorah said, stepping back, taking his hand in hers and bringing it to her lips for a kiss. "This..." she kissed his hand again, "my lips, your hand, this kiss, the soft breeze, birds singing, bright sunlight *-this* is God. *All is God.*" Lappodoth's eyes sparkled into hers. "Shame, fear, hatred - these are not of God, but are instead what we do when we forget we are one with God. Evil is not a power of itself, my beloved; it is simply the absence of God."

The breeze gusted strongly from the encampment, carrying the laughter and shouts of the children.

"Come, Devorah, Sar, Judge over Israel," Lappodoth said. "Your students," his eyes met hers, smiling, "your *other* students await."

As they walked carefully, hand-in-hand down the rock-strewn hill, the joy and blessedness again arose spontaneously in Devorah. *Thank you, Abba*, she thought. *I am so deeply grateful*. She squeezed Lappodoth's hand. *I shall not fear the Canaanites, but will deal with them from that place of deep serenity, invulnerability, calm assurance and joy within me, that is You. Thank You!*

# CHAPTER ONE

Twenty three children scampered around the well at the center of the large oasis in the hill country of Ephraim; their cries and laughter echoing up from the cool, damp depths. The children, ages three to thirteen, were gathered for Devorah's daily school. No other Sar before her had cared to educate the clan's children. Devorah believed instructing the children was a joy and an honor, not an obligation, and she enjoyed it mightily. She also had a weekly class for the older children. Still unable to conceive her own until recently, though not due to lack of trying, Devorah felt that all of these raucous, racing, little people were her own.

She even accepted Canaanite children into her classes. The oasis was after all, just off the main road. And her primary concern, both as a Judge and as a person, was peace. What better way to ensure peace than through mutual understanding and education? Yet in spite of her best efforts, perhaps at this very moment, Sisera was massing his war chariots.

She shut her eyes tightly, swayed, heard the thunder of horses' hooves and saw the heavy iron chariots' wheel scythes turning and flashing, blood and flesh dripping from them. She reached out her arm and Lappodoth steadied her.

*Fear not my daughter, in whom I am well pleased; for I am with you.*

"Yes, my Lord. Thank you," she whispered.

"Are you well?" Lappodoth asked.

"A moment husband," Devorah said. "But a moment." It was too much at times. After all, she was only human. And this understanding of what He, or It was… He was not like Baal or Toth or the gods of the nations surrounding them. He was not like a 'He' at all. Much more like an It - a presence in, around and through her, everywhere equally present, all knowing and *oh wonder*, all loving.

"Then why these ceaseless wars, *Abba?*" Devorah whispered. Yet the joy and the deep sense of connection, even in times of danger, remained. When she was able to come from that sacred inner space, all would be well.

"What?" Lappodoth asked.

She opened her eyes and smiled. "To the children," she said, taking his hand and stepping out on the downward sloping path. "Then the majlise." She laughed softly.

"What?" Lappodoth asked warmly.

"Oh, I was just thinking that perhaps my concern about the Canaanites is a bit misdirected. My first concern will be our own people, and getting the priests at Shiloh and the twelve tribes to agree."

"Indeed!"

Soon they heard the yelps of the children mingling with the flapping of the tents, and the braying of camels and donkeys. The sounds of civilization. A dog with a stumpy tail raced around Devorah's feet, almost tripping her. The aroma of dung fires, unwashed people, animals and roasting meat filled the dry air.

"I have very often wondered," Lappodoth said, "why we can not live in houses like other peoples."

"I have also wondered, husband. I think some day we shall. But now, too many think cities are unclean and ungodly. And consider how very many of our people who have settled in the cities have since gone over to the gods and goddesses of our neighbors."

Lappodoth nodded. They were almost to the encampment. "Yet we have been here, in this place, without breaking camp from before I was born."

"We have always wandered in search of Him...." She said.

"But if he is everywhere, as you have said, can he not be in the cities of Moab, and Jerhico and Hazor? Did not Joshua purify those cities in the Lord's name?"

"He did, Lappodoth," Devorah said, "almost two hundred years ago. But now King Jabin, Sisera's master, rules in Hazor."

Lappodoth spit at the names, scowling; he stopped walking and turned to face her. "How long will your gracious God allow us to be tormented? It has been nearly a generation since Shamgar, son of Anath, was Judge over us and subdued the Philistines. Will Jabin's atrocities go un-avenged?"

"Do not blaspheme, Lappodoth." Devorah's voice was low and rough-edged, very like a growl. "Have I not been a good Judge over

Israel?  Have I not nurtured Barak and our army?  Am I not a good daughter to my parents and wife to you?"

Chagrined, not wanting to attack or upset her, but only wanting to relieve the anger and distress in his own heart, Lappodoth stepped forward and enveloped Devorah in his arms. "Forgive me, my Queen," he said. "I meant no harm to you. And I meant no blaspheme. But, *when?*"

Shouting and laughing, a young boy, Kenaz, 12, and a young girl, Abishag, 11, ran up to them.  Kenaz grabbed Lappodoth's robes and pulled him in the direction of the well.  Abishag did the same with Devorah.

"You are late, teacher," Abishag said to Devorah.

"Yes," Kenaz said. "We are tired of waiting. We want to hear the rest of the story."

Lappodoth broke free of the child's grip. "Yes," he said, turning to Devorah to lightly brush her cheek with his lips. "Finish the story. I must relieve Daniel with the flocks. I will stop at your father's tent on my return."

"Thank you, Lappodoth," Devorah's smile was weary. "Until this evening."

"Come!  Come!" Abishag called, dancing around her.

The children led Devorah through the bustling encampment toward their meeting place at the well.  The hill country of Ephraim was steeper and rockier than the name suggested, Devorah thought, as she walked past the looms, tinsmith, grain and butcher's stalls that lined the upwardly-sloping main path.  But the rugged terrain gave them security, as did their nomadic ways. Tents could be struck quickly and easily, at the first sign of trouble. The steep rock-strewn inclines were easier to defend and made the use of chariots impossible. And since the land was useless for farming, their neighbors had no need of it and left them alone.

Yet over the last decades, as they prospered and their numbers increased, the Ephramites needed more food and land they could farm. Their movement down to the fertile soil of the Jezreel valley and the villages of the Canaanites, once gradual - a family here, a family there - was now accelerating.  Her own sister, Micah, her husband, Ehud, and their six children had been living among the Canaanites for eight years. Abishag, the child who was tugging at her arm, was the oldest of them.

The land was theirs. God had given it to them and Devorah felt the Covenant keenly.  It lived deep in her heart and illuminated her soul and mind. Never could she even contemplate living among the unbelievers. Being near their gods and goddesses, their rituals of death and fornication, were an anathema to her. Yet, here was the beautiful, no radiant, Abishag, healthy, intelligent and no worse for her family's living among the unbelievers for eight years.

Lappodoth *had* touched a nerve though. More and more of Jacob's descendants, especially the tribes of Judah, Nephtali and Zebulon, along with her own, were living in houses and farming, acting as merchants and artisans, and, as they expanded, took root, traveled to trade and visit, their Canaanite neighbors were threatened and the violence against them increased. Only the most heavily armed caravans dared travel.

The taxes and the money the Canaanites extorted from them for protection was unconscionable. Hadn't the Lord given this land to *them*, the Israelites? The time for action was fast approaching, but her General, Barak, was a weak reed. Still, Lappodoth's question remained in her mind: were not their so-called 'enemies,' the others surrounding them - the Kenites, Sidonians, Canaanites, Moabites, Philistines and Jebusites - also made in the image and likeness of God...?

Devorah welcomed all to partake of the Covenant. Birth mattered not. To experience the reality of the One God as she experienced it, to know the everlasting love and forgiveness, and to live from that place was the greatest blessing one human could give another. Bestowing that blessing was the focus of Devorah's life. So, Abishag had brought Kenaz, son of the Canaanite iron worker, to the class with her.

The One God Devorah worshipped did not require punishment, attack and destruction. He, or It, was about asserting the good, the true and the beautiful - not eliminating evil. There was no opposition to It's Oneness. It was whole and complete, abiding in all of Its creation, human and inanimate. It's greatest joy, and the greatest joy of Its servants, was to awaken human beings to their birthrights: the reality of being spiritual beings having earthly experiences.

Kenaz reached his small hand up to Devorah's. "Faster, Devorah, faster," he called. "You think too much. Your mind wanders."

She smiled down on him. He had no idea of the danger his presence here created for himself and his family. Not from Devorah or the Israelites, but from his own people, the Canaanites. Only two months ago, their king, Jabin, had decreed it a crime for iron or any iron-making technology to be given to the Haibrus. The king feared it would be used as he used it, to make weapons.

*Devorah* 9

Devorah saw the humor, thought that God enjoyed a good joke. How much was enough? King Jabin, ruler of Hazor, and his General in Chief, Sisera, already had 900 iron chariots and 40,000 soldiers armed with iron-tipped spears, knives, swords and shields. While the children of God (well, yes, they were all children of God, but those who had a Covenant with the One God) had all of 10,000 soldiers armed with older bronze weapons—one or two weapons per man, not the spear, sword, knife and shield of *each* Canaanite soldier.

But of course, that was adequate for the Israelites. What else but faith in the One God was necessary? Devorah laughed out loud; would that were true! She shook her head, sadly. *God does help, but I have a people to govern and defend.* Devorah knew that Barak is a fine General, but one could not fight chariots of iron, wheel scythes twisting and gleaming, with stones - though they did have those in abundance. She kicked one away and it rolled, harder than she'd intended, into an old man sitting beside the path.

"Forgive me, Sire," Devorah bowed.

"No forgiveness is necessary, daughter," he responded.

A few more paces and the children engulfed them.

"Teacher! Teacher!" they shouted. "Finish the story."

"I can not finish the story, my darlings," Devorah said, settling herself cross-legged, her back against the well. "It is too long. But I can continue it. Where did I leave off?"

Hands shot into the air accompanied by a chorus of, "Me! Me!"

Devorah remembered very well where she'd left off, and her heart raced with enthusiasm and her eyes shone with an eagerness to resume. Being an excellent teacher, she held her tongue, waiting to see her young students share her enthusiasm and be actively involved.

"Marni," she said, pointing to a tall girl of 10 with tight black curls and penetrating blue eyes.

Marni stood up. A hush fell over the group. Devorah welcomed the sounds of the busy camp, the animals, people talking and even the wind in the palm trees. "You told us that we had come to the sea and could not cross; that behind us was Pharaoh's chariots. We were trapped!" Oos and ahs of approval and anticipation rippled around the group.

"Yet we are here," Devorah said, motioning Marni to sit. "So we must have escaped." The children nodded. "How did we do that?"

"God!" Jesse called out to a chorus of agreement.

"And why would God save us?" Devorah asked

"The Covenant!" They all stood, repeating it over and over until Devorah gestured for them to be seated. Heart racing now, eyes almost sparking fire, Devorah then stood. *How wonderful*, she thought. *If they could only retain this zeal.*

"Yes," she said. "The Covenant—our promise to serve the One God and It's promise to guard, guide and prosper us in return. Where is this One God?"

They jumped up again, each with their left hand on their heart and the right on their forehead. "It is within, Devorah," they chanted. "It is within every one of us."

"Is that all?" Devorah asked.

"No," Jesse said.

"It is everywhere," Eliazer proclaimed. "The water, earth, sand, sky, clouds and animals."

"And how do we serve It then, if It is everywhere?"

"By honoring all things," Marni said, "and respecting all things; beginning with ourselves. To be good stewards of creation, by being kind and gentle and respectful."

"And to obey the Laws and Commandments," Eliazer added.

"Yes!" Devorah said. "When we do this, we serve God and are one with God. In return, God will guide, guard and protect us. But first is the Covenant. First is our knowledge that we are one with God and It is one with us. As long as we remember our oneness with the great creative power of all that is, and we choose to live, feel and act from this place, we are serving God and cannot act amiss. But...."

"If we forget our oneness..." Jesse said excitedly, and then quieted, wanting Devorah to continue.

"Yes, Jesse! If we forget our oneness and partnership with God," Devorah continued, "then we are on our own, have ceased to serve God and will bring trouble and difficulties upon ourselves. Many will say God is punishing us for disobeying Him. How many of you have heard this?" They all raised their hands. "I do not think God punishes us. Most people will disagree with me. But I want you, my best students, to know what is in my heart. I think God is one loving power, that only loves and does not punish. What feels like punishment is only our choice to be separate from It - our mistaken belief that we are alone and apart from It. In truth, we can *never* be separate from It!" Devorah's eyes blazed with light and she seemed to be floating an inch above the ground. "We have only to remember the Covenant - God's promise to us and our promise to God - to claim or birthrights, to know the truth of our partnership and claim our Oneness and our lives will change."

The children's eyes glowed with excitement.

"And so," Devorah continued the story. "Moses heard God say, 'stretch out your staff over the waters.' Moses did so, and a great wind came and parted the waters of the sea and we walked across on dry land."

Loud, frightened voices behind Devorah interrupted the story telling. A soldier, covered with dust, thick leather vest speckled with bright blood, face bruised and bronze helmet askew, raced through the circle of children and stood before Devorah. He dipped his head as a sign of respect. "Jeremiah's caravan was attacked on the road to Hazor two hours ago. Jeremiah and four others are wounded, three are dead. Everything was taken. The survivors are on their way here."

"Who were the attackers?" Devorah asked.

"They wore no uniforms," the soldier said. "But their swords and knives were of iron. I think they were Canaanites; Sisera's men."

---

Yael followed her husband to the edge of the oasis. She was tired to the depths of her bones. The trip to Hazor had been profitable, but tiring. She preferred their tents in the open wind-swept spaces to the tight jumble and noise of the city. Especially Jabin's city. The Canaanites were fine merchants and artisans, good designers and engineers, too. But, Yael wondered, to what end? She shuddered, closed her eyes yet could not escape the mental images of the Festival. The smell of burning human flesh, and then, only hours later, the scent of sensual abandon from the writhing sexuality of Astarte's worship.

Her flesh crawled, yet tingled, too. Yael couldn't help comparing herself to the lithe temple maidens who danced so seductively and dared to make love out in the open, in public. Her body was as good as theirs. She too, could dance and sway hypnotically. Her face too, was as attractive, yet without the kohl and rouge and other tricks they used, not nearly as wanton and seductive. She pursed her lips and slid her tongue out to moisten them, to make them shine.

There was something else, too, at the edge of her awareness - attraction, sensual attraction. Yael had never seen female flesh so naked before - bare breasts, arms, legs, and the graceful curves of feminine buttocks. She'd seen glimpses of these in the mikvah, of course, but even in the ritual baths, the women bathed in their robes. Never had she seen such easy, graceful and sensual nakedness before and it aroused her.

Almost everywhere she and Haber went, especially around the Temple, Yael saw naked and partially naked female flesh. It fascinated her. She stared so much that Haber asked her about it. But Yael felt drawn to it, in spite of her self. Aroused and repulsed at the same time, she would look away, but her eyes were pulled back to it again and again, especially to the breasts and buttocks.

Now the vision of feminine nakedness displayed so publicly and casually for all to see, danced at the edge of Yael's heart and mind. Those women *wanted* to be stared at, *wanted* their nakedness admired and appreciated, even by other women. They did not cringe with shame and want to hide and cover up their nakedness as the Haibrus did. What would it be like to be as they were; to be naked and to display oneself that way?

Yael patted her own buttocks and lifted her breasts. But oh, what was she doing? What was all this about, she wondered? There was no need of feminine tricks and sensual nakedness here with her husband. Haber, though eight years older than her twenty-two, was still vigorous and a fine figure of a man, who knew how to make love to her. But it was plain, unadorned procreation without much allure or passion, leaving Yael with a sense of lack.

Haber was a righteous Kenite artisan, a tinsmith, a trade much in demand; passed down in his clan from the time of his forebear, Jethro, and from even as far back as the exodus. I have no *need* of kohl, rouge and passion, she thought. But something in me burns for it. I am still young and without children. She shuddered at the thought of children, the pain of childbirth and the drudgery of caring for them. The elegant, regal ladies of the Canaanites, if they bore children, had slaves to care for them. Ah, to be as they were; or to be one of their slaves....

Haber released the pack mule's lead and the animal wandered a few feet, then bent its head to nibble the succulent grass. As he loosened the carefully arranged packs, Arak came and asked about the cooking pot Haber was making for him. They wandered off and it fell to Yael to finish unpacking. The last and longest bundle was the tent. She unrolled the stitched-together skins and removed the mallet and the sharp tent pegs stored at its center. Yael's movements were deft and rapid. She enjoyed this work and was good at it.

She paused and stared at the mallet, as if seeing it for the first time. She picked up a wooden spike, touched its sharp point with her thumb. The tent pegs started out much longer, but after each use, Yael sharpened them. Her eyes clouded over and her heart beat more rapidly. She felt frozen in time, tense, waiting. An image of a handsome man in armor, Canaanite armor, drifted before her. She looked down; he was lying at her feet in a fetal position. Yael felt a thrill and her nipples grew taught. She felt out of control yet guided by an inexorable power. It was hard to breathe. She could hear the blood pounding in her ears. She gripped the tent peg, pointed it down and reached for the mallet.

"Yael," Haber was calling her. She shook her head to clear it. The vision lingered, then was gone. Her body returned to normal and she sighed.

"Yes, husband," she answered.

"Arak tells me of another Canaanite raid." Haber gestured to the older man and he came nearer, smiling at Yael. She nodded, acknowledging his presence.

"It has been the second time in two weeks," Arak said. The older man had been a Haibru soldier and had a long, white scar from his left ear to his chin. Yael always cringed when she saw it. "We do not give our traders enough protection," he said.

"And our weapons are inferior," Haber added. "We need the iron of the Canaanites."

Yael's mind wandered to the sensation in her hand as she'd held the tent peg. She'd heard this talk of protection and weapons her whole life. The palm of her hand seemed to tingle.

"Your cousin, Jereboam, was taken prisoner," Arak said.

Yael's heart stopped. She looked to Haber to be sure she'd heard correctly. He nodded then wrapped her in his arms. She sobbed. Jereboam was her mother's sister's first born and her favorite cousin. "Did he resist?" Her voice was hoarse and strangled. It was well known what the Canaanites did to Haibru soldiers who resisted them.

Arak nodded.

"Was he wounded?" Haber asked.

Arak nodded.

"Where?" Yael asked. "Where was he wounded?" Arak didn't seem to understand. "On what part of his body? How badly was he wounded?"

"I was not there, Yael," Arak said, his voice soft with sympathy and grief. "They say it was Sisera's men, not bandits. They wore uniforms. Perhaps they will make a prisoner exchange...."

Haber laughed. "Exchange? Who have we to exchange?"

Arak looked down and shook his head.

Yael stepped from her husband's embrace, bent and retrieved a tent peg. Stabbing downwards and brandishing it, she said, "Maybe we will capture one of them to exchange for my cousin." Her voice was matter of fact, as if she were talking about a trade of wheat for barely. But her eyes blazed fiercely and her voice was tinged with anger.

"We will talk with Devorah," Haber said. Arak nodded.

Yael looked sharply at him. "She has done nothing yet. Nor has our brave General, Barak," she said this last sarcastically. "Why would you think now would be any different? We - you, me, and Arak here, are the ones who must act." Her voice shook and she sobbed. "You can at least learn the secret of iron, Haber. Then at least our weapons will be a match for theirs." Yael threw the tent peg to the ground and stepped into her husband's open arms; her body convulsed with sobs and despair.

"I have begun, Yael," Haber said, stroking her flowing black hair. "I know some of it. I will learn the rest. For you, Yael." She leaned back and looked into his face. "And for our people."

Yael kissed him on the mouth. He pulled her close and she felt him stiffen. "Help me with the tent, husband," she said, voice full of promise. "We can tell Devorah later."

---

In her royal suite, three stories above the Temple of Astarte in Hazor, Sisera's mother, Betheena, peered through the palm wood lattice screening the solarium window. She longed for her son's return, with a lover's longing. And once again the pangs of that deep emotion bothered her. Such feelings from a mother for her son were not seemly. She had never acted on them; never even hinted at them. But ever since Sisera's father had been killed by the Haibrus seven years ago, and Sisera had accepted the role of protector of the house, Betheena had felt a new, deeper, almost sexual (she blushed at the admission) feeling for her valiant son.

When, two years ago, Sisera, then twenty eight had been elevated by King Jabin to command first the palace guard and then the corps of chariots, Betheena had felt her longing become tinged with worry and concern that sometimes bordered on pain. Sisera's duties required him to be away from Hazor often, and though she was forty-four, with a comely body and the vigor of youth, Betheena kept to herself and was lonely without her son.

It need not have been that way, for Betheena was a princess of royal blood, being Jabin's half sister, they had the same mother, also of royal blood. Perhaps the longing was in her blood, a thing passed down through the generations. Something she must simply learn to bear, a dull ache that was always present, sometimes stronger than others. Yet it did seem as if there had been a time, when she was twelve, before she'd spent her first month in the Temple of Astarte, when the ache had not been with her.

Even royal maidens offered themselves as sacred prostitutes, though they lived and served in the Temple's inner-most courtyard, the one reserved for the great leaders of the nation.

Betheena saw a cloud of dust on the horizon, between the city's twin guardian peaks. Sisera! Her heart leapt. *Gently*, she said to herself, it may not be he. Yes, gently. She studied the cloud for a moment. Her vantage point on the third floor gave her a good view. It was not a large cloud; probably not chariots, perhaps one or two riders on horseback or a small column of men on foot.

The sounds of the city drifted up to her and Betheena looked down. Across the street immediately below her were the King's granaries. A small group of functionaries were talking over a donkey laden with sacks of grain. Tomorrow, when the grain was distributed the noise would be deafening. Behind the granaries, was the slave market, with its stalls, and pens and platforms for showings. Some few merchants were walking their human property around the stalls, exercising them. Once a week, in two days time, the market overflowed with the color, noise and spectacle of the very rich in their finest regalia, buying from the very poor in rags. To the left were the public wells from which most of the noise came.

Betheena looked up. The dust cloud was dissipating. She could not see the great gate from her position, but if it were Sisera, she would hear his horse's hooves on the street stones in a moment.

Sisera had been born nine months after her first stay in the sacred temple of holy Astarte. Thoughts of the Great Goddess made

Betheena's heart race. She had lived a gentle chaste life outside the city, in a small quiet village with her amah. Her mother, who lived in the palace with the king, had little interest in Betheena; rarely came to see her and rarely invited her to the palace. Betheena was untroubled by this and thought it the natural state of affairs. She loved wandering bare foot in the lush fields and playing with the lambs. She actually saw the city for the first time when she'd turned twelve and her half brother Jabin, the King of Hazor, rode out in great state and pomp to bring her to the temple.

Betheena had never seen the shimmering fantastic colors of silk or breathed the mingled smells of oranges and lemons, dung and spice, nor felt the sway of horse and litter. All of this was bound up in her sensual memories of Astarte, Goddess of Fertility, and of serving Her in Her Temple, so that her heart still raced when she thought of it.

No sound of horse's hooves. Sisera had not returned. Betheena sighed and turned from the lattice. The sun was setting. Slaves were lighting torches and the quickening breeze sent a chill through her. Betheena pulled her robes more tightly about her, then she drifted back to her memories.

First, they had bathed her. Temple maidens only a few years older than herself, naked but for jeweled loin clothes that barely hid their clean-shaven genitals and slid suggestively into the clefts of their buttocks, disrobed her and led her to a pool of steaming water. Betheena had never seen such large quantities of hot water before. She dipped a toe in and drew back. The three girls waiting upon her tittered. One of them, a lithe red-head who she would come to know as Melka, took Betheena's hand and led her into the water.

Betheena had never, ever felt anything as satisfying as being in that pool. The girls stood away from the pool with their backs to Betheena as she acclimated herself. Betheena had not had an opportunity to study a naked person before and her eyes roamed hungrily over the flowing, full curves of the teenage temple maidens. *Do I look like that?* She wondered.

Melka turned, bent to pick up a sponge and came to sit beside Betheena in the water. Looking deeply into Betheena's eyes, Melka gently rubbed first Betheena's hands, then arms with the sponge. Betheena's heart raced and she felt her abdomen and genital areas turn to liquid. She groaned and closed her eyes, giving herself up to the other girl's ministrations.

After the bath, they gave Betheena a jeweled loin cloth like theirs and led her into the presence of the Goddess. Already in an altered

*Devorah* 17

state of sensual over-load, when Betheena smelled the hypnotic incense, and saw the bejeweled larger than life idol before her in the dimly lit sanctuary, she fainted - flopped to the floor. When she awoke, it was to a vision of the bare backs and buttocks of her sister temple maidens as they prostrated themselves before the Goddess. In a few moments, when her head cleared, Betheena joined them, prostrating herself as they did, in deep gratitude to the One who had granted her this blessing.

After a time, as Betheena's heart ceased its racing, Melka came and led her to a dimly lit alcove with a divan and a smoking brazier from which floated the same hypnotic incense. They sat on the floor.

"You are of royal blood, Betheena," Melka said. "A princess of Canaan. It is your duty to serve Astarte, Goddess of Fertility. The welfare of our people depends upon the Goddess' favor. If She finds favor in your service to Her, She will bless us with a good harvest and many children. Do you understand?" Betheena nodded. "You will now dedicate yourself to Her service. From this day forth and for the rest of your life, you will come here, to Her temple for one month each year and offer your body. You are Her slave, Betheena, Her willing and obedient slave. Do you understand?"

"I am Her slave," Betheena said dreamily and sensually, her body tingling and undulating slightly.

"Yes." Melka stroked Betheena's cheek, longing to take the comely virgin for herself. "Her slave." She stood and reached out her hands to Betheena and when she grasped them, pulled the new temple slave to her feet. "You will sit on this divan and wait, breathing in the incense of service, with every breath, reminding yourself that you are only a slave, here to serve whoever comes and commands you in the Goddess' name. Do you understand?"

"I hear and obey," Betheena said dreamily.

"Good, my little slave girl. I am pleased!"

Betheena's heart raced with joy.

"You will give yourself fully to what is asked of you," Melka said. "Trust the Goddess. She will guide you. Trust your body; your senses and feelings will guide you. Let your mind be asleep." She caressed Betheena's budding breast. Betheena moaned. Melka bent and kissed her nipple. Betheena moaned from the center of her being. *Oh, what sacred sweetness,* Melka thought. *Surely initiating this girl could not be a sin?*

"This is *love*, Betheena," Melka whispered in the child's ear; "sacred love. This is how you and I shall serve Astarte. This: what we are feeling now is how we are meant to feel and how She wants us to worship Her. You shall never know a greater, more fulfilling love, Betheena. You are mine in the Goddess' name!"

"Yours...."

---

A slave came to light the torches. Betheena tried to pull herself from the memories and focus on her son. He had not been her first born. Her first born had been sacrificed to Baal. She went to the table and poured wine into a beautifully wrought silver goblet, added water and drank deeply. In a moment, warmth suffused her chest. Downstairs, she heard the slaves preparing the evening meal.

Betheena drank again.

Melka, two years older and wise in the ways of the city, temple and palace had watched over Betheena in the weeks and months following the ceremony. It had been good with Melka. Later, in the days following her initiation, a few men had come to her and she'd learned to please and enjoy them in Astarte's name, but it had never been as good as that first time with Melka. Melka knew all the men allowed to visit the inner-most court of Astarte's Temple. She had lain with them herself. Four of them, all of the royal household, all had lain with Betheena. Atrim, father of Jabin, had been with Betheena most often; Melka counted 17 times. When Betheena conceived, Melka told her she was sure it was Atrim's seed that had quickened in her.

Had Atrim, the over-king of all the Canaanite city-states, known she was his daughter? At the time, Betheena had been shocked by the idea, but now, as she seated herself in the stiff-backed throne-like chair, she realized it had been an honor to be impregnated by her own father. After all, Baal and Astarte had been brother and sister, as had been Toth and Isis. It was the exception for the great mass of everyday people. But for the great ones, it was the rule.

They were at the very pinnacle of civilization, the intersection of the human and divine; far above the many others swarming in the streets around her suite in the palace. Betheena sighed, nodded knowingly and clapped her hands. Immediately, a handsome young male slave appeared and bowed deeply before her.

"Bring me a footstool and a table."

"Yes, Mistress." The slave obeyed, bowed low, and backed from her presence.

Betheena could have simply moved the furniture herself, but she hadn't wanted to. Awash in the glow of power as she contemplated her divine heritage, Betheena had wanted to be waited on. She could even have made the slave *be* her footstool. He would have eagerly complied, she had used him as furniture before, but she was not in the mood tonight.

She admired the workmanship of the finely wrought silver on her goblet. It was a scene depicting an olive grove and oil press. *We have a higher standard to adhere to,* she thought. It is our mission to keep and extend civilization; to honor our God and his Goddess consort; to protect them from the ravages of the desert nomads and their One God.

What could *they* know of God? They had no temples, lived in tents, had no iron. While we have beautiful temples, fleets of trading vessels, caravans that travel to Cathay and the Indies and a system of justice and sophisticated law resting on the will of the gods and on the divine power they have given to our priests and great ones.

The Haibrus were barbarians, nomads, threatening the roots of civilization. Betheena was proud of her General son's service to her half brother the King. Together, they were waging a relentless war of attrition against the nomad invaders, the desert aliens and jealous god who challenged their way of life and the greatness of the gods.

Yet there were alternatives to force and violence and the Haibrus were not so stiff-necked and un-educable as every one said. The handsome slave, for instance. He was a Haibru but under her tutelage had taken well enough to the worship of Astarte. Now he basked in his service to Betheena and devoted himself fully to her needs and pleasure, *because* she was of royal blood and a priestess of Astarte and to serve and worship her, was to serve and worship the Goddess.

But until they were tamed and trained, the Haibrus were fierce. Betheena feared for the life of her son and the lives of the brave Canaanites who fought with him. But it seemed that they had no alternative, no choice but to make war. Hadn't they tried to live in peace? Generations ago, when the Haibrus had first come among them, the Canaanites had welcomed them; encouraged them to camp beside their cities, water at their wells, live in the city walls, even join them in worshiping Baal and Astarte in their beautiful temples. They were tolerant of the Haibru god. And what had happened?

Betheena shifted in her chair, removed her feet from the footstool and returned them to the floor. Some, quite a few at first, had adapted to the life of the city and gloried in the sensual worship of Baal and Astarte, though, Betheena swallowed hard, the sacrifice of the first born male had been hard for them. Still, many of the Haibrus became as their Canaanite neighbors.

But their One God - One God - Betheena laughed aloud, how silly, grew jealous of Baal and Astarte and caused his more zealous worshippers to attack those that had fallen away; and forcibly return them to His worship, or kill them. Now there was little commerce between the worshipers of the One God and those of Baal and Astarte. In places they tolerated one another, but for the most part, they lived in separate enclaves.

Betheena stood and paced. Shadows from the torches danced along the frescoed walls. *Even this we tolerated*, she thought. But they breed like locusts. Now there are so many of them they are pressing upon our most fertile territories in the Jezreel and in Samaria. It was only a matter of *when* Sisera would fight the great battle to rid their land of these vermin.

*Vermin, Betheena, isn't that a bit strong?*

Lately, whenever she worked herself into a frenzy of hate, another voice, softer, deeply serene and gentle, came to her. It was something from her life before the initiation in the Temple of Astarte, a voice that sounded the way she remembered feeling when she was eleven wandering bare foot in the lush fields and playing with the lambs. Betheena stopped pacing and stood still, listening.

*Aren't they human, as you are? Do they not long for love, as you do; and worry for their sons and daughters?* She nodded and felt suddenly drained. Walking back to the chair, she sat heavily.

"But are we—Jabin, Sisera and myself, closer to the gods? Are we not the special and divine children of Baal and Astarte, with a mission ordained by them?'

*Do you really believe Baal and Astarte are gods? Do you feel their presence?*

"In the Temple, when I bow down before them. When we have the services to them, the rituals music, dancing; when I inhale the sacred incense..." Her eyes closed and she touched a hand to her genitals. "Yes. I feel them, then."

*But outside the temple, when you see a sunrise, taste the warmth of fresh bread, inhale the fragrance of the breeze from the sea; look at your child—do you feel Astarte's presence then?*

"I feel something, but it is not what I feel in the Temple. Perhaps what I feel is just the life force itself."
*Which is greater?*
"The life force."
*And Baal? Is he a god of life or of death.*
Clearly, he was a god of death. Betheena shuddered, remembering the sacrifice of her first born son. Because she had conceived as a temple maiden and was unmarried, there was no question that her son would be sacrificed to Baal-Malek at the next harvest festival.

Betheena had gone back to the country after her month in the temple. Amah and Melka had accompanied her. As her belly grew full, she ate and relaxed and gave herself over to life growing within her. The days passed in a gentle haze of sleeping, chatting and long slow walks beneath the dry blue skies. Then, a month before the baby came, Atrim, her Sire and her son's Sire, the great over-king sent for her. Melka went back to Hazor with the messenger and explained Betheena's condition to the king and begged his leave to attend him after the child was born. Atrim agreed.

The baby was a marvelous red-headed boy! A lucky child. Betheena nursed him herself. He was a sweet, good natured child, with big solemn black eyes. As they prepared to bring him to the city, the dread that she had been feeling throughout her pregnancy, threatened to overwhelm Betheena. She could no longer deny that he was to be sacrificed to Baal. That she had borne this sweet child to honor the god was one thing, but to have him be murdered before her eyes?

Melka tried to console Betheena, reminding her that this was the sacrifice of her first born male, for the good of the community and after this, all her sons would live; and surely, she would have many sons. Atrim would see to that. The festival and sacrifice were ten weeks hence, why not enjoy the child 'till that time?

Atrim, though married, had taken Betheena as a concubine and came often to her suite of rooms in the palace. He too, tried to sooth her, and Betheena, though deeply troubled and oblivious to the royal attention and lavish surroundings, had done her best to do what was expected of her.

Now was the moment of truth, the day of the Festival. Betheena had barely slept and when Amah awakened her, she had cramps in her calves and an ache in her head she thought would split her skull open. She could not keep any food down, but rushed to be with her son. She held him and cooed and rocked him in her arms, sobbing and would not be comforted. Melka tried to apply make-up, but Betheena laughed at the absurd idea.

"You are royalty. Your sacrifice carries more weight. You must look the part," Melka said.

Again, the absurdity of the idea of her sacrifice being any more important or meaningful than any mother's, twisted Betheena's mouth into a humorless smile. Surely if this god she was giving her first born to was truly all powerful, he would only give life, not take it. He is a god of death, not of life! She knew it and the insight settled her.

"You have a position to maintain," Melka said.

Betheena's eyes burned into Melka's. "You know all about that, of course, don't you, Melka?"

"I have had only girl children," Melka said, softly and looked away.

"I know that. But you know all about making other sacrifices to maintain your position. Love and friendship—mine, for example."

"I have always been loyal to you, Betheena!"

"A strange loyalty, Melka. Strange, indeed." Betheena's eyes were moist from her tears but she stared haughtily ahead, her heart cold and steady. "Apply the kohl and rouge, then. I shall maintain our position."

Silent crowds lined the twisting streets, hung from the balconies and craned dangerously from the roofs as Betheena walked, cradling her son, beneath a royal indigo canopy borne by four male slaves, naked but for loin clothes. Melka and Amah walked a few paces behind her. Betheena walked the two hundred cubits from the palace to the Festival alter, looking straight ahead, feeling nothing. The smell of burning human flesh was already adrift on the air. It was a distinctive, sweetish aroma, quite different from lamb or fish. Other women had gone before her. Later she found that thirty-seven women had given their sons to the god that day. She was to be the last.

As she entered the square, a sigh rose from the multitude. Atrim sat on a raised dais made of grey stone slabs with eyes that saw, but looked through her. How many of his children had he already sacrificed in this way? Indeed, she herself had been to the Festival sacrifices every year of her life in the city, and until this day, never experienced the pain of the mothers and the empty futility of the deed.

Sharing the platform with Atrim, was the god. He stood fifteen feet tall, wide mouth gaping, fire roaring in his wide belly; out-stretched arms tilting down to receive his beloveds and propel them into the flames. Four priests stood, naked, but for white linen loin cloths and gleaming gold bejeweled wrist and head bands, two on either side of the idol.

As Betheena reached the base of the platform, the two, to her right descended the ramp to meet her. One was carrying a chalice of drugged wine, the other took the child from her and held him up. The multitude cheered enthusiastically. They gave Betheena's son a drink, rocked him, gently, then ascended the ramp. Betheena followed. The two priests already on the platform led her to a place near the King where she stood and watched. They gave the boy another drink, lifted him again for the crowd and took their places before the great god Baal. The one holding the child aloft maintained his position while the others prostrated themselves at the god's massive feet.

Then, it was done. The priest lowered the child, took a step forward, laid the baby on the outstretched downward tilting arms and the child rolled into Baal's flaming belly. Betheena never once looked away but did choke a moment later when the wind wafted the scent of her son's burning flesh in her direction.

Two years later, Betheena had borne Atrim her second son, Sisera.

---

The squadron of five massive chariots reigned in before the brigade stables at full gallop, one after another, in faultless precision. The dust settled on the motionless drivers and spearmen; only the teams of splendid horses moved, stamping and neighing, nostrils flaring. The parade ground, too, though now crowed with uniformed men, was silent. A moment later, as Sisera stepped from the building's dim interior into the light, a cheer broke from every throat, and the soldiers banged their weapons on their shields. "Baal Hakim!" They shouted. "Baal Hakim! Baal Hakim!"

Sisera raised his arms above his head, fists clenched, and looked smiling into each of the cheering faces. He was tall for a Canaanite, bulky with a reddish-blonde beard and hair. He stood 5'10" and weighed 215 pounds. His size alone inspired confidence. But it was his deeds on the field of battle, his sense of justice, and his compassion for his troops that inspired ardor. Jabin, the Over King himself, was rumored to be jealous of him. But there was none to replace him. For sixteen years, Sisera had fought gloriously.

Yet he was getting tired. His warm brown eyes were tinged with sadness and he felt the corners of his mouth droop and his arms grow heavy. They were splendid soldiers and the drill they just completed had gone flawlessly. *Yet still I am tired. Their adoration strengthens me. Yet I can not do it all alone. It is necessary to bring forth additional leaders. Should something happen to me, the Canaanite Federation would be at great risk. This is not sound leadership.*

He let the sadness drop from him and gestured for his warriors to be still. At first they redoubled their clamor; finally, they fell silent.

"Soldiers!" he said to them. They cheered again. He waited. They fell silent. "This is the anniversary of our great victory at Hazor! The battle was fought by King Jabin's father's father to take back our capital from the Haibru invaders. Since that time we have fought again and again to keep these barbarians from destroying our culture. Their desert god knows nothing of the wealth and beauty of our cities; of our justice and the serenity of our fields and orchards. They foul our air and pollute everything with their sheep and burnt offerings. We try to live in harmony with them but they refuse to respect Baal and Astarte. There can be no god but their god; and they kill those of their kind who are tolerant, accept our gods and come to live amongst us. How long shall we allow this?"

"No longer!" the multitude shouted back at him. "No longer, Baal Hakim!"

Sisera allowed them to shout and clamor, then resumed. "My mother awaits me!" They cheered. "Your mothers, wives and sweethearts await you. We shall not tarry here much longer. I promise you! Soon there will be an end to drills." He raised his fists above his head, turned and re-entered the dim recesses of the stables. His soldiers broke ranks noisily.

But in the stable, the sounds were muffled and the heavy, sensual aroma of horse flooded his nostrils. Hay crackled beneath his heavy sandals. Pausing, Sisera inhaled deeply and pulled off his helmet. Sweat dripped, running down his forehead to sting his eyes. In the dim light, the scent of horse mingled with his own body odor, rekindling a memory of fornicating in the stables when he was a boy.

Walking quickly, he entered a stair well and climbed three stories to his command room. Sheepskin maps were strewn across the two large tables in the center of the room. On a smaller table next to the window overlooking the parade ground was a decanter of good wine from the Galilee and three golden chalices. Though not normally one for ostentation, Sisera did appreciate the finer things, and saw no reason to deprive himself of them unless absolutely necessary.

He poured the rich purple liquid, admiring its heavy flow and the contrast of its deep color with the shine of the gold, and drank greedily. *Oh, I needed that; how I ache!* He tugged at his heavy leather breast plate. As he poured to fill his cup again, Zeber and Sostrum, his two adjutants entered the room. They too, seemed tired. Though ten years and eight years younger, Sisera, knew the strain they were experiencing was as great as his. They tugged off their copper helmets and set them on the map tables.

"What you said out there about younger leaders," Sostrum said, "Is correct."

"But I said nothing about that, Sostrum," Sisera said.

Sostrum looked confused and Zeber laughed. "It's true, Sostrum, Sisera said nothing about younger leaders." He moved to the wine, poured a cup for his colleague, handed it to him, poured one for himself, and raised his chalice in a toast. "Here's to our companionship," he said spilling a drop for the gods on the rough hewn planked floor. "We understand one another's minds so well, we need not speak what we are thinking!"

Laughing, Sisera and Sostrum, spilled and drank deeply.

"But you did speak of our wives, sweethearts and mothers," Sostrum said, squinting in Sisera's direction. Sisera stood full in the glare from the large window and it was difficult to see his features. "Did you not, my lord?"

"I did, Sostrum. I did indeed. I know my mother misses me sorely, and again has plans to marry me off." Sisera shook his head. "I have enough of duty, here, with the Army. I need not have it in my bed, too! As Baal is my witness, when I need a woman, I will have her. I have no need of marriage to fornicate!"

"Well spoken, my good lord," Sostrum said, and Zeber nodded. "But we have been here in Charoshet for nearly a year. I know my wife and family...."

"And mine," Zeber echoed.

"...in Hazor are wanting to see me," Sostrum concluded, then added: "And I believe two thirds of the men feel the same."

Sisera had his back to them and was staring out the window, nodding. He'd heard and agreed with every word. The city bustling beneath them was a regional center of trade and moderately fortified. Caravans brought finished goods from Charoshet's many small artisans and factories throughout Canaan. There were temples and palaces, in fact he looked into the courtyard of Astarte's large temple, but they were not the temples and palaces of Hazor. The women were willing—more than willing; the wine was good and the food acceptable, even delicious at times. But it was not Hazor. There was no royalty here, unless one counted the merchant 'princess.'

"You are right," Sisera said, turning to face them and moving away from the window so they could see him more easily. "We have had enough of garrison duty." He drained the last of the wine and strode to the map table, gesturing the others to join him.

"Our spies tell us that Barak is concentrating a few hundred Haibrus here," Sisera put his index finger on the map, "at Mt. Tabor." Sostrum and Zeber leaned forward. "I propose we strike at him decisively, here in the valley before Megiddo."

"Yes," Zeber said. "In that flat land we can use our chariots to advantage."

"We can also bring infantry from Beth Shan and Taanach to form a great human barrier that will stop any escape to the west and south," Sostrum said.

"We already have the north blocked," Sisera said. "If Barak chooses not to fight, his only option is over the mountains to the Sea of Galilee and Ammon - and the Syrians are not likely to allow that."

"When will this begin, Lord?" Zeber asked.

"Our success depends on having as many Haibrus in the bag as possible," Sisera said. "We can not bother with a few hundred. We must have many thousands. All of their fighting strength if possible." Zeber and Sostrum nodded. "So we must continue our campaign of harassment and intimidation to provoke them to mass and fight."

Sostrum was not happy. "But this is what we are doing now, Lord," he said, tugging at his beard. "And here we are, away from our women and families, suffering. Can we not do something more to provoke them?"

"What would you suggest, Sostrum?"

"Maim prisoners, especially the soldiers; sacrifice prisoners to Baal."

Sisera's lip curled with distaste and he frowned. "We are soldiers not butchers or fanatics."

"True, lord. Yet...."

"... Yet we go on as we have been, Sostrum. I will, however, give more and longer leaves."

Sostrum bowed deeply. "Thank you my lord. May I have your permission to withdraw?"

As Sisera waved him away and Sostrum departed, Zeber said, "Think not ill of Sostrum, my lord. His wife is very sick and his children are not being well cared for."

"Yes, I know. It weighs heavily on me. We have many such amongst us. But we are not butchers or fanatics! I want to destroy the barbarian Haibrus, but not by destroying the very things, the civilization we are fighting for. Surely, you understand that Zeber?"

Zeber looked deeply into Sisera's eyes. Yes, Sisera thought, he does understand. "Please help Sostrum understand it also, Zeber. Watch over him."

"I will, my lord." Zeber turned and left.

Sostrum was waiting for him in the stables below. "We can not continue this futile war of attrition," he said.

"Indeed," Zeber agreed. "But you can not commit atrocities. Sisera will surely hang you if he finds out."

Sostrum leaned forward, touching his beard to Zeber's. "And who will tell him?" Sostrum's eyes burned into Zeber's.

"Not I," Zeber said.

"Good," Sostrum said, smiling. "I will visit the new batch of prisoners later. I recall one, a soldier who was wounded, but not too, badly. Perhaps if he is sent back without an ear or eye.... Perhaps then they will hate us enough to fight."

# CHAPTER TWO

Yael sat before Devorah in the majlise. She'd come as did many other men, women and children to seek answers to the oppression and lack of safety they'd been experiencing. But she did not have high expectations. She knew Devorah to be an exceptional woman and a good and fair judge, but a woman, nonetheless. She also knew of Devorah's reputation as a prophetess, but was unsure of how this 'ability,' if that was the right word, worked. Did God take over her body? Did she writhe and twist, yell or speak softly? Or did God just take hold of her mind and mouth?

Yael was curious, not only about Devorah's relationship to God, but about her own. Her recent few experiences suggested 'taken over' might not be too far from the truth. Though she hadn't writhed or yelled, Yael had seen things, real things, too: just as in life.

The people milled around in the grove. Now there were perhaps two thousand men, women and children. Haber moved a few feet ahead of Yael to the front and center of the throng. He stopped a few cubits from the slight elevation Devorah would sit upon and spread his blanket. Yael joined him and they sat down. A few men in what passed for military uniforms were on either side of Devorah's place. Seeing them made Yael think of Jereboam, her captured cousin. She closed her eyes and prayed silently for his safe return. I will ask Devorah about this harassment from the Canaanites, she thought. Something had to be done.

Lappodoth, Devorah's husband came forward, spread a carpet on the rise and sat down. The murmuring from the multitude grew louder. Yael had seen him before, but not this close. He was bigger and younger than she'd thought, with rough features but a gentle demeanor. No fighter there, either, she thought. Then she caught herself. *How fierce you've become, daughter!* Her cheeks flamed. It's so; but the times demand fierceness, she thought. We're naked here; we have NO protection; and they're deliberately provoking us!

Lappodoth stood as Devorah came forward. The crowd quieted down. She too, seemed younger than Yael remembered. Her jaw was chiseled and set and her green eyes blazed with banked fire. No lack of fierceness there, Yael thought. She has enough for us all. *She has to.*

Devorah gestured for the multitude to rise.

"The Lord God, Yahweh, is the One God," she prayed, arms outstretched, palms up, head tilted back, eyes closed. "His love brought us forth from Egypt. We are his chosen ones, made in His image and likeness. What can befall us?" Devorah gestured for then to be seated.

"The Canaanites." It was a man's voice, deep and rich, without anger or fear. It came from behind the multitude. Devorah's guards stood taller, hands tightening on swords, necks craning.

"Indeed, brother," Devorah said, opening her eyes and looking around. "Would you stand that we may see you?" Her voice was deep and soft.

A man with one leg pushed himself up leaning on a rough-hewn crutch. Yael thought he was in his mid-thirties. A jagged scar ran across his clean shaven face from where his left ear should have been to his jaw. He wore a clean, short, white woolen tunic that ended at his knees.

"The Canaanites took your ear and cut off your leg?" Devorah asked.

The man nodded. "I am Dovid ben Ami of the Nephtali."

Devorah smiled warmly. "A fine and stalwart tribe."

"Indeed," Dovid said, smiling back as warmly. "Those at your left side are Nephtali and on the right, Zebulon." Devorah bowed her head in acknowledgement. "Two tribes that will forever put the People of the Covenant before their own smaller interests."

"Oos" and "ahhs" from the crowd as some agreed; grumbles and coughs from those of Asher and Benjamin and the other tribes who disagreed.

"Yet you seem in good spirits, Dovid ben Ami of the Nephtali; even grateful," Devorah said.

"I am, Devorah, Sar of Israel."

"But when I prayed acknowledging God's power, you spoke of the Canaanites."

"I did."

"Are they," Devorah asked, "separate from God's power?"

He smiled more deeply, held out his right hand to her, the hand not holding the crutch, palm up and cocked his head to the left. "Devorah, you of all our people." He shook his head. "How can *you* ask that?" Dovid paused. "Of course they are not separate from God's power. They are the instruments of God's power, chosen as we are chosen."

A gasp erupted from the multitude, punctuated by muffled shouts of, "shame" and "blasphemy!"

Devorah raised her arms for silence. The voices died away.

"Go on, Dovid. Complete your thought."

"It is said that all things, good and bad, are echoes of the voice for God." Devorah dipped her head in agreement. Yael did also. Though she hadn't heard that phrase before, it resonated deeply in her and Yael thought there was a great truth in it.

Dovid continued: "The Canaanites befall us, because it is God's will that they befall us. And when we are ready to return to God's will, they will cease to be a problem. It is not God who makes the Canaanites a plague in our lives, but our own imagined separation from God. When we no longer feel separate from the all encompassing power It is, but accept responsibility for our actions and the uses we make of It, then we shall be victorious.

"So long as we *feel* like a divided petty people," he gestured to the men of Asher and Benjamin, "we will think and act and so become a divided petty people. The power does not need us to be great or petty. The power is indifferent to us; It is ours to use."

Dovid sat down and Devorah continued. "But the Covenant is a commitment to greatness, not pettiness. The Covenant calls us to greatness. The Covenant says, 'do ye thus, and thus shall be done unto you.' It is a promise. If we honor our part, the all-power we call God, will honor Its part." She paused, looked at the hundreds of faces before her and saw doubt, confusion, fear and emptiness in most, and comprehension and acceptance in only a few. I will speak to those, she thought, but *for* those who do not understand.

"My people, my family," she said, voice eager and enthusiastic, "brothers and sisters, wise ones, mothers and fathers, soldiers, shepherds, farmers, merchants, artisans, children," Devorah extended a hand and the young people stood and cheered.

"All things *are* echoes of the voice for God. Dovid, our brave warrior, is proof of this great truth. Is Dovid, happy, content and productive?" Many nodded. "Did God punish him?" A chorus of "no!" echoed around the crowd. "Did God allow the Canaanites to take his ear and his leg?" Hesitation. "Who made the decision to defend his people?" "Dovid!" "Who knew what could happen in war?" "Dovid." "So, who made the decision to risk his leg and ear, Dovid or God?" "Dovid."

"God allows everything and nothing. God allows the rain to fall on the just and the unjust alike. My people," Devorah reached up and out in a wide, inclusive gesture, "God is the ever-present power within and around us; you, me and everyone, even the Canaanites." Angry shouts of "no!" "They worship Baal!" "They blaspheme!'

"Justice is mine, sayeth the Lord," Devorah said. "This means the deed itself, carries with it it's own reward or punishment. It is not for us to punish. How can it be, if God Itself shuns it? Dovid lost an ear and a leg. Is that punishment or reward? Judge for yourselves. Look at him and judge! He chose with divine guidance to defend his people and though he seems punished, he is not.

"What we take to be real and true are only temporary conditions, appearances. The greatest reality is here," Devorah touched her heart, "and here," she touched a finger to her head. "These are the places we comprehend and experience God's eternal reality. The Covenant lives here, in everyone, whether they know it or not; even in the Canaanites. It is here, not in the Ark, or temple. It is for this that we have been chosen; to awaken ourselves and all human kind to the truth of our being and our relationship to God.

"And what is that truth? All things are echoes of the voice for God. We are to love first; we are to honor the divine within and around us; we are to be mindful and responsible for our thoughts, feelings and actions, first, and then respect and enable every person's power to do and be likewise. The Covenant tells us, as ye sow, so shall ye reap. *This* is God's will for us and in this way do we best honor and use the power that God is.

"Once there were people who experienced the fierce power of the Covenant directly. They were our ancestors. They witnessed the parting of the Red Sea, saw the Pillar of Fire, ate Mana. Now we have only the law and the tales to tell us what it was like. We have no direct experience of the Lord's fierce power for ourselves.

"Now we have only It's gentleness and the still small voice within. But this is enough! *If* we honor and attend to It. The Law and the tales are helpful and we use them, but they are not the thing Itself. They are reminders, mile markers; the finger pointing to the moon, and once we see the moon, we need no longer point our finger.

"The power that is God is always responsive to us; returning what we put into it, what we sow. Use the Power that is God consciously, instead of unconsciously. Always present and receptive, It receives the impression of our everyday, habitual thoughts and feelings and returns to us what we dwell upon. Therefore, raise your hearts and minds, lest you attract what you do not want. True worship is awareness of how Spirit works and acceptance of our responsibility for how we use It, not empty ritual and slavish obedience to the Law and the tales."

But their faces told Devorah that the Law and the tales were their meat, their bread and honey; all they wanted. *Oh, Abba*, she prayed, *if only I can waken them.* But really, what chance did she have, a mere woman, when even Moses with all God's miracles, could not bring them to an awareness of their divinity, and they bowed down before the Golden Calf and wandered in the desert for forty years?

She *had* reached a few though; Devorah saw awareness in a few more faces as she looked around. *All I can do is be a clear channel for, You, Abba*, she prayed again. *To keep myself mindful, open and aware and share what You give me to share.*

Then, as it had many times before, time stopped and Devorah heard His voice. Not a *voice*, actually, and certainly not a male voice. She called it "Abba", the masculine form, because she was comfortable with the tradition of her people. But really, and she'd thought about this often and deeply, if one were to reflect seriously about it, how could the One God be masculine? If it was 'one' wouldn't that have to be *both* feminine *and* masculine? The masculine without the feminine was bereft, out of balance, lacking wholeness, and hardly 'one.'

There was no voice, really, for the power was not human. It was beyond everything human at all. The ideas simply filled her, her head and heart, and she knew with every fiber of her being that this was good and right and healthy and should be acted upon or shared.

*I am well pleased, daughter. To keep yourself mindful, open and aware is all I ask. You cannot behave appropriately unless you perceive correctly. Since you and your neighbor* are *equal members of one family, as you perceive both so you will do to both. Look out from the perception of your own holiness to the holiness of others. You are the work of God, and Its work is wholly lovable and wholly loving. This is how you must think of yourself in your heart, for this is what you are.*

Devorah blinked. The ideas were hers now. The Majlise continued. A family of shepherds wanted a better price for its wool. The merchant resisted any change, then, as they dialogued, he agreed to an adjustment. Devorah had done nothing. A question of boundary stones was also amicably settled in the same way. A young woman rose. Devorah nodded to her.

"I am Yael, wife of Haber the Kenite, descendant of Jethro."

"Speak, Yael."

"I have a cousin very dear to me, Jereboam, who guarding a caravan, was wounded and taken in a raid. I would like him restored to us."

"That would be my wish as well," Devorah said.

"What you said earlier," Yael continued, "about all things being the echoes of the voice for God and the Canaanites being chosen as we have been chosen to share the power of God." She paused.

"Please continue, Yael."

"I have prayed and Jereboam has not returned. Must I pray to Baal to send my cousin to me? Is Baal the equal of Yahweh?"

"Baal is an idol empty of power." Devorah looked hard at Yael. "But you know that, don't you Yael?" Yael nodded. "Then why...."

"I am tired of pious words," Yael said bitterly, long black hair swirling around her head and full breasts shifting as she gestured aggressively. "Actions; deeds are called for! We have prayed for 20 years and now, each year, the Canaanites become bolder and bolder. I say, enough! When will we fight, Devorah?"

Dovid stood. "I am ready!" he said. "Who will stand with me?" The guards around Devorah stepped forward; here and there in the crowd a man stood, altogether perhaps 16 or 17 in a multitude of 2000. Yael looked around her and spat.

"Our people are not yet ready, Yael," Devorah said, gesturing for those standing to be seated.

"Will they ever be?" Yael said, staring down at her husband who looked away.

"They will, Yael," Devorah said. "Some of us will; you and I," she gestured, "those standing. We will feel the guidance and act upon it. Not everyone, and not a great many. But enough will be called and heed the call as our good Dovid has done and then, the Lord God of Hosts will be with us. To act before we feel the power, without being called, to act from an empty, heathen space will destroy us."

"And in the mean time?" Yael's voice was sarcastic, her pretty face pinched.

"Make yourself and yours ready. Open to guidance. Help others be guided. Feel your love and compassion for Jereboam; live from your heart out and know the truth of your own divinity; as you sow, so shall you reap."

Haber was pulling on Yael's hand trying to get her to sit. Yael, who'd been staring deeply into Devorah's eyes, nodded and sat. Perhaps, she thought, she would accept her anger and frustration; if all things were echoes of the voice for God, then these too, were of Him. Not accept them and do nothing, not feel guilty and suppress them, but accept them as part of her guidance; to embrace them and move to include them productively in her life. She glanced at Haber, squeezed his hand; he squeezed back without looking at her. Perhaps her sexual disappointment with Haber, her desire for something more exciting, even glamorous might be embraced also. Yael smiled, could the desires she'd been suppressing and denying most of her life also be echoes of the voice for God, too?

---

Jereboam screamed. Sweat ran down his face, burned his eyes and he soiled himself again. How can one body have so much fluid in it? Despite the excruciating pain, the sense of humor that so endeared him to Yael still twitched in his battered psyche. He longed for the simple gift of being able to reach up a hand and wipe the sweat from his brow. Naked, arms extended above his head, he was shackled to a wall by his wrists; his feet dangled inches above the ground. All feeling had fled his hands a day ago and he'd understood to stop twisting, realizing he was scraping the skin and even the flesh from his bones. He'd never hold a sword and shield again.

Jereboam screamed again as the spasm in his chest bent him forward. He prayed in a hoarse whisper, choking back the nausea, licking the blood and sputum from his lips, "Yahweh! Dear God, is this not enough? How shall I bear it? Allow me to know You are fully present, here and now. Let me feel Your blessings. I adore you and the Covenant is everything to me!"

*It will not be much longer, Jereboam. Stay with Me. Breathe. Sing of Our love. From the perception of your own holiness, look to the holiness of others. Welcome the Host within and the stranger without, as an expression of who you truly are. Bring in the stranger and he becomes your brother.*

Jereboam inhaled deeply, choked and spat blood. He inhaled again, this time without choking or coughing. He opened his eyes and saw the bearded Canaanite, obviously a noble and military leader, staring at him. Jereboam inhaled again, held it and sang the first notes of the Schma—'Hear of Israel, the Lord our God, the Lord is One. Blessed be the Name of His glorious Kingdom for ever and ever." Gloriously defiant; the pain was forgotten.

The Canaanite General walked up to him, disbelief on his blood-stained face. My blood, Jereboam thought and inhaled again, coughing, on my brother's face. The Canaanite reached up both hands and began strangling him. The pressure in his lungs and on his throat was intense; Jereboam began to black out.

"Sostrum, no!" A voice rang out. "Do not kill him! Remember, we want to send him back with the others. Sisera wants to provoke them ever so gently."

Sostrum did not let-up.

Zeber grabbed his arms from behind and pulled them from Jereboam's throat.

Sostrum back-handed Zeber and sent him reeling, turned and again locked his hands around Jereboam's throat.

Zeber rose, shook the straw and filth from his arms, took out his dagger and pushed its point into the small of Sostrum's back. "Release him, Sostrum." Sostrum hesitated. Zeber pressed the point more firmly. "Release him." Panting, Sostrum dropped his arms. Zeber backed from him, dagger at the ready. Sostrum's breathing slowly returned to normal and he smiled thinly. "You would have killed me for this filth, this Haibru?"

"No, not killed you; merely stabbed you."

"And what is he to you?" Sostrum asked.

"Just a man. Like you and me," Zeber said.

"No," Sostrum said. "Not like you and me! He is a Haibru. He would use his life to destroy everything you and I hold dear; our gods, our culture."

"If we must preserve our gods and culture with this hatred and torture, perhaps they're not worth preserving," Zeber said.

"You sound like one of them," Sostrum pointed to Jereboam.

"Perhaps. But it is our prince and master, Sisera, my words and deeds are meant to honor. He would not tolerate this, Sostrum."

Sostrum's breathing had returned to normal. His anger was gone and he was loath to threaten his colleague. "I meant no disrespect to Sisera. You know that, Zeber."

Zeber sheathed his dagger. "I know," he said. "Will you order him taken down and released?" He gestured to Jereboam.

Sostrum nodded and called, "Guards!" Two large men naked but for skimpy loin clothes appeared. "Take him down," Sostrum ordered. "Dress his wounds and send him back with the others. How many are we releasing?"

"Twenty-six, Lord," the guard replied.

Sostrum turned to Zeber. "Well, at least this one will never use sword and shield against us again!" He said, proudly.

As the guards led the whimpering Jereboam away, Zeber put his arm around his colleague's shoulders and they moved toward the passageway. "They *are* like us, Sostrum," he said. "Surely you can see that?" Sostrum said nothing.

Why did Sisera of all people, the heir and commander of the host, and a good and decent soldier like Zeber not see the threat the Haibrus posed? *Yes, alright, of course they were human beings*, he thought, *but they were foreigners and their god would not tolerate our gods*.

Baal and Astarte welcomed the Haibru god and asked only that His worshippers also bend the knee to them once a year. Was that too, much to ask? But it was! Thou shalt have no other gods before Me, the Haibru Covenant said. Yet how many of them had accepted the compromise with Baal and Astarte? Hundreds of them, perhaps thousands! Only a group of the stiff-necked kept to themselves, honored their Covenant and challenged the authority of royal Canaan.

And though they did not threaten militarily, and though we have iron weapons and many chariots, the memory of the Haibru destruction of Jerhico and occupation of Hazor were fresh in Zeber's heart and mind, and in the minds of most Canaanites—kept that way by biannual festivals and rituals. Never again would Canaan be overwhelmed by the Haibrus and their One God! Only Barak, the Haibru General, had any military skill. But he seemed unable to muster an army, much less equip it. The Haibru's twelve tribes were too fractious and seemed unable to cooperate. All true, but somehow his unease lingered.

Sisera knew Sostrum and Zeber were right; that they and all their people on garrison duty were being stretched beyond what was healthy for effective morale and good discipline. Sisera took a sip of wine, put the magnificent chalice down and breathing deeply took quill to papyrus. "Orders of the Day," he wrote. "Troops will begin a series of three week leaves in rotation. Beginning with the King's Own, here, entire cohorts including officers will, when their turn comes, be paid in full, including back pay, and will be issued rations for the journey to their home bases...."

Sisera set the quill down and shut his eyes as a vision of his mother, Betheena, staring out through the latticed window of her apartments, overwhelmed him. His heart thudded, perspiration stood out on his forehead and his hands shook. He thought of her often, too often, if truth be told. She was still beautiful and her strange blend of sensuality, fragility and arrogance kept him fascinated; perhaps, because he too, had those qualities. There was also an under-current between them, a heat; that was more than the stimulation of their arguments, no, discussions of gods and goddesses, life and death. Unusual topics for a mother and son to discuss, but entirely natural for his mother and him.

She was after all, a priestess of Astarte, not a high priestess, he smiled, Betheena lacked the ambition for that, though not the sensuality and intellect. Those she had in abundance. Now the vision of her leaning against the lattice work screening of her window glowed in Sisera's mind's eye. She was dressed as a maiden in flowing white robes, face bright with anticipation, head covered, cheeks and lips modestly rouged surrounded by her handmaidens, also dressed in white.

She was waiting for someone. For him! But he wasn't coming. He was dead. Sisera shuddered violently and stood. No! This was a mistake. He was here, alive and well and about to issue orders that would bring him home within days. An evil vision. He inhaled deeply to steady his stomach and shaking limbs. He *was* prescient. He had had visions before and they had come true. His mother also had this gift. But never had he experienced anything like this. Not a vision, really, but the certain knowledge that his mother waited in vain and he was dead.

Sisera paced, sipped wine, stretched his 5'10" form, large for a Canaanite, but couldn't shake his feeling of dread. He looked out the window overlooking the parade ground and saw Zeber and Sostrum

*Devorah*

supervising the gathering of some Haibru prisoners to return. looked quite battered and bloody with wounds unlikely to ha from combat. *The condition of those men will not endear u͟ ͟͟͟͟ͅ͏͞ Haibrus,* Sisera thought as he turned away.

He still shook, but less. Another sip of wine would help. And it did. Whatever that vision was, it was not about now. He would be seeing Betheena soon, in the next few days. She would not be waiting in vain—she would not be waiting at all, for his return would be a surprise. The tension drained from him as he imagined how they'd talk and argue, hug and kiss.

---

Barak wanted to believe, he just couldn't. It didn't work for him; he felt nothing. And these public meetings, this majlise...! For the tenth time the General scratched his sandy-colored hair, a nervous tick he was well aware of. As the voices droned on around him, he looked up to see Devorah staring at him with her steady, unwavering gaze. When their eyes touched, hers smiled briefly into his. She was another thing Barak had difficulty believing in. No, that wasn't quite right. He believed in her, the person, and thought she was an excellent Sar. His problem was with her, the prophet.

Barak stretched his thin, wiry frame as best he could without disturbing the family in front of him. The ground was hard and he wasn't used to sitting. Plus, they were all jammed in here. Maybe two thousand of them, with nearly no security; sitting ducks! He'd posted reinforced patrols at all possible points of ingress and they were well away from the busier roads; but still....

Why did these ceremonies have to be so long? Every minute they spent together, increased the likelihood that Sisera's mercenaries would stumble onto them. And for what? Was the risk worth the reward? Did Yahweh really require them to do these rituals? Clearly, the priests and people thought He did. But did He, *really*? And how different were these rites from those their Canaanite enemies performed? Of course we don't sacrifice infants or have sex in public. But otherwise.... Barak had been to Canaanite services and found the similarities amazing. If I were to push a little deeper, he thought, a wry expression on his face, I might see those similarities as proof of our One God idea, though I'm certain the priests on either side would disagree.

One thing is certain, the power was not in the rituals, words and ceremonies themselves. That was a belief Barak shared with Devorah. Solidarity, a feeling of belonging, and obedience to the law came from the rituals—all good and useful things. But what about God? Where was God in all of this? "I am, that I am," God supposedly said to Moses from the burning bush. What does that mean to me, in a practical way? How does God help me through the day, and to win against the Canaanites?

Frustrated because he hated superstition, didn't see how God worked and was completely certain that the rituals and ceremonies were unrelated to making God work, Barak scratched his head again. There were real challenges ahead for them and he needed all the help he could get. Rather than reassuring him, the story about Joshua and the walls of Jerhico, aggravated him. Too many thought that story meant the people did not have to prepare for war: to arm and train; that God would save them with a miracle.

Barak thought a miracle would be fine, but you couldn't count on it. One, especially a General, had the obligation to use the resources God gave in an intelligent, realistic way. It was good to entreat for God's support, but also necessary to move one's feet in the desired direction. It would be suicide to take on Sisera's chariots with stones; though they had those in abundance!

Besides, Barak knew the truth about Joshua's great victory at the walls of Jerhico was preparation, strategy and tactics. First, Joshua sent Rahab, the prostitute, to spy out the city. Then, Rahab and his other scouts reported his famous seven days march around the walls led by priests carrying the Ark of the Covenant was designed to increase the fear and uncertainty. Second, because of the length and girth of the walls, 900 cubits of perimeter wall, 2 cubits deep, Joshua was able to easily encircle it with only 8,000 soldiers before overwhelming it, 1 cubit of ground, six men deep. Third, the tactic of surprise through a ruse: on the seventh day the silent though armed religious procession led by priests carrying the Ark, changed into an assault column which scaled the walls and passed through the portions damaged by recent tremors.

Barak smiled. That was the 'miracle,' recent tremors had damaged parts of the walls and made the assault easier. And the super-natural power of the Ark of the Covenant? What part did it play? Did it help

# Devorah

with the miracle? Barak thought not. Yes, the priests carried it around the walls, but that was more for morale, for building and maintaining the faith of the fighters. But even that was not essential to the Haibru victory. For though few knew it, Joshua himself and a few hundred of his men, were trained professionals, actual mercenaries, recruited by Moses. Their faith in Yahweh was strong, but not stronger than their faith in their weapons, training and tactics. Miracles matter, but skill, discipline and professionalism are necessary, too.

*Our entire military heritage shows that*, Barak thought. We're more guerilla-like than organized and we're still using the single-edged sickle swords, spears, bows, slings, and daggers of Joshua's day, but our faith, skill and zeal give us strength and bring victory over our better armed opponents. And Joshua's focus on light infantry in small irregular bands that perfectly mirror the uneven terrain of our hills, is also still good. Even the circular slashing sword for cutting muscles and blood vessels Joshua preferred worked better for us than the Canaanite thrusting swords for penetrating vital organs.

Barak inhaled deeply, feeling clearer. We must re-kindle the pride in our military prowess, he thought. Devorah, offers our best hope. She might awaken the people and rally them to a more active faith and pride. She might also teach *him* how to have a relationship with God. For, though he did not believe, he *wanted* to believe - and he struggled mightily to do so. And clearly, Devorah *had* a relationship with God, an excellent relationship. It shone in her eyes, words and grace—in everything she did. That meant it could be done, that there *was* something beyond what he could apprehend with his senses! After all, something had caused the tremors that weakened Jericho's walls.

Barak shifted again, stood briefly, stretching to his full 5'7", then sat back down. A smile crossed his weathered, beardless face. What if he *could* lead the people to both prepare for war *and* have faith? Wasn't that what Moses did, and Joshua? Feeling less frustrated, Barak, settled back, resolved to talk with Devorah immediately after the ceremony. He sighed and caught himself actually enjoying the singing, even joining in, in a few places.

Devorah was encouraged by the changes she was seeing in Barak and planned to talk with him about the deteriorating military situation when the services were over. They'd chatted before and found common ground in their beliefs about God. He could almost grasp her sense of God as a present power, not some far off being. But he was so unremittingly practical and results oriented that he lost patience quickly. She had to be patient and go carefully with him because when he lost patience his ego and pride dominated him totally and he would say things, and stick to them, even to his own detriment.

Devorah had had only one formal negotiation as Sar of Israel, that with a Syrian minister, a very dignified, stiff and prickly man with a creative mind, and now, as she contemplated meeting with Barak, the idea of a 'negotiation' seemed apropos. Walking on egg shells, her mother used to say. Devorah grabbed her stomach as the pain shot through it. Shutting her eyes she pressed her lips together and struggled for breath.

Beside her, Lappodoth put his hand in hers, leaned closer and said gently, "Perhaps it will pass, my Queen."

Devorah nodded and did her best to smile; took a breath, then doubled over with the pain.

"Let me bring you back to the tent," Lappodoth said, "*please!*"

"Yes," Devorah said, "good. But we must wait for the cramps to subside. I do not want to stumble here." Lappodoth nodded. A few moments later, she squeezed his hand. He stood and reached down for her; she rose, steadied herself, then using him as a crutch, moved slowly through the crowd. The ceremony continued. People seemed to ignore them. Devorah had one more severe cramp before they cleared the crowd, and Lappodoth had to bear her full weight.

Whatever she needed, he was completely and fully present for her. As soon as they cleared the crowd, he scooped her up in his arms, whispering blessings and nothings in her ear punctuated with adoring little kisses.

"I felt our child move inside me, husband!" she gushed, as he laid her down on the mound of cushions deep within the cool half light of their tent.

"We are blessed, Devorah!" Lappodoth said. "I wish only that it was not so painful for you. I would do anything to ease your burden, my Queen. I want to do more for you."

"You do too much for me now, husband," Devorah said, happily. "All the other women think you spoil me."

"Perhaps so," Lappodoth agreed. "But you are my Queen and I love you very much." He knelt and kissed her chastely. She returned the kiss with passion, pulling him down upon her. "The baby!" he said, recoiling.

"No, husband! We are not made of glass. You can not hurt us now." She opened her arms to him, hands beckoning. "Not at this early time. We will know what to do and when. Come to me now, I want you! The baby has made all my appetites stronger."

"And the cramps?"

"Gone!" she said.

Still, he hesitated. "But the services…the people…"

"The tent flap is lowered?" she asked. He nodded. "Then come to me! Let us enjoy ourselves while we can. Soon enough I will be too big for easy love-making." Devorah set her feet flat, shifted her weight to the small of her back and lifted her robe.

Lappodoth admired her dexterity and adored the sight of her glistening sex. Eagerly he pulled his robe off over his head and knelt between her wide-stretched legs, engorged penis jutting before him. The scent of her sexual secretions filled his nostrils and inflamed his senses. Everything seemed to be brighter, clearer, as if it were happening more slowly.

Devorah reached up a hand and pulled gently on the top of his head, guiding it down, toward her moist and glistening vulva. Her smell grew stronger, more entrancing as Lappodoth allowed her to guide him nearer and he found himself empty of all, but the desire to please his Queen and serve Her sex with his mouth. She had trained him to do this for her in the first weeks of their marriage. He'd resisted at first, for it was a thing quite foreign to his masculinity. A thing he'd heard the Canaanites did. But as his love for her grew, so did his desire to please her. The smell of her sex excited him now, and his ability to please her in this unique way, made him proud.

Devorah was moaning as Lappodoth used his lips and tongue and teeth to pleasure her. His face was sticky with her juices, and gradually, to serve her better, he lowered himself, so that now he was flat on the rug-covered ground before her, crushing and grinding his penis beneath him, hands wrapped around her buttocks; she leaning further back, bare feet resting on his shoulders. He saw the puckered opening of her anus and thought he smelled it, too. Sometimes its scent was strong and repulsive, today it smelled exotically sweet, like night blooming Jasmine.

"Yes," Devorah moaned. "Oh, please, husband; lick me there!"

He touched his tongue to the soft puckered flesh and found the taste to be mild, even sexy.

Devorah leaned back a bit more and opened her legs wider to give him greater access to her. "Oh, thank you, husband. You serve me so well."

Lappodoth alternated between her vulva and anal opening until Devorah had an enormous orgasm. Then, partly as she'd trained him to do, and partly as he'd learned on his own, he orgasmed, too. After a moment, he licked her clean; she removed her feet from his back and he knelt up, wiping their sexual juices from his face, body and the rugs with a small cloth. He stood and put his robe on; she pulled hers down to her ankles; sat up, opened her arms wide to him. He sat down, cradled between her thighs and arms.

"You please me beyond words, Lappodoth!"

"Thank you, Devorah. I am well pleased also!"

"We can have sex this way right up until the baby is born, husband," Devorah said.

"Yes," Lappodoth agreed. "We can. But I also like putting my penis where my nose was."

"Yes, of course!" Devorah was quick to reassure him. "Yes. It is good, all good, is it not?" Then changing the subject: "Did you notice Barak earlier, during the services?"

Lappodoth smiled. "I saw him," he said. "Just when your pains started." He stroked her hand. "He seemed more content than usual..."

"Yes," Devorah's voice was enthusiastic. "That's what I saw, too. Could it mean he's changing?"

Lappodoth snorted. "Not likely," he said. "But it is possible." He shifted his weight and turned to face Devorah. "I would not want his responsibilities, Devorah." His voice was filled with compassion.

"The task is mighty," she agreed, eyes mirroring his feelings. "But so is our God. Barak fights not only Sisera and the Canaanites, he fights himself and God, too. I am afraid he is unequal to the task. No," she leaned forward just inches from her husband's face, "and you can understand this too, my passionate one," she patted his groin. "*He* is not unequal to the task, his *beliefs* are unequal to the task. Barak must get out of his own, and God's, way! Look at us," she said, sitting back and allowing more space between them. "I am pregnant! Finally! We kept our faith, allowed for a miracle and kept having sex, all the time and...."

*Devorah* 45

Lappodoth dipped his head. "Yes, I understand, but this is not about having a baby, it's about fighting a war."

Devorah frowned at him. "The principle is the same, my husband. God is the same. It makes the tiniest seed grow and great kingdoms arise and wither."

They heard footsteps in front of the tent, then a man cleared his throat. "Devorah? Lappodoth? It is Barak. May I come in?"

---

Devorah flashed Lappodoth a look of triumph. See, her look said, the power is always at work; ask, and you shall receive; knock and it shall be opened unto you. Lappodoth dipped his head, acknowledging Devorah's wisdom, then invited Barak to join them. "Please, Barak, you are most welcome. Come in!"

The entrance flap drew back. "Would you prefer it open or closed?" Barak asked.

"Thank you. Open, please," Lappodoth said, rearranging the cushions to make a place for Barak and sliding the cloth he used to wipe their spendings beneath them.

Barak entered, his tall wiry body and nervous energy transforming the space. Like the sensation in the air before lightening strikes, Devorah thought. He paused and sniffed audibly. My God! Devorah sucked in her breath as she sniffed. Could our musk be lingering still? Her eyes darted to Lappodoth's. He too, sniffed and looked down as his face reddened. Barak looked quickly from one to the other and cleared his throat.

Devorah was grateful to him when he seated himself and said nothing; though she was certain Barak smelled their musk. "May I offer you something, General?" she said smiling.

"Water would be appreciated, Sar...er, Devorah. Thank you."

She arose, went to an earthenware pitcher and goblet set on a nearby table; poured and handed Barak his drink. She looks even more radiant, he thought, gazing into her unlined, full-cheeked face.

He drank thirstily, held out his cup for more and Devorah refilled it. He looked around the smallish tent. Nothing special: worn rugs, three cedar chests, plain earthenware jugs for water, sheepskin blankets. Even his own battle tent had more character than this. But all was neat and in order.

"The services are so long, are they not; and in the hot sun, too?" He looked hopefully from Lappodoth to Devorah for agreement.

"Indeed," Lappodoth said.

Devorah smiled. "I find them quite tedious at times," she said. "As I know you do, Barak." She gazed at him with her almost palpable stare. He gazed back calmly. "But before I had to leave, I thought I noticed you enjoying yourself a bit more than usual."

Barak's eyes widened slightly. "You are most perceptive."

She bowed her head, acknowledging the compliment. "You knew that, General," she said.

"I did; and it is good for our people that you are as you are, Devorah."

She silently acknowledged his compliment.

"The Canaanites are pressing us harder," Barak said. "You are aware of that?"

"At the last majlise," she said, "there were a number of questions about it. The attacks seem to be more brutal, too. Many of our soldiers are being maimed."

Barak nodded. "That is a two-fold strategy: to provoke us *and* to insure those men can not bear arms against them in the future." He paused and looked long into her eyes. "It is working on both counts," he said.

"Are we ready to fight, General Barak?" Devorah asked him.

He did not look away from her steady gaze. "We have talked about this often, Judge over Israel. I am loath to fight if we can not win."

"But now, we must fight, mustn't we?"

"We still have a few options...."

Devorah nodded. "We do. But don't we want to use those in service to our strategy of seizing the initiative?"

"We.... We are not well prepared."

"But soon," she said, "If not now, we must fight soon, mustn't we?"

He looked down.

"Be not downcast, General Barak," Devorah's voice was lilting and almost musical. He looked into her face, seeing the fire in her eyes and the glow surrounding it. "If we are agreed we must fight, then the time is right. It is the appointed hour; the time of our victory! God is showing us. He shows us the time—now. Next we are to be open and ready for what is to follow. Do you not *see*, Barak?"

*Devorah*

"I see that we must fight soon against great odds."

"So we are agreed that the time is nigh and that we must prepare?" Barak nodded.

"What steps shall we take in preparation?" Devorah asked; pressing her advantage, driving him on, heart leaping with joy. *At last!*

"We must rally the people," he paused. "*You* must rally them. And…." Barak looked down.

"And you want some rallying for yourself," Devorah completed his sentence.

"I think we face great odds," Barak said, voice heavy. Devorah nodded. "I would like to believe that we have a chance," Barak said.

"I think we have more than a chance, General! I think, no, I *know* we have God on our side and so cannot fail!"

"But, Devorah," Lappodoth said, "the Canaanites pray to their gods as fervently as we pray to ours…." Devorah nodded. "Why will we win and they be defeated?"

She smiled at him. "We do not pray for victory, my husband, as they do. In fact, we do not pray for things or events in the world. We pray for the realization of the Covenant, for the experience of our Oneness with God. The God of the Covenant is not about setting boundaries, raising crops or winning battles. It is the one power in everything—seed, soil, rain and crop; but most especially within our hearts and minds.

"When we are aligned with It, we feel clear and sure, not the sureness or arrogance of puffy self-importance, but the calm certainty that comes from fulfilling our heart's desire. That desire and passion, if it be loving and compassionate, and attacks no others, *is* God. When we come from that place, we are one with Sprit, acting in accordance with Its will.

"I often think of such passion as glue, and of the world as a broken pot. Each of us is born with a way to bring the pieces together again, to make the world whole, what we call Tikun Olam. That way, that contribution, is buried in our hearts and minds. When we act from that desire and passion with love and compassion, we are the glue that holds the shattered pieces together, we contribute to Tikun Olam."

Devorah looked deeply into Barak's eyes. "Your contribution, your great passion, Barak, is to be a strategic leader, to plan and train and execute a strategy for victory. My contribution is to help you. God's contribution, which of course we and our desires already are, is to see to the final result. There is our part and God's part.

"Neither of us is responsible for the final result, Barak." He was smiling at her, nodding. "But we can know the result will be taken care of; if we go forward, passionately, with songs of thanksgiving in our hearts, to do what is ours to do, to the very best of our abilities."

"That doesn't sound like sitting back, praying and hoping for the best." Barak said.

"Absolutely not!" Devorah answered.

"We will act, pay careful attention to the conditions within and around us, but maintain a deep conviction in the oneness of God and our manifestation of that oneness. Even were we to lose, we would still know that we are one with God, that It is good, all the time, and that perhaps next time, we will do a better job of it."

Barak was agreeing, nodding, then, like a cloud passing across the sun, his face darkened. He looked deeply into Devorah's warm eyes, saw nothing but love there and shook his head. "There is much at stake here, Devorah. We will have only one chance, one chance in this generation."

Devorah's smile faded but the warmth still shone from her eyes. "What I am trying to tell you, Barak, is very different; very different from everything you believe and have been taught to believe. It was handed down through the generations and originated with Moses himself. Few understand it and fewer still are capable of using it." She turned to Lappodoth. "Even my beloved husband," she caressed his cheek, "does not understand it." Lappodoth blushed and looked down. "Though, I have tried mightily to help him and teach him."

Barak was becoming impatient. He arose and stood with hands on hips looking from one to the other. "One chance," he repeated, energy rippling down his torso into his shifting legs and feet. "In a generation." His hard, unyielding eyes bore into Devorah's calm ones. "If we fail now, we will not be able to produce a sufficient force of men for a generation." He shook his head. "Enslaved for a generation.... And maybe more. We might be so badly beaten that we will never recover. That's what we're contemplating."

"I know the stakes, Barak," Devorah said, her voice even, the warmth still in her eyes, "perhaps better than you. It is always we women who bear the load. We who must find the food and cook it, raise the children, tend the sick and the wounded; suffer the privation and sexual abuse and bury the men."

She tilted her head as if listening, closed her eyes, stepped forward and touched Barak's cheek. "Barak, hear me!" Her eyes searched his. "It's *always* one chance. But we must act! You yourself said it, a moment ago. Did you not?" He nodded, looked away from her, then looked back, fear in his tight lipped expression. Devorah touched his shoulder. "We can not be paralyzed by fear. Do you agree?" He wanted to, but fear had the upper hand. He swallowed hard. Devorah wanted to hug him.

"I too, have moments of immobilizing fear, Barak." She patted her belly. "I am going to have Lappodoth's child." Barak smiled at her, a truly warm and appreciative smile. "But I know that I have a choice: to be loving or fearful. Each is a seed and whichever I think, is the seed that I plant." She patted her belly again. "For this unborn life," she looked at him with shining eyes, "and for all the unborn lives, ours as well as the Canaanites, I must choose love and plant seeds of love." He began to object. She raised a hand to stay him. "Yes," she said, "even in war it is still possible to love and to remain loving. It is not *either* love or war, my General, but *both* love *and* war. Even fighting and killing we can come from the place of love and oneness, planting the seeds of peace instead of those of the next war."

Barak was hearing her, beginning to understand. "It is a paradox, Barak," she continued, eyes shining. "It can not be understood with the kind of thinking we use everyday. That is why it is so different, as I was telling you earlier. *This* is what was handed down from Moses to our own time. *This* is the Covenant. What our people were chosen to give the world, but have failed, not only to give and share, but to use ourselves."

Barak wanted to object. He opened his mouth to speak.

"Hold," Devorah said, stretching out her hand. "Hear me. I mean no disrespect. When you have heard, you will know I speak only the truth."

Barak shut his mouth and folded his arms.

Devorah smiled. "Thank you, Barak." She gestured for him and Lappodoth to be seated. "One God means it's all god, everything—humans, dogs, stones, wheat, water, clouds - all made of one substance, one energy. This energy is invisible, formless. It shapes and takes shape. *It* is what spoke to Abraham and the ears with which he heard. *It* was the flesh and blood Abraham was, the joy in his heart and the consciousness in his mind. Abraham understood this as did Isaac and Jacob, Joseph and the others from then 'till now."

"How can this be?" Barak's eyes were wide with disbelief and he seemed ready to stand and move around.

Lappodoth, too, was agitated, though not as much as Barak. "Yes, Devorah," he said. "You've explained this to me many times. I know it is correct. You wouldn't lie. But it is difficult to understand."

Devorah nodded agreeing with them. "It *is* difficult to believe! But how else do you explain the Burning Bush, the Parting of the Red Sea, Joshua's destruction of Jerhico and all the other miracles God has wrought for us? There is a power in everything that God is able to use and that we, too, may use, because not only are we made in the image and likeness of God but of the same substance."

"Image and likeness I have heard before," Barak said, "but not of the same substance. That is new to me."

"And what do you understand image and likeness to mean?" Devorah asked. "Certainly not that god looks like us?" It was her turn to be unbelieving.

Barak looked sheepish and nodded. "Not like you, a woman," he said. "But a man, like me."

"So," Devorah stood, hands on hips, glaring at him. "What's the difference between us and the idol worshipping Canaanites and Egyptians?"

"Yahweh is stronger than their gods," Barak said.

"He *is* stronger," Devorah said, "but not because He is as they are, only stronger. He is stronger because He is *not* like them or us and our idols. 'His image and likeness' means His ability to create, to use the power He is to manifest, to give form to the formless.

"Our God is not like other gods, merely a human being with super human appetites, jealousies and power - puppet master making us dance to his tune or an alien will outside our own. Our God is everywhere, equally present. Most meaningfully, It is the still, small voice in our hearts and minds, guiding us. Our Covenant with It is to remember this, to pay attention to It and to honor It. To always act with love, respect, compassion; for our word is law, whatever we say, think, feel and do is returned to us; as above, so below. Evil comes when we do otherwise, when we forget the Covenant and the power we wield.

"God does not punish us. What befalls us, good or evil, is the consequence of the thoughts, feelings and actions we have put into the Law, the seeds we have planted. As we sow, so shall we reap. As we lose sight of our inner power and the Covenant and become ever more like our idol-worshipping neighbors, planting as they plant, we reap what they reap and our lives and fates become more like theirs.

"There is a part of us that denies our power and responsibility within the Covenant; denies God and denies our oneness and reality

# Devorah

as spirit. This part is entirely earth-bound and cannot imagine being one with the Creator of all that is. For this part, appearances are real, all that matter. It knows nothing of faith, wisdom and belief. It knows and believes only what it can sense. Full of fear and bounded by the flesh and blood our bodies, this part is our everyday consciousness, our small "s" self.

"The Covenant teaches that we are more than this, yet even when confronted by evidence of our spiritual reality, as with the miracles of Exodus, our small self still wants to know where its next meal is coming from. To remember and live from the Covenant is to welcome God and act from our big "S" Self, knowing His love and compassion in all that we do.

Barak was grinning and nodding. "True, Devorah," he said, "very true!" He stood and walked about, affirming his understanding. "That's the way I am. I'm more with my little self, and you are more with your big "S" self."

Devorah smiled. "Most people are like that, Barak. But the big Self is still always there; always available. It is to seek and awaken this that we have been chosen and to do that for all peoples: Haibru and Canaanite.

"Both selves are necessary. That is what it means to be human, to be both spiritual *and* physical."

"Yes," Barak said. "That is the lesson of the battle of Jerhico! Joshua used both faith and preparation. We will need the Ark of the Covenant."

"That will not be easy to obtain," Devorah said. "The High Priest, Malachizer, is not on our side." Barak nodded. "But it is my job to deal with that, General," Devorah said, shaking her head and scowling as if she'd tasted something bitter.

"In fact," Devorah said, "Malachizer is the perfect example of what we were just talking about, of how the two parts do not understand one another very well. Spirit knows itself in the body, but the body denies Spirit. Working from the body, the purely physical, one would never acknowledge and experience Spirit. But working from the spiritual, one can access both spirit and body.

"That is what I'm trying to teach, even to the High Priest who should know. The Covenant is about working from the Spiritual first, then the physical, instead of what we always do—work from the physical to the spiritual. It's all God; that's what the oneness means. But when we work at the level of purest spirit, the innermost, ignoring appearances and conditions, that's when we get the best results—an easier, faster change in the physical conditions and appearances we're most concerned about."

Barak paused in his pacing. "Yes," he said, "as a General, conditions and appearances are my main concern."

"Indeed," Devorah said, rising, going to him and touching his shoulder. "And for the High Priest as well. He is strictly about appearances and what is written in the scrolls.

"But surely, Barak, you see that the more we dwell on the appearances and the more power we pour into them, the realer they seem. We must go from the inside out; from the vision of what we want, not what we don't want. It's like trying to change your shadow, by trying to touch or move the shadow. How silly, yes? Everyone knows the shadow is an effect of your body. The same is true for spirit and physical. The teaching says that your physical body is an effect of your spirit. One is cause, the other, effect. We keep failing to understand it is the same with the conditions of our lives. We keep trying to change the conditions, the outside, the shadow, by working with the conditions, touching the shadow; when what we need to change is our spiritual, mental and emotional states, our inner awareness, too."

"I see clearly now that we must do both," Barak said. "We have to pray *and* take practical action; to take practical action while praying; to act from a place of inner knowing and connection with our reality as spirit. We have to do both the right things, with the right attitude. One without the other will fail.

"Yes, General!" Devorah said. "We are a natural team you and I, Barak. You know the military arts and I the spiritual arts. As we go forward together, as God intends, I must become a bit more of the General and you a bit more of the prophet." She put both hands on his shoulders and smiled into his face. "Agreed?"

Barak took her hands in his, returned her smile, and said, "Agreed!"

"And you both must become more of a politician," Lappodoth said.

They turned and looked at him, their almost euphoria, evaporating.

Lappodoth nodded. "I see you understand my meaning," he said. "The challenge is getting the tribes to come together."

"I'd rather fight the Canaanites," Barak said, bitterly.

Devorah was, for once, momentarily without optimism. She shook her head sadly. "Truly, that is our greatest challenge. I think we can count on half of them: Zebulon, Naphtali, Issachar, Manasseh, my own Ephraim, and Asher."

"It saddens me," Lappodoth said, "that my own Judah is unreliable."

"With all due respect," Barak said, dipping his head to Devorah, "They duel with Ephraim for influence," Barak observed.

Devorah was unaffected. "You are correct, General," she said. "My kinsman have been dominant in this land from the very beginning."

Suddenly, the normally dour Lappodoth smiled and spoke with uncharacteristic hopefulness. "Come, General, wife," he said. "This too, is part of God's good will for us. Let us enumerate; look at each tribe individually and then decide how to proceed."

---

At the same moment, one hundred and forty leagues away, in the provincial garrison of Charoshet, Sisera sat in his tower suite with Zeber and Sostrum doing a similar enumeration. The town was strangely quiet. Most of the troops had gone home on leave. One company of cavalry and a handful of staff officers remained. The late afternoon air was hot and very dry. The sun beat down. Even in Sisera's high, open tower, the heat was oppressive.

"Thank the goddess, the light is fading," Zeber said, wiping his brow. "Shall I summon a slave to light the torches, my lord?" Sisera seemed not to hear him. *He's in a strange mood*, Zeber thought. *Almost like the fading light itself.*

"My good lord," Sostrum said as he put an arm around the General's shoulders. "Why so cheerless?"

Sisera shrugged off the comradely arm and stepped to the map table. "The twilight is right for us." His voice was low and listless. "Do you not see?" He turned and looked into Sostrum's face, then Zeber's, staring hard into their eyes 'till they looked away.

"I do not see it, Sisera," Zeber said with uncharacteristic bluntness. "And I will not allow you to continue in this fashion! You are the Lord General! We have 1,000 iron chariots and 30,000 heavily armed men. Against what?" He beckoned for Sostrum to join him.

Sostrum nodded and came to the map table. "Look my lord," he said, gesturing to the maps. "The kings have banded together, under your uncle Jabin. The biggest and strongest fortifications are in our hands. All the main highways are under our control; while the Haibrus are scattered and badly divided. It's every tribe and everyman for himself. We have oppressed them with our taxes, our laws and our military might. Our culture, cities and trade are superior to theirs in every way."

Zeber too, pointed down to the map. "The tribes east of the Jordan—Dan, Reuben and Gad, especially, are far removed from the main body of the Haibrus. And according to our spies, even more so in spirit than in actual distance. That is not to say that on this side of the Jordan all is harmony and peace. Far from it. Judah and Simeon in the south have troubles of their own, being plagued intermittently by famine, our allies the Philistines, and the Jebusites.

"Judah is also playing a double game with Ephraim—proud, arrogant Ephraim, ever spoiling for a fight. Ephraim, Naphtali, and Manasseh are the biggest threats. Judah feels it gains either way—if the Haibru's win and if Ephraim looses. Zebulon is the most accustomed to bearing our yoke; and Asher, who feels his interests lie with Sidon—his neighbor and our good ally—rather than with his fellow tribes."

Sisera still seemed distracted. "I am aware of all that you say." He looked from one to the other. "Yet I have a sense of foreboding, almost of dread. How can you forget Jericho and Joshua?"

"My Lord!" Zeber said. "That was two hundred years ago! The solidarity that united the Haibrus is long gone. Each tribe goes its own narrow way. The only thing they seem to have in common is their willingness to suffer our taxes, torture and tribute. No Haibru in his right mind will use the open highways. They seek out the narrow, winding, lesser known mountain paths."

"And, My Lord," Sostrum stage whispered, "our spies among them tell us their spirit appears to have been similarly afflicted: narrowed and shrunk. Their Torah, the word of their so called One God, is ignored as are many of the teachings and laws of their ancestors. Many are moving to our cities, becoming farmers and merchants and even worshiping our gods."

Sisera nodded. "I have heard this. But remember," he looked at them wild eyed, "their god is still the god of Moses and Joshua." They looked away from him. "Our spies also talk of their Sar and Prophetess, Devorah; she of the very same proud and arrogant Ephraim you said is ever spoiling for a fight. She is leading a spiritual revival and also stiffening Barak's spine.

"They say her wisdom and insight are extraordinary—divinely inspired. She has earned the respect of Ephraim and many of the other tribes. Day after day she sits beneath the palm tree in the oasis between Ramah and Bethel, dispensing justice, righting wrongs, and restoring law and order where before there was chaos and anarchy."

"But My Lord," Zeber said. "Even if this is true, of what use is that against the iron of our swords and chariots? Besides, she is only beginning and we are ready, now!"

Sisera stared hard into Zeber's face, then Sostrum's. The whites of his eyes shone eerily in the gathering gloom. "But that is the point! Don't you see? That is my concern! She can re-connect them with the power of their god; the power Joshua used against us. We were better prepared then, too." He paused and looked around suspiciously, as if to be sure no one was listening.

"We are dealing with powerful spiritual forces that we barely understand," he said. "You have heard the rumor that Devorah is none other than Anat, our very own War Goddess?"

Zeber stifled a grin. "I have, My Lord. But...."

"It is said She is angry with Her brother Baal and with us for ignoring Her."

"And the proof of her anger, My Lord?" Zeber asked.

"You have but to see the large number of sacrifices being offered to Anat's brother, Baal at the temples here. My mother writes that in Hazor a new temple to Anat has been erected and many sacrifices have been offered."

"But My good Lord," Sostrum said. "Even if this could be so, Devorah has done nothing yet."

"Indeed," echoed Zeber. "And perhaps she never will."

Sisera laughed. "Concerned as I am, we must hope she will not wait much longer, for *we* can not wait much longer. We can not maintain our state of readiness for another six months! You know that. We must take them all in one battle, where our chariots will dominate. But we cannot until she calls the tribes to rally to her."

"I think her call will come soon. Our strategy of harassment is working, My Lord," Zeber said.

"I concur," said Sostrum.

"Very well." Sisera smiled, seeming to have regained his strength and purpose. "We know Barak has concentrated fighters around Mt. Tabor. In four weeks, after our soldiers have returned from leave and are refreshed, we will mass here," he pointed to the map, "south of

Mt. Tabor in the Jezreel valley, along the banks of the Kishon river. We will form a continuous line girded by our fortifications from Charoshet in the west to Beth Shan in the east and thus cut off the north from the south their main source of reinforcements. We will force them down from Mt. Tabor and the hills to the valley where our iron chariots can annihilate them."

"Yes!" Sostrum and Zeber saluted.

Yael too, was thinking of Mt. Tabor. Cousin Jereboam would soon be making his way there to join Barak and the other seasoned Haibru fighters. But what could he do, Yael wondered? The monsters at the fortress in Charoshet had broken both his arms and wrists. He could barely hold a bowl of stew, much less a sword or lance.

Now he was working the bellows as Haber prepared the molten tin for the mold. He said he felt no pain, but Yael noticed him wince if he held something at an awkward angle or if the weight was not right for his grip. She loved her cousin almost as much as she loved her husband. Jereboam was her age and was the son of her mother's sister. They had played together when they were babies and youngsters. Yael felt nothing but fondness, perhaps for her own gentle and sheltered childhood, when she looked at him as she was doing now; quickly followed by a flame of anger at the Canaanites who had crippled him, so fierce that she was blinded by rage.

"Oh, Lord God," she prayed. "Grant me the opportunity to have justice in Your most holy name. Grant me the opportunity to take an eye for an eye as You have decreed, not only for my cousin who honors You and fights against Your enemies, but for all Your people who have been treated unfairly by the Canaanites! May the most mighty among them be laid low and may my hand be Thy instrument! Amen."

Haber and Jereboam were working rapidly now, but with a grace and calm that reminded Yael of the sure-footedness and peace of God. They had laid out six molds and were pouring the steaming molten tin into each, before it cooled. She was proud of Haber. He was a good provider, a good lover and compassionate. He had taken Jereboam in happily. And though Haber was older, his passion for sex, nearly matched her own, even tho his lovemaking was quite prosaic.

*Devorah*

Haber allowed, no encouraged, Yael to take the lead in their lovemaking. Though she had been a virgin at the time of their marriage, simply by following her instincts and not holding back, Yael led them, and was still leading them, to joys and passions that more than satisfied him and often satisfied her. Yael licked her lips, thinking of Haber's erect penis. What would it be like to ride him in public, at the majlise, with everyone watching? She touched herself, there. How wicked!

Could sex like that be of God? The Canaanites thought it was. Why did her people have to be such stick in the muds? To them, if it was daring, wild and exciting it had to be evil. But really, where else but God could it come from? It was just pure, spontaneous passion. She had no evil intent. She merely wanted to express herself.

Yael sensed that Devorah and Lappodoth had a similar, but more fulfilling relationship. Perhaps it was her attitude - that openness to all the manifestations of spirit in and around her - that made Devorah so attractive and effective. Yael had gone to Devorah's majlise last month feeling angry and upset, and had come away feeling calmer and maybe a little optimistic, even though Devorah had promised no new action and had not issued the call to arms Yael thought necessary--that everyone felt was necessary.

Then a few weeks later, as if by magic, Jereboam appeared. And though no call to arms had been issued, men and supplies were flowing to Barak's strong point at Mt. Tabor. God did work in mysterious ways! And here was Yael's beloved Jereboam! Though permanently crippled, his eyes still burned with his characteristic contradictory combination of soft compassion and fierce zeal. Yael felt both comfortable and intrigued by him.

"Now then, cousin!" She said when he walked into their encampment as if he'd just been with them yesterday afternoon. "What brings you here?" She threw herself into his arms and he embraced her with his one good arm.

"God is good, cousin!" He said. "Is it not so?"

"To see you is good, cousin; to see you thus is sad. Was it as terrible as it looks, Jereboam?" She asked, stepping back to take him in at arm's length, compassion flowing from her eyes with her tears.

Jereboam heaved a sigh; looked down, smile gone; looked back into her eyes. "It was, Yael. It was terrible. Often I begged Yahweh to take me to Him. But each time he encouraged me and blessed me with strength. He even encouraged me to sing The Schma, which I did;

felt good doing so; but was only beaten more severely by Sostrum, Sisera's adjutant." Jereboam shook his head. "That man, Sostrum, must die," he said.

"He shall, cousin," Yael said, "God grant me the skill and I will do it myself!"

Later, as they sat by the tent flap taking their ease, Haber talked about how their weapons might be made the equal of the Canaanites. "This iron is not so difficult to work with, from what I've been told," he said.

"The difficulty is in acquiring the ore," Jereboam agreed.

"It is against the Canaanite law," Yael reminded them. "It is death to work iron."

They both looked at her and smiled tolerantly, as one would at a child.

"Your love is a treasure, wife," Haber said, "and I know you worry about us. But I also know you would never be governed by an unjust law, much less an unjust Canaanite law."

"You are right, husband," Yael touched his cheek and smiled into his eyes. "And I do love Justice; and think we can no longer go on as we have."

"Iron weapons would level the field," Jereboam said. "What is to prevent us from sending our brave men to sea to get it wherever the others are getting it?"

"But we cannot make the tools in any case," Yael said. "As it is we use a foreign blacksmith and he keeps his art a well hidden secret."

"Not so!" Haber said. "There is a blacksmith in Megiddo whose 'secret' has long been common knowledge. Practically every farmer of Mannasah has iron tools. We must get their expertise to Barak. If the other tribes with access to the sea, if especially Asher were to show some initiative we might get the ore; and together with the skill of Manasseh we might have the weapons of iron we need."

"We must bring this to Devorah's attention!" Yael exclaimed.

"I will tell her of it," Jereboam said, "on my way through Ephraim to Mt. Tabor. But I must tell you," he took Yael's hands and gazed deeply into her eyes, "that I think this time it is too late for iron weapons. It will take time to produce enough and we cannot wait. We will have to fight within the month."

# CHAPTER THREE

Yael would be so pleased, Jereboam thought. Not only am I here with Devorah, but she looks like she's going to give birth any day now! I must find a scribe and try to get word to her.

"Jereboam, thank you," Devorah was saying. "You and your cousin and indeed your whole family are the kind of people who make my duty worthwhile." Devorah sighed and shrugged. "Of course I serve all our people, but...."

"No need to explain, Sar," he said respectfully. "You are human, with likes and dislikes as we all have." She looks so good, and healthy, Jereboam thought. Vigorous, bold, yet soft and cuddly. At one with the new life filling her belly. She is truly a blessing!

Lappodoth came in and nodded to Jereboam who was a stranger to him.

"Husband, this is Jereboam. He is a Judean and was recently released from the fortress of Charoshet after being tortured."

Lappodoth frowned and embraced Jereboam. "I am so sorry kinsman," he said.

"It is what is, Lappodoth. I have been a soldier of Israel for thirteen years." He turned to Devorah. "Sar, I have come for two reasons." She nodded to him. "First, I beg you on behalf of our people and with all the judgment and experience of my years of military training—call the tribes to battle. It is time."

"I agree, Jereboam" she said. "And so does Barak. Your second point?"

"We can have weapons of iron. The ore can be obtained overseas from the same sources the Canaanites use, and we have skilled blacksmith among our brothers of Mannasah."

"Yes. Thank you. We are aware of that. We have asked Eli of Asher to outfit a ship, lay-up trade goods, olives, oil and grain, and go to Macedonia where the ore can be obtained. Barak now has three blacksmiths from Mannasah with him on Tabor. They have raided Acco and have a sufficient amount of iron ore for 1,000 swords."

Jereboam was ecstatic. "That is excellent news!" he said. "Why have we not heard of this?"

"It must be kept secret from the Canaanites," Lappodoth replied, "for obvious reasons. We cannot afford to provoke them, nor do we want them to ask the Sea Peoples to help them find our ship." Jereboam was nodding. "They know about our raid on Acco, of course, but do not know exactly how much ore we have taken."

"Jereboam," Devorah said, "you have shown yourself to be a brave and intelligent man. May I ask you a spiritual question?"

"Please, Sar."

"Devorah. Call me, Devorah."

"Thank you, Devorah."

"Our ability to win in battle against the Canaanites, given the facts, is non-existent."

"It would take a miracle," Jereboam agreed.

"I believe a miracle is possible, because I believe the One God is everywhere equally present—in us, the sky, the clouds, rain, in the Canaanites, the hills, the forests." Jereboam nodded, not having any difficulty with what Devorah was saying. "I believe that the power we call God is a natural power like lightening or the wind, and that just as we may use the wind to sail our ships or run the pumps that bring water up from our wells—once we have learned its laws, so can we use the power of the One God within us to connect with the power of the One God that surrounds us."

"I feel what you say is clear," Jereboam said, "and perhaps even true. But it is not what the priests say."

"I *feel* God, Jereboam; *commune* with him. Don't you?"

"I do; with no need of priests and ceremony."

"Yes!" Devorah said. "Yes! That is God. But as you said, the priests are not happy about that. I would have the priests be happy before I call the tribes to war. Half the tribes are already doubtful. The priests might provide the last excuse they need not to fight. If I am a blasphemer, how can my call be honored?"

"But you are not!" Jereboam exclaimed.

"In their eyes, perhaps I am. No ritual, nor ceremony, nor priests do I require to be righteous and serve the One God, our people and myself. And I think I have done a pretty good job of it."

"You have!"

*Devorah*

"The personal experience of connection is more powerful than any ritual. In fact, that is what the rituals, ceremonies and priests are intended to do, to make that connection and help us experience the One God in and around us. Yet now the rituals have becoming a purpose in and of themselves and people are pining for the lack of true connection.

"General Barak is one such. He has the skill and intelligence, but too often doubts his connection and faith. He feels alone and in danger. If he had an experience of his connection with the One God, he would be unbeatable. I will have to supply that connection for him.

"It is the *fact* of our connection—our Covenant, our belief and faith in it, with or without the rituals—that will sustain us and bring victory. The priests believe in a god that is little more than an idol, like the gods of Egypt and our neighbors. Yes, we make no graven images. But the priests' god lives in the ark in the temple and can only be approached through ritual and ceremony."

"That is not the god I experienced in the torture chambers of Charoshet," Jereboam said. "Yes I sang praise, but that was not to invoke him, for I felt him first, within me. I sang the Shma for the joy of the feeling in my heart; for the sudden realization of the truth of my being and connection to him even as they broke first one arm, then the other."

Devorah nodded. Lappodoth came and put his arms about her, kissed her on the cheek and turned to Jereboam. "We are few, Jereboam, very few. Devorah would call the tribes to rally to her, but what of the priests?" Jereboam nodded in agreement. "And besides," Lappodoth said, patting her belly, "I think we have five or six weeks to go, then a few weeks of recovery before Devorah can be actively involved."

"Need she be 'actively involved'?" Jereboam asked. "What of Barak?"

Devorah shook her head, sadly, "Barak, as we have said, has little faith. I will have to be with him."

"He is a good tactician and General," Jereboam said.

"Indeed," Lappodoth said. "Many admire his skill and will join with us because of him. But his heart is not in it."

"It is not that, exactly," Devorah said. "He can not over look the odds against us. He can not imagine how we can triumph, even under the best of conditions. He wants more men, iron weapons, cavalry and a few chariots. I do not blame him. I want them, too. He knows we must fight and soon, but he can not see a way to win. A stale mate is the best he can see.

"I do not see a way to win, either. But I know we shall. We must plan and take the steps we can then trust in the rightness of our cause. A battlefield is a fluid place, is it not Jereboam?" He nodded. "Much can go wrong," Devorah continued. "The weather, for one, can be quite treacherous." As if on cue, masses of heavily laden rain clouds darkened the sky. She smiled. "Our opportunities will arise and we must be prepared to seize them. We have what we have, what we've been given. It is good and enough. Let us make the most of it."

Devorah's smile turned to a grimace. She staggered. Her eyes rolled up into her head so that only the whites were showing. She moaned and collapsed in a heap. Lappodoth, nearest her, crouched and lifted her head to his breast. Jereboam also knelt, panic in his eyes.

"Fear not, Jereboam," Lappodoth said. "She is well. See her chest rise and fall with her breath? She is having a vision. Usually she receives guidance in less traumatic ways, but often it takes this form."

Twenty minutes later, Devorah stirred, opened her eyes and blinked. Normal consciousness had returned. Jereboam felt himself begin to breathe again. She made to stand and Lappodoth helped her up. Jereboam stood with them. She smiled and sought to put her visitor at ease.

"It is fine, Jereboam. I am well." She paused. "I must go to the priests of Shiloh before I call the tribes to war."

Jereboam was disappointed. "The priests are important. But the call to arms.... The call will take time - to reach the tribes and to have them respond. Could you not issue the call and while you are waiting for responses, visit Shiloh?"

Devorah smiled. "I had thought it was either one or the other, Jereboam, but now see that both the call *and* the visit can be done almost at once. Thank you! It shall be as you say." She paused to consider. "I know you were on your way to Barak. But would you wait a few hours, until I can compose the call, then take it to all twelve tribes?"

"I would be honored, Devorah!" Jereboam looked down and swallowed, not wanting to contradict her a second time. "May I suggest that I take your call to Mt. Tabor and that you send twelve other messengers simultaneously to all the tribes? That would be faster."

Devorah looked at him steadily then smiled. "Again you are correct, my kinsman! More proof that the One God is fully present in

*Devorah* 63

everyone and everything. It shall be as you have said. Go now." She made gentle shooing motions. "I will compose the call, opening myself to our father. Lappodoth will give it to you when it is completed."

Jereboam bowed and left the tent. "He is unusually nationalistic for a Judean," he said.

"Indeed," Devorah agreed. "They are a proud people. Almost a nation unto themselves."

"That is putting it mildly, wife." Lappodoth looked deeply into her eyes. "Surely you know how they foment doubt and mistrust with Dan, Simeon and Reuben so that the interests of Judah triumph?"

"I am aware, who can not be? The High Priest is Judean. Yet they are all not that way. What of Jereboam?"

"The exception to the rule," Lappodoth said. "The leadership of Judah is not like Jereboam. You have heard the reports of our spies, there is some reliable evidence that they connive with the Philistines."

Devorah nodded. "'Connive' and side with in a war involving their own people are two different things."

"True. Yet they are fully capable of staying 'neutral' and sitting the war out."

Devorah shook her head wearily. "Yes. Please, husband, leave me now so that I may compose the Call to Arms."

Lappodoth dipped his head, kissed her on the cheek and left the tent. Devorah collected the papyrus, ink and quill and seated herself and the writing table. She closed her eyes, allowed her breathing to slow and heard the busy sounds of camp grow muffled and distant. "Oh, Abba," she said. "I am so blessed to be Your daughter. Thank you for my life, the unborn life within me," she patted her stomach, "and all the lives everywhere around us. I know you intend the world to be a joyous life-affirming garden for all humankind; that we are to be good stewards of all You have given us: plants, animals, fish and birds. But we have forgotten this. We have lost sight of our oneness with You and of our Covenant. We have used Your gifts to harm one another, cause injustice, pain and suffering. I want to turn from all of that, Father, and return to Your dream for us.

"I want to rally the Haibru people to me, that they may act lawfully within Thy framework and use Your power to correct the injustice, pain and suffering they have been experiencing - that they themselves have created using Your power. Now is it time to use Your power differently, to see ourselves and our neighbors not as oppressors and ourselves as victims, but to stand before You, ourselves and our neighbors as people of strength and substance willing to assert our claims for justice, joy and sustenance."

Devorah's heart throbbed and leapt at her word/thoughts. How right they felt! How timely. "Now, Father, I claim my birthright as Your daughter and ask that You give me the words that will rally the Your children to me. We must stand, Father, and assert ourselves. You know that it is long past time for us to do so. I call for justice, not retribution; for freedom, not for slavery. I know I speak the truth, that we are one and that as I speak these words and release them into Your law, this will surely come to pass! Amen."

---

She fell into a deep sleep and dreamt.

A city, large and of great beauty was spread before her, surrounded by high, crenellated walls of huge, square, baize stone blocks. The space between the walls was filled with green date palms and pools of water scattered amidst white, one and two story wood and stucco homes. Dominating the western quarter, a great building made of the same baize stone blocks stood four stories tall. Surrounded by four courts, each separated by gauzy draperies flapping and blowing in the wind, the building seemed to be a temple. Smoke from cooking fires, sacrifices, blacksmiths, tinsmiths and other artisans rose and drifted in the cool brisk air. Sounds of hundreds of busy residents drifted up to her and she saw men and women, children and animals living full lives in the city. Some were clearly Israelites by their clothes, others Egyptian and many others whose garments she did not know.

Birds dipped and soared and chirped in the lush olive grove surrounding her. A warm green-growing smell filled the cool air. Light streamed through the trees and sparkled on the leaves.

Devorah felt joy as she looked down upon the city even though she did not know its name or where it was. The brown hill she stood upon and those around her and stretching off into the distance, meant she was probably in the south, in the land of Judah. She knew too, somehow, this was an Israelite city; its neat clean streets, happy and prosperous people the promise of things to come. How glad Lappodoth would be - no more tents!

Another vision of the future appeared. Devorah was no longer in the promised land, but in some far off place with totally different trees, weather and terrain. Cold desolation and an empty, dry, used-up feeling replaced her joy and warmth; and she was afraid, deeply afraid. Shuddering and wide-eyed at the sight of her breath congealing in the freezing air before her, Devorah stood in what she knew to be snow, even though she'd only seen it twice before. Words to describe what she was experiencing were hard to come by because she'd never experienced anything like it before.

Beneath her freezing bare feet, was a thick, rough hewn wooden plank. Another, similar plank was a foot away, and another, and another, stretching away, like some kind of track or road, into the distant silhouette of a two story walled enclosure. Metal, perhaps, iron, lay in two parallel rows on top of the evenly spaced planks and gleamed in the dim moonlight. Damp freezing air hung in grey vaporous clouds obscuring the faint disc of the moon. Every few moments, a great light stabbed into the darkness and swept around her.

The beams of light came from the sharp roofed towers surrounding the distant enclosure. Black flags with a twisted, red symbol in the center, snapped in the wind. Further ahead, beyond the towers and the enclosure, a tall chimney pierced the low lying mists to spew thick coils of oily black smoke into the air. A filthy, greasy stench burned Devorah's eyes and throat and made her gag. Large, heavy, black vultures dipped and wheeled in the frigid air.

Wails—shrieks of unbearable unimaginable pain and human suffering, muffled by the snow and vaporous air, barely audible to her ears, crashed and echoed in her heart like the waves in that cavern at the edge of the Great Sea. What was this place? Could it be Gahanna - hell? Perhaps, but Devorah's senses told her it was definitely real; a time and place very different from her previous vision, but just as real. But what time and place? There was a cold starkness, a bare inorganic squareness, that was the antithesis of the soft, organic roundness of her own time and the time of the first vision. It was a distant future in a distant part of the world.

She closed her eyes, but still felt the shrieks of pain vibrate through her heart and her bones. Please, she sobbed; please, let it stop! How can this be real? One future bright, followed by another of unimaginable horror! Would she contribute to this? Were these visions the result of actions she was *about* to take, or had taken already? I have always been guided, she sobbed, gulping the cold air and choking on the stench.

*You are part of this daughter, but not* the *cause.* She felt calmer, opened her eyes and again found herself on the high place above the city in Judah. A third vision of the future. The western wall was still there along with remnants of the northern wall, but now the walls gleamed white, and at their center were wondrous, gleaming tall buildings. Man made objects flew through the clouds above, while in the city, other man made objects resembling carts and carriages raced through wide, paved streets without making dust - but without horses or donkeys to pull them!

Devorah closed her eyes, opened them again and was in her tent. She looked about her. The familiar smells, sounds and sights, the touch of the sheepskin and warmth of the dry air comforted her. She felt the new life stir in her belly and smiled softly.

"What shall be, shall be for you my daughter," she whispered to the unborn child. "Life is our gift and we shall use it up. I had wanted to spend these next few days and weeks quietly, here in our tent, communing with you. I see now that I am called to wage war on the Canaanites, prop up Barak and soothe the priests of Shiloh.

"I take heart in knowing that as I do all of this you will be with me and I will be thinking of you, praying constantly and that we will be constantly guided, guarded and protected by the one power that sustains us both and the universe." Devorah patted her belly and arose.

"Lappodoth," she called. He came to her. "Let us make preparations for Shiloh."

"What of the call to arms?" he asked.

"Indeed," she smiled. "Thank you!" She kissed his cheek. "I had forgotten it. Prepare for our journey, food, escort, animals and," she seated herself at the table and drew the writing implements to her, "by the time you have finished, I will be done."

"My brothers," she wrote. "Some of us have enough, others struggle and some suffer in dire need. The best, most fertile land belongs to the Philistines, Canaanites and Moabites. We are oppressed with armed might and unfair taxes. We cannot use the highways. It is not safe to trade. We live in tents, instead of houses. Brothers, our work is incomplete!

"What one of us can not accomplish, many of us might. Community has ever been our strength and reward. I now call upon you to set aside individual and tribal differences, remember our connection to one another, and come together as brothers of the Covenant. As one, beneath God's banner, we shall stand and assert our Father's blessings.

"We are all His children: Haibru, Philistine, Moabite, Egyptian, Canaanite—all His children. But for too long we have not claimed our rights at His bountiful table. It is time now to cease dwelling upon our sins and failures, refrain from thinking and acting like victims and, like deserving children, ask our Father for His bounty.

"This is, first and foremost about us—our people, our tribes, our Covenant with the One God. And has nearly nothing to do with the other peoples in this land. For, though He is their Father, too, it is about *our* Covenant; *our* responsibility and *our* deeds!

"We will come together believing in the rightness of our cause. We will gather our weapons, assert our just and legitimate claims for fair and equal treatment, negotiate and trust that justice will be done and our needs will be met. We will fight and fight fiercely! But our whole effort is to live in peace and equality with our neighbors. We do not ask God to do to them what they have done to us. Rather we ask that He bless us as He has blessed them.

"We come together, sons and daughters of the Covenant, greatly outnumbered, under-trained, and ill-equipped, knowing we shall be successful only because we have no choice *but* to rely upon our relationship with the One God. And what, truthfully, could be more powerful than the one—omniscient, omnipotent, omnipresent God, alive in you and me, in the stars, clouds, rain and the desert? Can Sissera's 900 iron chariots equal Its power? We take solace and strength and hope in the rightness of our cause, as the Covenant has taught us to know that rightness; and we know now that as our awareness stays steady and fixed on the eternal Presence in and around us, we shall be successful!"

Devorah handed Lappodoth the papyrus. He read it without expression.

"There's not enough red meat in it, wife," he finally said.

Devorah was disappointed. "You don't like it?"

"I do like it! It comes directly from your relationship with the One God—beautiful and just, clear and honest."

"Well...?" she asked.

"You're asking the tribes to send their able-bodied men. You're asking women and children to pick-up the slack. You're asking for economic hardship. You're asking people to risk life, limb, family and homestead."

"Yes...?"

"They need flame and ferocity, blood, guts and red meat to motivate them!" He looked at her, then raised his arm for emphasis, saying, "'Victory! Defeat of our foes! Death to the enemies of God and Israel!' These are the words they will want."

"Is that really necessary? We will be as bad as the Canaanites if we act from that place."

"It has always been so, wife, and probably always will be."

"You're right, my husband." Devorah smiled and leaned forward to kiss his cheek. "It will always be thus, until it is *not* thus. Now it is not thus. This," she took the papyrus from him, "is the new way, a different call, not to war, but to fierce, armed assembly. War will come if the Canaanites do not deal fairly with us."

"I understand and agree, Devorah. But I think others will not. I think the tribes will make their economic and political judgments on their narrow, individual self interests. They would do that no matter what you wrote. Community and nation-hood are non-existent, probably always were nonexistent. But a fierce and bloody call to arms might push some in the councils to joining us. That document won't."

"I honor your wisdom, husband. It will no doubt be as you say. But those who come and respond to this," she held the papyrus up, "will be of a different quality than those who might come for blood. They will be closer to the One God, fiercer, more committed, more cunning and will demonstrate more staying power. And, when we are successful, they will build a better peace."

Lappodoth dipped his head. "I'm nearly done assembling our things for the trip to Shiloh."

"Good!" Devorah strode out of the tent, looking for Jonah, her scribe. Seeing him, she called and - possessed by a new urgency - began giving him instructions while he was still a few yards away. "Make twelve copies of this. Give this one to Jereboam and give the copies to twelve messengers, one for each Tribal Council and send them off immediately. As soon as you complete a copy, find a messenger and send him. Instruct the messengers that they are to wait for a response and we would encourage the Councils to respond in seven days. I am going to Shiloh."

As Haber caressed the warm flesh of Yael's breast, her nipple erected. He bent to take it's firmness into his mouth and laved it with his tongue. His penis jutted erect against her thigh. Yael, eyes closed and sighing with the tingling passion of her husband's manhood,

*Devorah* 69

her fingers in a hollow fist up and down its length. He moaned and squirmed trying to re-position himself to enter her.

"Take my other breast, husband," Yael said, not granting him entrance. Obediently, Haber switched his attention to Yael's other breast. But that only inflamed him more. He reached down to spread her legs. She resisted. His hand was wet with her juices; the tent redolent with their musk.

"Oh, Yael. Enough! Your smell and taste, the feel of your wondrous flesh have made me nearly insane with passion. Open your legs! Allow me to come inside you. I want children."

Yael moaned, covered his mouth with hers and rolled on top of him. Her weight was warm and rich, fertile to him. It pleased him to be her couch, the cushion she rested upon. He reached up to stroke her firm fleshy buttocks, the desire to be in her vagina momentarily forgotten. She moaned, kissed him more deeply and ground her hips on his penis, her large, firm breasts resting on his chest. Haber moaned and returned the pressure of her hips with that of his own. He was near, she thought, very near.

"Please, Yael. Allow me to enter you. I.... I.... ahh, ahhh, ahhhh." His orgasm was intense and prolonged. Yael rolled off him and took a bit of fleece near their sleeping carpet to wipe his spendings from her belly and pubic hair.

"Why, Yael? Why will you not allow me to give you my seed? I want children! I am growing old. I am already 8 years your senior."

"Are you not satisfied, Haber? Do I not please and satisfy you? Don't you delight in my body?"

"I do. But it is not enough. I want us to have a child, many children."

"Well, I do not," Yael said, and stood.

The sight of her voluptuous curves towering above him, and the fresh wave of odor flowing from her body, reinvigorated Haber's diminishing erection.

"Please, Yael. Let us try again, now. Look! I am ready."

She looked and smiled down at him. "I do adore your penis, husband, and love holding and fondling it, and loved riding it. But I think we have been blessed all these years without children and I do not want one now."

"What do you mean? How dare you!"

"No, Haber," Yael said eyes flashing with a disdain that frightened him. "How dare *you*? You are aware of our lives here and the potential for war. Should we lose that war, what will happen to a child of ours, to any Haibru child?" Haber shook his head. "They would," Yael continued, "if they lived, be used as slaves. All our people would again be enslaved.

"And if we win against the Canaanites, we will still have the Moabites and Philistines... and ourselves! Have you heard how the priests of Shiloh attack Devorah; suggest that she blasphemes? How could you ask me to bring a child into such a world?"

Haber stood, penis shriveled, and looked levelly into her eyes; wordlessly, a stunned expression of deep sadness on his face. In the silence, the sounds of the camp—sheep bleating, goats and chickens calling, bells on animals clanking and chiming, dogs barking, human voices, the soughing of the wind and children laughing and crying—drifted in to them.

"Life, Yael," Haber gestured to the tent flap. "Life knows itself. Life can not be denied. Children are part of that, Yael."

She shook her head and returned his look, starring deeply and steadily into his eyes. "It is *not* inevitable, Haber. We have been given reason; we can choose. I choose my life and your life. We need not add to this. We have enough. We have each other." Yael shuddered and looked away. "I am speaking from my heart, husband. Sometimes I feel like the angel of death. Strange dreams and visions haunt me. I see murder...."

Haber hugged her; the shuddering subsided.

Yael broke from his embrace and took a step back. "Am I losing my mind?" she asked, then rushed on, not giving him an opportunity to respond. "No, I think not. I think: death is a part of life. Death culls and removes diseased tissue. There are those among us and many among the Canaanites who I would gladly give to death."

"Enough!" Haber exclaimed. "Yael, please stop this talk." He took a step towards her, his arms open. She retreated, glaring, teeth bared, a growl-like rumble in her throat.

"I am telling you what is in my heart, Haber. We have been too long together for me to hide this from you."

"I have never seen this thing in you, Yael, never heard it, before. Perhaps, it *is* an illness. Perhaps you might visit Hakim Saul in Charoshet...."

Charoshet! The moment she heard the name, Yael knew she was to go there. "Perhaps so, my husband. But Charoshet is Sisera's garrison. It will be strongly fortified, with many soldiers and so will not be safe for a decent woman."

"Sisera has given leave to much of the garrison," Haber said. "My niece and nephew have lately passed thru there. They saw Hakim Saul, too." He reached for the purse, dangling from his belt. "Here." He took out five silver pieces. "This is more than enough for food, lodging and the doctor." She hesitated. "Take it, please", Haber said. "You must be well. Thank God we have the money to pay."

"But no doctor can help with what I feel."

"Please. Go and find out. Besides, the change will be good for you."

Yael nodded, smiled cunningly and reached out her hand.

---

It had taken only two days and three nights to reach Charoshet. Yael had disguised herself as a Moabite and joined a small Moabite caravan under the protection of their Proctor. The lingering anxiety she'd been experiencing, morphed into a perverse thrill of anticipation, a kind of looming dread; a sense of impending great fateful deeds, the moment she took the silver pieces from Haber. Though the trip had been peaceful and uneventful, Yael's sleep had been fitful, with dreams of bloody wounds and ethical turmoil - worse than any she experienced in her husband's tent.

It began the first night out when she helped to pitch her tent. The mallet she selected, seemed to move in her hand, as if with a life of its own. She picked up a very sharp wooden spike, eight inches long and touched its point with a finger tip. Her eyes clouded and her heart beat more rapidly.

This had happened once before, when she and Haber had returned from Hazor. Yael felt frozen in time, tense, waiting. An image of a handsome man in armor, Canaanite armor, drifted before her. She looked down; he was lying at her feet, asleep in a fetal position. As in that first vision, Yael felt a thrill and her nipples grew taught. She felt out of control yet guided by an inexorable power. It was hard to breath. She could hear the blood pounding in her ears. She gripped the tent peg, pointed it down towards the man's head and reached for the mallet....

Yael shook herself awake, panting and soaked with sweat. Had she cried out? No, all was dark and quiet around her. She breathed deeply, grew calmer, and felt the sweat begin to dry on her face. Murder. She was going to do murder in the dream, and, if the Canaanite shamans were correct about such powerful waking and sleeping visions, would actually do murder in real life.

Who was that handsome warrior at her feet, the man she would kill? Clean shaven, same age as Haber but better in build, more masculine with a longish straight nose, high cheekbones, square jaw and reddish blond hair. No dream figure had ever been more vivid. And his armor! Not worn, scraped and caved-in like the rare bits of Hebrew armor she'd seen, but fresh, well-tended and imposing.

The kind of armor noble men in Hazor wore for ceremonies at the temple of Baal. Her flesh crawled, yet tingled, too. She had crept into the first courtyard of the profane temple in Hazor while Haber had been in the marketplace. Even now, Yael couldn't help comparing herself to the lithe temple maidens who danced so seductively and dared to make love out in the open, in public. Her body was as good as theirs. She too could dance and sway hypnotically. Her face too, was as attractive, yet without the kohl and rouge and other tricks they used, not nearly as wanton and seductive. She pursed her lips and slid her tongue out to moisten them, to make them shine.

Oh, but what was all this about? She had no need of such things with Haber. But that was plain, unadorned procreation without much allure or passion and it often left Yael with a sense of lack. Enough! She inhaled deeply striving to turn her mind to more decent things. I have no *need* of kohl, rouge and passion, she thought. But something in me burns for it. I am still young.... Finally, she fell asleep.

The dream returned on the second night. This time when she awoke in the pitch black silence, damp with sweat, she also noticed the dampness between her legs. Had that been there last night? It had. Somehow, the murder was bound up with the heathen temple and the sex they practiced there. Was there a temple in Charoshet? She'd ask a Moabite in the morning.

"Indeed!" said the Moabite soldier. "There are many. But the most sacred and most beautiful is the temple of Astarte, sister and consort of Baal. They do no human sacrifices to the mighty Astarte, but instead offer only love in Her name. The most comely of all sacred prostitutes offer themselves there. It is said that the Goddess may enter any woman in the precincts of Her temple, possessing her so that woman will offer herself to whoever will lie with her."

Yael's mouth fell open and she stared.

"Come, lady!" the Moabite guard said. "Certainly you have heard of Astarte?"

Not wanting to be seen as what she was, a Haibru, Yael quickly recovered. "Yes, of course. I had no idea she had such a fine temple here."

"Indeed, She does! And many are the women taken by Her and made into willing and lustful sacred prostitutes. I myself have lain with one; and it is said the great Sisera, General of the Canaanite Armies, also serves the Goddess there."

Yael reached down, touched the cloth of her robe to be sure the moisture between her legs was not coming thru. "Thank you. Where in the city is Astarte's temple?"

"You can't miss it. It's not far from the caravansary and near the garrison fortress." He looked at her, a gleam in his eyes. "I could take you there, if you like."

That was like a slap in the face. He was battle worn, bruised and old; not more of the same, she thought. "No. No, thank you sir. You have been most kind." She dipped her head and returned to her tent.

What was happening to her? How could she be thinking and feeling what she was thinking and feeling? Her entire life was about duty, family and the One God. Where was this coming from; this deep almost overpowering urge to serve an idol as its sexual slave; the need to offer and expose herself publicly? And to use the mallet and tent spike to murder that beautiful Canaanite warrior?

She was dizzy and sat down. The noise around her was increasing. They were breaking camp. She had to arise and do her part. "Oh, Abba," she prayed. "This feels so wrong, so unlike my devotion to you, almost like someone else has taken control of me—my heart and mind. But I know, Abba, that my soul is Yours and I do only that which You would have me do, which fits Your plan. Though I do not, and cannot know what part I am to play in Your grand design, I know that I do have a part, and will play it gratefully. I beg you to guide me, and will go forward with the sure and certain knowledge that I am doing what I must do. Thank you!"

For a brief moment, she felt soothed, clear and at peace. Then she got up, stepped out of the tent and saw the Moabite soldier she'd been speaking to; and when she felt his yearning, hungry eyes caress her, the uncomfortable longing returned to pulse in her veins.

A few hours later, they arrived in Charoshet. Since their conversation, the Moabite warrior had hovered around Yael like a bee around pollen. Such flirting was unusual among the Haibrus and Yael felt both gratified by the attention and repelled. As he and the others unpacked the mules and camels, Yael walked rapidly to the street of the doctors, to find Hakim Saul's home. She was more hopeful now, that he might be able to help her manage her strong urges. After all, his skill was given him by the One-God....

But did not her own urges come from that same source? Was He not fully present in all people, places and things? In the Temple of Astarte, too? Yael stopped walking and looked around her. If she went to the left, she would soon be at Hakim Saul's. If she went to the right, where she saw the battlements of the garrison fortress rising above the street, she would be near the Temple. Which way?

The thudding of her heart and tightness in her throat, was that fear or fulfillment? Clearly, the Temple was not consistent with the life she had known. But did that mean it was not of God? She was here, wasn't she? There was no question she had some destiny, some larger fate to fulfill. Her urges, the almost swooning, damp passion told her the Temple was meant for her. But what would happen there? She could not see past just going. Her sex was dripping. She'd never been so aroused before. What could this possibly have to do with God's plan for her?

But what if her entire normal way of thinking was not the only way of thinking? What if her 'normal' way was actually impeding a better way, the true way, keeping her from being one with God? What if the urges were a truer, better way to God? If that were so, wouldn't she have to release the old ways so the new ways could come thru? And wouldn't the new ways be urging her on, while the old ways fought to keep their place?

The Temple was the next step. Could she go back to Haber afterwards? Perhaps not, but probably yes. She would be changed, but after all, she was still who she was. That would not be wiped out by a visit to the Temple of Astarte. Perhaps, she would return better and stronger for the Temple experience; embodying both the new ways and the old ways. Yes! That was it! And what of the murder, was that to happen here, in her own tent, or not at all? Something to do *with* the murder, but not the murder itself, would happen here.

Yael closed her eyes and spun herself around. I will go in the direction I am facing after the spin, she thought. All is God, and God is good, so if I go to the Temple or Hakim Saul's it will be well. She spun herself vigorously, wobbled, then opened her eyes. The battlements of the fortress loomed ahead of her.

Astarte's Temple was indeed beautiful. Yael felt feminine grace and flowing energy in its open spaces and elegant curving arches. Tall, two story date palms, spaced at close intervals, surrounded its curving forecourts creating the feeling of an oasis. Musicians walked about freely, strumming lyres and playing pipes. Water danced in bubbling fountains. Merely to enter the Temple precincts was to sigh and unwind; which Yael did as she seated herself upon one of the many elegantly carved stone benches, facing the pool at the entrance to the second court.

*This is a sin,* part of her screamed as she began to relax and give herself over to the peaceful refreshing rhythm of the place. *Idols are worshiped here and shameful sexual practices done.*

I see none of either, Yael responded, relaxing further.

*But what awaits in the courts beyond? You* are *going to go further aren't you?*

I am, after I rest here awhile.

*Be careful! You are weak! You identify too strongly with the flesh and sensual things. You would adorn your body and have men desire you.*

Yes. I want that. You are right. Will my desire for it go away if I starve and punish it?

*Yes! Yes! Of course it will. Starve and punish it. Deny it. If you dwell upon it, it will overwhelm you. Please!*

"No!" Yael said it aloud, vehemently. A musician near her stopped playing his lyre and turned to look at her, as did a priestess passing by. No more punishment, she continued in her thoughts. Will it grow if I give in to it, or will it be resolved once and for all; or will something else come of it? I know not, but feel guided to this place. I know also that if I act from the place of deepest calm and sincere passion, which is where I am now, all will be well.

*But you're excited, aroused, tingling with fear and anticipation.*

Even as I am also calm. God is not bound by our rules for Its power and manifestations. God has not agreed to be bound by either/or thinking—either I'm calm or excited, or sinful or holy. Such is our, human, way. Right now, the fact is, I am both—sinful *and* holy; excited *and* calm, and God contains me, as I am. All things are echoes of the voice for God; Devorah had said that.

The priestess that had stopped to look at Yael a moment before, when she had cried out, drifted back to her. "Are you well, my child?" she asked.

Yael looked up at her. The woman was in her late thirties, with warm, brown eyes and smile lines crinkling at their edges. She was beautiful and serene with just enough kohl and rouge to seem worldly and sophisticated. Her reddish-brown hair was artfully done up; a few strands dangling at her temples to give her a piquant look without disturbing her sophistication. The gauzy silken material she wore rippled in the soft breeze, barely concealing her firm breasts and shaven pubis. Heavy, heady perfume floated around her. Yael felt an overwhelming combination of admiration, lust and a willingness to tell all.
But all she could do was stutter, "I...I...."

"May I sit?" the priestess asked; her voice lulling like music. Yael nodded, mouth agape almost able to taste the woman's perfume. "My name is Asmara," she said, "Priestess of Astarte. You're new here, aren't you?" Yael managed to nod. "I thought so." She looked Yael up and down appraisingly. "Not from Charoshet, either, I think." Yael nodded again. "The West, I would say, from the look of your robes."

Yael's eyes widened with appreciation. "Why, yes. How did you know?"

"I too came from that part of the country."

The phrase, "from the West," Yael knew, was a code word for Haibru. "You?" her voice was full of awe. "You're so elegant and beautiful and ...."

"Cultured?" Priestess Asmara's eyes smiled deliciously into Yael's. Yael nodded. "It is the Goddess Astarte, child," she said. "I became what you see by serving Her here, in this beautiful temple."

Yael's heart skipped a beat. This aloof, magnificent creature had once been as she was now, a lowly Haibru. Amazing! Could this be her path, too? Asmara was everything she admired, had been secretly dreaming of, even as she feared and hated it.

A passerby in rich robes greeted the Priestess Asmara and bowed low in deep respect. She acknowledged him and raised a soft, pampered hand to Yael's chin, blood red nail polish gleaming in the bright sunlight. The lyre player came up to them. Asmara turned to him, nodded, and said, "The sacred induction music." He dipped his head and began a repetitive, almost monotonous, pattern of chords. Gently Asmara turned Yael's head, first to the left, then the right, admiring what she saw. "You have excellent bone structure, child." She lowered her hand, leaned back, tilted her head and appraised Yael with unsmiling eyes. A pipe player joined them, weaving his plaintive sounds in and out of the lyre's rhythm.

A shudder ran through Yael. Asmara's sudden shift from warmth to cool seemed so, harsh! Yet, feeling great power in this woman, Yael was willing to be judged by her. Besides, the music was comforting, soothing, and she didn't really want to disappoint Asmara. Where had this sudden passion to please come from? Yael took a deep breath to calm herself and inhaled the powerful scent of her appraiser's perfume. How delicious and erotic! She squeezed her thighs together.

"Astarte is a generous, loving Goddess," Asmara said.

"Yes," Yael responded, dreamily, drifting on the priestess' fragrance and the hypnotic pattern of the music.

"She is accepting of all who give themselves to Her."

"Yes."

"I think you would find favor in Her eyes, were you to give yourself to Her."

"I...I...."

"You would become beautiful in Her service, as I have. You would no longer be from the West, but serve Her here, in Her beautiful temple. You would apply Kohl and rouge, and adorn your body. You would dance before Her and the assemblage on Feast Days. You would, after a time, have your own slaves, to wait upon you, hand and foot." Asmara gestured to a dusky heavy-set woman around Yael's age standing a few yards away. "That is my slave, Elkanta." Yael looked at the comely woman and felt a stab of jealousy. Where did *that* come from? "Elkanta adores me and adores serving me. It gives her pleasure to wash my feet and paint my nails." Yael felt the breath catch in her throat. "You see she wears a good robe, has painted her face with kohl and rouge and has adorned her body with bracelets." Yael felt the attraction.

Asmara looked deeply into her eyes and Yael felt a click, first in her heart, then in her head, as if a key had slid into a lock. "Many come to the service of Astarte first as slaves to Her priestesses." Yael's eyes were wide and glazed, her breathing deep and regular, Asmara's perfume and the repetitive music dulled her mind. "As My slave, not only would you experience the joys of service to My body," she ran her hand along her flanks and cupped her breasts, "but you could experience the joys of service to the Goddess. You would accompany Me to the offerings on Feast Days and you would be naked in gauzy garments, adorn yourself and become one of Astarte's handmaidens, offering yourself to men in Her holy name."

Yael blinked and coughed. "Breath deeply, my child. Allow yourself to drift on My scent, the scent of My body and My perfume and the mesmerizing rhythm of the sacred music." Asmara sat more erectly, leaned toward Yael, offering her naked breasts. All of Yael's buried thoughts of sensual feminine nakedness blossomed. "Admire My beauty, My elegance and allow your deep desire to please and serve pour into pleasing and serving Me and the great goddess Astarte."

"Astarte," Yael repeated, mindlessly.

"You are becoming My Haibru slave girl; My oh, so willing and eager Haibru slave girl," Asmara said.

"Your oh, so willing and eager Haibru slave girl."

"Look more deeply into My eyes, slave girl!"

Yael obeyed.

"What is your name?"

"Yael."

"Good, Yael. Now tell me, have I been right about you? Do you admire My beauty and sophistication, My sensual nakedness?"

"I do, Priestess, I admire your beauty and sophistication, and your sensual nakedness arouses me. I want to be like you."

"Good, Yael. What more? Do you wish to be someone of sophistication, to adorn your body, be naked, and be attractive to men and women as I am?"

"Yes, oh, Yes!" The sacred music and powerful scent inflamed Yael's senses, even as they dulled her mind.

"And if I agree to take you into My service, to train you and mold you, will you be grateful; will you show your gratitude by dedicating yourself to My pleasure and service?"

"I will, Priestess. I long to please and serve You."

The Priestess stood and pointed to the ground at her feet. "Kneel, before Me," she said.

Yael slipped from the bench to her knees. What was she doing? Her heart was pounding, throbbing in her chest. She could barely breath. Her feelings and mind, her entire life, seemed altered, so that this, now - being on her knees before this gorgeous woman, about to become her slave, felt like the culmination of her entire life—the purpose for which she was born.

The red polish gleamed on the toe nails of Priestess Asmara's excellent feet in Her elegant leather sandals and Yael imagined herself washing and serving those feet before being granted the privilege of painting the toe nails. The smell of leather mingled with the scent of Asmara's perfume and Yael inhaled it greedily. The music fizzed in her ears and bubbled in her blood. Never had she felt such anticipation, such unearthly bliss and delight, such empty fullness, such release and freedom. Truly, all things were echoes of the voice for God! Yael closed her eyes and gave herself over to the sensations.

A small crowd had gathered round them attracted by the music; two soldiers, a temple maiden, three slave girls. Though not unusual for priestesses to take slaves this way, when Asmara was involved it became an event. She had recently enslaved the son of one of the Ache, the ruling council of Charoshet. The fourteen year old boy had been so taken with the Priestess, that when commanded by her, he gave up his privileged life and joined the Army to please her.

Now, Asmara smiled down upon her captive. "Raise your eyes to Mine, Yael."

Yael obeyed and felt a raw power streaming into her from the Priestess that made her even more eager to obey. Asmara smiled and Yael felt a wave of pure bliss flow through her body.

"I am pleased, Yael. You have pleased Me and from this moment forward, pleasing Me, obeying Me and serving Me is your sole reason to live. It is your purpose. Tell me, Yael, why do you live?"

As she responded, Yael felt a thrill of ecstasy deep in her chest. "I live to please, obey and serve You, Priestess Asmara."

The people "oo'd and ahh'd," proud of Asmara's power, titillated by it, but in awe and frightened of it, too; it could easily be one of them entranced on their knees at Asmara's pampered feet.

"Good, my child. Now, by the power invested in Me by the Great Goddess Astarte, I, Asmara, priestess of Astarte take you, Yael, as My personal slave, hand maiden and body servant. You may acknowledge your acceptance of this by kissing My feet."

Feeling wildly endangered, yet elated; evil, but ecstatic to her core, Yael bowed her head, lavishing wet kisses on Asmara's precious feet, with their red painted toe nails, in their elegant leather sandals. She heard Asmara's voice, not with her ears, not outside of her, but in her own head, *inside* her. "Grovel, slave! Abase yourself before your Mistress. Make yourself low; but keep your servile lips on My sacred feet." Yael eagerly obeyed.

"Rub your unworthy body in the dust of the ground. Feel your abasement. Know that only in My service and in the worship of the Great Goddess Astarte can you find any value or worth. You are lower than the dust and dirt beneath My sandals, but as you serve and obey, you are redeemed. Glory in giving yourself to Me without limits."

Yael squirmed, moaned, burned and dripped with a passion she had not known possible. Now she heard Asmara's voice outside her.

And though her mind was nearly obliterated by pent up passion, Yael sensed the presence of others. Asmara spoke to them, raising her arms and opening them wide.

"Worshipers of Astarte, bow down, you are on sacred ground!" No one moved. "Obey Me, oh beloved! Now, here before you, in the Goddess' holy name I take this Haibru peasant to be My slave, and as My slave, the Goddess' slave." The three slave girls dropped to their knees. Asmara pointed to the others. "Bow down!" she commanded. "Do not blaspheme. Honor She who rules over you. Bow down and give obeisance to the power of the Female." The others knelt. "Pray to Me in Her name. Let your devotion flow forth and into this lowly unbeliever that she may find peace in her slavery to Me and devotion to the Goddess." Mumbled prayers filled the air and others walking nearby, came, knelt before Asmara and joined in the prayers.

Asmara re-focused her attention on Yael. "Feel the power of your Goddess as it surrounds you, slave Yael. Surrender to it! Die to your old ways and be re-born in sacred service to Her and to Me. Are you near to orgasming?" In answer, Yael moaned. "In a moment, I will give you permission and you will have many orgasms…for Me. Your orgasms will be the final act of sanctification, consecrating you to My service and the worship of the Great Goddess.

"From this time forward, you belong to Me. I own your body and you will be able to orgasm only when I command it. Do you understand, Me, slave?" Yael moaned. It was all she could do. "When you orgasm, it will be like no other you have ever experienced, and you will know that this ecstasy comes from Me alone, by My grace, and from your adoration of the Great Goddess Astarte."

Grinding and moaning in a rapture of nearly mindless servile adoration, Yael heard and accepted all her Mistress proclaimed.

"Are you near, slave?"

Yael moaned.

"No matter what you do or wither you go, no matter how your adoration and servitude may wax and wane, you are now and forever more My servant and will always submit to My will. In the name of the Great Goddess Astarte, orgasm and become Her slave and Mine, forever!"

Yael orgasmed over and over again, moaning, screaming and rolling around at her Mistress' feet. Mind nearly gone, wiped away by the power unleashed in the release of her long repressed desires, the ritual and now this soul shattering orgasm, Yael heard the sacred music, and

*Devorah*

the prayers and shouts of Astarte's other worshippers on their knees around her, dimly, as the sound of far off rumbling. Reborn into the Mighty Astarte's service, Yael wanted nothing but to serve and obey her glorious Mistress and be allowed more orgasms like these.

---

Devorah, Lappodoth and a small company of armed men arrived at Shiloh on the evening of the third day after their departure. The ride had not been too difficult, but this was only the third month of her pregnancy. The morning sickness however, was becoming a problem. The trip had to be made in any event, no matter her condition. Thank God Lappodoth was as attentive and helpful as usual, and the soldiers did the heavy work of setting up and tearing down their small camp. It was good to talk with the people they met along the way, but Devorah was disappointed that only a small majority of them were in favor of war with the Canaanites. That made the priests of Shiloh even more important.

Though she hoped it would be otherwise, Devorah felt she would not be well received. Unlike the great majority of Israelites, the people of Shiloh lived in houses. They still tilled the soil and tended flocks, but being in the fertile plain instead of the rocky highlands and sharing the town with Moabites meant developing habits of a less nomadic more settled nature.

The streets were emptying as their small caravan, entered the town square. Women were filling their water jars, lamps were being lit and flocks of sheep and goats were lowing on their way to their evening enclosures. To the west of the fountain, Devorah saw the outlines on the Temple which held the Ark in its holy of holies. As Lappodoth looked after their mules, Devorah drifted towards the Temple. Torches were being lit in its four watch towers. The streets nearest the Temple held the dwellings of the priests. The homes were modest one story buildings, the roofs serving as cooking, sleeping and social areas. Canvas awnings of various colors and patterns flapped on poles. The whole gave her a sense of calm, well being. Not the kind of situation that suggested a need for war. At the corner, near the main gate leading to the Temple's first court, was a house larger than the others. This must be Malachizer's home, Devorah thought.

Malachizer had been High Priest for the past twelve years, ascending to his position three years before Devorah had become Sar. The two positions, High Priest and Sar, had a history of rivalry. The High Priest dated from the Exodus, 180 years ago, while the Judges had been in existence for only sixty years. Malachizer had more than just the traditional power position differences with Devorah. She was a prophetess, too, and with a foot in both camps, he felt threatened more often. Yet, on the two occasions they had met, Devorah had found him set in his ways, but compassionate.

"Perhaps his compassion comes from his ever growing family," Lappodoth said, coming up behind her and seemingly reading her mind. "It can't be easy to live with so many people, even in a large house."

Devorah turned to face him, glad of his familiar presence in this foreign place and threw herself into his open arms. "How big is his family now?" she asked, as he took her hand to lead her to the caravansary.

"I don't know if 'family' is the correct word," he said, looking down into her upturned smiling face as they walked. "He has a wife of course, and four concubines; between them, they have nineteen children."

"Nineteen?"

"That is my understanding."

"And we're going to be overjoyed with one." She patted her belly. "How many do you think we'll have, husband?"

He stopped walking and embraced her. "As many as you want and can bear safely, Devorah - one or ten, I will love them all."

They walked in silence for a few minutes and arrived at the inn. Their escort had unpacked. Their bedding and cooking implements were in a large room with a fireplace and a stairway, instead of a ladder, leading to the roof.

"Can we sleep on the roof, husband?" Devorah's voice was filled with child-like enthusiasm.

"Yes. Of course! We can cook up there, too, if you like."

"I would like."

Lappodoth took the sleeping gear, Devorah, the cooking implements and up they went. It was quite special up there. Devorah, could see the high temple walls and Malachizer's larger house next to them. "Thank you, Abba!" she thought. "For this interesting place, our safe journey, my loving husband, the new life inside me and this opportunity to reason with Malachizer. I know everything is unfolding for the highest good of all concerned!"

A priest came to the door while they were breakfasting on the roof. The sentry showed him up. He bowed stiffly to Devorah, too stiffly for one so young. He seemed officious with a neatly trimmed beard and well-tended priestly robes. "My master, the High Priest, bids me welcome you and invite you to sup with him for the noon meal in his home."

Devorah rose and smiled into the young man's stern face. Were they all like this here in Shiloh? "Thank you, young man. Please tell your master I look forward to his hospitality." The priest/messenger dipped his head and turned to leave. "A moment," Devorah said. "What is your name?"

"Eleazer, Sar."

"Eleazer, what is being said about the reason for my visit to Shiloh?"

"I am reluctant to carry tales, my Lady."

Devorah gestured dismissively. "I am interested. Please. You may speak."

"It is said you are here to call for war with Canaan and want the High Priest's blessings."

Devorah, nodded. "And what is your opinion of such a venture, Eleazer?"

The priest looked her directly in the eyes, pulled himself to his full height and said in a petulant tone, "We are at peace here, Lady. We share a good life with the Moabites. There are some Canaanites among us, too, and we have no quarrel with them."

Devorah stared back at him. "Is this how the other priests feel?"

"Not just the priests, Lady. It is how most of our people feel."

"I see. Well, thank you. Please tell the High Priest I will join him in his home at noon."

The priest dipped his head, turned and left.

"Your task will not be easy," Lappodoth said.

"When has it ever been?" She smiled up at him. "But when I am in the place of the Lord, the path will be made straight before me."

"Amen!" Lappodoth said, fervently.

Malachizer had welcomed her warmly, embracing her as a long lost sister. Now he sat opposite her across a smooth and polished board laden with lamb, fish, eggs, vegetables, fruits and still warm breads. He poured himself a goblet of wine, picked up the goblet in front of Devorah, to fill it, but she shook her head, no.

"Just half, please, my brother," she said. "I am newly pregnant and do not want to intoxicate the new life within me."

Malachizer's face lit-up. "Congratulations, Devorah! Children are a true blessing!" He gestured out the window to the court just below them, from which the sounds of children at play drifted up to them. "As you can see, I have a school of my own here."

"Indeed. God has been good to you, Malachizer."

"He has and I am grateful." The smile slipped from his face. "He has rewarded my devotion and obedience to His Laws. The Law and Tradition are everything. He tells us what He wants us to do and we must obey and do it."

Devorah smiled ruefully. "Would it were so simple, my priestly brother. As Sar, I have heard many difficult situations in which the clarity you speak of eluded me."

Malachizer frowned. "I know you to be a Godly woman, sister; a prophetess, greatly favored by Him. It pains me to hear you have such doubts. How is it you have become so disconnected from Him?"

"I am rarely disconnected from my Father, Malachizer. What I am saying is that His will is not always so easy to discern."

"Indeed?" The High Priest's tone was huffy. "Isn't it spelled out in the Holy Testimonies?"

"As far as they go, yes, but there are things and conditions now that the Holy Testimonies did not foresee."

"The Law is the Law. Those who disobey or break it must be punished."

"That is too harsh for me."

"That is because you are a woman."

"No, my brother. I am a woman, as God made me. But that has no effect on my judgment. It is too harsh because simply reviewing the facts in a situation to first determine if even a Law *has* been broken, is quite difficult. And, if a Law *has* been broken, is punishment the best response?"

*Devorah*

"Yes. Always. If a Law has been broken punishment is required."

They were staring at one another now, glaring, all thought of the feast before them forgotten.

"Is this what God wants?" Devorah looked earnestly into the High Priests unusual blue eyes. "Do we inflict pain even unto death in His name?"

Malachizer moved his head up and down, eyes cold. "It is in the Law."

"What if 'the Law' is not of God, but merely our interpretation of God? What if it was written by men full of the fear of God, rather than the love of God?"

"We have no way of knowing. It is written."

"But we do have a way of knowing!" Devorah's voice was full of enthusiasm. "We can be with God now, can we not?" She searched his face. It was impassive.

"What do you mean?" he asked.

"You can experience God now in the lives of your children and the joy they bring you."

"Perhaps. In a manner of speaking. But I experience Him in the temple, in the trembling of my heart when I prostate myself in the Holy of Holies."

"You do not feel him in the flight of a bird, the blossoming of a flower, the setting and rising of the sun?"

"These are beautiful, even wondrous things, caused by God, but not God himself. God is in His Law, in the Holy of Holies, in the heart of righteous men."

"Ah, yes, in the heart...."

"Yes, but only in the heart of the righteous—righteous are those that follow the Law. All others are not of God and must be brought to Him or punished."

"The fear of God, then, is more potent than the love of God."

"Many have been brought to love through fear."

Devorah was becoming frustrated. "I have seen you when you speak of your children. I detected no fear there. That is the kind of love I have for God and it leaves me almost fear-less. It is from that place that I connect, commune and prophecy."

"I can not prophecy." Malachizer sounded sour, almost jealous.

"It is not given to everyone."

"Obviously. So, you have come about a call to arms and you want my blessing, the temple's blessing." He looked at her steadily.

She returned his gaze without blinking. "Eleazer told me the sentiment here is for peace."

Malachizer nodded. "Not only will we not bless your call to war, we will speak out against it."

Devorah had been prepared for this, but still, hearing it was a blow. She sighed and felt as if the wind had been knocked out of her.

"I do not understand," the High Priest said, "how you can speak of the love of God and war in the same breath."

Devorah sighed, then looked at him brightly. "It is not war we are about but love and peace. There is an imbalance between our people and the Canaanites that must be corrected. We will negotiate with them before we fight. But unless we are ready to fight, and they know we are ready, our negotiations will be a waste of time. Surely you see that, brother?"

"So, you are asking me to endorse the call to arms to give your negotiations a chance of success." Malachizer looked down and combed his beard with his hand. "What if the Canaanites will not negotiate? What if they attack us, here, in Shiloh, first, before you are ready?"

At first Devorah thought he was joking, but the deep fear in him was palpable. "Barak believes Sisera's deployments are no threat to this place," she said.

"Barak is a good General, but he can not know, for sure, what will transpire."

"Our focus must be on what we want, not what we do not want."

"Indeed," Malachizer said. "But we can not avoid facts. Our people are badly outnumbered and under-equipped." He looked down. "And, I do fear that God has abandoned us."

"What do you mean?"

"Many of our people are inter-marrying; worshipping idols; moving to the cities; failing to obey the Law. Perhaps what is being visited upon us now, the imbalance you speak of, is our just punishment for turning from Him."

"All you have said is true, Malachizer, yet I do not believe it is a punishment, for I do not believe in a god of vengeance and punishment. I think God loves us and wants the best for us, but we must use God's love and grace correctly. When we become full of fear, envy and self-importance, and when we use the Power of God for those things, then those things are what we receive. It is not God punishing us, but simply the inevitable consequences of our misuse of what the Power God is.

*Devorah*

"We plant seeds, Malachizer. Our thoughts, feelings and actions are seeds. What we sow, is what we reap. We have been planting injustice, imbalance and fear. Now we need to rise up together in community claiming our good and go forward to achieve it, even tho we are outnumbered and ill-equipped, knowing that God - and God alone - is our salvation. My call to arms sows the seeds of self respect, community, love and righteousness. With or without you, we shall be successful, because we are planting the seeds of success."

For a moment, the look on Malachizer's face made Devorah think she had reached him. But then his canny expression returned and she knew more talk would be useless. She turned to the table, broke bread, poured olive oil on it, laid a piece of fish on top and ate hungrily. Malachizer watched her. She smiled at him and spoke with her mouth full. "This is excellent food, my brother. Thank you!" He made a gesture of gracious generosity and joined her in eating.

"We will need the Ark of the Covenant to precede us into battle," Devorah said, sipping her wine.

Malachizer choked and sputtered. "Uh, uh, I, I, uh......"

Devorah smiled inwardly, enjoying the hypocrite's discomfort. "It is still housed here in Shiloh, isn't it?"

"Why, yes, of course! But.... But it is dangerous if not handled properly."

"I am aware of that, Priest. I would leave the handling of it to your priests. No one else would handle it. Barak wants the Ark used as it was at Jerhico in Joshua's time."

"And if you lose, what will become of the Ark?"

Ah, that was the priest's main concern! And not even that, Devorah thought. His main concern is, 'what would the Canaanites think of him, Malachizer, and what would they do to Shiloh if the Haibrus lost?'

"We shall not lose, Priest," Devorah said, trying to conceal her scorn. "In any event this is not negotiable! As Sar, I order that it be done!"

"Yes, of course," Malachizer said.

"No one will think the worse of you, Malachizer, if we should lose. You were only obeying your Sar."

"Yes, of course," Malachizer said.

"And while the Ark will contribute to our victory, it will in no way equal the contribution of Judah's full support. Do the elders of Judah, feel as you do?" She asked him.

His eyes touched hers then darted away. "They do," he said softly.

"Judah's participation would make all the difference." Devorah's eyes held his.

"Judah has always gone its own way, as is the prerogative, no, the necessity of the natural leader of our people."

"Judah is blessed with excellent land, talent and prosperity," Devorah said.

"It has been thus for centuries; even in Egypt; even in the desert. God has marked Judah and its people."

Devorah smiled and nodded. "Yes. I am aware of that. Perhaps one day community and the Covenant with all the people will matter more than pride and prosperity." She took another bite of the fish. "Ah, but this is excellent fish, Malachizer."

"We will get no help from the priests of Shiloh," she said to Lappodoth upon her return. "We will stay the night and in the morning return to our oasis." Lappodoth hugged her, feeling both her disappointment and resolve, then went outside to inform their escort that they would be leaving at first light.

---

Barak watched the men drilling. Nearly 2,700 had joined him on the western, windward slope of Mt. Tabor, and more were drifting in every day. This, without Devorah's call to arms fully ratified by the twelve tribes! Encouraging. The group before him of the Nephtali, thrusting and parrying with wooden swords and shields, were among the best. They needed more training, much more, but the raw material was there. And speaking of raw material, there was another cause for optimism. The iron ore taken from Acco was now being forged into iron swords and spear tips in the new armory run by seven experienced blacksmiths and their teams from Mennasah, who in turn were training twelve local tinsmiths. As of now, there was not enough ore to equip all he had in camp, yet he remained optimistic because word had come that the ship they sent to Macedonia was returning fully laden with more ore.

They were even becoming more like an Army. He had an aide de camp - Jereboam, a Judean - recently come from Devorah and too badly mauled in the dungeons of Cheroshet to fight, but with a ready mind and a strong sense of tactical and strategic issues. He also had a great love of the Covenant and the people. And the Nephtali before him had a Captain. One of their own and elected, but a Captain nonetheless. They obeyed him, too. Now their Captain had them working in three groups, in twenty pairs, each group under the direction of a lieutenant appointed by the Captain.

Barak himself was self-taught in military affairs. The Israelites had a proud military tradition developed under Joshua, but that had long ago disappeared as the nation drifted asunder and soldiering ceased to be an honorable profession. Now men at arms were little more than fighters for hire, self-trained and self-equipped. The idea of a disciplined Army, with uniformity, tactics and strategy, was almost unimaginable.

Barak had studied the records of Joshua's battles, big and small, and applied them. Barak had a war band of his own in the old days and shadowed the movements of Philistine, Canaanite and Moabite armies while skirmishing against them to test and refine what he'd studied. The more he learned, the more effective he became, and men rallied to him as his reputation grew. His plan was to develop his band as a cadre from which to form the officer corps of a much larger force. He had spies in all the armies of his neighbors, and had even parleyed with Sisera and other non-Israelite military leaders. He thought Sisera a capable leader and a decent human being, who had wicked men around him.

One of those, a demon in human form named Sostrum, had been responsible for the murders of Barak's parents and his pregnant wife, Marni. He ground his teeth and the breath caught in his chest as he recalled the scene of the massacre—blood, hacked-off limbs and severed heads in the tents and common areas, the well polluted with blood; fires burning, the stink of charred flesh, survivors keening and wailing. It had been thirty years ago, but the sensations - sounds, visions, smell and feel, would never leave him.

He had been a carpenter then. Only years later, when he'd taken up the warrior's path to avenge his family, had he found the name of the man responsible for the massacre: Sostrum. The Canaanite had been an ambitious sheriff in Cheroshet, with a plan to drive all the Haibrus from the area. He raided small, defenseless settlements to set an example. Sisera was just beginning his military career and did not know Sostrum then. Sisera did all he could to suppress the tactics of terrorists like Sostrum as he accumulated sufficient power.

For awhile, the desire for vengeance had consumed Barak. He tamped it down and used it for fuel, so that its white heat radiated a cool and focused power that he put to excellent military use. When he finally found that Sostrum was the man, both he and Sostrum had become Generals and it was not possible to deal with him one to one. Yet Barak had no doubt that the time would come, and soon now, when he could strike the demon dead.

Barak had also learned much about military strategy, tactics and logistics from studying Egyptian campaigns. They set the standard for formal armies. Though Israelite strategy and tactics were those of lightly armed, mobile irregular infantry and little resembled those of Egypt, Barak knew Sisera, too, studied the Egyptians, and that if he were to beat Sisera, he'd have to devise some twist on the classical, big army methods. That 'twist' Barak sensed, was near at hand, somewhere in his own background and culture, but he could not nail it down.

He'd discussed this idea at length with Malachizer, the High Priest, when both of them were younger and less eminent, when Barak studied the scrolls on Egyptian methods in the library of the Temple in Shiloh. During that time, Barak learned that Sostrum was responsible for the massacre that took his family. He burned with hatred and a desire for revenge, and Malachizer had helped him deal with that.

"I have found, brother," Malachizer said, putting an arm round Barak's shoulders as they strolled in the forecourt, enjoying the cool March breezes and the hint of new growth, "that we cannot know God's plan for us in advance. Something terrible and evil like the massacre of your family and pregnant wife, serves a greater purpose beyond our ability to know."

"That thought crossed my mind, Malachizer, and has given me some peace. Yet it is not enough."

"Indeed," Malachizer said, "the wound is yet too fresh. Time and your desire and willingness to come to understand God's purpose will be salutary."

Barak nodded. "But what of sin and punishment? Has this befallen me as punishment for my sins, and is that not true for our people as well?"

"I am on the cusp with that, Barak; balanced between two ways of understanding. One is yes, indeed, God's commandments and the Holy Writings contain all we need know, or ever know, about how to live and worship Him. Those who disregard the word of God are sinners and must be punished. On the other hand, I sense that the only punishment is that we ask for too little; that God is a God of love and abundance.

"That it is done unto us as we think and believe, and that if we dwell in fear, lack and limitation, this is what is returned to us. In this view, there are no punishments, simply the consequences of our own thoughts, feelings and actions. For things to be different, *we* must be different. If we want peace and love and prosperity, we must *be* peaceful and loving and prosperous."

"So," Barak said, "the power is ours." He smiled. "The soldier in me likes that. That's why I am here, to be knowledgeable, clever and wise. That is why I study the best Military in the world."

"Yes, good!" Malachizer patted his back. "We once had a glorious military tradition. Perhaps through you, we will again."

Barak turned to face Malachizer. "That is my fervent hope and greatest goal; what I believe I was born to do!"

Malachizer hugged Barak and resumed strolling. "Though the second point of view—that there is no punishment and by inference, no sin, but a mistake—warms me, I am coming to the conclusion that if I wish to be High Priest one day, I must refrain from such unorthodox thinking and remain focused on the Law and Tradition: the belief that we can and do know what we are to do, that God has already given this to us in the Law and Tradition, and that to disobey these is sin and worthy of punishment."

"Ah," Barak said, "as a military man I must question the underlying idea in your 'punishment and sin' point of view - the idea that we can know in advance. My experience has shown that we can know in advance only in the most limited way. We can plan, gather facts, be prudent, but we can't *know*. The whole of military history shows the unpredictable nature of battle and that the most flexible army, the one with the greatest ability to change on a moments notice, is victorious. Too much planning, training and equipment are an impediment to victory."

Why were his own words from long ago returning to him, now? He smiled. Why? Because they were the words he needed to hear, now! *We will never have enough men and material to match the Canaanite Federation.* He had to face and accept that. Only fear made him dwell on what he didn't have. God knew he didn't want more of that! Faith was the strategic and tactical twist he was looking for, the missing element in his own tradition.

We can't know *how* victory will come, only that it *will* come. I do not have to make it happen, I just have to focus on it. God, what Devorah called the big Self of which I am a part, will do the rest. My little self as Barak can't know all of *how* it will be accomplished, just that it *will* be accomplished. We go ahead as we have been—planning, arming, training and, when the time comes, we will seize the day by being flexible, mobile, enthusiastic and full of faith.

Indeed, such faith was the core of their great military tradition, supported by Joshua's six strategic elements. The first of these, the hill strategy based on the terrain they occupied and fought in, required a mobile fighting force, lightly armed with their circular slashing swords, bows and spears, deployed in small contingents of a hundred, was natural to them. If they could re-arm with iron, instead of copper, they'd have one of the best irregular, guerilla forces in the world!

The wind whipped around him, stirring up dust devils. Barak shook his head and looked down. The second of Joshua's classic strategies, to exploit the disunity of the Philistine and Canaanite city states that occupied the coasts and plains, seemed to be working in reverse just now. It was the twelve tribes that were disunited and unlikely to come together. Yet, though their enemies were united politically, Barak had plans to exploit their geographic dispersion. Surprise and guile, covert infiltration and enticement, the last of Joshua's strategies, were chief among these. He and Devorah were finalizing plans for feints north and west from Tabor, under cover of night movements.

Jereboam approached and saluted. Barak returned the salute, eager to hear what news Jereboam had to share. That gesture, the salute—fist clenched, arm across the chest vertically—though a cherished part of all military life and a sign of mutual respect and common purpose, was something quite new to this generation of Israelite soldiers. Barak was pleased. Though a little thing, the salute bespoke a greater thing—that the rag-tag Hebrew volunteers were becoming a proper army.

Jereboam's face was impassive. *Bad news*, Barak thought. He was right. Through most of the Judean's report, Barak maintained his new found sense of connection. But as the list of problems lengthened, Barak began to feel overwhelmed, set-upon, and alone. A tiny part of him knew that those feelings were an invitation to pray, to give it over to God, and keep moving forward. But that part, too, was, for the moment, overwhelmed.

# CHAPTER FOUR

Yael found service to Asmara to be much like the service in her own tent that she so detested. But not at first.

Immediately after the consecration ritual, Asmara took Yael to her apartment in the Temple of Astarte and taught her how to pleasure a woman. Initially hesitant, under the priestess' hypnotic control, Yael learned quickly and enjoyed servicing her Mistress for many hours.

Asmara taught her new slave how to bathe and anoint her, paint her face and toe nails and dress her. Asmara was gratified by the speed with which Yael learned and the depth of her devotion. She thought the Haibru now belonged to her, body and soul. Yet she knew from sad experience that promising beginnings did not happy endings make. One or two more rituals over the next day would be required to bind the woman to her forever. She much preferred being served by a willing and eager convert like Yael than a market slave like Elkanta. Elkanta was obedient but unenthusiastic.

Now, as Yael knelt at her feet, gazing adoringly up at her, Asmara held her gaze, feeling her control deepen, then said, "Astarte requires my devotions, slave. Obey Elkanta as you would me."

"Your will be done, Mistress." Yael tingled with the thrill of deep surrender and eager servility mingled with the gratitude of lingering sensual arousal.

"Elkanta, use the slave as you will." Asmara said and she left for the public rooms at the front of the Temple.

"Yes, Mistress." Elkanta was dark and swarthy and heavy. Not fat, Yael thought as she gazed up at her Mistress' slave, heavy.

Elkanta looked down upon her. "Kiss My feet, slave!"

"But…but…." Yael hesitated.

"Did you not hear what the Mistress said? She told Me to use the slave as I will and she told you to obey Me as you would her. What of that do you not understand?"

"I…I…."

"Enough of this! Obey! Kiss My feet!"

Yael crawled to Elkanta and kissed her feet. Wasn't this wrong, licking a slave's feet? It was nasty and humiliating, dirty and sexy. But hadn't her Mistress told her to obey Elkanta? And pleasing her Mistress was so arousing. Soon the kisses she was giving Elkanta became more passionate and less perfunctory.

"Good, slave girl. Good," Elkanta said. "Adore My feet. It is all you Haibrus are worthy of." A knot formed in Yael's belly, but was quickly lost in the ecstasy of obeisance as Elkanta walked about the apartment and Yael crawled after her on her belly, kissing the woman's smelly feet whenever she could. "Perhaps," Elkanta said, lifting her robes to reveal plump, well-shaped buttocks, "the Haibru slave girl might also be worthy of kissing My buttocks. Crawl around behind Me and gaze at them." Yael obeyed, looked up and thought they were beautiful buttocks indeed, and worthy of being kissed. "But only if you beg." There was that knot again. But she was so far gone, she *wanted* to beg. The slave's buttocks looked good to Yael, very good and very sexy; she wanted to press her lips to them and feel their warmth and resilience, and she wanted to smell them.

"Kneel up!" Elkanta commanded.

Yael obeyed. Elkanta's gorgeous buttocks were just inches from her mouth and their scent, a blend of sweat, perfume and feces, filled her nostrils. Yael shut her eyes, inhaled the odor more deeply and felt aroused, soft, and submissive.

"You like that smell, don't you my Haibru slave girl."

"Yes, Elkanta," Yael said between deep mind wrenching breaths.

"Beg for more, you worthless Haibru she dog! Beg for more of your Mistress' beautiful hypnotic ass."

Though the knot in her stomach had grown more troubling, the obsequious passion rushing through her blood and nerves from the hideous smell and fleshy vision drove Yael on. "Please, Mistress Elkanta," she begged, "allow your worthless Haibru she-dog slave to smell and kiss your beautiful buttocks. I am unworthy of Your glory. But if you give me an opportunity to please and serve You, I swear I will satisfy You."

"Yes! Good. I am pleased," Elkanta said. "So I am your Mistress now, and you are My slave?"

"Yes, Mistress Elkanta. I am Your Haibru slave girl, Your she-dog, Your bitch!" Yael was panting with desire, the smell and view driving her mad. This was her place, the place of the Haibru, to be the slave of a slave. What joy to surrender to it, to submit to the power of it!

"And you long to adore your Mistress' buttocks—to sniff them, kiss them and worship them?"

"I do, Mistress Elkanta. I long to serve and adore Your buttocks."

"Then you are My ass slave, the slave of My ass." Elkanta arched her back and her buttocks jutted touching Yael's face.

"Yes. I am Your ass slave, the slave of Your ass." Oh, God, how low, how gross, how delicious; the slave of this swarthy, heavy female slave's ass. Yael's tongue darted out and touched the sacred flesh before her.

Elkanta took a step forward. "Did I say you could touch My sacred flesh, slave?"

"No, mighty one, forgive me! I could not help myself. You are so glorious and powerful and I, so low and vulgar! Have mercy on your filthy slave, please, I beg you!"

Elkanta took a step back and touched her ass cheeks to her worshiper's face. "Once again your words have found favor with Me. I will have mercy upon you. Kiss My left buttock first, then My right, then you may burry your face in the valley between them."

Yael hastened to obey, quickly orgasmed and collapsed beneath Elkanta.

"Get up, Haibru she-dog slave!" Elkanta kicked at Yael's prostrate form. "Get up. I command you!" She kicked Yael again.

Freed of the trance by the orgasm, Yael moaned and shook her head to clear it.

Elkanta kicked her again. Instinctively, Yael reached up and grabbed Elkanta's foot, pulled and the woman fell, heavily on her back, the wind knocked out of her. She recovered quickly and flung herself on the still groggy Yael. They were scuffling, pulling, slapping and rolling on the floor when Asmara returned.

"Stop!" Asmara's command was imperious and impossible to disobey. The two slaves stopped - instantly frozen in tangled positions. "On your knees!" They obeyed. "It is a good thing, I returned for my amulet," she said. "I do not know what this was about. I do not *want* to know. It is over. Elkanta, you have no power over Yael. Yael, you need not obey Elkanta. Now both of you, there is work to do here. Do it!" Asmara took her sacred amulet from the ebony jewel box, slipped it around her neck and left.

Elkanta got up and resumed her chores; Yael, being too new to have chores, sat and thought. Haber's face, then Jereboam's drifted across her mind's eye. She sighed. Then, Asmara's imperious face stared at her, eyes sparkling, getting larger and larger until there was nothing but her Mistress' eyes. Yael heard Her voice, *You belong to Me, Yael. You are My Haibru slave girl; you belong to Me, body and soul.* "Yes, Mistress," Yael responded, "body and soul." Yael sat in that semi-conscious state until Asmara returned, and called her to tend her in her bath.

That night, Yael slept naked at the foot of Asmara's couch. Her dreams were full of terror. She again saw the warrior in golden armor curled in a fetal position at her feet, while in her hands were the wooden mallet and a sharpened tent peg. He was to die and she was to kill him. When her Mistress stirred, Yael awoke, drenched in sweat. As she tended to her Mistress' toilet, holding the earthenware pot for her, and then licking her clean, Yael felt a further shift in her heart and mind. So much had happened in such a short time!

Asmara sensed the shift in her slave's demeanor and knew it was time for another consecration ceremony. One or two more, and the Haibru would be her slave forever. "We will go to the Temple, slave Yael. I will consecrate you again and you will serve as a sacred prostitute. I will dress you and adorn you so that you will find favor in the Goddess' eyes."

Yael's heart thrilled at the idea of being made beautiful for a public ritual. "Thank you, my Mistress!"

"We will dress you in the robes of a sacred prostitute. Your nakedness would be on display for all to see," Yael tingled. "You will wear kohl and rouge and jewelry to make you a pleasing offering."

"Thank you, my Mistress!"

Asmara clapped her hands. "Elkanta! Bring breakfast." The slave placed the Mistress' elegant ceramic bowl on the table while she and Yael sat at Asmara's feet and ate from a worn wooden one. Afterwards, Asmara dressed and groomed Yael then led her, half in trance, to the Court of the Sacred Prostitutes. Asmara planned to conduct the re-consecration ritual there, and then give Yael to the crowd. But, as they entered the Court, a messenger from the High Priestess came and Asmara left Yael on a bench with instructions not to move until she returned.

Yael obeyed, drifting in and out of trance on the warm breezes, sensual music, heavy scents and sights of beautiful women. Then she saw him, at the same moment he saw her—the disgusting soldier she'd talked with in the caravan, the one who'd ogled her. He was still dressed in his military garb - sword and leather buckler, scruffier than before.

She was totally repulsed. Why was he coming toward her? Then she realized she was dressed as a sacred prostitute in the Court of the Sacred Prostitutes, of course he was coming to her, to lie with her. Yael gagged, felt as if she wanted to vomit. Not this man, please Astarte! Soon he was at her side. She rose to leave; he grabbed her wrist.

"Hello. Fancy finding you here! I had no idea. I thought you were Haibru and now I find you are a sacred prostitute."

"I am not, please!" She shrieked, gagging at his unwashed odor. People looked at them. Off in the distance, at the far end of the Court, a handsome warrior in golden armor, glanced their way.

"Not what?" The disgusting soldier said, his sour breath spilling across Yael's face. "Haibru, or a sacred prostitute?

"Not a sacred prostitute. I am Haibru. Please, let me go!"

"No, I want *you*. If you are a Haibru wench, that is all the better! Besides, you are here looking like a sacred prostitute. I have made my offering to the Goddess and I may have any woman in this Court." He leered at her, reached out and touched her robe. "I fancied you in the caravan and have thought about your firm flesh and womanly roundness." He drooled, pulled Yael to her feet and dragged her toward the private area.

Struggling, Yael scratched his arms and face. He smacked her with his open hand. There were two heavy rings on his fingers. Blood flowed from her split lip, nose and eyebrow. He was much bigger. Yael struggled again, all thoughts of Astarte, Asmara, sexual servitude, jewels, clothes and exhibiting herself, gone. He let go of her wrist, grabbed her throat with one big hand and slapped her face again, harder. The force of the blow coupled with the pressure on her throat, nearly knocked Yael unconscious. She slumped; he gathered her up in his arms and strode to the private area.

A crowd had gathered and cheered him on. He waved and smiled at them as he carried Yael away. In the dim cool recesses of the alcove, grunts, moans and shouts—the sounds of sex from other, nearby alcoves drifted in to them. He laid Yael on the couch and hurriedly removed his sword, buckler and smock. She moaned, but her eyes were still closed. He bent over her, hands shaking and gently, more gently than he thought possible, peeled back her robe to reveal her breasts.

He sighed at their magnificence. "Thank you, oh Great Goddess Astarte for this sacred prostitute." He removed his kilt and stepped out of his loin cloth. His massive erection bounced in front of him. Yael opened her eyes, still dazed, saw the immense penis inches from her mouth and screamed. The soldier slapped her face, once with each hand, and she slipped into unconsciousness. He climbed on top of her, pulled the robe down partially off and roughly spread her legs to reveal her sex. Behind him came the sound of the curtains to the alcove being drawn back.

"She said she was not a sacred prostitute," the man's voice was deep and full, rich with power and authority. "I believe her, why don't you?"

The soldier turned quickly and saw a warrior slightly larger than himself, dressed in gleaming gold armor; clearly an aristocrat, perhaps an officer. The soldier knew the type, but this man was the real thing. He wanted no quarrel with him. "Does that really matter, brother? She is here looking like she belongs here. We are here." He gestured with his palm open. "I will gladly share her with you, when I am done...."

"She does not belong here." The golden warrior's voice was flat and matter of fact. "She is not a proper offering to the Goddess. Neither of us will have her. Choose another or go."

The soldier's erection shriveled away. He did not want to fight, yet he picked up his sword and withdrew it from its scabbard. "Who are you, brother? Why do you dictate to me? Are we not all brothers in Astarte's sight?"

"We are," the golden one said. "I am Sisera, General of the Armies, nephew of the High King and priest in Astarte's service."

The soldier returned his sword to its scabbard, went down on one knee before Sisera and bowed his head. "Forgive me, Lord! I had no idea. Of course you are right. The wench is a Haibru, very comely, but there are many such here."

Yael moaned, opened her eyes and slowly took in the scene before her. It was the golden warrior of her dream! She sat up, realized she was naked and clutched the robe to her.

Sisera gestured to the soldier to go. He stared wordlessly at Yael the whole time the man dressed until he left.

"You seem familiar to me," he said, distractedly. "Yet I know we have not met."

"Yes," Yael said. "And you to me. I am Yael, wife of Haber the Kenite."

Her eyes glowed into his with a strange blend of admiration and fear. Sisera was used to women's admiration, but the fear, even a touch of horror, he saw in Yael's face and eyes troubled him. "You need not fear me, Yael. I will not hurt you. I am Astarte's true and devoted slave. I would do nothing to offend Her, and forcing you to offer yourself here, would offend Her. Please, put your robe on."

Yael pulled up the robe to cover herself; blinked, letting the horror and fear drift away, and responded to the everyday normalcy of their conversation. "I was enslaved by Asmara. I wanted to come here...."

Sisera smiled sympathetically. "Asmara. Yes. A powerful witch. She has brought many to the Goddess. Come," he gestured for her to arise and walk with him. They stopped at a nearby fountain and he wiped the blood from her face with a piece of cloth. "Your wounds are not serious. I have seen many and know. Would you like a cup of wine?" She nodded her acceptance; they walked out into the sunshine. "What brought you to Charoshet, Yael?"

She could not believe she was walking and talking with the monster, Sisera, enemy of her people! Not only had he saved her, he was offering refreshment and carrying on a sincere, compassionate conversation. "I came to see Hakim Saul. My husband wants children, but I do not. I can not imagine bringing children into a world like this." She looked up into his warm, blue eyes. God, he actually understood her!

"You said your husband was Haber the Kenite?" Yael nodded. "I know him. He is a coppersmith, is he not?" Yael nodded again. "He is a good man. We have done business together. You are comely, Yael, very comely." His eyes ran appreciatively across her body. She tingled. "I would have remembered you. Why have I not seen you before?"

"I know not, Lord." Yael said, warming to him and his courtly, virile sexuality. *Perhaps I can repay him for his kindnesses to me. What would it be like to lie with one such as he, one who is so obvious about his desire for me, here in this exotic city? None of my people would know, and besides, only an hour ago, I was prepared, no thrilled, to be a sensual sacred prostitute, to offer myself to a man, to be used by a man, many men.*

As if sensing the direction of her thinking, Sisera stopped walking and turned to her. The sounds of the city, the shouts, creak of carts and buzz of many conversations, swept over them. Again he ran his eyes over her. She felt them on her flesh like drops of hot water. "You are indeed a lovely maiden in distress. On my honor, I would not interfere with you further, especially since I know your husband. But there is something about you, Yael - something compelling. I feel both drawn to you and repelled by you."

Yael dipped her head in agreement, his glances fueling the growing heat of her own desire. She shifted her weight to reveal more of her shapeliness and leaned closer to him. "I too, feel a strong attraction to you, my Lord."

She looked around; they had not gone far from the temple. She took his hand. Electricity snapped between them. Sisera drew back, but then allowed her to continue holding his hand. She felt in control of him, and the situation. "We have not gone too, far from the temple, my Lord." Her eyes bore into his. Her heart leapt and the perversity of it! He gripped her hand more tightly. "Perhaps we can return there and I can show my appreciation for your bravery and," she raised a hand to his cheek, "your beauty." He said nothing as she turned and led him back to the Temple of Astarte.

Afterwards, Sisera said, "Let us go for some refreshment."

"Thank you, my Lord. I would enjoy that." Yael paused and leaned against his strong body. "And thank you for being with me, in the temple. I have never experienced anything like it!"

He smiled. "You are most welcome. I know of Hakim Saul," he said. "He has not attended me, but he has others of my suite." They entered a small courtyard with elegant divans and tables holding wine, goblets and trays of fruit and cakes. They sat down and he poured, handing her a goblet. The Canaanites did not water their wine. Yael drank, draining the cup in a moment. Sisera gestured to the trays. "Please, eat." She helped herself and ate hurriedly. Sisera watched her as she ate. "Didn't Asmara feed you?"

"Nothing so good as this, my Lord."

"Well the Goddess be blessed; eat your fill!"

Another officer, older and nasty looking, entered the courtyard, strode to Sisera and saluted. "Ready to return to the Fortress, My Lord?"

"In a moment." He gestured to Yael. "This is Yael. She is here by mistake. Asmara brought her." The officer nodded, knowingly, looking Yael up and down. "She wants to go to Hakim Saul. Will you be so kind as to take her, Sostrum?"

Yael, stared. Was this the same Sostrum, the monster Jereboam had told her of?

"Of course, My Lord," Sostrum said, saluting.

"Good." Sisera turned to Yael. Seeing her face blanch as she stared at Sostrum, "Are you alright, Yael?"

*It is him! Got to keep my face composed*, she thought. "Yes, my Lord," she said.

"Good," Sisera said "Go with this man. He will take you where you want to go. I am sorry for your inconvenience."

Yael smiled. "Thank you, Sisera! I will spread word of your decency and compassion when I return home." She stood to go, wiping her mouth. "One more favor, my Lord?" she asked.

"Of course, my gracious lady."

She blushed at his courtliness. "After Hakim Saul I wish to return to my husband's encampment. I want to go on my own. I will need weapons to protect me."

"Quite the independent adventuress," Sisera said admiringly.

"Can your officer procure them for me?"

"Indeed he can. When you have finished with Hakim Saul, go to the Fortress, ask for Sostrum and he will give you what you need."

"Thank you, my good Lord!"

"You are most welcome, my lady." Sisera dipped his head in appreciation and turned to Sostrum. "I will see you in the map room." Sostrum saluted, took Yael gently by the elbow and guided her to the street.

Sisera sat for a moment, watching Sostrum and Yael disappear into the crowds. Then, sighing, he stood, blinked and looked about him. The sky was a deep blue punctuated by puffy white clouds. The wind was cool and brisk; the shrubs and trees splashes of deep green amidst the white-washed stucco walls. Everything was good and normal, and better than good. Yael *had* been worth the effort. He inhaled deeply.

He had not planned on getting involved with the Haibru woman. But in the brief glimpse he had as the mercenary dragged her off, something about her spoke to him. She was familiar in an unearthly way. As he contemplated what to do, a series of disorienting feelings—deep, peaceful resignation followed by vague alarm raced through him. His sense of everyday civility and honor urged him to confront the uncouth mercenary and free the women, Haibru or no, after all, the Goddess wanted only willing servants. Yet something, perhaps the vague sense of alarm, restrained him.

Still, he drifted nearer the corridor they had disappeared into. Sounds of blows being struck, clothes tearing and struggle grew more distinct. His resolve also became more distinct and in the few feet it took to reach the alcove curtain and draw it back, his mind was made up. It hadn't been difficult after that. The mercenary was a bully and quickly acquiesced to Sisera's demands. The woman had been a different story.

Not that she resisted. Quite the contrary. She was as grateful as he'd expected her to be, but her gratitude was tinged with a strange fear, even horror. She seemed to recognize him too, and her expression of dread increased as she listened to him talk to the mercenary. When he told the mercenary who he was, she shut her eyes and looked away. But then she'd warmed to him, and he being one never to ignore an opportunity with a beautiful woman, even a Haibru woman, had lain with her.

He walked from the tavern, through the streets and to his headquarters, smiling and chatting with people. He was one of the last of his garrison to go on leave, and it was long past due. When he returned he would finalize his battle plans, mass his 40,000 well-armed troops, 900 iron chariots and destroy the Haibrus once and for all. The irony of that wholesale destruction and his recent saving of one Haibru woman, was not lost on him. Soon I will be in Hazor. With Betheena. He smiled at the thought of being with his mother again; the good food, pampering, and fiery discussions.

---

Hakim Saul was not as old as Yael expected him to be. His beard and hair were mostly black with only a few streaks of grey, and his black eyes sparkled with compassion and lively good humor beneath bushy brows. He had greeted her in the courtyard of his small work place. There was a fountain and a few heavily leaden date palms. His voice was deep and gentle. "Your husband sent a messenger inquiring after your well being, Yael. I had no idea of who you were, but told the man to return today."

The doctor looked deeply into Yael's eyes. She felt his deep desire to understand. "I was guided to do that by some deeper intuition. Normally, I would simply have told the truth that I had no knowledge of you, and sent the messenger away. In your case...." The smile lines around his eyes crinkled; he didn't finish his thought. "So. Why have you come and where have you been?"

Yael felt at ease and safe with this man, wanted to trust him, hoped he might be able to help her. Perhaps all of this *was* part of God's plan

*Devorah* 103

for her and her people. "Thank you for your kindness, Hakim Saul." She was quite weary but managed a smile.

"Let us go inside. Here," he said, gesturing to a large cushion. "Sit; rest. Tell me." He seated himself across from her.

"I have been dreaming of murder for the last several months." The doctor's mouth dropped open, his eyes grew wide and he gestured with his head for her to continue. "At first it was only fragments. I held a tent peg, a mallet, a figure lay at my feet. Then, over time the fragments grew clearer and coalesced—the mallet was my own mallet, the one I use to hammer the pegs to our tent; the pegs were shaped and sharpened as I shape and sharpen them. The figure became a man, then a man in armor, then a tall handsome man in gold armor.

"He was a guest in my husband's tent. He slept in a curled position. I approached, raised the mallet with my right hand crouched, held the stake above his ear and drove it home. I exulted as the blood spurted forth, soaking my hands and robe, this was an enemy of Israel and I was granted the privilege of killing him. But...."

"But...." The doctor repeated.

"But today I met him. He saved me from being raped in the Temple of Astarte. He is a good man. He is Sisera, the Canaanite General."

"You think this is a dream of power, foretelling the future? You think you will kill Sisera?"

Yael looked away from the doctor, swallowed and shook her head affirmatively. She felt a sadness, a deep sense of loss she had not felt before in connection with the - what else could she call it now, but *murder*. "I think I will not glory in it as I once thought I would. I think I, of myself, no longer want to kill him after what he did for me today. But I think it is God's will and that I must do it."

"But this is not what brought you to me originally, is it Yael? You said this incident with Sisera happened hours ago. What was it you wanted my help with?"

"The dream is part of it, hakim," she said. "But it is children. That is why I have come and why my husband Haber let me come. He wants children and I do not. He thought you could help me think differently about children."

"You are physically able to have children, your blood flows, your body is normal, but you choose not to, is that it?" Yael nodded. "Why do you not want children, Yael?"

"I am a beautiful person, a person of fiery passion and pride. I want more." She smiled ruefully, a vision of herself on her knees gazing adoringly at Elkanta's gorgeous ass cheeks flashed through her mind, the deep longing to kiss them tenderly and smell their odor inflamed her heart and groin. "Until a few days ago, before I came here and fell into the hands of Asmara...."

"Asmara the Priestess of Astarte?"

"You know of her?"

"Everyone in Charoshet knows of her. You are indeed lucky to be whole." He leaned forward and looked more carefully into her face. "You *are* whole, aren't you?"

"I am not sure, Hakim." She paused. "Yes, basically I am whole, but I am also deeply wounded. A part of me, something I barely noticed, some part I thought so small was seized upon by Asmara and came to rule over me." She shuddered. "And would rule me again were I to return to the priestess' presence. Who could bring children into a world in where such things are possible?"

"I understand, Yael. But this with Asmara is not the reason you came to me, it but adds to your original reason."

"Yes, Hakim, you are right. I did not want children because our people are oppressed, God has abandoned us to our sins and lecherous evil ways, He allows the Canaanites to torture and humiliate us. And I might soon be a murderer. How can I bring a child into this? And the future seems to hold more of the same. We must rise up, but seem unable to." She leaned forward, the dullness in her eyes shifting to softly glowing radiance. "But I think our time is at hand. I think that is what my dream is about. Sisera is a good man. I would not kill him, but for the fact that his death, will mean our freedom. It is not personal, but duty." She looked down. "In fact, if it were personal, if it were up to me, I would not kill him, but lie with him again."

"Then perhaps," the doctor leaned back, "when you have killed Sisera it might be a better world in which to raise a child?"

Yael thought this was a revelation. After a moment of hesitation, her face lit up, eyes widened and she grinned. "Yes," she said. "Truly."

"Good," the doctor said. "And what of Asmara?" Yael frowned. "Did you not tell me that her power over you came from a small part of yourself?"

"Yes." She looked searchingly into his face, again silently asking, *May I tell you the Truth? Can I trust you?*

"You must trust me, Yael. I can only heal you and make you whole by helping you embrace all the strands of your life."

She nodded, reassured. "Do you think I truly will kill Sisera, that it is God's will?"

"It made you happy to think so, didn't it? A little sad because you now feel something personal for him, but happy and relieved."

She shook her head, 'Yes.'

"I, of course, have no way of knowing," he said. "Yet I put great stock in power dreams. My experience shows that it will work out if you simply allow. Do not judge yourself or the conditions, choices or situations in your life with your everyday consciousness; simply allow. Neither you nor I can know *now*, what we will do *then*, when then is now. To me, it seems unlikely you will have an opportunity to kill Sisera, but I am thinking with my everyday consciousness now, about then. If you do have an opportunity to kill him, decide then using your greater awareness—the part of you that sent the dream. Does that work?"

She shook her head, 'Yes.'

"This part of you that Asmara used and you said she could use again, tell me about that."

"I am beautiful." She looked deeply into his eyes. It was a statement of fact. "Don't you think so Hakim Saul?"

"I do," he said.

"I want to be admired, appreciated, perhaps even worshipped. I want jewels, silk, fine creams and unguents to anoint my body." She ran her hands seductively along the contours of her breasts. "I wanted to be waited upon and not have to work so hard. I thought, and Asmara promised, I could have all that if I became her slave and through her, Astarte's slave." The doctor leaned forward, encouraging Yael to continue. "Asmara saw my desires and reversed them, bringing out their opposites - if I wanted to be worshipped, I would first have to worship. If I wanted to be waited upon, I had to first wait upon her and her slave, Elkanta. I wanted more than the gentle sex I knew with Haber, and was given soul shattering orgasms from kissing a slave woman's filthy feet and sniffing her smelly buttocks...." Yael sighed, felt the heat coming upon her.

"Good," Hakim Saul said. "Enough. Thank you for sharing this with me, Yael. I understand how difficult it is to reveal these things to another person, especially a man." She dipped her head, eyes never leaving his. "I sense that the passion is still strong in you."

"Yes." Her lips were a tight line.

"What you have been through, Yael, has been the equivalent of torture on the wrack. The foundation of your life has been almost completely shattered. I have seen Asmara's and other priestess' victims and they rarely return to a life outside Astarte's Temple. They have given themselves and are slaves forever. This did not happen to you, though you gave of yourself fully, perhaps because God *does* have a larger purpose for you, perhaps represented in your dream of Sisera.

"What do you know of the Covenant God has with our people?" Yael frowned, looked down. "From your expression, not a great deal, true?" Yael dipped her head in agreement. "But you are an Israelite, even tho you are married to Haber, a Kenite?" Yael nodded, eyes on his. "How old were you when you married?"

"Fourteen."

"And how old are you now?"

"Twenty three."

"And for how many years have you been desiring to be admired and appreciated?"

"As long as I can remember."

"Good; thank you," Hakim Saul said. "I understand better now." Yael nodded.

"I asked about the Covenant because our power—the human ability to do things and be effective in the world—my power, your power, even Asmara's power - comes from our connection or covenant with Spirit, our greater Self, the Self that is all-powerful, loving and always with and available to us. The more you rely on It, the more peaceful, powerful and joyous you are.

"Awareness of this connection/relationship with Spirit is what our people call, 'The Covenant.' It is our realization and awareness that God is not elsewhere, in the sky or on a mountain top, but here," the doctor patted his chest, reached across and patted Yael's. "And here," he said as he tapped his forehead and hers.

"Struggle, suffering and pain come when we forget our natural connection to Spirit and try to do things on our own by relying on our own meager strength." He sighed, leaned back and smiled peacefully. "Our little selves are so pathetic; relying on them is like expecting a child to raise a tent by himself. When we rely on our little self, we tend to judge ourselves as wrong, guilty or evil. Have you heard these ideas before, Yael?"

"Once," she said, "at a majlise with Devorah."

The doctor smiled. "Ah, yes," he said. "I have heard Devorah is an excellent champion for this view of the Covenant. But I have never met her nor heard her speak. Yet, I think she is an excellent Sar for our people." Yael nodded. "The more common, dominant view of the Covenant is that God is far off, in the sky or on a mountain top, making rules, judging and punishing and the Covenant is our promise to obey His rules and serve Him with rituals in the Temple.

"You will not recover from what you have been through if you follow this view of the Covenant, feel guilt and judge yourself." He leaned towards her. "What do you think," he asked. "Could you use what you've been through as an opportunity to develop a relationship, a Covenant, with your inner power, your big Self."

"Perhaps."

"It will be worthwhile; but you've got to know you will not be able to do this in a few weeks. It will take months, even years. Can you allow yourself the time you'll need to become whole again?" Yael nodded.

He looked deeply into her eyes. She felt her breathing slow. His eyes seemed to glow as he stared fixedly at her. She looked back, her eyes unable to close or even blink. He made a gesture with his hand across her face and eyes. Her breathing entrained with his. He made another gesture.

"Relax, Yael. Feel yourself becoming completely relaxed and open; receptive to what I tell you. There is a place deep within you that has never been broken, harmed or wounded. Do you believe this?"

"Yes."

"It is your big Self, your greater awareness, the awareness of all of life, beyond your everyday thinking. It is the place of the Covenant, the place from which, more and more, you consciously choose to act, feel and think." He made another pass across her face. "It is the place we are now expanding so that its boundaries encompass everything in your life, good and evil, life and death. From that place you are able to embrace your perfectly healthy desires to be waited upon, worshipped and beautified. From that place you are able to accept that you want those things and not judge, condemn or punish yourself because you want them. It is human and natural to want them. It is your traditional, everyday thoughts and their vision of a demanding and punishing God that fears what you want, even though you can not help wanting. Do you feel this, child?"

"Yes, Hakim Saul."

"Good! Judgment, condemnation and punishment are not of God but come from another part of you, your small fearful self, the censor. This part only judges, condemns and punishes for that is its sole mission in life. You can never please it, no matter what you do, do not even try. *It* is the part that does not want to bring children into this world. You, as many of us do, have confused the voice of the censor with the voice of God. In reality, God is that part of you that only loves and blesses, is incapable of judgment and punishment and has never been broken, harmed or wounded - your greater awareness, joyous, optimistic, loving, creative, and daring." The doctor made another pass across Yael's expressionless face.

"Look upon your normal desires to be waited upon, worshipped and beautified from the place of greater awareness, not from the place of the censor. Forgive yourself for being human. Cease judging and punishing. Know that this is difficult, moment to moment work. But you are strong, powerful woman, Yael and you will learn to do this, becoming more and more successful at it. Do you understand and accept all that I have told you, Yael?"

Yael dipped her head in agreement, eyes still locked on his. The doctor's hands made two swift passes across Yael's beautiful face and she blinked and her breathing returned to normal. She regarded him thoughtfully, right on the edge of being overwhelmed. "You have told me a lot, doctor." He shook his head, *yes*; "I think I understand a portion of it. I wonder how, when I have returned to Haber and my people in the West, will I remember the rest?"

"We have planted seeds, Yael, they will blossom in their season."

"But seeds must be tended and nurtured."

"Indeed," he smiled warmly at her and she smiled back. "You will nurture them with your awareness and your everyday living." She cocked her head with a question. The doctor responded before she could speak. "Use the place within that has never been broken or hurt that is full of love and optimism; it is always available. When you find yourself thinking of Elkanta, Asmara and Astarte, allow those thoughts. Do not resist or judge them, for what you resist, persists.

"Simply be aware of them and welcome them as an opportunity to go to the place of your greater awareness. The thoughts of sensual glory and slavery, of not wanting children will come often; allow them and turn them over to your greater awareness. Take them to that place that has never known pain and failure and from *there* you can choose to see them as God sees them, not as the censor sees them." He looked deeply into Yael's face, held her gaze for a long moment. "Can you do that my daughter?"

*Devorah*

She smiled softly, eyes warm. "Thank you, doctor. I will do my best."

"Good. The idea is to just keep returning to that place and renew your Covenant with God. It is *not* to change your mind about Sisera, Asmara, Haber or yourself. It is to forgive yourself for your so called evil thoughts about murdering Sisera, being a slave to Asmara or not having children. The idea is not to decide anything on your own, but to join with Spirit, then decide. Whatever you decide from that place and guidance, will be good for all concerned."

"Not judging myself will be difficult." She smiled at him. "I have such passionate, evil thoughts." He began to speak, but she held up her hand to stop him. "I know," she said, "so called *evil* thoughts."

"Yes. Good!" He patted her shoulder. "The trick is to love what is especially deep in your heart. You can not repress that; to do so will sicken you and cause you to choose wrongly. Go through judgment to passion and through passion to serenity."

"I have much passion to go through, doctor."

"I can see that, Yael. You are a magnificent woman, destined to do great and wonderful things."

"Thank you, doctor."

He stood. "Ah, one more thing. What I have told you is a bit more than half the battle; it will help you cope with temptation and put you in the place of power to access to your greater consciousness. You also want to have a vision, a goal, something to focus upon, pour your energy into and work towards—something equally as deep as your passion to be admired and appreciated." Yael's face was clouding over. Her eyes darted around the room, avoiding his.

"I know this will be especially difficult for you, Yael." His voice was low; his eyes sought hers. "For most people this is about family and children, but that is not possible for you just now." Her eyes came to rest on his. "What would give your life meaning and purpose?" She shuddered and looked away. "Is it killing Sisera?"

"Yes," she whispered getting up and pacing.

"You know that is not enough." She paced without answering. "When that opportunity comes, *if* it comes, you will deal with it. But what about now, tomorrow, next week?"

"Is it being Asmara's slave?"

Yael stopped pacing and turned to face him. "There is something there. Asmara has marked me for life, but no, that is not it. My cousin Jereboam is serving with Barak. He was tortured and made unable to fight by the Canaanites. Soon Devorah will issue a call to arms. My husband, Haber is a tinsmith, but he is interested in learning to work with iron. Barak will have need of men in his armory. I would speak to my husband and see if we can go to Mt Tabor to prepare for war."

"You think Haber will agree?" Yael nodded. "And what would you do there?"

"Cooking and cleaning, not so exciting, but it will be with our Army, for our Army!"

"I fear that is still an insufficient focus, Yael."

"Yes." She looked down. "I have talked with Devorah. Perhaps, I might serve her, help her organize things. There will be much to do."

"Yes," he said. "That would keep your mind deeply active...."

"I might also be a spy!"

"A spy?"

"Yes. I have learned a lot about being a sacred prostitute. Perhaps I can go to Hazor and learn of the Canaanite intentions. She paused and grinned at the doctor. "I already have one piece of information that might be useful to Devorah. You probably know it, too!"

"What is that, Yael?"

"Many citizens, common soldiers and ranking officers think Devorah may be the incarnation of their war goddess Anat."

Hakim Saul nodded. "And this will be useful to Devorah, how?"

"It means they fear her and also feel bereft of their own spiritual support. They fear that not only has their goddess abandoned them but She has chosen the Haibru Devorah instead. This is an important advantage. If Devorah can secure just one or two victories, they will give up hope and can be easily beaten."

Hakim Saul smiled at Yael. "Very insightful; and I think you have made the correct interpretations. Good! And you would be a spy here in Charoshet?" Yael nodded. "What about meeting Asmara and Elkanta again?"

She looked down and swallowed, then looked back at him. "That would be exciting work and full of the glamour I seek."

Hakim Saul nodded and smiled at her. "Indeed. And dangerous, too."

"Yes!" She was quite enthusiastic, and girlish. "But that is the thrill, Hakim Saul, to be independent, on my own, relying on my beauty and brains! And think of the good I might do! And once the war is over and I have killed Sisera, perhaps I might be able to return to a more normal and traditional life."

# Devorah

The doctor opened his arms, she stepped into them and they hugged. "God speed, Yael," he said.

"May I see you again?"

"You may, but I think you will not need to. Shall I make arrangements for your return to your husband?"

"Ah, yes," she said thoughtfully. "That must be done. But, let it be a test for me, doctor, to do on my own; a taste of what I will experience as a spy in Hazor."

---

Betheena looked through the lattice of her third story window. Sisera had sent word of his immanent arrival and she wanted to go to him the moment he arrived. Much of Hazor lay stretched before her and, as it often did, her heart swelled with pride at the beauty and cleanliness of the royal city. What a shame that the slave barbarians escaped from Egypt and chose Canaan as their dwelling place. They were dirty, uncouth and had no arts, music or anything approaching culture; certainly nothing to compare with ours, or the Philistines or even the Moabites.

They did have one interesting idea, she allowed. The concept of one God. Now, there was a thought whose time has come - not for everyone, obviously, but for her and her son. Betheena thought the rituals for Baal and Astarte were almost laughable and she knew Sisera did, too. How ironic that they both had key parts to play in those activities by virtue of their births and position in society. Some aspects of the rituals approached beauty—a few of the psalms, dances and costumes. But most of it, especially the prayers were silly, especially the fertility rituals.

Quite sexual at forty four, Betheena found most of what she was asked to do in Astarte's name, not sexy or arousing at all. *Probably all in my head*, she thought. No doubt, because almost everyone else in attendance always seemed quite aroused. Her taste ran less to passionate abandon and more to dutiful service. Betheena preferred private sex with well trained and obedient partners and slaves, male and female, to the wild drunken bacchanal of the public fertility rites.

Still, rituals did have a place in her private sex life. Done correctly, as she did them, they heightened and enhanced sexual experience almost to transcendence. Perhaps it was these peak experiences that helped her appreciate the Haibru's one God idea. She had taught Sisera quite a few of the rituals and knew that he too, found them potent and compelling.

The rustle of clothing and the flip-flop of sandals on marble caught her attention and Betheena turned to see the King entering her chamber. At 54, Jabin was still a fine figure of a man, tall, firm of flesh, complexion ruddy, brown eyes sparkling, hair and beard full, black and tinged with grey.

"Ah, sister," he said, striding toward her with open arms, smiling. Betheena opened her arms in turn and went to meet him. They hugged then she stepped back and curtsied, deeply. "Your majesty," she said. "May I offer you some refreshment?" she asked as she stood, gesturing to the heavily laden table.

"Yes, thank you. Figs and grapes, please." He seated himself on one of the four backless chairs arranged in a group near the window. "With pleasure, Sire!" Betheena fixed a plate, brought it to him, bowed deeply and offered it to him. He held her hands in his, and as she looked up, he gazed deeply, perhaps longingly, into hers. Gently, she extricated her hands leaving him holding the dish. "It has been too long Sire, too long."

"Indeed," he said. "Arise and sit." Betheena obeyed. "I am here about my nephew."

"Sisera?"

"He is thirty now, is he not?" Betheena nodded. "And still unmarried."

"My lord," Betheena stuttered. "He has been most busy of late in your service...."

"And before that what was the excuse?" The King's voice was gruff, unyielding.

"Majesty, I know not...."

He raised a hand to still her. "I know we are about to launch the final campaign against the Haibrus and I want my General's mind clear and uncluttered. So, we will not speak more of it now. But I want you to know, when the campaign is over, our victorious Sisera is to be married." Betheena gulped, looked down and nodded. "A likely mate for him is Delilah, our cousin Lotar's daughter."

Betheena suppressed a gag. Lotar was a buffoon and his daughter, though comely, almost brainless. Not her choice. But, as her brother said, the wise course was to leave be until after the victory parade.

"I will be leading the services tomorrow at the Temple of Baal and look forward to you and Sisera having parts in the rituals. I want

*Devorah* 113

to show the people a strong, united royal family leading them to victory. Sisera will have a major part." She nodded and he smiled. "Not anything you haven't done before—but perhaps more important this time."

Betheena arose and bowed deeply. "It will be an honor, your Majesty."

The King also stood. "A pleasure, always, sister," he said, taking her hand and bringing it to his lips. "Until tomorrow."

"Until tomorrow, Sire."

Betheena watched Jabin depart, her mind aflame. *Sisera will not be happy serving in the rituals to Baal,* she thought. *He would also not be happy with Lotar's daughter, Delilah. Poor dear! Not the homecoming she wanted for him.*

As it happened, Sisera did not mind the King's invitation and had, on the long ride home, anticipated it. Passing through the dry, water-starved countryside, he prayed for rain and renewal and made a truce with Baal, Astarte and Anat. *Whether you are real or not,* he had prayed, *or whether there is something greater that works through you, I know not. I wish only to be guided, guarded and protected. I want to lose myself in the oblivion of faith and belief. To be empty of nagging doubt and full of fervor.*

When, upon his arrival, his mother met him in the stables and told him about the temple rituals and what his uncle the King required, Sisera was almost eager to worship and serve in the rituals to Baal. He would have liked to clean himself up before seeing Betheena, but her enthusiasm for him, dust and all, eased Sisera's mind. Her love and adoration enveloped Sisera and he sighed, swept up in the power of her emotion. For the first time in months, he felt safe and peaceful.

Betheena large brown eyes widened and glowed with deeply banked passion as they rested upon him. *Perhaps it is time to revive our own, private rituals...*

Still in the stable, with the smell of hay, manure and horse sweat surrounding them, a slave brought a moist warm cloth which Betheena used to gently mop Sisera's brow and face; another slave brought a chalice of iced wine which he drank in a gulp of gratitude. It was good to be home! Hand in hand they climbed the broad stairs to her third story hide-a-way. She seated him in the same chair the King had recently occupied. The slaves had followed with more wine, fresh cloth and a golden bowl of water. Betheena dismissed them and knelt next to the bowl at her son's feet.

"Please, mother!" He said. "It is not fitting that you do this."

"Nothing could be more fitting. You are magnificent! I am proud of you; you are my son and it is fitting that I serve you." She removed his sandals and golden leg armor then laved his feet, legs and thighs with the moist cloth. The water quickly turned muddy. She clapped her hands and a slave brought another golden bowl with clean water, a fresh cloth and took away the dirty cloth and water.

Sisera inhaled deeply, sighed and felt the tension drain from him. After a moment, he reached up and undid his breast plate. He felt slightly vulnerable and uncomfortable, his broad chest covered now only by a flimsy tunic. He was not used to being so unprotected in strange surroundings. But these were not such strange surroundings, really. He'd been here before and his mother had ministered to him this way then.

He looked down at her and their eyes met. She was still amazingly beautiful, the Goddess incarnate! He was truly blessed. She gazed at him momentarily, and then went back to her task, humming. Sisera allowed no one else to serve him this way. He had no body slaves Nor servants. When he offered his seed to Astarte with the temple prostitutes, it was all very straight forward without warmth or passion.

Betheena laved his thighs, pushing his legs apart to give her easier access. He heard her inhale deeply, drinking in the warrior's scent of sweat, leather, horse and urine. His penis trembled, began to stiffen.

"You know, mother," he said to take his mind from the sensual bliss of her ministrations. "I think my deployments for the forthcoming campaign against the Haibrus are quite strong. But I have one key concern about the placement of the main body of my chariots."

She shifted her attention to his other thigh but did not stop her stroking. Looking up at him she said, "I am no expert on military matters, my son. You are, and in this situation I think the answer you seek is already within you." She leaned forward and placed a long lingering kiss on his thigh near his groin. "I think that the power of the gods will guide you; that once you are fully relaxed, without resistance and open to them, the answer will come."

Her kiss caused his muscles to flex involuntarily. "Perhaps. But talking to you is also helpful."

"Please, then talk to me."

"My captains think the best disposition for the chariots is across the Kishon River Valley. I have a map in my saddle bags. I can show you later. Such a disposition makes the most sense. With this drought,

# Devorah

the river itself offers no obstacle, and a line there would make escape from Mt Tabor impossible and reinforcements from the south equally impossible. But, something bothers me...."

Betheena stopped her laving and looked intently into her son's face. "You are beloved of the gods, Sisera! Feel that, embrace that and the certainty you seek shall be yours!"

He smiled, stroked her hair and she laid her head on his thigh. Even after bathing him, the smell of horse sweat, leather, man sweat and urine lingered on his hairy flesh and filled Betheena's nostrils. It was an erotic scent, many-layered and potent. She lay still, inhaled it deep into her lungs and felt a tingle in her vagina. He continued stroking her hair. After a moment, she leaned forward and up, pushing her head against the fabric of his short tunic. The smell there was even more potent. Her tongue flicked out teasing his inner thigh and tasting the harsh tang of his dirty body. He sighed again. How delicious! His muscles twitched. He shifted his weight and broke contact.

"Mother...."

"Shhh my son. Allow me the pleasure of serving you in this way."

"I don't think...."

"Remember, how I used to bathe you and kiss you?" She leaned forward and placed a moist kiss on his thigh.

"I was a child then, mother."

"It is even better now, Sisera." She kissed him again and licked all the way up to his groin, nuzzling him there and inhaling deeply of his fragrance. "Now you can truly appreciate what I am doing." His penis stirred. "See. You *are* appreciating my attentions."

"I...."

She stopped licking him, raised her eyes to his and said, "We are both adults, Sisera; wise in the ways of the world and the Temple of Astarte. Let us not play at innocence here! We love each other too much and time is short. I shall leave you if that is your wish."

"No, mother; don't leave me, please. Forgive me. No one loves me as you do, please, continue."

"You are sure?"

"Yes, please. I am sorry. Make love to me."

Betheena smiled and returned to kissing his inner thigh. But a moment later, as Sisera's manhood swelled, she broke off again. "Your tunic is in the way. Remove it."

"Yes, mother." Sisera stood and quickly obeyed Betheena's command. "May I sit again?"

"No, I think not." She eyed his naked body, large half erect penis bobbing in front of him. The scent of his body odor was stronger now without the tunic; that and the sight of his splendor inflamed her. Warm liquid heat throbbed in her loins. She would take her pleasure first.

"I would have you serve me, now." She looked deeply into his eyes until he looked down, then in one fluid motion slid her robes up, over her head and revealed herself to him. His eyes widened as he drank in her supple nakedness; the breath caught in his throat. She raised her slender arms above her head and gently turned. Sisera's penis grew to its full size. His voice was hoarse. "You are still a magnificent woman, mother."

She smiled and seated herself, regally. "Worthy of your adoration and worship?"

"Oh, yes!" His voice was low and husky with passion.

Betheena gestured to the floor before her. "Kneel." Sisera knelt. "Bow down before Me, prostrate yourself, show Me your adoration." Sisera obeyed, his naked body rising and falling in worshipful obeisance. Betheena moved her fingers against her clitoris, reveling in the sight of this handsome, powerful man abasing himself at her feet for her pleasure.

"Enough!" She commanded. Sisera stopped instantly, gazing blankly into his mother's eyes in a trance of willing, slavish adoration.

"What are you doing?" She demanded, beginning their private ritual.

"Worshiping you."

"Why?"

"Because you asked me to."

"Do you enjoy it? Do you enjoy worshiping Me, obeying Me and pleasing Me?"

"Oh, yes." Sisera's eyes gleamed with muted passion, pre-cum dripped from his penis.

"And who am I?"

"You are my mother."

"Yes. And who else am I to you?"

"You are the goddess incarnate, the great goddess Astarte in the flesh."

"And who are you?"

"I am your son and your slave. I have been consecrated to your service in your temple since I was seven years old."

Betheena leaned forward and passed her hand across his eyes. He did not blink; he was deep in trance. She could wait no longer. "Serve Me now, slave!" She said, shifting her weight and opening her legs to give him access to her vagina.

Sisera leaned forward as he had been trained to do and inhaled the hot, tangy stench of his mother's sex, filling himself with its aroma and deepening his trance.

"Begin!"

He gave her inner thighs soft gentle kisses, then licks and gradually licked in to her vagina, expertly working his tongue across her labia, then gently opening and parting them so her clitoris stood revealed, proud and erect. Soothingly, tenderly he touched his tongue to it, tasting its unique flavor, then lavished wet kisses upon it, finally enveloping it with his warm mouth.

Above him, the Goddess moaned with pleasure, and Sisera felt that amazing empty-fullness that came from fulfilling his deep desire to please and serve Her, to be one with Her, embraced by Her forever. She spoke to him. He was aware of Her commands and obeyed them instantly, but was in another world, free of his everyday fears and concerns, duties and responsibilities. Empty of need, yet full of potential, he existed only now, one with Her divine transcendent power. There was nothing else. What else could there be? She spoke again, he obeyed and had one of the most powerful orgasms of his life.

He awoke slowly, slightly dazed but refreshed. His mother was on her knees, robes draped around her, head on his inner thigh; he was dressed, seated on the chair.

She was smiling into his eyes as he opened them. "Better?" She asked.

"Oh, yes! I'm feeling clearer, too."

"Yes? About what?"

"The Kishon River Valley. I *will* put the main body of our chariots there. The drought has nearly dried up the river completely and we will have a great strategic advantage."

Betheena stood and opened her arms. Sisera stood and stepped into them. "Good my son! Very good. You have the clarity you sought. The Goddess has answered you."

---

The strident blast of two hundred braying horns hung in the air, echoing through the Temple courtyard and out into the packed city streets. As the sound died away, ten thousand voices roared their approval. Then, to the rhythmic pounding of two hundred drums, Jabin, his Queen, the High Priest of Baal and the great lords of Hazor stepped forward onto the dais erected before the great god. Betheena and Sisera were in the second rank of dignitaries. The cheering of the multitude was awe inspiring, but deafening.

Sisera saw his mother's lips move but could not hear a thing; first the horns and drums, then the cheering. Nonetheless, the enthusiasm and spectacle were infectious. Sisera felt himself caught up in the spirit of it. He again looked at his mother and saw she, too, was moved, her habitual, tight lipped expression replaced by wide eyes and soft lips. He sighed deeply. How she moved him and how grateful he was to have her in his life. "Thank you, thank you, thank you," he said, feeling ready, even eager to do his part in the forthcoming rituals.

As the cheers died away, the priests, hundreds of them, arranged around the inner and outer walls of the Temple so that every inch of space was occupied, naked but for spotless white loin clothes, began their hypnotic rhythmic chanting.

Betheena, too, seemed ready. Her face even more animated now, eyes wide and moist staring at the great stone god, tongue flicking back and forth across shining lips, supple body swaying with the chanting. With breasts bare in the ceremonial dress popularized by the Cretans and transparent diaphanous pants held by a wide solid gold belt that rode up and down on her swaying hips, she was a sight to behold.

Sisera, too, began swaying with the chant. Also nearly naked but for a golden loin cloth, not white like the priests, but golden, spun of threads of gold, he felt his member stir. 'Wait. Save yourself for the ritual.' Turning his mind back to his solitary ride through the desert, he recalled the power of pure spirit he'd felt there, grateful for that simple untainted experience of heart and mind. Now, feeling the overwhelming force of fleshy, voluptuous sensuality, he realized how rare and worthwhile that solitary time in the barren wilderness had been. The purely spiritual and intellectual aspects of worship had their place, but they could barely compete with the carnal, eroticism he felt now. A truly successful religion needed both sensuality and spirituality.

Similarly, the private rituals he and his mother cherished were excellent, but public rituals offered something, as well. The thousands of witness/participants, the grandiose music and costumes were aphrodisiacs in their own rights. The Temple grounds were overflowing: the noise, smells, sounds and colors nearly over powering. Two thousand people, many with babies in their arms and young children on their shoulders, were jammed into a space designed for half that number. Flowers and shrubs were trampled, fountains and pools stopped up. Beyond, in the streets surrounding the Temple, another ten thousand were packed in. Strolling merchants shouted and waved their wares, some selling small clay idols of Baal, Astarte and Anat, others hawking incense sticks, wine, goat and vegetable kabobs. Towering over it all were the great white-washed stone columns and towers of the city center. Sisera thought Hazor was one of the cleanest, best organized cities in all of Canaan, a land noted for its fortified cities.

The priests stopped chanting. The drums took up a more strident, rapid beat. A moment later, the horns sounded the melodious chiming call of the Royal Procession. King Jabin, golden crown sparkling, heavy maroon robes fringed in gold, stepped forward into silence as the instruments abruptly fell silent.

"Kinsman!" His voice boomed out over the crowd in the courtyard and was audible even to the thousands in the streets. "God is great! May Baal rule over us ten thousand years!" The multitude roared back the refrain, "God is great, ten thousand years!" The King continued, "We are gathered here to invoke the god's blessing on a holy war against the Haibru barbarians!" Cheers.

The sun was directly before the King and shone brightly off the burnished shields, weapons and jewels of the crowd. Jabin squinted and raised his arms. "Look about you! See how the sun shines brightly on the glories of our civilization—the stout walls of our beautiful city, the burnished iron of our weapons and the dazzling sparkle of our jewels. Our flesh is firm, hair fine and oiled, bellies full and robes of fine material. Our fields flourish, our merchants prosper and our artisans are among the best in the known world. Do you want to see all this trampled beneath the filthy sandals of Haibru slaves?"

"No!" A mighty ocean of sound swept him up.

"What?" He asked them.

"No!"

He stared straight ahead, as if he hadn't heard.

"No! No! No!" They chanted.

"No!" The King said. "No. We shall not let them have one lamb, one olive tree, one tael of iron ore. No, no, no!"

The crowd roared its approval.

"We have the best Army, too!' More cheers. Jabin gestured to Sisera, who took a step forward and stood hands on hips head tilted up. The cheers grew louder. Jabin gestured and Sisera stepped back.

"The Haibru slaves invaded our land one hundred and seventy six years ago. We lived here at peace with those around us: the Philistines, Moabites, and Syrians. Somehow the Haibrus escaped Pharaoh and fell upon us, like a swarm of locust. At first, they took us by surprise and won battles. But many of these so called 'victories' were the result of treason and betrayal, as at Jericho. But the great god Baal favored us and each year we took back more and more of our land, driving the invaders into the hills and converting many of them to our ways and the service of our gods.

"Now the time has come to convert them all. We do not wish them ill. But if they would live in Canaan, they must live here as Canaanites. They must give up their uncivilized filthy ways and become clean and dutiful. They must pay our taxes and worship our gods!" The multitude roared its approval.

"Those who will not be as we are, will be enslaved. We will make war on them now, to eliminate any possibility of resistance. Our victory will be swift. After the battle we will welcome the Haibrus as Canaanites and help them become as we are, so that one day soon, they too, may have full bellies, fine oiled hair and bow down before Baal and Astarte."

"God is great! May it come to pass!" The multitude chanted.

Jabin raised his arms and gestured for them to be still. "We will now offer sacrifice," Jabin said, stepping back, as the High Priest stepped forward.

The High Priest was a tall man in his fifties, wearing only the ceremonial white loincloth of the priesthood. A wide golden slave's collar and bracelets, marked his office. His well toned muscles rippled as he moved. In a voice equal to the King's he said, "Beloveds we will invoke the blessings of heaven on our endeavors. First we will sacrifice to almighty Baal, then, to Astarte."

He turned and gestured to the nobles assembled behind him and they stepped aside, revealing the great stone god and the roaring fire in his belly. Five priests stood on either side of the fifteen foot tall, stone figure. The High Priest turned to face the courtyard, and said, "Behold the servants of the god!"

At the far end of the courtyard, at the place where the central aisle met the outer wall, a door way opened and two young people, a boy and girl, stepped forward. The crowd began to chant, softly, "God is great, blessed are his servants." The sacrifices were beautiful, unblemished virgins - as required. Both twelve years old, they had been raised from birth in Baal's service, trained in his adoration and worship, knowing only the life of Temple slaves. They had but one purpose, one desire, to give themselves to their god. They could conceive of nothing but this, knew nothing but this. Now was the zenith of their lives, and they were happy.

Youthful bodies supple and lithe, care-free smiles on their faces, they almost ran down the central aisle. At the base of the dais they prostrated themselves and crawled on their bellies up the twenty steps. Sobbing and moaning, quivering and shuddering in ecstasy, they crawled on hands and knees to the priests who stood facing them and waited. The High Priest came and stood behind them. At his command, the boy and girl knelt upright. Their breathing became more regular, their bodies softened and they gazed longingly at the god. Another command from the High Priest and they raised their arms at right angles to their bodies, palms flat facing forward, as if some one were pointing a weapon at them, in the position of adoration.

The five priests on either side knelt and assumed the same position. At the High Priest's command, they and the sacrifices bowed down before their lord. The drums beat a steady rhythm, the horns blared once and the worshippers kow-towed, rising and falling with the drums steady rhythm. The High Priest gave another sign and the horns blared once, the drums stopped, and the young boy and girl rose to their feet. The boy took the girl's hand and at the High Priest's command, they ran forward and threw themselves into the god's fiery belly.

The High Priest turned to the multitude, raised his arms above his head and the people roared. They began chanting, "God is great, blessed are his servants." A moment later, the High Priestess of Astarte stepped forward. She was bare breasted in the Cretan fashion and wore only a golden girdle around her ample hips.

"The great mother, the goddess Astarte, blesses you," she intoned. They cheered. "The god taketh, but the goddess giveth." More cheering. "Now it is time to honor the great mother. Who better than the King's sister, Betheena and her son, Sisera, the King's nephew and General, to enact the fertility ritual? As above, so below. As the goddess gives life to our wombs, fields and beasts, blossoms and blooms, so Betheena has given life to Sisera. Now he honors her as the Great Mother." Scattered cheers.

The High Priestess raised her arms and gestured for silence. "Witness this sacred ceremony in the silence of awe and deep appreciation of the mystery it represents. We are puny, fragile beings subject to the whims of Nature. But the Life Force that animates us and reproduces Itself through us is strong and almighty. We can know only a little of It's ways. In this ceremony we honor what we know and what we do not know." She stepped back and gestured to Betheena.

The crowd murmured appreciatively as she stepped forward, bare arms raised and outstretched above her head, naked breasts thrusting. She had painted the aureoles with dark rouge and the nipples a shade of deep orange. The effect of this made her breasts seem larger and her nipples moist as if she had been nursing. The bright sun sparkled off the rings on her fingers and glinted from her golden girdle.

Betheena lowered her shapely arms and cupped her breasts, offering them to the multitude in the universal gesture of nurture. As she did this, Sisera came forward. He walked around his mother seven times, then knelt before her. He raised his arms to the position of adoration, palms flat facing front, arms at right angles to his body, and gazed adoringly at she who had become the Goddess incarnate. She remained as she was, legs slightly parted, hands cupping her breasts.

"Worship!" The High Priestess commanded.

Sisera began to kow tow before his mother.

"Pray to Her!" The High Priestess commanded.

Continuing to kow tow, the muscles in his handsome body rippling seductively, Sisera prayed. "Oh, Goddess! Oh, Great Mother! Thank You for my life. You are almighty and all powerful, the Life Force Itself. I am a mere man, your humble servant and adoring slave. I worship to show my deep gratitude for all You have given. I worship because I adore You. I worship because it is my place to worship and abase myself before You. I am nothing and You are everything."

"Serve Her!" The High Priestess commanded.

Sisera stood, removed his loin cloth and freed his massive erection. He turned slowly so that the multitude could see him. He faced his mother again and knelt before Her as She moved her hands onto her hips and leaned back, thrusting Her vagina forward. Her genital region had been shaved, Sisera himself had done it, and Her nether lips had been rouged a deep red. He leaned forward and sniffed loudly. He kissed Her labia, then sucked loudly on Her clitoris. At first She was un-responsive to his ministrations. But as he reached up and stroked Her buttocks and anus, while continuing to suck, Betheena became aroused. Her hips began to gyrate, her fingers stroked his hair and her eyes, which had been coolly observing the multitude before her, shut tight. In moments he brought her to a series of increasingly violent orgasms.

"Enter Her!" The High Priestess commanded.

Sisera stood, his mouth and nose smeared with his mother's vaginal fluids. He wrapped his arms around her, tilted her back and put his engorged penis into her moist vagina. He thrust gently at first, gradually increasing his rhythm so that by the time he orgasmed, they were a blur of motion.

"Rest!" The High Priestess commanded.

They collapsed in a heap, side by side, wrapped in one another's arms, smiling; deafened by the people's cheers.

# Part Two
# The War

They were at Devorah's favorite place, the summit of the highest hill in Ephraim. The encampment and oasis spread below them. Late afternoon sun burnished the brown hills and a cool breeze blew from the ocean-sea in the west. *Hmm*, Devorah thought, sniffing loudly. *Is that a hint of rain? How good!* Indeed; but only a hint. What a blessing that would be! Lappodoth wrapped his arms more tightly around her. But, with her back to his chest, he could barely get his arms round her big belly. The baby would come in perhaps six, more likely four, weeks. "We are so blessed, my husband; are we not?" Devorah said, feeling warm and safe.

"We are. God is good. This beauty," he gestured, "and air and the scent of growing things! See how this light illuminates the hills and casts those rich, purple shadows?"

Devorah sighed. "Even as I marvel, I am sad for how we diminish It, cut It down to human size; we often ignore and take It for granted." She leaned forward, pressing against his strong arms and gestured to the panorama around and below them, "This is God embodied - the miracle of everyday life - the growing things, hills, rocks and pebbles; the clouds, sky, and light! How did it all get here and come together so we might live?"

"It is a mystery," Lappodoth said.

Devorah turned and smiled up into his face. "It is so beyond us that we can barely comprehend it. We give it names: God, Baal, Astarte, but what, really, do those names mean? They capture our awe, wonder and gratitude. But naming is just another way to cut the vastness and ineffable magnificence down to human size."

She took a step, her belly jutting 24 inches ahead of her, and pulled Lappodoth forward. "We must get out of It's way, Lappodoth! Allow the Power to use us. Acting as if we know what we're doing is not working; probably will never work. For our lives to be different, *we* must be different, fundamentally - how we think and relate. The Power Itself is only always good, isn't it?"

"Yes."

"It is our use of It - our *misuse* of It - that is the problem! If we can only be still and know Its calm, love, simple acceptance and be-ingness. If we can only get our bloated nothingness—our fear, hatred and doubt out of the way of the divine circuits, heaven would be present for us." She bent and picked up a piece of shriveled palm leaf. "Look. See the detail, the design, the obvious plan. This is at work in our lives too, right now."

"Truly," Lappodoth said. "Not only is It there, It goes on and unfolds with or without our awareness. Everything matters and nothing matters. We must choose and decide, there's no escaping that, but we can choose and decide with It's guidance," he patted her ripe belly, "or without it. I choose *with* It."

"As do I. There is so much more than we can comprehend. We are designed to be narrow, to function in a limited zone of comfort. But there is clearly much more. Dogs hear more than we do, cats see more. What understanding we have is gleaned through our physical and cultural experience, which is but a fraction of all that Is." She turned to him opened her arms and they hugged. The sun sunk lower, the breeze picked up and the air grew colder.

"Our priests and great teachers, even Moses, barely touched the hem of Its garment. We will always, always have this longing to know God. Our teachings are helpful, but they are not the thing Itself. Learning is a pathway to illumination. But it is only when we become still and quiet, and let our everyday minds go, getting our bloated nothingness out of the way, that we *know* and can embody a greater portion of the Divine that dwells within us. Experiencing a personal communion with God, even in what we take to be difficult times such as these, is our purpose - what the Covenant is all about."

"I want our child raised in this belief, Devorah." Lappodoth's face was intense. "You and I are an island of sanity in a sea of fear and terror. Your vision, our vision, is what I choose to honor."

She put a hand on his cheek and smiled into his eyes. "Oh yes, my husband! Everything matters and nothing matters, but we choose this now, in our moment of personal communion." A chill in the air made her shudder. She pulled her robe more tightly about her.

Lappodoth thought she shuddered from a momentary dread. "The news has not been encouraging of late," he said. "The messengers from Asher and Dan...." She leaned forward and kissed him gently on the lips both to stop him from talking and for the sensation of it.

"This is what faith is for, husband. As we said, we can know but a tiny fraction of what there is to know and experience. We can not know what lies ahead. But our belief in God's goodness, in His love for us and in our Covenant with Him we *can* know. We can believe more strongly in that, than in our fear of disaster. Let us put into the Power our hopes and dreams and allow It to return them to us. This is a great opportunity for us to relinquish our limited fearful human perception and rely upon the Divine Power. We have taken, and shall continue to take, all the actions our everyday minds direct us to take, while remaining open to God's whispers through our intuition.

"Appearances are deceiving, even facts such as Sisera's overwhelming advantages are only temporary conditions, 'advantages' only in a particular context. Should that context change, those advantages could become disadvantages. Sisera is relying on that context, which exists in our limited human thinking. Yet that context is beyond his control. It is under God's control, Nature's control. Anything is possible. You and I, and to a more limited extent, Barak, are not relying on that context. We see it, acknowledge it, but see it as malleable, conditional, the result of limited human thinking - a mere fragment of what is possible. We know that with God, anything and everything is possible. God is not bound as we are bound, and when we are with It and allow It, we are as It is. This makes us more fluid and flexible so when the current situation changes, as we are praying it will, we shall be better able to take advantage of it."

"Yes," Lappodoth agreed. "This is what faith is for. I do not know how the change will come, but I have faith that it will. So, everything matters and nothing matters, yet I choose to have faith that what you and I do to get our bloated nothingness out of the way of the divine, will matter."

Devorah patted her belly, "Especially for this one."

Lappodoth turned her, pulled her back to his chest, and reached around her to stroke the new life within her. "That is the best we can do, my queen. And I trust it will be enough. Your call to arms has not been well received. Dan and Asher are the most recent to reject it. We have not yet heard from Reuben...."

"It matters not! We have six of the tribes and will have the 10,000 the Lord asked me to rally. Another boatload of iron ore has reached Barak, and his armory is forging weapons day and night. We will be well armed."

"The Canaanites will be fierce. They are fighting for their very way of life." Lappodoth said.

"As are we, husband, as are we! We are fighting for justice and freedom in God's name. We are fighting to fulfill the Covenant and take the land promised us!"

"I understand, Devorah; but the other tribes, Dan, Asher, Reuben - why do *they* not understand? Are they not of our people? Were they not also promised the land and included in the Covenant?"

Devorah's face softened. "They, as each person, must decide on their own. Their decision affects us, but ultimately, it is about them alone, not us. Their choice does not make our choice invalid. Their misuse of the One Power, does not foreshadow our misuse of It." She touched his cheek, smiled. "We will wrap ourselves in our faith, and our faith will work miracles for us. What those miracles might be, I can not say, but I believe we will see them."

# CHAPTER FIVE

Barak and Jereboam stood on the upper deck of the two story watch tower at the summit of Mt. Tabor. They were able to see fifteen miles in all directions. The wind was fiercer up here, but that just added to Jereboam's feeling of exhilaration as he surveyed the chariots massing eight miles away on the banks of Kishon in the south west.

A gentle stream now, barely worth the name 'river,' the Kishon was known to become a raging torrent when swollen by hours of heavy rainfall. Jereboam smiled. Right there, the plain in which Sisera had placed his chariots, could become a deadly swamp, making the chariots useless after only a few hours of normal rain.

The mid day sun glinted off their wicked wheel scythes. "They don't usually mount the scythes until their ready to attack," Jereboam said.

Barak, grunted. "True, but they're not ready yet. Look to the north east."

Jereboam saw lines of large carts heavily laden with hay, grain, jugs of oil, wine and food stuffs moving slowly on the trails two miles away, round the base of their aerie.

"Their supplies; from Hazor," Barak said. Jabin's capital was invisible, just over the horizon. "Let's send some of our people to slow them up."

Jereboam smiled. "May I go, sir? Who shall I send, Nephtali or Zebulon?"

Barak smiled back. "No, you may not go. Ask Ben Zvi and his company of Nephtali if they would like to go."

"Ha! Of course they'll go!" Ben Zvi is one of the most blood thirsty captains we have."

"My compliments to him, nonetheless, and invite him," Barak said. He was in an excellent mood. Perhaps it was the wind, or the view, or…who knew? Maybe it was the hint of rain in the air. Whatever it was, Jereboam was glad of it. He slapped his arm across his breastplate. "As you command, Tzevah!" and climbed down the ladder.

Barak's mood lightened further as he surveyed the streaming columns rolling in from the north. *Our plan is working! What Devorah and he thought Sisera would do, he is doing. That's something of a miracle right there. God helps those who help themselves.*

Indeed. This foray of Ben Zvi's was about more than just harassing the enemy. It was a preliminary maneuver in the two pronged attack he and Devorah had discussed. She would feint to the shores of the Ocean Sea, with fifteen hundred men from Issachar and Manasseh gathered at her oasis sanctuary in Ephraim, threatening Dor, the Canaanite city most dependent on Hazor for protection. This would draw Sisera away from his encirclement of Mt Tabor. Then Barak would feint towards Hazor, putting additional pressure on Sisera to divide his force and further weaken his concentration at the base of Mt Tabor. Once Sisera divided his force, Barak and Devorah's feints would wheel and attack Sisera's main body from the rear at Mt. Tabor.

Still, the bulk of the chariots would remain in the south and west at the base of Mt. Tabor in the Kishon River Valley. Sisera would not send them to Ephraim, the country was too hilly. Some of them might be drawn off to defend Dor and Hazor, perhaps one or two hundred, but the rest would still be his to deal with.

Barak sighed and prayed—*Abba, here I am again, thinking about the 'facts' and how limited I seem to be. I know that with You, all things are possible. I want to think with that limitless part of myself that is You and be open to the possibilities my small self can not see or even imagine.* Just praying and asking helped him shift, made him think he could manage to do that, and he felt that that place with his Father was real and available to him. He felt better, his racing mind calmer and the fear less intense.

*The slingers!* The deeper calm gave him an insight into a strategic repositioning of his six hundred expert slingers. This unit of boys and young men had a well deserved reputation for accuracy and deadliness. Their well-worn leather slings and pouches filled with smooth, river-washed stones were all the weapons they needed. They practiced constantly and had an effective range of one thousand cubits. What Barak now realized was he wanted his slingers to attack the chariots, not as they charged, but as they slowed to turn and charge again. He could accomplish this by repositioning his slingers just a bit higher up Mt. Tabor's slopes than he'd originally planned. This would give them more time to select targets as the chariots were forced to slow and turn to charge again. How good! Another gift from the inner connection with spirit!

Jereboam returned and saluted smartly, much better than a few moments ago. A good omen? "Ben Zvi will be moving out shortly. He was quite enthusiastic."

"Good. Thank you!"

"I have news."

"Tell me."

"Devorah is on her way with Lappodoth and her guard contingent. And another shipment of iron ore has arrived!"

"Excellent. Soon every man will have iron weapons. Is Devorah coming from Ephraim?" He should have seen her dust if she had been.

"No. Shiloh."

"Shiloh? Perhaps she had another run at Malachizer...."

Jereboam shook his head. "It is probably easier for her to get through Sisera's lines from that direction."

"Yes," Barak said, "Of course. Their lines are still not at full strength. I understand Sisera himself is still on leave in Hazor."

"Have you heard about that obscene ritual he is said to have performed with his mother?"

Barak looked briefly into Jereboam's hate-filled face. *We must be careful not to become the thing we fight against*, he thought. "I have. These things make clear why we fight."

Jereboam nodded. "Indeed," he said.

A clamor from below drew them to the opposite side of the tower; looking down, they saw Devorah and her guard contingent beginning their ascent. Half of them, sixty in all, were mounted on horses and mules. Barak easily identified Devorah's heavy body, sitting side saddle on a black mare. "May she have time to deliver her child before we must attack," he said.

"It is our most fervent wish," Jereboam said, saluting and turning away. "I will go prepare her quarters."

Barak turned to follow Jereboam down the ladder. A cool breeze brushed his face. He sniffed, then sniffed again. Rain? He looked up at the sky, turned in a circle, saw no clouds nor any sign of precipitation. Hmm.... It did smell like rain. He shook his head and climbed down to meet the Sar of Israel.

She looked adorable, even sweeter and more innocent in the bronze helmet and bronze and leather armor strapped around her ponderous belly. Warmed by the affectionate yet respectful expression on her General's face, Devorah smiled contentedly and opened her arms to embrace him.

"My warrior queen and mother to be," Barak said sincerely and tenderly.

"My fierce Tzevah. Thank you for your most kind and gentle greeting."

*My, weren't we being courtly*, Barak thought. Yet it was sincere. "How many are in your escort? Will they be part of your column to the sea? You can't possibly lead an attack in that condition!"

Devorah smiled; this was Barak at his best! "I have 122 fully armed warriors in my escort; they will be in the attack on Dor, *and*, God willing, I will not have to attack in this condition," she soothed her belly, "The ride has moved things along quite nicely."

"You're not bleeding?" Barak's alarm and concern were genuine.

Lappodoth who had just walked up to them, put his arm round her shoulder and said, "She is in magnificent condition! The ride did her a world of good. I am sure our child will be strong and healthy, a true Son of the Covenant."

"And if it is girl?" Devorah looked at Lappodoth with a mock scowl.

"Then a true Daughter of the Covenant!" He opened his arms and they embraced.

"Did you stop in Shiloh?" Barak asked.

Devorah tilted her head, squinted and looked up, into his eyes. "Why yes; why do you ask?"

"You approached the camp from that direction," Barak said simply. "How is my old friend Malachizer?"

"You were bar mitzvah together, weren't you?" She stared intently into his face.

"Yes," Barak said. "Why do you stare so?"

"Your old friend might be a traitor," Lappodoth said.

Barak's mouth dropped and his eyes widened. "No!" he said.

"Perhaps not," Devorah said. "I do not want it to be so. I left a small contingent, 25 men we could ill afford, to remind them of their obligations. Malachizer is a Judean. The Judeans are going to sit this fight out, perhaps hoping we will win, but no matter who wins, planning to be even more ascendant than they are now. We have been told, reliably, that they are leaning toward Sisera. Shiloh is a hot bed of secret activity - men, supplies and material, in support of Dor and Canaan, some from as far as Moab and Edom."

Barak nodded. "A clever double game...."

Devorah's lip curled nastily. "A kind way to describe it," she said. "Treachery is more accurate. The death and maiming of my brave Ephramites when we feint towards Dor will be their burden unto eternity."

Barak bowed his head. "A strong and powerful malediction, Sar. Surely you do not wish it to unfold? They are, after all, our own people."

"I do not wish it upon them; by their own deeds, they will bring it upon themselves." She shut her eyes and rocked slightly. Lappodoth put his arms round her shoulders to steady her. "The Judeans shall bring greatness and ruin to us. They are the mobilizing factor. They, *we*, shall all reap what they sow—both the glory and grandeur and unimaginable horror shall be ours because of them." She shuddered. "I have seen and felt a thing," she choked and tears came to her eyes, "that will befall our people.... It is fierce, monstrous beyond our ability to imagine."

Lappodoth and Barak looked at her openmouthed, eyes wide, speechless. Finally, Barak spoke. "Come, Devorah. You are weak from your ride. Let us go for some refreshment in my tent and continue our conversation there." Devorah nodded her acceptance.

Seated on full cushions in the shade of the tent awning, faces refreshed with splashes of water, goblets of water in hand, Barak resumed their discussion. "But Jereboam is Judean. Surely this great calamity is not the fault of *all* Judeans? Is, God so unfair?"

Devorah looked at him, head tilted to the left and thrust forward aggressively. "How can you ask that?" she said, as if to a thoughtless child. "Of course He can be unfair! Look what we're experiencing now and have been for a generation! And think of our exodus from Egypt. It was the Pharaoh who would not let us go, correct?" They nodded. "Why, then, did God find it necessary to kill the first born of *every* Egyptian? *That* is unfair." As they looked at one another silently, the noise of the camp drifted around them.

Devorah caressed her belly. "It kicks like a boy, Lappodoth. Here," she took his hands and placed them on her belly, "feel."

Lappodoth felt his child move and his face lit up. "God is good," he said.

"Yes," Devorah agreed. "Oh, yes, of course It is!"

"Then how can He also be unfair?" Barak asked.

"He—the Power we call 'God'—I is actually neutral, Barak. We have spoken of this before. Is the wind 'unfair' when it blows down our tents and 'fair' when it cools us and dries the sweat from our brows? No. It is wind, a neutral part of our experience here. We, by our behavior, make it fair or unfair. *We* choose. Knowing the wind and understanding it, it is up to us to adequately stake our tents and tie up our camels and donkeys.

"We can, of course, blame the wind, but, if we are honest, we will see it is our choice and our responsibility to learn from our mistakes and choose more wisely." Barak and Lappodoth nodded their heads in agreement. "The vision I have seen, which may or may not come to pass, depending on the choices our people make, is the result of choices Judeans are making now and will make. If they do not make other choices, and the other tribes follow them and do not choose differently, as they tend to do, then great waves of killings and terror will befall us." Again her face was grim, jaw set, eyes narrowed.

"What are we to do? When will this happen?" Lappodoth asked.

"I know not when. The very distant future, hundreds or thousands of years hence, I think. What we can do is honor the Covenant and live in It's spirit. Not simply, the forms and rituals, as the High Priest does in Shiloh, but It's true spirit—love, respect and community, instead of narrow self interest. The Judeans do not do this. They mistake the glory of their tribe for honoring the Covenant. To them, the greatness of Judah equals the greatness of God and Israel. That is simply not so, though many will live and die that it be so.

"These are the seeds they sow and we shall all—Ephramite, Benjemite, all—reap the whirlwind." Devorah gripped her stomach. "This one wills it be otherwise," she said. "Abba grant him the strength to make a strong contribution."

"Like his beautiful mother," Lappodoth said.

"Amen," Barak agreed.

Yael saw Devorah talking with Lappodoth and Barak, and then watched as they walked off together.

She had managed to return from Charoshet alone and as a result, was more assertive and self confident than ever. After leaving Hakim Saul, she determined to return to Haber and have children by him; her former doubts gone. She had gone to the fortress and, as Sisera

*Devorah*     135

had promised, Zeber obtained a steel sword and two daggers for her. She also begged Zeber for food and water for the trip, and though he grumbled, he bought it to her. Yael felt the trip to Charoshet and her brief time as Asmara's slave had served her well.

The journey to the border of Ephraim had taken only two days! [Three and a half days had been needed with the caravan.] She'd traveled from dusk 'till mid morning and encountered no one. Arriving at the Kenite encampment, she found that Haber had joined Barak and was working as an ironsmith in the armories on Mt. Tabor. She was glad that Haber had chosen to cast his lot with the Haibrus. He could just as easily have gone to work for Sisera, for the Kenites were a neutral people respected by both Canaanite and Haibru. In fact, Sisera himself had once visited the Kenite encampment, located strategically between Mt. Tabor and the heart of Ephraim.

Haibru by birth, but Kenite by marriage, Yael was returning from the Mikvah. She felt clean and centered. Haber adored her, accepted her new sexual proficiency and was grateful to have her maintain their tent, not far from the armories. She had told him of her desire to spy for the Haibrus and now that she had a sword and two daggers, perhaps even fight as well. He had been skeptical and told her that once she was pregnant, she'd feel differently. She agreed but observed she wasn't pregnant yet, and besides, Devorah was a woman and if she could fight, so could Yael. The dreams of murdering the golden warrior came less frequently and were less intense.

Now, here was the Sar of the Nation, the Sar's husband and the Tzeva! God had placed them in Yael's path. *This* was the opportunity she sought. She had to say something to Devorah. Would the Sar remember her from the majlise a few months ago? Yes! Yael made eye contact with Devorah, and Devorah smiled and nodded. Yael dipped her head.

Of course Barak knew her. The wife of one of his ironsmiths was an important person. "Do you know each other?" he asked them.

"I have spoken with this woman in majlise but do not recall her name." Devorah said.

Instead of waiting for Barak to introduce her, as would have been proper, Yael extended her hand and Devorah took it. "I am Yael," she said. "Haibru wife of the Kenite ironsmith Haber, who works here for Barak. I am overjoyed to see you again, Sar." Yael gestured to Devorah's armor, "dressed as you are." Yael's smile was broad and attractive.

Devorah returned Yael's enthusiastic smile. "And to you, Yael. Thank you for your service to our people. What is your tribe?"

"Judean."

Devorah's face clouded, momentarily.

"A good Judean, Sar Devorah," Barak said. "My lieutenant Jereboam's cousin."

"Ah!" Devorah exclaimed. "Now I remember! You were quite articulate at the majlise."

Yael's smile broadened. "I have grown more so, Sar."

Devorah nodded and looked sideways at Yael. "And what would you like to say now, Yael? A moment. May we sit here beneath your verandah, Barak?" Barak nodded and as the two women seated themselves.

"I would like to fight, Sar Devorah! To don armor and join you. I have an iron sword and two iron daggers from my recent trip to Charoshet. I am quick, resourceful and intelligent."

"You made the journey from Charoshet to the Kenite encampment in Ephraim alone?" Devorah asked. Yael nodded. "How did you come to be in Charoshet in the first place?" Yael recounted the whole story, her slavery to Asmara, most of the encounter with Sisera, but nothing about her dream of murdering him.

"You know Sisera?" Devorah's voice was disbelieving.

"I have told you the story, Sar." A touch of impatience tinged Yael's voice.

"Yes. Of course. I meant no offense."

"None taken," Yael said.

"Your knowledge of Sisera and Charoshet could be quite useful to us."

"I thought it might," Yael said. "In fact, I have one bit of intelligence that might be useful to you."

"And that is?" Devorah asked.

"Many citizens, common soldiers and ranking officers think you may be the incarnation of their war goddess Anat." Devorah's eyes flashed. Yael continued, "That means they fear you more than they should; and also feel bereft of their own spiritual support. They fear that not only has their goddess abandoned them but She has chosen you, the leader of the Haibrus instead."

"This is an important advantage," Devorah said, and beaming she reached out for Yael's shoulders with both hands and squeezed them. "Thank you for bringing me this information." Yael smiled back, face reddening. "If we can secure just one or two victories," Devorah mused, "they will give up hope and we can beat them more easily."

Devorah stepped forward and hugged Yael again. "Thank you, Yael! Thank you." Devorah's face was alive with wonder. "What you have told me is also a sign, Yael," she said. Yael looked confused. "It means the God of the Covenant is already working for us! That without true earthly power, without proper weapons and organization, we are already on the path to victory!" Yael nodded tentatively. "And now you want to fight…. How? Certainly not as a soldier in the line?"

"I am not sure," Yael hesitated. "I want to kill. I have had a dream of killing a man in golden armor…in my husband's tent…by hammering a tent peg through his skull…."

Devorah, Lappodoth and Barak shuddered at the image Yael conjured; such a violation of the obligation of hospitality was nearly as heinous as the killing itself. Devorah looked into Yael's eyes and saw no shame or hesitation. "You have lived with this dream for some time?" she asked.

"Yes," Yael said. "At first it repulsed and frightened me. To kill a guest in my husband's tent. But as the dream recurred, those feelings left me and in their place grew a feeling of destiny, of duty, even of exultation…."

"I understand, Yael. I too, have powerful visions." Devorah stretched out her hands and Yael took them. They continued staring, wordlessly, into one another's eyes. The men grew embarrassed. Lappodoth coughed and Barak shuffled his feet. "I will keep you with me, Yael," Devorah finally said.

"Yes, Sar," Yael said. "Thank you! Oh, thank you!"

"I will be here six or seven days conferring with Barak. Then we will leave to strike at Dor. You may serve in my personal bodyguard." Yael dipped her head. "Until then, carry on as you have been."

Yael saluted smartly. "Yes, Sar. Thank you."

Barak, who'd been chafing with anger and disbelief during most of this conversation, could contain himself no longer. "We are not talking about preparing a meal, ladies! We are talking about combat - blood, limbs hacked off and guts spilling out!"

Devorah and Yael scowled at him. At that moment, Jereboam joined them. "Tell them Jereboam!" Barak said.

"Tell them what, Sar?" he asked.

"We want to fight," Yael said, gesturing to Devorah. To show how war-like she was, Yael thrust her chest out, put her hands on hips, standing immobile as the wind blew her luxurious long hair into her face.

Jereboam stared into Yael's eyes, his mouth set in a tight lipped grimace. "It is Devorah's duty, as our Sar, to lead us. You need not expose yourself...."

"But I *want* to, and it is my duty, too, as a Haibru."

"Do you want to die?" Jereboam's voice was soft. Yael had to lean forward to hear it.

"I won't die!" she said.

"How do you know, cousin?"

"I have had a dream. I won't die before I fulfill my part in the dream."

"Are you prepared to be maimed, or scarred, then," he pointed to the three lived scars on his face, "as I have been? To lose the use of an arm or leg, or, God forbid, all your limbs? Or perhaps a brain injury, so you would be as an infant and have to be taken care of for the rest of your life?"

"My dream...." Yael asserted less forcefully, swallowing hard.

"Are you prepared to risk all this because of a dream?" Jereboam put his good arm on her shoulder and leaned forward to stare more intently into her face. "Think cousin. Think!"

"I did not dream the dream once, Jereboam," she explained. "I have dreamt it many times over the last many months and was aware of no wounds on my body." But she was clearly less confident.

Jereboam pressed his opening. "You are courageous, brave and strong enough to fight, and it is your duty as a Haibru to do so. But you need not seek combat. There are other roles...."

"I have offered Yael a position in my personal body guard," Devorah said.

"And I have accepted!" Yael said.

Jereboam looked from one to the other. "Good," he said. "You may have to fight, probably will, but you will not be in total combat for long periods as would a soldier in the line." He paused and again scanned the women's faces. "Listen to me. Combat is pure evil and horror. I love and respect both of you and know you will handle yourselves well. But I would spare you that horror, and would ask you to spare yourselves."

He looked down, then up at them, his eyes wide and sad. "I want you to understand what it is. In my last battle, the fight in which I almost lost the use of this arm and received these two scars," he touched his face, "and others you can not see on my chest and thighs, we were 210 against 400. We were on flat ground, just east of the Salt Sea. Judah claimed the land from Moab. The Moabites had twenty chariots...without scythes. Each contained an archer and a driver; each was pulled by one horse." Jereboam paused. "The sounds the horses made when we wounded them...." He paused again. "A plaintive, wailng screaming I can still hear—horrible, heart rending.

"I myself killed one of them....

"We were in squads of 20, armed with shields, spears, daggers and curved slashing swords," he patted the sword in his belt. "We were in phalanxes, in the Philistine fashion; each phalanx 100 cubits from the other; to make it more difficult for the chariots to cut us down." Barak was nodding, seeing the dispositions.

"As we took our positions we sang. I was afraid. My mouth was dry like sand. My heart shook my chest. I had been in battles before but never like this, standing and waiting for the enemy. As they drew nearer our singing stopped.

"They were still too far to see individuals, but it was clear from their mass that we were greatly outnumbered. I looked at Malamud, beside me. We had been together since the beginning of the campaign. He was more frightened than I.

"They came nearer and were 600 cubits from us when they loosed arrows. We crouched and raised our shields above our heads. The arrows whizzed and made a dull thud when they struck a man's body, or a flat clunk when they bounced off our wooden shields or stuck into them. While we were thus protecting ourselves and unable to observe the enemy's movements, they advanced upon us.

"Malamud shifted his shield, stood up to observe, and cried out a warning. I stood, too, and as I did, I heard the dull thud and saw Malamud clutch his face, screaming soundlessly; blood rushing forward over his eyes and mouth. An arrow stood straight up from the top of his head. Malamud writhed, the blood from his wound splattering me, getting in my eyes, blinding me temporarily. I gathered him in my arms and he continued his tormented shaking, a gurgling sound came from his throat and more blood spurted from his nose and mouth.

"The others in my phalanx had risen and were screaming. The ground was shaking and I heard a roaring thundering. I wiped Malamud's blood from my eyes, and saw a chariot not ten cubits from me. I fell to the ground, rolled, pulled the daggers from my belt and as the horse pounded over me, thrust upwards into its belly. I held on for a second and its momentum ripped its flesh open. The horse kept going forward, but its blood and guts immediately spilled across me. Instinctively, I shifted to avoid the gore and one of the chariot's wheels grazed this arm." Jereboam rubbed the spot. "Another inch and it would have been severed.

"We did not win that day, and many good men lost their lives." He looked at Barak. "We are not soldiers, to stand on an open field, in military formation."

Barak nodded his agreement, "We are warriors. We swoop down from the hills on an unsuspecting column of enemy. Surprise and mobility are among our greatest assets. It is difficult for us to stand toe-to-toe with a trained soldier."

"But this is not all of what I wanted you to understand," Jereboam said, looking into Yael's sympathetic face. "I wanted you to understand about the blood, fear and terror. Do you?"

"Yes, thank you, cousin, I do," Yael said.

"And you are willing to face all of that?"

Yael nodded. "Then God be with you, cousin! For tho I hear you say you understand, I know you do not. Until one experiences it, it is impossible to understand." He stepped forward, opened his arms to embrace her, then he and Barak walked away.

Left standing alone, Yael reconsidered Jereboam's story and advice. Why indeed would she risk her life and limb, willingly subjecting herself to the horrors of battle? Yes, she believed in Devorah, wanted to be like her and wanted the Sar of Israel to be proud of her. But she was angry, too; angry about what Asmara and Elkanta had done to her and wanted revenge.

She was also angry with herself and ashamed and wanted to erase that shame and make up for what she'd done in the Temple. For truth be told, whatever the Canaanites had done to her, she had allowed them to do.

Unaware of her surroundings, Yael strolled ahead. I will become a fierce warrior, she thought, well practiced with the sword and shield and spear. I will kill many Canaanites and no one, no one--Canaanite or Haibru, would ever imagine I could have been the willing slave of Asmara's slave, she shuddered, the slave of a slave.

Lappodoth held Devorah's elbow as they climbed the slight incline, then edged down to the foundry pit where Haber and two assistants labored. Baskets of iron arrow heads and sword blades lined the rim of the pit. Haber paused as they approached; mopped the sweat pouring from his hair and face with a ragged sheepskin. An assistant offered him a wineskin, he took it and drank deeply.

"Sar of the Haibrus," he said, dipping his head respectfully. "This is an honor."

"For me as well, Haber. Thank you for joining our cause." The big man dipped his head again. "Yael, had told me of your ties to Sisera."

Haber smiled. "'Ties' is perhaps too strong a word. We have done business in the past."

"He trusts you then?"

"Up to a point."

"If you were to tell him what you've been doing here, and went to him with information about our plans and troop movements, would he believe you?"

"He might."

"You know we are badly outnumbered. Our success requires stealth. We need him to believe what I will ask you to tell him."

Haber bowed. "It is an honor to be even more a part of your victory, Sar." Devorah dipped her head. "There is a good chance he will believe the words you put into my mouth."

"Thank you, Haber."

The ironsmith bowed. "Will you tell me what I am to say now?"

Devorah gripped her stomach. "I had planned to tell you now, but I...." Liquid dribbled down her legs. She gripped Lappodoth with both arms. "It is time husband!"

---

Sisera woke with a start, panting and soaked with sweat. His heart beat so ferociously he feared he was dying. He opened his left eye tentatively. Light from the sentry fire outside the tent cast shadows inside, along the walls. Light gleamed on his armor; he shuddered and closed his eye. Enough! He said to himself. You've had this dream before. Yes, but never this real, never this intensely. He felt the sharp point on the top of his head, a tingle, anticipating the blow, then the explosion of unimaginable pain. He sat up, leaned forward, reached both hands to his head - nothing; just hair, damp with sweat.

*Aiyee, aiyee; enough; let's be done with it. I want no more! By all the gods if this is to be my fate, let it be done now. Now, Baal, please, this minute! Anat and Astarte, if this is Your will, so be it; I submit. All I ask is that you take me now! Please! No more torture.* Silence was his answer. A vision of Betheena, leaning against the lattice work of her withdrawing room window in Hazor, drifted across his mind. His heart stopped racing. His mother had a sad smile of longing on her elegant, youthful face. He sighed. He wanted her to be proud of him. How proud would she be if he was disabled by fear and could not fight because of a dream?

He sat up; felt the cool breeze dry the sweat on his face. He stood and paced, naked but for a loin cloth. The sentry firelight burnished the muscles in his calves, buttocks and thighs as he moved. Betheena would ask him what he was worried about. If she were here, she would remind him of his power and beauty, his royal birth and the hundreds of iron chariots at his command. She might even caress his body and nibble at his ear. His penis stirred. By the glory and power of Astarte, this was the way to overcome a nightmare!

But this was more than a nightmare. Had he told his mother of it, its history and power, she would probably warn him to be careful. He stopped pacing. He *was* being careful! But one could not lead an army from one's tent. The Canaanite Federation demanded its Generals be statesmen, too. Out and about in the public eye, appreciating both the military and political situations, his duty was not just to win the war, but keep the Federation content.

Up till now, that had not been difficult. But now that the Ephramites, at the very center of travel between Moab, Canaan and the Philistines were committed, he had to be sure none of the weaker members of the Federation were unprotected. The ancient maxim was: *Never divide your forces*; but he might have no choice. Sisera began pacing again. He'd already had to send a strong column to the north east to counter a force Barak sent to interdict Sisera's supply and communication lines to Hazor. Also, his people in Shiloh had word of a possible movement towards the Ocean Sea, perhaps against Dor. If that happened, Sisera would have no choice but to prevent it, or failing that, destroy the enemy's ability to attack anywhere outside the Jezreel Valley.

No easy matter. He'd rather avoid the potentially swampy regions south west of Tabor, concentrate his forces and press Barak to do battle on the flat banks of the Kishon River, where his chariots could chew him up.

The reflected light from the sentry fire grew duller as the rays of the rising sun grew brighter. Feeling clearer, the horror of the dream less intense, Sisera went to the basin on the camp stand and splashed water on his face. His stomach rumbled with hunger. Voices and sounds of early morning stirring in the camp comforted him. I'll eat with the men this morning, he thought. Splashing more water on his face and upper body, Sisera dried himself and slipped on a plain tunic. As he stepped from his tent, Sostrum, in armor and full battle dress, strode up to him. The captain saluted smartly. Sisera was not happy to see him. He'd wanted a slower start, a peaceful breakfast with the troops.

Sostrum sensed his mood. "My General," he said, "I would not disturb you but I have two important pieces of information."

"Yes?" Sisera glared at him.

"Our spies on Tabor report that Devorah gave birth to a boy four days ago."

In spite of himself, Sisera smiled. He was actually glad for her, and for himself. That meant she would soon be ready for military action. Perhaps.... "You said four days ago?" he asked Sostrum.

"Yes."

"And she is well and the child is well, also?"

"Yes."

"That means she will attack in three or four days."

"That is correct, Sire," Sostrum said. "Do you remember Haber the Kenite?"

"Of course."

"He is here." Sisera's eyes widened. Sostrum shook his head yes. "He arrived last night. He has news of their troop movements."

"Excellent! Bring him to me." Sostrum saluted, pivoted smartly and left. Sisera smelled the cooking - sizzling grain patties and sausages, around the sentry fire, which the men had allowed to shrink to the size for cooking. "May I join you?" he asked the group nearest him.

"Of course, General," a bearded older man said, arising and bowing deeply. "You honor us."

Sisera bowed in turn. "Thank you," he said. "Please sit." The man crouched scooped the food from the pans with a big piece of flat bread and heaped it on a tin dish and handed it and the bread to Sisera. Sisera accepted, squatted, and ate with gusto. The food tasted marvelous! He'd nearly finished when Sostrum returned with Haber. The bearded soldier handed Sisera a ceramic cup of mulled wine. "Thank you!" Sisera said, accepting the steaming beverage. "What is your name?"

"Anlin, my Lord," he said smiling, staring directly into Sisera's eyes.

"Thank you, Anlin. I am sure you have a leadership role with these men," he gestured to the soldiers sitting around him.

"I do my lord."

"I sense a wisdom in you I would have near me. Could you arrange for someone to take your place?"

Sostrum and Haber were at Sisera's side. Anlin looked at a large young man with the beginnings of a beard. "Kiva, you have heard our General. Would you assume my position so that I may serve as he asks?"

"I can," the younger man said, standing and dipping his head. "Thank you for your confidence, Anlin." Anlin dipped his head in return, turned to Sisera and bowed deeply. "I am at you service, Lord."

"Come, then," Sisera said, and followed by Haber and Sostrum, they walked along the avenue of tents that made up the center of the Canaanite encampment.

Sostrum used the period of silent strolling to review his sense of outrage. First he had to cater to this Kenite, then walk behind Sisera and this common soldier! Sostrum strenuously objected to the General's fraternization with troops of the line. He had told him so frequently. He thought it degraded the soldiers' respect for authority. That the men loved Sisera and were eager to follow him, a thing that made Sostrum quite jealous, was beside the point. True respect required reserve and distance.

He cleared his throat. "My Lord," he said. "Will you hear Haber's report?"

The men gathered around their cooking fires waved to Sisera and he waved back, smiling. We must fight wisely, he thought; with as little loss of life as possible. These are good, brave men.... Sisera stopped, turned, opened his arms and greeted Haber as if he were his long lost brother, not a foreigner. Sostrum bit his lip. "Good to see you, Haber! How is your beautiful wife? What have you been doing?"

Haber returned Sisera's warmth. "I have been making iron weapons for Barak with ore we stole from you."

Sisera's smile slipped a bit, but he appreciated the Kenite's candor. "And your wife? I don't think I have met her."

Haber laughed softly. "Perhaps you did my Lord, and don't realize it. She was recently in Cheroshet and had a bit of difficulty at the Temple of Astarte."

Sisera blinked, shut his eyes; thought, but decided, no, that would be too much of coincidence. "Sostrum said you have information for me."

"I do, my Lord. That is one of the benefits of using your ore to make weapons for Barak." Sisera nodded. "You have heard that Devorah has had a son?"

"I have."

"In seven days they will send a strong force west thru the narrows between the Carmel and Tivon hills, out of the Jezreel and into the coastal plain. I have heard mention of Dor."

Sisera turned to Sostrum. "You believe Haber's information to be credible?"

"I do my Lord."

"And the seven days?"

Sostrum smiled wickedly. "With all due respect to Haber," he bowed slightly, "I think the time is the trap. I think they will move sooner, in perhaps five or six days, and will prepare an ambush for us. The passage between the Carmel and Tivon hills is the perfect place to do it."

Sisera turned to Haber, whose expression remained calm and bland. "Would they deliberately have misled you?" he asked the Kenite.

"It is possible, my Lord," he replied. "But I *asked* no one. The seven days is a number I deduced from watching their preparations—supplies, animals, water and feed. It did not seem to me as if they would be ready sooner. Besides, Devorah needs time to recover."

Sisera shook his head. "I agree…with both of you. It may be anywhere in the range of five to eight days. We will go in four and be waiting for *them*! Thank you, Haber go back to Tabor before you are missed." The Kenite bowed and left. "Sostrum, prepare two thousand light infantry, that you will command, to march on the evening of the third day hence." Sostrum saluted and left.

For a moment Sisera felt decisive, wise, proud, and confident, until Haber's words drifted through his mind. "Perhaps you met her, and didn't realize it. She was recently in Cheroshet and had a bit of difficulty at the Temple of Astarte."

---

The baby came forth quickly, as befitted the son of a Sar of Israel girded in armor and ready for battle. He had a full head of reddish hair, green eyes, and fair skin, all of which made his dark haired, brown eyed, olive complected father wonder.

"He is marked for great things," Barak said, upon seeing him. The proud parents did not argue, but simply wondered.

"We shall name him, Abimelech," Devorah said, "'friend of kings.'"

"I like the sound of it," Lappodoth said. "But our people have only one king—the Lord God."

"God will always be the king of kings," Devorah said. "But it may be that in the future, we shall need more than a Judge to rule over us."

Lappodoth nodded. "He should also bear the names of Ruben for my father, and Ehud, for yours."

"Yes," Devorah said. "Ruben Ehud Abimelech." She sat up, held the child to her breast. He suckled vigorously and Devorah enjoyed the sensation. "He is so quiet, husband," she said.

"Indeed. He did not cry when he breached and has not cried much since. Perhaps he is unafraid."

Devorah smiled radiantly. "What a wonderful thought, husband! Yes, perhaps he is unafraid of the world he finds himself in." She looked down at the baby; he stared back at her solemnly. "Are you unafraid, Abimelech?" She said, leaning forward, touching his tiny nose with hers. "Is that why you are so quiet?" The child stopped suckling and stared into her eyes. "Oh, he is so wonderful," Devorah said, rocking him.

Barak, Jereboam, and Yael entered the tent.

"Haber has gone to Sisera's camp," Barak said. "He should be back tomorrow evening."

"Good," said Devorah. "Abimelech's delivery was nearly bloodless and pain free. I am strong and ready."

Lappodoth, standing at Devorah's side, stroked her hair. "Give yourself time, wife. It is true you are not severely impaired, but it has been a shock for your body. You needn't go so soon, especially to fight."

"I will protect her," Yael said, immediately sensing the folly of her words in Jereboam and Barak doubtful smiles.

"Thank you, Yael," Devorah said. "And you, too, husband. I shall rest. Let us have the bris and enter our son into the Covenant, the day after tomorrow. Then, I can decide if we are to march on Dor that day or the next."

"The sooner, the better," Barak said.

"Yes, Sar," Yael said. "I understand."

As the warriors filed from the tent, Yael hung back then went to have a closer look at the baby.

"Would you like to hold him?" Devorah asked.

Yael recoiled at first, but then considered the idea and found it good. "Why, yes, Sar, I would. Thank you!" She held the baby close to her bosom, rocking him gently.

"You look perfectly natural with him, Yael," Lappodoth said.

"Thank you!" she said, staring into the baby's unblinking eyes. Then, turning said, "Lappodoth, would you mind giving your wife and I a moment's privacy?" He looked doubtful. "Only a moment," Yael said. "Women's talk."

"Oh," he said, smiling, and turned to follow the others out of the tent.

Devorah looked at Yael.

"How did you know you were pregnant, Sar?" Yael asked.

Devorah smiled. "You think you're pregnant, Yael?" she asked.

"I have had some upset in my stomach and cramps," Yael answered. "The other women say this is one of the first signs. I know it is different for each woman. I wanted to ask you, because I think I am more like you than the others."

"When was the last time you laid with Haber?"

Yael blushed. "The last time, the *very* last time?" she asked.

"I don't wish to embarrass you, Yael," Devorah said. "I know you served as a sacred prostitute in Astarte's temple. None of your earlier encounters have made you pregnant, if indeed, you are pregnant. So it must be someone more recent."

Yael scowled and tensed. "As it happened, Sar Devorah," she said, voice tinged with hauteur and annoyance. "I did not lie with *many* men in Charoshet, but one. I was seduced by the charms of other women."

Devorah's eyes widened. She had heard whispers of such sexual practices, but never met anyone who'd done them. Her curiosity was aroused. "What was it like?" she asked softly.

Seeing Devorah's interest to be sincere, Yael relaxed and decided to be truthful. "It was amazing, Sar," she said, "All-consuming and enslaving."

"I have heard whispers of that," Devorah said.

"It is good that it is only whispered of," Yael said with a smile, "for if everyone knew, there'd be no children."

"Better than with a man?" Devorah's tone was disbelieving.

"Different, Sar, different," Yael paused. "Please, now, about your pregnancy. I know what the other women say, but I am most interested in how it was for you."

Devorah swallowed and looked down. She still wanted to know more about sex between women, but responded to Yael's question. "For me, it was about timing. When was the last time you lay with Haber?"

"Last night," said Yael. "But he did not come inside me. He did not orgasm at all. He has difficulty staying erect."

"That is too bad," Devorah said. "But, no; last night would be too recent. It would have been six, seven or eight weeks ago, when you...."

"When I was in Charoshet," Yael said. "Haber is not the father then, if indeed, I am pregnant."

"If you are having stomach cramps and nausea, you are probably pregnant. Have you vomited in the morning?" Yael nodded. "Have you missed your blood?"

"Twice," Yael said. "It is four days late for the second time." She looked down. "It was that last time in Cheroshet," she mumbled.

"Then you know whose seed quickens within you?" Devorah asked.

"Yes," Yael said, standing taller, a strange, rueful, sad smile pulling at her mouth. "It is indeed true that the Lord works in mysterious ways." She patted her belly. "This child, if it survives, will be a miracle child, just like Abimelech. Its contributions to our people will be beyond our imaginings."

"Tell me," Devorah said.

"There may be nothing to tell. It may all be for nothing, Sar. Let us wait to see if it lives." Devorah looked disappointed. "Please, Sar Devorah, I mean no harm. Please, it is too difficult for me to explain now. Will you forgive me?"

Moved by Yael's earnest request, Devorah saw the younger woman in a new light and wanted to honor her. She kissed Yael's cheek and put an arm round her shoulders. "Of course I forgive you, sister!" she said. "In fact, there is nothing to forgive." She brought her arm to her side and took Yael's hand. "Come," she said, moving toward the map table. "Let me tell you of our strategy. Barak!" she shouted. Barak entered as Devorah unrolled a map parchment to show Yael their feint toward Dor.

---

Betheena felt cold and old. She drew her elegant, purple dyed wool cloak more closely around her, clapped for the slave, and continued pacing. A moment later, her favorite male slave presented himself, bowing low before her. For a moment she admired his grace and the easy flexing of taught muscles beneath smooth, shiny skin. But only for a moment. "Braziers for warmth," she snapped, turned and resumed her pacing.

*There was a time I would have had sex with him to warm me*, she thought. *But now....*

*You're not that old*, another part of her responded. She held out her arm and saw the skin still taught and wrinkle free. Her graceful, ring-clad hands were also firm and unblemished. *See, not that old.*

No, not that old. But old enough to want a grandson.

Ah, yes! Not just a grand*son*, a grand*child*.

Indeed. A grand*child*. But how can I have a grandchild if my son doesn't return to me?

Three slaves entered carrying large copper braziers. Placing them around the room, they lit them and departed.

We have talked of that, she thought. Your concerns have no basis in fact. *We* are the power, not the Haibrus. The military might is ours!

I know, yet my intuition cries out!

*Soothe it. Amuse yourself; distract yourself. Call again for that gorgeous slave. Let him warm you and make you feel young and alive. Take your mind from your fears; do not nourish them.*

Yes; good. She clapped her hands and the handsome slave reappeared. This time he knelt at her feet. With trembling hands, Betheena reached out to raise him up.

Devorah's strength returned rapidly. She decided to have the bris a day earlier than planned, which would give them one more day ahead of Sisera's blocking column. Haber had returned and confirmed that Sisera accepted the story about the Haibru plans to strike at Dor thru the narrows between the Carmel and Tivon hills. Haber also told of the strength of the Canaanite encampment and how the idea of the Haibru's breaking out of the Jezreel and into the coastal plain had really worried Zeber, Sisera's second in command.

Devorah was glad of Yael's companionship. She'd never had a woman she could count on and confide in. She also found Yael useful as an aide de camp. Not only could she read and write, she was a quick learner and very reliable. Devorah could entrust Yael with things that fell somewhere between what she'd have done herself or asked Lappodoth to do. In just a day she'd narrowed the 20 women Lappodoth had talked with about serving as Abimelech's wet nurse to three for Devorah to choose from. Yael also worked well with the Ephramite clan captains in Devorah's escort to ensure that each militia man had enough food and water for their return to Ephraim.

Yael was shocked and disturbed to find that each soldier had to provide his own food, water, clothing, weapons, tent and other equipment. She had never fully understood how the militia system worked. Not that she was ignorant, she had simply been uninterested and uninformed. Like everyone else, she just accepted that things worked and had no curiosity about *how* they worked.

The idea of expecting fighting men - men who were about to risk their lives - to supply their own food and equipment started Yael thinking. That may have made sense long ago, or when troops were mustered from their own villages, but here, on Mt Tabor, Devorah's escort were visitors, without any way to fend for themselves. Barak agreed with her. "The traditional supply system is dysfunctional," he told her. "Our people will never be able to count on a real army, or put a force in the field to stand and fight until the militia are only ancillary, not the core of our forces."

In the evening, after the bris, as she combed Devorah's hair, Yael talked with her about what Barak had said. Enjoying Yael's ministrations, Devorah had turned the question back at her. "What do *you* think?" she asked.

"Barak is right," Yael said. "And I like him."

"He *is* right and I like him, too." Devorah put her hand on Yael's writs to stop her combing and turned to look into her eyes. "Barak is a good soldier and a good man. He needs me, and now you, to remind him of that and to keep his faith in God strong. We are all lost without faith in God."

Yael looked down. When she looked back at Devorah, her eyes were clouded. "I have faith in you, Sar. I am not as sure about God."

"I am as I am, *because* of God, sister." Yael said. "And what is true of me, is true of you also. You too, are of God."

"And Sisera," Yael flung the words at Devorah. "Is he too, of God?"

"Oh, yes. Yes! He, too, reflects God's love and compassion. He has a mother, who it is said, he loves."

"They have sex together. What of that?"

"That is not our way," Devorah said. "But I think he still feels a deep filial love for her." Yael half nodded. "More importantly, though, is how he fits the larger plan, God's plan, if you will." Yael looked puzzled. "The decisions he makes as a General can favor us. I choose to think that if his decisions allow us victory, then that is of God. Sisera is the right man, at the right time; chosen, after all these years, that we might end our oppression." Devorah was proud of the way she put these ideas and thought they would allow Yael see things more clearly.

"Hmm," Yael said. "Now, can we go back to Barak's ideas about the army?"

Taken aback by Yael's blasé response, Devorah's head snapped back as if she'd been slapped. Swallowing hard, she gulped air, her face reddened and her body trembled.

Not understanding what she'd done, but unhappy with Devorah's reaction, Yael asked for forgiveness. "I'm sorry," she said. "I didn't mean to anger or upset you." Devorah stared, speechless. "Please, excuse me, Sar. I thought you had completed your comments." Devorah's coloring and breathing were returning to normal. "I meant no disrespect. I understand what you meant about God, I am just more interested in military affairs now, since we are about to go into battle."

Devorah still trembled and her voice shook. "All the more reason to be concerned about God, don't you think?" Yael shrugged. "What if you are killed? Aren't you concerned about what happens to you after you die?"

"No," said Yael, smiling. "I am not concerned. I don't think about that. However, I shan't die until I have murdered Sisera in Haber's tent."

"*What?*" Devorah's eyes were wide with disbelief and her mouth hung open.

"I have had a dream, Sar. I've dreamt it for many months. At first it was shadowy and vague. Now it is clear to me. It is my destiny, where I fit in God's plan is to kill Sisera. I won't die until I have murdered Sisera in Haber's tent."

Devorah shut her mouth, held Yael's eyes with her own, saw no guile or doubt, then nodded. "I too, have prescient dreams," she said. Yael nodded. "Do you have any idea of when this deed will happen?"

Yael looked back evenly. "I don't understand your question, Sar," she said.

"Do you kill him before or after our great battle?" Devorah asked.

Yael smiled. "Yes," she said, admiring Devorah's practicality, "that *would* be good to know. But, no; I do not know when I kill him."

Devorah shut her eyes. It didn't matter, did it, she thought. Either way, his death would be an opportunity for them. But it *would* be good to know when to take full advantage of it. *Ah, well, now see who's the one who needs to have faith?* Devorah opened her eyes and smiled. Would this change her plans for Yael? Was there something she, Devorah, had to do for Yael to fulfill her destiny? She thought not. "Will your service to me prevent you from fulfilling your destiny?" she asked.

Yael stood taller; looked directly into Devorah's eyes. "My service to you, here and now *is* my destiny, Sar. Now, for the first time, I feel my life is fulfilled." She stepped forward and put a hand on Devorah's shoulder. "Please, give this no more thought. I do not think of it as I used to. Is it not as you have said, that we are in God's hands - guided, guarded and protected - each playing a part, and that as the Canaanites also believe, our destinies are written in the stars?"

Feeling the tension drain from her, Devorah sighed deeply. She hugged Yael, then stepped back and smiling broadly, she held the other woman at arms length and said, "Indeed, sister! Perhaps it is as you say."

"Good, then," Yael said. "Now, can you tell me what you think of Barak's view of our army?"

Devorah's smile deepened. "Persistent, too; you have many excellent qualities, Yael!"

"Thank you, Sar," said Yael, hands on hips, waiting for her answer.

"I think I did tell you; I agree completely with Barak. We are not capable of fielding an army because we are not a nation. We are nothing but a group of tribes, not even a confederation like the Philistines and Canaanites. They are nations and can field a disciplined force because they are rich enough and organized enough to have full time soldiers. We are nothing like that. I called upon all twelve tribes to join against the Canaanites; and how many came?"

"Sorry," Yael said. "Before yesterday, I was not paying attention to these things, Sar. Eight?"

"Ha! Six! Six of twelve; how pathetic! Barak and I look forward to the day Israel shall be a nation with a full time professional army. My body guard and Barak's cadre, perhaps 460 men in all, are the closest we are to a full time professional army." Devorah shook her head sadly. "It will be one hundred or two hundred years at least, before we will be there. Why, we're still living in tents! What kind of a nation lives in tents?"

Devorah shuddered, shut her eyes and gripped her skull, shrieking softly. Once again, the horrible pressure in her chest and the awful, depthless agony and despair swept through her. She saw once more the stark, bleak snowbound landscape with row upon row of long wooden buildings, and watch towers, all surrounded by frozen strands of metal glinting in the dull winter light. And at the center of it all, three of the highest chimneys she'd ever seen spewed thick, stinking black smoke to the heavens.

"Sar! Sar, are you alright? Sar!" Yael was shaking her.

Devorah's eyes opened. "Yes, Yael," her voice was flat and unbelievably sad.

"What did you see?"

"Something I have seen once before; something that awaits our people; our fate; where our lives are leading; something that makes a mockery of my simple faith in God's goodness. Ah...." She shuddered to her core. Yael embraced her tightly. "I can not go forward if this is to be our fate, Yael. But yet, as you know your dream of murder to be true, so I know this dream of mass murder to be true." She sobbed. A moment later she inhaled deeply and stepped from Yael's protective embrace. "I also know deep down, and have faith that what I have seen though true, is not the whole truth. It will not be the end of our people. From that unspeakable horror, a new nation of Israel will be born."

Yael smiled. "A new nation; good. But, when will there be a first nation?"

"That is what we are about now, sister. Perhaps not in our lifetimes, but soon."

---

From the tower in the Fortress, Sisera watched the strong column of 2,500 under Sostrum wind its way from Charoshet. He was concerned, but had no choice under the alliance, but to protect Dor from the Haibru threat. The column was leaving a day later than he'd wanted but still, if Haber's information was correct, they'd be early enough to ambush the Haibrus.

Sostrum had seemed reluctant to go. That was not a good omen. He was a nasty one; enjoyed torturing prisoners, and jealous, too. Sisera would have dismissed him a year ago by making him military attaché to Moab, but with this campaign on the horizon he hadn't wanted to disrupt the army. Now, Sisera realized, with this bad attitude of his, he should have trusted his intuition of a year ago.

But wasn't that the thing about intuition? The priests said it was the whisperings of the gods, but one just couldn't be sure which were the whispers of the gods, and which of the demons.

The last of the supply wagons rolled out of sight. Sisera sighed and went inside. He still had a smaller column of 700 men on the road from Hazor to prevent the Haibru bandits from disrupting his own supply lines. He paced, restlessly. He'd just have to wait for word of these two columns before taking further action. He wandered to the maps and put his finger on the chariot emplacements around Tabor. It really didn't matter about those two columns. Here, he tapped his finger, is where the battle will be won or lost.

He shuddered. Yes, it could be lost. Then what would he do? He couldn't show his face in Hazor. His mother would be shamed. But he couldn't lose; it would take a miracle. He walked back to the window. Yes, a miracle. But wasn't the God of these Haibrus the one who humbled Pharaoh at the Red Sea and tumbled the walls of Jericho? What of it? We have 900 iron chariots and 40,000 heavily armed, well trained soldiers against maybe 10,000 ill trained, poorly equipped militia men.

He could not lose! But what if he did? Could he go on living if he lost? Perhaps, but not as a lord in Hazor. Sisera paced in front of the window. He'd have to go to Egypt or Moab as a mercenary. Skilled military men were always in demand. Losing would not be the end of his life, just the end of life as he lived it now. He'd have to start over elsewhere. Who knew, but that might not be so bad.

What kind of traitorous, defeatist thinking is this, Sisera thought? You sound like you have a little Sostrum inside you. A moment, Sostrum is many things but not a traitor. Perhaps he has betrayed your honor and ideals, but he would never betray our cause. Besides, what could the Haibrus possibly offer to tempt him? They have no land, money or anything of value. True.

---

Devorah was elated as she reviewed their plan and considered all that had happened in the past few days. Everything had gone perfectly, exactly as she and Barak had planned. *Oh, thank you, Father! Thank you.* Immediately after the bris, she and her escort, Yael, Lappodoth, and Abimelech and his wet nurse had left Mt Tabor for their encampment in Ephraim. Abimelech had barely cried as his foreskin was removed. Lappodoth retrieved the tiny piece of flesh, washed it and placed it in a pouch which he wore on a rope, round his neck.

Leaving the baby, Lappodoth and 400 heavily armed militia at the encampment, Devorah, Yael and the 1,500 men from Issachar and Manasseh force marched into the narrows between the Carmel and Tivon hills, in an amazing day and a half, to take up positions to ambush the Canaanite column as it marched out of the Jezreel and into the coastal plain to protect Dor. Devorah knew that timing and coordination with Barak were essential if the rest of their strategy was to succeed. They planned to keep communication up to date by using a series of relays with the fastest ponies and best riders available.

In the north east, after capturing and interdicting the Canaanites' supplies flowing south from Hazor, Ben Zvi was to notify Barak, then force march to Hazor so that King Jabin would panic. To ensure the panic was deeply felt, Barak would send a small column of 500, disguised to look three times its size, to reinforce Ben Zvi. This, it was hoped, would cause Jabin to order Sisera to divide his force and direct large numbers of chariots and troops to defend the capital.

It was imperative that Devorah's ambush in the narrows coincide as closely as possible with Barak's dispatch of the 500 to reinforce Ben Zvi.

Devorah's force had been ready and hidden for an afternoon and a night. She and Yael were at the highest point, five hundred feet above the rock and boulder-strewn canyon floor, at the place where the canyon walls were only twenty feet apart, with a view of almost the entire narrows, a half mile in either direction. Morale was high and the troops were proud to have the Sar of the Israelites as their commander.

Once the Canaanite column penetrated to the center of the narrows, the plan was to roll already prepared boulders down the hillsides, blocking both retreat and forward movement. In addition, clumps of dry sage, cactus and brush were strategically placed along the road to be ignited with flaming arrows. Then they would charge down the hills to engage the survivors of the arrow attack. Veteran fighters thought this a splendid plan that would bring an easy victory.

Yael was the first to see their own scouts galloping into the ambush area. They waved, pumped their arms up and down, to signal that the enemy was approaching, then galloped on to stow their horses and join the ambush. Thirty minutes later, the Canaanite scouts trotted into view. They rode through the narrows looking cautiously about them then, near its end, seeing nothing, turned and galloped to the main body. As soon as the scouts had departed, Devorah raised the shofar to her lips and blew four times. At this signal, the militia men at the far end of the narrows, rolled down their boulders.

Now the Canaanite main column, 2,500 strong, was in sight and Yael recognized Sostrum at its head. He looked much as she remembered him, mean and wary, perhaps more wary now. She whispered, "That's Sostrum, Sisera's right hand man," to Devorah.

"Ah," Devorah said. "So that's him. He's more of a butcher than an officer. He's the one responsible for torturing Jereboam." Yael snarled and gripped her sword more tightly.

The Canaanite column was well into the narrows. Any moment, Sostrum would see the boulders blocking their path and know he was in a trap. Devorah raised the shofar to her lips. Sostrum shouted, his horse reared and Devorah blew one long continuous blast on the shofar. Shouting, the Israelite archers stood, ignited their arrows and let them fly into the bundles of brush. There was a whoosh of flame and instantly it seemed as if the whole narrows trail was ablaze. At the tail entrance, the Israelites rolled the huge boulders into place. The trap was sealed. As terrified Canaanite soldiers turned to retreat, the Israelite archers picked them off.

Devorah and Yael stood watching the progress of the battle. "It will be a massacre," Yael observed, coolly.

"Yes," Devorah said, gesturing to the nearby messenger. "You see what is happening?" she asked him.

"Yes, Sar."

"Good! Ride swiftly to Barak and tell him the Canaanite column is destroyed and that in two hours we shall turn and attack Charoshet, then Sisera's rear, as agreed. How quickly can you reach him?"

"Five or six hours, Sar."

"Good. Go!" As the messenger ran for his horse, Devorah noticed the sky was darker than it should have been. It is the smoke, she thought, but when she looked up through the wisps of smoke, she saw that massive clouds were indeed blocking the sun. She sniffed. "Rain!" she shouted. "It will rain." She raised the shofar to her lips and gave three sharp blasts, waited, then three more - the signal to charge.

"Why charge now, Sar?" Yael asked. "Our archers can still kill many of them with no risk to our men. So what if it rains?"

In the midst of the tumult, excitement and nearly overwhelmed with gratitude, Devorah still felt a bottomless reservoir of patience deep within her. She turned to Yael, her armor gleaming in the rays of light that pierced the massing clouds and said, "Rain, sister, is the miracle I have been praying for. Rain! It means that the place where Sisera has massed his chariots, the dry swamps on the banks of the Kishon will soon become actual swamps. It means his chariots will be useless to him. It means his order of battle will be useless to him. It means Barak will be able to fall upon him and use our light infantry, guerilla tactics to great effect. It means, victory!" Devorah shouted, "VICTORY!"

Yael's eyes were wide and her mouth hung open, but she understood what Devorah was telling her.

"I want us to finish here," Devorah said, "as quickly as possible so we can attack Sisera on this side of the river while Barak attacks him from the east. We haven't a moment to lose!"

"But it is not raining yet, Sar," Yael said.

"You are right, but it will be. We will need at least eight or nine hours of forced march before we reach the Kishon, and, if we do force march, we might be too tired to fight effectively. We will skip Charoshet for now, we can go back when we have destroyed Barak's forces." Yael's eyes narrowed and glittered. "I know you were looking forward to entering Charoshet as a conqueror," Devorah said. "And to see those women from Astarte's Temple... ah...."

"Asmara and Elkanta," Yael said, eyes still narrowed, tongue flicking across her lips.

"Yes," Devorah said. "Well you shall, only not right now."

The archers had dropped their bows and quivers and swarmed down the hillsides with the other militia to throw themselves, hacking and slashing at the disorganized Canaanites. Yael made to join them, but Devorah restrained her. "No. Your place is with me. You are my aide."

Sostrum was picking his way through the flames and sword fights on foot, making for the trail entrance. "Look," Yael shouted, gesturing. "He must die! I must go and kill him, in Jeroboam's name."

"No," Devorah said. "Your place is with me. Sostrum may, I say 'may' escape this fight. But he will not escape altogether. He shall die. Fear not, one of us will kill him."

Yael twisted, pulled and tugged at Devorah's hand on her wrist. Her eyes were wild and staring, froth white on her lips. Devorah slapped her with her free hand; slapped her again. Yael blinked, wiped her mouth, took a more normal breath and said, "Forgive me, Sar. I have never experienced anything like this before."

"Nor have I Yael."

"But you are so calm, able to think and strategize."

Devorah smiled softly. "It is God, Yael. Here, amidst all of this horror and tumult, I feel as close to It as I do on my hill in Ephraim."

Yael saw the Presence in Devorah and knelt at her feet.

Devorah pulled her upright. "Do not kneel to me, sister, but to It, the power that you and," Devorah gestured to the melee below, "each of them is a part of. Now has that power aligned with us and our vision. We are blessed! Thank You, thank You, thank You!"

It had grown quiet below. The fires were nearly out; the smoky pall was lifting. Now they saw hundreds of human carcasses littering the trail and hillside. Some were not yet dead but twisted grotesquely and moaned. Hacked off pieces of men, arms, ears, heads, hands were strewn everywhere.

Devorah gaped at the horror, tears streaming down her cheeks.

"Once each of them had the spark," she said. "Now It has departed from them. How fragile we are and how easily destroyed." Choking back her tears, she raised the shofar to her lips and blew one long blast, the signal to regroup. "Let us go down," she said to Yael.

As they neared the narrow trail, Devorah saw Israelite's hacking the hands off fallen Canaanites. "No!" she shouted. "No. We, I, will not tolerate this! I know it is an ancient, even honorable custom, but I find it offensive. Stop and re-form." As the men formed a column of twos, Yael walked the line, talking to their captains, counting them.

"We are 1,350, Sar," she said, returning to Devorah. "We have lost only one hundred and fifty of our people! It is a great victory! We have killed nearly 2,000 of them."

Devorah acknowledged the information. "How many prisoners?" she asked.

"Nearly 200," Yael said. "We can not spare anyone to guard them. It is best that we kill them."

Devorah looked at her sadly. "You are right, of course. But," she gestured to the bodies and pieces of bodies scattered around them. "I can not bring myself to add to this. Leave 20 men and enough food and water for a day. After that, they will be irrelevant. We will have won."

"As you wish, Sar," Yael dipped her head.

Going to the head of the column, Devorah climbed the hillside till she could see them all. "God has given us a great victory today!" The men cheered long and loudly. Many were wounded, some grievously. "Look up!" she said, pointing to the cloud covered sky. "It will rain soon." Silence. "Who among you understands what this means to us?"

"Victory!" a number of voices shouted. "Victory at Mt Tabor," they said.

"Yes!" Devorah screamed. "Victory at Mt Tabor! Rain, when it comes, if it comes in torrents, will make it impossible for Sisera to use his chariots against us."

A roar, deep and fierce, rose from the column.

"I want us to go quickly so that we can add our strength to God's miracle and slaughter the enemy on this side of the Kishon River. I want us to run, who will run with me?" As the distant thunder rumbled, and drizzle began to fall, and all around the Sar of Israel, an even deeper and fiercer roar swelled the air.

Sisera had been watching the sky.  Clouds had swiftly gathered almost as soon as the blocking column departed for Hazor.  It was going to rain, he could smell it.  The only question was, how hard?  A light rain would be annoying, but that was all.  A heavy rain would make it impossible for both sides to maneuver; a deluge would destroy him.  Not only would his chariots be useless, but his heavily armed and armored troops would have to slog through muck, tire more quickly and be unable to defend themselves, much less attack.

Thunder rumbled in the distance, lightening arced between the clouds.

What to do?  He could reposition his men and chariots, but that could take hours and if there was no deluge would leave him vulnerable to Haibru attack while he was maneuvering.  And where to reposition them to?  No doubt the Haibrus were also watching the sky.  They would have massed lower down Tabor's slopes to prevent Sisera's troops from taking higher ground.  He could move his army back, away from the river, but that would break the siege and Barak's forces would be lose to ravage the countryside.  On balance, it was best to stay where he was and pray the rain was not too bad.  He shouted down for his horse and personal body guard.  "We ride to Tabor!" he shouted, thinking to make what positioning shifts seemed best, but basically to remain in place.

Barak was overjoyed.  *Thank you, thank you, Abba*, he chanted silently over and over.  It was raining!  Not yet enough to turn the Kishon's banks into the swamp they became when soaked, but a good beginning.  If it kept up like this for five or six hours, or got heavier, the threat from Sisera's chariots would be eliminated.  He grinned; it was the miracle Devorah had counted on.  She had never, or almost never, stopped believing.  Without her, he would have given up in despair.  They were a natural team: she the eternal flame of spirit and faith, he the mighty arm and logic of know how.

*Devorah*

Jereboam approached and saluted. "A messenger from Devorah. She has routed the Canaanite column in the narrows, has turned and will attack Cheroshet." Barak's grin deepened. "Tzevah," Jereboam said, "you've been grinning for hours!"

"Isn't it wonderful, Jereboam!" Barak looked up, arms open wide. "In spite of me! In spite of my little faith; this simple natural phenomena will bring us a victory as great as Joshua's at Jericho. What a team Devorah, God and I make! I am so happy!"

Jereboam grinned back, nodding. The rain grew steadily heavier. "Shall I send our people further down the slopes to deny the enemy access to them?"

"Indeed," Barak grinned. "They'll be desperate for higher ground soon. What news of our feint towards Hazor?"

"Nothing yet. It's probably not raining as much in that direction." Jereboam saluted and went to reposition the troops.

---

Within three hours of his arrival, Sisera saw that the chariots were useless. All was lost. The water hurried and rushed in streams that had not been there just two hours earlier. As it crept over its banks, erasing the boundary between itself and the land, the river added its flow in pulses to the accumulation from the downpour. Neither the horses' hooves nor the chariot's wheels could gain traction. Worse still, in some places, both vehicle and beast were already sinking or stuck.

Forward motion against the Haibrus now descending the mountain on the other side of the river in force, was impossible because the boundary between land and river had disappeared. One couldn't go in the direction of the river on either bank for fear of drowning. That meant the Haibrus couldn't cross it either, thank the goddess!

Drenched and shivering, Sisera wiped the rain from his eyes. But the Haibrus *were* crossing; they were swimming across! Sisera couldn't believe his eyes. Swords, bows and quivers strapped to their backs, hundreds, perhaps thousands of Haibrus left the deep water and were massing a mere 500 cubits from where Sisera stood.

Up stream and down stream, they were coming across. Where were his commanders? *Am I the only one paying attention to this,*

Sisera wondered. He looked wildly about him. He had wandered here to where the river bank used to be, to reconnoiter, and now stood alone and separate. Everyone else was 600 or 700 cubits behind him, busy with the chariots. Now the Haibrus had seen him! His golden armor shown brightly even in this wet gray light. He turned and dashed through the ankle deep water, kicking up spray, debris and hacked off body parts. *Got to make it to my commanders*, he thought. The shouting behind him, diminished and was lost in the roar of the pouring rain.

Sostrum turned and saluted as Sisera ran up to him. Sisera returned the salute. "Sound the alarm! The Haibru's have swum across the Kishon," he shouted breathlessly over the sound of the rain. "They are only lightly armed. No shields or spears, just slashing swords, bows and daggers. Form the men into phalanxes!"

Sostrum gestured to the trumpeter who stood nearby, then he convulsed and fell forward, an arrow through his throat. As Sostrum's blood splattered his face and armor, Sisera tore the trumpet from the trumpeter's hands, raised it to his lips and gave three mighty blasts, paused, and sounded three more blasts.

The twenty men nearest turned to face him. "The Haibru's have crossed the river! Even now they are out maneuvering us upstream and down. Go. Each of you, ten upstream and ten down, sound the alarm. Tell them my orders are to form phalanxes and to stand and fight. The chariots are useless. Forget them. Form phalanxes. Go!" Haibru arrows were now raining down upon the Canaanites almost as densely as the rain.

Two of the messengers were cut down before they took two steps. Sisera stepped over Sostrum's body and made for a nearby chariot. Unhitching a horse from its traces, he bounded upon it and raced upstream shouting the alarm and his orders. Gradually, the heavily armored Canaanite soldiers formed into phalanxes and the phalanxes took defensive positions a few cubits from where the river's edge used to be.

The lightly armed Haibrus who attacked these phalanxes frontally, were massacred. Sisera did not wait to see more, but dug his heels into the horse's flanks and turned to rally his troops downstream.

But it was too, late. None of his messengers had gotten through. A few phalanxes were in place, but they were isolated and could not attack. Haibru militia swarmed around them, but did not attack frontally. Everywhere, Canaanite bodies floated, pierced by arrows or hacked to pieces. Sisera's horse reared as an arrow struck its hind quarters and he fell off, rolling up into a defensive crouch, sword drawn. Five Haibru's swarmed him. He killed two rapidly, but then, from the right, was slashed in the left shoulder, and seconds later, from the left, a sword cut across his chest.

They were not mortal wounds and he dropped onto his chest, rolled over and hacked the legs off both his attackers. The fifth left him alone. In the momentary respite, Sisera checked his wounds then surveyed the battle as it swirled and ebbed around him. The Haibrus were definitely winning. He decided to go back upstream, to the phalanxes that had been holding their own.

He moved west away from the river and the worst of the fighting, then turned north. He was able to trot and in five minutes returned to the general area the phalanxes had controlled. Now, aside from a few groups of Haibru militia, nothing remained standing. Bodies, pieces of bodies, reeking, steaming guts and bloody weapons were strewn around him where his proud warriors had once stood. *All is lost!* Attracted by his golden armor, two Haibru militia rushed him. They fought well, but in moments, Sisera had killed one and wounded the other. But it was over. *I must get back to Charoshet*, he thought. *Maybe the column from Dor has returned and linked-up with the one from Hazor. If that is so, we can return and finish this.*

---

They ran, then trotted, then walked. Devorah had dismounted and ran with them. The men cheered. They'd been running for three hours when the drizzle turned to heavy rain.

Now running was difficult, but for Yael, the noise of the downpour and the rhythm of her body put her in an altered state that not only made the running seem easier, but turned her effort into a kind of moving meditation. Thoughts of Elkanta and Asmara drifted through her mind. Her feelings about them, though still intense, were not *as* intense. The child that she was now sure she carried, what would become of it? Would she still be capable of murdering its father? Yes, she thought, she was. Sisera's death was ordained by God. She was merely His instrument. But she did have a choice, didn't she? And things had changed, hadn't they? Yes. However, Sisera was an enemy of her people and she would probably kill him if she could - if not in battle, then in her husband's tent.

Devorah ran beside her. "How are you feeling, Sar?" Yael asked her. "You look pale."

"You do, too." Devorah responded. "Who wouldn't in these conditions?"

"Are you spotting?" Yael went directly to the crucial issue. "It's been only five days since you gave birth. Are you bleeding?"

Devorah slackened her pace and moved to the side of the column. Yael followed. Devorah slowed, stopped and drew her left hand under her crotch. There was blood. Not much, but any amount was a problem.

"We will wait for your horse," Yael said. "You shall ride."

"But the horses are at the end of the column!"

"Yes," Yael said. "What of it? When they arrive, you will mount, as will I, and we shall ride to the head of the column. No one will think the worse of you."

Waiting for the horses was more difficult than running and trotting. Yael felt cold and sodden to the bone. The water poured down ceaselessly; she caught herself wiping her face, only needing to wipe it again a second later. Devorah was in the same condition. Only three or four more hours to go, Yael thought. The horses finally came. The men cheered as they rode by, Devorah smiling and waving. Yael was simply thrilled by it all, despite the danger, fear and discomfort, and she wondered how she could ever go back to being just Haber's wife?

They heard sounds of the great battle before they saw it. Devorah unsheathed her sword; Yael did also. "Ride back along the length of the column and charge each man to fight for God and Israel!"

Yael frowned; she did not want to miss any of the fighting. "Why not blow the shofar, Sar?" she asked.

Devorah smiled and looked deeply into Yael's eyes. "I know you want to be in the vanguard, Yael," she said. "And you shall be. But seeing you..." Devorah paused and looked Yael up and down admiringly, eyes wide and appreciative before she continued, "Seeing you will truly inspire them. You are like Anat, Yael, the Canaanite Goddess of war come to life. Show yourself to them! Inspire them. Lead them to victory!"

Yael bowed her head briefly in deep humility and pride, then turned with a roar and—waving her curved slashing sword above her head—galloped along the column shouting, "For God and Israel! Slay them! Cover yourself with blood and glory. For God and Israel! Slay them!" The men roared the words back at her as they increased their pace. As she rounded the column and galloped back to Devorah, they were running almost as fast as Yael's horse galloped.

Two phalanxes, with scant space between them, were immediately before them. Screaming and shouting, swords slashing, Devorah and Yael led Devorah's personal body guard, the first two hundred men of the column, into the narrow space, widening it and making both phalanxes more vulnerable. The power and thrust of the forward momentum of the running militia slammed the normally impregnable wall of shields, pushing it apart and sending the heavily armored Canaanites tumbling over one another. Like ants devouring a drop of honey, the Haibru militia engulfed the two phalanxes, and in moments, hacked every man within them to death.

The Canaanites had not anticipated an attack from that direction, and the force of their attack - and the surprise of it - put Devorah, Yael and their body guard at the very tip of the spearhead. Devorah leaned down from her charging horse and hacked the head off a man with her first swing, blood from his body spurting and running from her already soaked cloak in pink rivulets. Momentarily repelled, she wiped it from her face, then having no choice, swung again and again almost exalting in the rhythm of it and the feel of the sharp blade parting flesh.

Yael had planned to stay close to Devorah, but as she, too, swung again and again from her galloping horse, protecting her leader, time and distance became meaningless to her. Even as her arm grew tired and the taste of blood was salty in her mouth, Yael could not stop; did not *want* to stop. All fluid motion, she was the angel of death personified. Nothing, no thing, could compare to this! Exhilaration filled her to overflowing. Time stood still. She saw her opponents as if they were still, like paintings on a temple wall. First, she pierced them with her shriek, then watching their amazement at her approach, she had time to observe and cut them to the quick.

The hundreds of on-rushing men behind the two hundred in Devorah's spearhead, divided elegantly and flowed around the two now-destroyed phalanxes, to slam into and in the same way, devour, another, make phalanxes singular, before their moment dissipated. Then, the fighting degenerated into a series of individual combats. The only semblance of ordered military action was the discipline of Devorah's body guard as they fought in a lose circle around their leader and her aide. Yet were Yael and Devorah covered with blood and gore.

*How many have I slain?* Yael wondered. The noise had lessened; the salty taste of blood, less strong. Devorah rode up to her, covered in mucus, bits of flesh and blood, some of it her own seeping from wounds on her left forearm and left calf. She needs protection on her left side, Yael thought.

"Yael!" Devorah raised her sword high.

"Devorah, my Sar. A great victory!"

"Indeed! Look at you. Does it hurt?"

"What?" Yael answered.

"Your left cheek and right thigh; you're wounded. But I think most of the blood covering you is other people's."

Yael's eyes flashed. "Aieee!" she shouted. "For God and Israel! Slay them! Cover yourself with blood and glory. Slay them!"

Devorah looked up; the rain still gushed down on them. "At least we won't have to bathe to get this gore off us," she said.

"For me, my Sar," Yael said, eyes gleaming, "I fear blood stains my soul now - blood that shall never be washed away. Though this battle be nearly over, I am not yet done!"

For a long moment, Devorah stared into Yael's eyes. "You are a splendid woman, Yael!" she said. "The world has not seen your like before nor may not again. Peace be upon you. You do indeed have a mission to complete that goes beyond what our small earth-bound brains can comprehend. Go now and do what you must. But guard the life within you and return to me soon." They leaned toward one another, embraced, kissed deeply, and then Yael turned her horse and rode toward the Kenite encampment.

# CHAPTER SIX

Sisera stumbled through the deluge, falling over debris and bodies floating beneath the surface of the nearly eighteen inches of water that covered everything, everywhere he looked, across his entire field of vision, for 360 degrees. There was no escape from it. Nearly all the familiar landmarks were washed away. He was able to navigate only by means of Mt Tabor; by keeping it behind him and to his right, he was able to move in what he thought was the general direction of Charoshet.

His mind barely functioned; stunned and bewildered all he could do was think about lifting one foot laboriously out of the water, putting it down and lifting the other. He was past cold - overwhelmed in an experience he had never known before and wet beyond his previous understanding of wetness. Safety, in a dry warm place, was all he could think about. How long had it been raining, pouring like this? Ten or twelve hours? He knew of no comparable phenomena, not in his life time. How long had he been trudging alone through this deluge? Three, maybe four hours?

Ugh! A horse's carcass swept into him, driven by the powerful current, which he had to move against, knocking him down. He fell on his back and for a moment, his head was underwater. Sputtering, he got to his feet, momentarily disoriented. It was getting dark, darker actually. He turned round three times before he was able to find Mt Tabor and begin moving forward again. His body ached and his wounds throbbed.

The battle was lost - *all was lost!* Life as he knew it was over. But life, *his* life, still had to be lived.

Just ahead, at the limit of his vision, he saw a group of tents on a hillside, perhaps 200 cubits away. Fire glowed; warmth, dry safety. He redoubled his efforts and in ten minutes, reached the small encampment on the plateau above the deluge and collapsed. No one was out in the downpour, but backlit by their fires, he saw movement in the tents. He did not have enough energy to cry out, he just lay on his side gasping, trying to keep the rain out of his nose and mouth. After awhile he was able to sit up, and shortly after that he managed to crawl into the nearest tent.

---

Yael looked at him; horror, fear, compassion, anger flickering across her face. "I have been expecting you," she said softly.

"You! Yael." Sisera's voice was weak and hoarse as he staggered to his feet; his eyes wide—first with surprise, then with pleasure. "I can't believe my good fortune! Even though they have destroyed my life, the gods have blessed me by bringing me to your tent."

"The tent of my husband," Yael corrected him.

"Where is he?" Sisera asked, looking hurriedly around him.

"With Barak. Why are you here?"

"Your God has won the battle for you. This," he looked up and gestured to the downpour, "has destroyed my chariots and armored divisions." Then, as if seeing her for the first time, noticed the blood-splattered armor round her chest and the well-used weapons on the floor rugs. "You are dressed as a warrior, Yael," he said, dismayed. "And a fierce one at that," he said, eyes narrowing. "I see blood and gore all over you - in your hair, on your face and clothes…"

"I was with Devorah," she answered, staring back at him levelly. "We destroyed the column you sent to Dor, then joined the battle at the Kishon."

Sisera threw his arms open wide and stuck out his chest. "And now, oh, great Haibru warrior, you may slay me, the General of the enemy host!"

Her hand went to the dagger in her belt. Two feet from him, it would have been an easy matter to impale him. But no, she thought, this was not the way. "Perhaps letting you live with the shame of your defeat by a rabble of barbarian militia would be punishment enough, my lord." She bowed deeply.

He smiled. "It would be a shame if that were the case. But I was not defeated by them, but rather by their God. There is no shame in that."

Yael nodded. His smile was magnificent. In spite of herself, she felt her loins warm towards him.

"It is a wise man who knows a superior force and bows before it," she said, eyes twinkling into his. "But you can not return to Hazor. What will you do now?"

He started taking off battered, tarnished armor, then his clothes. "Get out of these uncomfortable wet things and get warm beneath a blanket." He looked her up and down. "You need to change, too. You must have arrived only minutes before me." He was naked now, small wounds on his neck, shoulders and left thigh seeping, but otherwise virile body glowing with strength in the firelight.

Yael nodded. "As you say." And she too, pulled off her armor and clothing, enjoying the passion in his eyes and the stirring of his manhood as he beheld her nakedness. She walked to the tent wall, bent, returned with two woolen blankets and handed him one. He took it, dropped it and reached for hers. "Come," he said, "Let us share; we will become warmer sooner." Sighing, Yael stepped forward, spread the blanket round their shoulders, and together, they sat before the fire, wrapped in it.

*He is the father of my child*, Yael thought, *a truly magnificent man*; and her heart softened further. "Where will you go, Sisera?" she asked, eyes full of compassion.

"There is always a need for men with my skills." He smiled into her eyes. "I might go to Moab, or Syria, or even Egypt. *I* am still undefeated. Your god defeated my gods. People will understand that." He leaned forward and kissed her lips. She returned the kiss more than he thought she would. "Besides, with a woman like you, at my side, a beautiful warrior princess, I could not fail." He yawned.

Yael stood; her firm, muscled flesh gleamed voluptuously in the firelight. Leaning down, she pushed him gently to his side and covered him with their blanket. "Sleep, my good lord," she said. "Rest. Tomorrow is time enough to talk more of this."

"As you say, my Haibru princess." Sisera closed his eyes and slept soundly.

Devorah and Barak embraced. "My, Sar," he said, stepping back and smiling joyfully into her eyes. "You were completely correct about the miracle! Thank you! You never lost faith."

Dripping with blood, water and gore in what had been the Canaanite command tent, a commodious affair, complete with couches, beds, a commissary and numerous map tables, Jereboam handed them cloths to wipe themselves and went back to preparing hot chai.

Lappodoth joined them. Devorah hugged him. "How is Abimelech?" She asked.

"Our son is well and strong. He nurses fiercely and I had to find another wet nurse for him."

"Two wet nurses!" Barak exclaimed. "That's quite a baby."

"He follows his mother," Lappodoth said proudly.

Jereboam handed cups of chai to Barak and Devorah, and then returned with one for Lappodoth and himself. "Let us sit," he said, gesturing to the chairs; and they all sat.

"We have won the war," Devorah said. "Now must we secure the peace." The men nodded.

"We can take all of Canaan now, from Hazor to Egypt and Moab to the Ocean Sea," Barak said. "We can pull down their idols and raze their temples!"

"I think not, Barak," Devorah said thoughtfully. "No one can doubt the power of our God now, not after the miracle of this deluge. No, I think the Canaanites and the others will flock to us if we leave them alone. But if we attack their gods, they will defend them."

"Yes, that makes sense," Lappodoth said. "It is only natural; we would do the same."

"You are thinking," Barak said, looking deeply into Devorah's eyes, "that our main concern is with our *own* religion." Devorah nodded. "With the Judean Malachizer, high priest in Shiloh."

Devorah dipped her head in agreement. "Shiloh was ready to tilt toward Sisera. I stationed badly needed troops there to prevent an outright break with us." She looked around and into each man's face. "Now that the Canaanites are done, we have no greater threat than from our own people. Remember, only six of the twelve tribes joined our fight. The rest will be still for the moment, but we must act towards them in such a way as to secure their complete commitment. Especially the Judeans."

"What does all that mean in practical terms?" Barak asked.

"Thank you, Barak; always the practical one." Devorah smiled at him; he smiled back and dipped his head. "First, it means I want you, Barak, to concentrate on building a first rate, standing army."

The General grinned broadly. "That will take a long time and much money."

*Devorah*

"Time we have," Devorah said. "The money will have to be found. But we will find it.

"Second, and the point of the army, is I want to garrison our troops, much as the Canaanites had garrisoned theirs, in the larger cities, strategically placed to cow both our own people and potential marauders." She paused and her face lit up. "That's it!" she said. "Potential marauders! We will use the protection money the Canaanites extorted from our merchants, to build and support the army." Barak and Lappodoth nodded enthusiastically.

"It will be difficult to get the merchants to pay, at first," Barak observed.

"True," Devorah agreed. "That is why you and the members of our army-to-be will collect the money." Barak smiled, nodding.

"Third," Devorah continued. "To govern the garrisons and the surrounding territories, we will install proven leaders. You," she pointed to Jereboam, "Ben Zvi, Yael, and others who distinguished themselves in combat."

"The tribes will be threatened by that, and may resist," Lappodoth said.

"Judah for sure," Jereboam said.

"Yes," Devorah said. "You are right; we'll have to anticipate that. But we will never become a nation among the nations until we weaken the power of the tribes." Her eyes shown with vision. "Our continued well being requires a strong central administration." She paused, looked down, then into each of their faces. "I may never live to see it, but my children's children will!"

---

Yael was soothed by the warmth of Sisera's body and nestled closer to him. The rain had stopped a few hours ago and the silence still seemed strange. He really needed a bath; his body odor was intense; but she found it oddly erotic, too. I, too, must smell quite strong, she thought. A sudden burst of bird song hinted at morning. The touch of nausea that seemed to rise with the sun, made her think of the life within her; the life she had created with this man.

Morning was coming. Best get it over with, she thought. Yes, but. *Are you prepared to leave your people and go with him to a foreign land? It might not be so bad to learn another tongue, different food, strange gods? What about leaving Devorah?* Yes, that would be difficult; I've come to love her. *And what of your oath to avenge Jereboam and all your kith and kin?* Her face clouded over. She stood, walked to and fro, and then went to the wooden cabinet holding the mallet and tent pegs.

She stared down upon it as it grew lighter, and her gorge rose. *It is for everyone's good. He would not be happy as a mercenary. He might love our child, but he would not be a good father. He is a prince and not used to mundane life and hard work. It is his destiny to die at your hands, Yael - and yours to take his life.* She bent and lifted the lid. Voices broke the stillness. He will awake soon. She leaned forward and removed the mallet and a tent peg. The peg was sharpened to a fine point.

She turned and walked to the sleeping man, knelt by his side. For a moment, a wave of passion, then sadness swept through her; then she felt nothing. It was as if she were someone else watching Yael, wife of Haber the Kenite and aide to Sar Devorah, place the sharp point of the stake gently on Sisera's temple, raise the mallet, then bring it down fiercely, squarely on the tent peg, driving it into the sleeping man's brain.

Sisera twitched, sighed and lay still. Some blood flowed, but not much. Remembering what the soldiers said about head wounds, that the brain itself felt no pain, she was glad. Months ago, this death had been personal; now it was not. Not exactly an execution, but close to it. His head looked so incongruous with that piece of wood sticking out of it. She reached out and tenderly neatened his hair. A sob wracked her chest, then the morning sickness reasserted itself and Yael stood, dropped the mallet and walked from the tent to vomit into the waste trench.

---

"Abimelech!" Devorah shouted happily, opening her arms and rushing to take the baby from his day nurse. She held him close, cooing, then looked down into his innocent big blue eyes. "My you've grown!" she said. "In just nine days, you've really grown!" Abimelech grinned and gurgled and squirmed. Devorah bent her head to his

*Devorah* 173

and nuzzled his nose. The baby cackled and scrunched up his face. "Oh," Devorah said, "you like that, huh?" She nuzzled him again.

"Oh, God," she sighed, holding him close and turning to Lappodoth. "This is what life is for. Isn't it my husband?"

He smiled broadly and put his arm round her shoulder. "It is, my Queen. May he be the first of many!"

"Amen!" she said.

Yael strode into the tent, her face stern and cold. "Sar," she said, saluting, then bowing from the waist, her chest armor gleaming in the torch light. As she took in Devorah, Lappodoth and their son, her face softened. "The perfect Israelite family!" she said.

"Speaking of families," Devorah said, "how is your morning sickness?"

"What?" Lappodoth exclaimed. "You're pregnant?" Yael nodded. "Haber is a lucky man. I know how thrilled I was to hear Devorah was finally pregnant."

"Haber does not know," Yael said.

Lappodoth's mouth fell open. "Not know?" he repeated, trying to understand.

Devorah put her hand on her husband's. "Haber is a kind and generous man he will be a good father to Yael's baby. We need not make it harder for him than it is."

Lappodoth nodded. "I understand," he said. "But who is the father?"

"Sisera," Yael said.

Now Devorah was as surprised as Lappodoth. "*Sisera?*" they both said.

"Yes. And I just killed him, yesterday in Haber's tent; drove a tent peg through his brain as my dream foretold. He died peacefully." Her eyes moved from one to the other. "I see you wondering how this could be, and how I can seem so dispassionate about it." They nodded. "I too, have wondered and am still wondering. I can say to you only that in each step of my journey to this point, I have tried to sense the best path, in the moment, and follow it."

Yael's voice was low and even, her eyes moving easily from Devorah to Lappodoth. "It would be arrogant for me to say I felt guided, as you do my beloved Sar. Most of the time, I was confused and afraid, and was able to decide and act only in the immediate moment. I laid no plans, had no strategy." She smiled radiantly at them. "But now, though I still have no plan, I am at peace, and ready, no eager, to bear Sisera's child."

Devorah rushed forward and threw her arms around Yael. "Yes." She said, hugging her tightly. "Yes! You *have* been guided. Not like me, but like you. You were asked to do extremely difficult tasks - things beyond the bounds of our culture. You did them, suffered, worried and wondered, and now you are home, rooted in the most essential element—life, new life." She patted Yael's belly. "Here. A thousand blessings and a thousand more!"

Yael took Devorah's hand and kissed it tenderly. "Thank you, Sar."

"Ah, Yael," Devorah said. "Do not thank me. We are one heart, one spirit; sisters, supporting one another; going forward together. And," Devorah stepped back admiring Yael, "I am encouraged that you still have your war-like mien and," she thumped Yael's armored chest, "armor. For I have an assignment I wish you to undertake, should you want to." Yael looked a question. "I want you to be Military Governor of Charoshet."

Yael's jaw dropped and her eyes went wide. "But but I have no experience, Sar Devorah!"

"You are resourceful, compassionate, have courage, good judgment and some recent military experience. I had no experience either, when I started! I have no experience now, of what is next. We will learn together. What do you say?"

Smiling radiantly, Yael hugged Devorah. "I say yes! Oh, how grand. What an opportunity!" Then like a torch going out, her smile faded. "I do love Haber. Not the passionate love of a bride; but rather with gratitude and serenity." She looked down, then back into Devorah's eyes. "Let me talk with him; tell him everything. If he agrees," she bowed from the waist, "I am at your service!"

"Excellent," Devorah said. "Go to him; I await your response."

---

Abimelech cried, but it was not an angry cry. Devorah had tried nursing him herself, but she didn't have enough milk. 'Oh, well,' she thought. 'One cannot be all things to all people.' But she was disappointed. After all, she was born a woman, being Sar and Seer, General and Politician were all secondary. *But oh, thank You, Abba, for Abimelech and all that I* do *have*, she thought.

She and Lappodoth were back at the oasis in Ephraim; but it was too cramped to be a seat of government. She laughed at that idea, 'seat of government.' But with their victory at Tabor, their territory had nearly quadrupled and wherever the Sar was, there was the seat of the nascent Israelite government.

She involved Lappodoth more actively in making decisions, and between them, they employed twelve scribes! Before, she needed only one scribe, occasionally. There were also foreign emissaries and ambassadors to deal with, and her relationship with the tribes, especially the six that had opted out of the war, were almost like handling foreign delegations. She longed for the days, only four short months ago, when she had communed with Spirit on the wild splendor of her hill top.

Yet again, did the gratitude well up in her, for she felt deeply and understood that this work, these challenges were what God wanted her to do. Actually, she communed with Spirit now, even more frequently than she used to, several times a day, in the flow of her governing. She had no choice. This was all new to her and the only thing she knew to do was to go within and ask Its guidance. She could not judge nor decide on her own, because she simply didn't have sufficient, facts, experience or wisdom.

But It knew everything and It was always, always there for her. She had but to ask, be open and receptive, and an answer would come. The forms the answers took were often everyday occurrences: a child's laughter, a boys' game, a bird's flight or a falling palm frond. There were no burning bushes or commandments carved on stone.

Devorah simply went to the Tabernacle within, became receptive and made sense of what she saw around her. And, most of the time, her understandings were wise and effective.

Lappodoth and Barak had suggested that they move the seat of government on an annual basis, spending a year in the territory of each tribe, so that each tribe felt more a part of the whole. Devorah was committed to nation building and wanted to knit the tribes together, but she could not bring herself to so honor the tribes that had opted out of the war. In fact, she was having difficulty even seeing those tribes as foreign allies, much less kin. Part of her wanted to punish them, make an example of them. But her guidance did not support that. If she was willing to forgive the Canaanites and govern them justly, she'd have to do that for the six errant tribes as well. She was especially bothered by Malachizer and the Judeans. During the campaign, Shiloh had cost her time, men and money.

In all of this, Barak was turning out to be a wiser, better politician than she was. Since the victory, he was more centered and peaceful and, though he did not rely on Spirit as she did, Devorah knew he communed often and in his own way. "We can not punish Shiloh or the High Priest in any way," he counseled. "The great majority of our people believe deeply in the Scrolls and their God of rituals and punishments. The priests serve this God. To attack them is to attack the people's God, and they will not stand still for it.

"They know not your version of God, nor your Teaching." He smiled at her sympathetically. "And they probably never will, ever. The God you worship - and taught me to worship—is, I believe, the God of Moses. Yet the priests and people know Him not. They are unable to make the effort to know Him as you do, and instead, they worship His appearances." Barak touched Devorah's cheek. "We will simply do what is in our hearts, worship as we understand to worship and commune constantly. We need not force our ways on everyone, but let people come to awareness on their own. Those that do this, will have a lasting impact. Meanwhile, for those who lack this awareness, we must be seen to honor the God of the Scrolls."

Devorah knew Barak was right, but it rankled. There was absolutely no denying that the concept of God she had and the experience of worshiping as she did, did not come easily; they took more time, skill and discipline. But once done, the experience of inner connection—the peace, insight and the improved performance and results that came from first seeking the kingdom within—made it all worthwhile. Yet, as Barak said, it could not be forced—and Devorah knew the people would have to discover it for themselves. For those who wanted to learn to develop a day-to-day relationship with Spirit, she would set up groups to support them and, through these groups, extend this new teaching. 'New,' wasn't really the correct word, for it wasn't new. All the original information and history in the Scrolls was there, they just interpreted it differently; had a more personal, inner relationship with it.

"What do you think of setting up the government in Shiloh?" she asked Barak.

He grinned broadly and patted her on the back. "Now you're learning," he said. "Spoken like a true politician. You're thinking that if we set up there, we'll co-opt the Temple and priests, right?"

She nodded. "I'll have to visit with Malachizer first, alone." She paused. "I'll take Lappodoth and the baby; the official reason will be for the High Priest to bless the child."

"Excellent!" Barak said. "Excellent!"

Devorah discussed the whole thing with Lappodoth and he agreed with Barak that it was a fine plan. "Spirit was with you when you thought of that," he said.

*Funny*, Devorah thought, *it didn't feel the way Spirit usually felt.* "Good," she said aloud, more brusquely than she intended, feeling a bit off balance. "Shall we leave for Shiloh tomorrow morning?"

Lappodoth agreed. "I'll send a messenger ahead so Malachizer can prepare accommodations for us," he said. Devorah dipped her head in approval.

---

Shiloh was bustling more than it had been on their last visit, ten months ago. With peace, it was safe to travel and many Israelites were making pilgrimages to the Temple. Also, because travel was safe now, but for the occasional bandits which the rejuvenated local militia hunted down ruthlessly, many more foreign traders were present to offer their wares to the pilgrims. Clean, new caravanserais lined the two boulevards leading to the Temple.

Malachizer had made arrangements for Devorah, her family, the two wet nurses and three heavily armed bodyguards to stay in his compound. It had only been a large house on their previous visit, Devorah noted with wry satisfaction. Now, it was a compound—and a rather large one at that! *The war has been good for Shiloh*, she thought; and was aggravated.

As they neared the town, Lappodoth dispatched one of their body guards to ride ahead and alert Malachizer. The High Priest was waiting for them as they rode up. Beaming, he took the unprecedented action of holding the bridle of Devorah's horse as she dismounted.

*My, my*, Devorah thought, *how things have changed! I take this as a good omen.* "My good lord," she said aloud. "How kind of you to receive us yourself."

Malachizer handed the bridle to a nearby attendant and bowed deeply from the waist. "The Lord our God has smiled upon us, Sar," he said in his booming voice. "And upon you. The future looks bright."

He had gained a bit of weight and his full head of hair and beard were grayer, but otherwise he was the same. Devorah stepped into his open arms and they embraced. Lappodoth had helped the wet nurse carrying Abimelech from her horse, took the child and now presented him ceremoniously to the High Priest.

Again, in an unusual act of personal support, Malachizer reached out and gently took the baby from his father's arms. "Oh, my," he exclaimed looking at the boy's fair skin and green eyes, "this is a truly amazing child. And what a grip!"

"We have come for your priestly benediction for him, Malachizer," Devorah said.

"Of course, of course!" he said. "I have arranged a ceremony for tomorrow. Will that be convenient, Sar?"

"Yes. Thank you."

"And you will be my guests tonight and we shall talk," the priest said.

"Indeed," Devorah responded. "We have much to discuss." She winked at Lappodoth, who winked back.

---

After bathing, changing and being present for Abimelech's feeding, Devorah and Lappodoth left the child with his nurse and went to the High Priest's bright and airy dining room; sconces hung from the walls and oil lamps from the ceiling and were placed strategically around the table. The food: humus, pita, dates, cucumbers, berries and roasted lamb, was simple but quite tasty.

Malachizer's wife, Ruth, and four of their eight children joined them at dinner. Their talk was general and of no consequence other than to create a warm relaxed atmosphere. After dinner, Lappodoth went to the roof top verandah with Ruth and her children, leaving Devorah and Malachizer at the supper board to relax and converse privately.

Malachizer spoke first. "I know why else you have come, Devorah."

"You do?"

"Our world has much changed since you were here last; you know that: you did it." She smiled at him and dipped her head in appreciation. "We can no longer pretend to be nomadic innocents. We must overcome our fear of cities and foreign ways. Now, because of your

*Devorah*

victories," he nodded, acknowledging her success, "we have thousands of Canaanites, Philistines, and Moabites within our borders."

"True. But of all people, do you - Malachizer, the High Priest - talk to me of tolerance for foreigners? That is hard for me to believe! I am glad to hear it, for I believe all people are God's children, but you have never espoused broad-mindedness before. You have always preached fear of the Lord, His wrath and punishment for those who do not follow His laws. Does your open-mindedness extend to their religions, to idol worship?"

The priest smiled at her. "We can not condone idol worship, Sar, but we need not aggressively root it out. If our neighbors choose to serve their gods by worshipping graven images, that is their choice. It is not for our people, but these others are not our people: they are our neighbors. We are responsible only for our own, and for the safety and prosperity of all within our borders - idol worshippers included."

"Things *have* changed, Malachizer," Devorah said, smiling back at him. "What else besides practical necessity brings you to this point of view?"

The High Priest leaned towards Devorah across the supper board, eyes large and shining into hers. "I was wrong, Devorah. When last you were here, I thought our people would lose the struggle with the Canaanites. Your faith was greater than mine; your faith never wavered and the Lord God Yahweh, honored your faith and showed me the error of my ways."

Devorah could hardly believe she was hearing this. She pinched her thigh to be sure she was awake. "God is grateful, Malachizer," she said. "But could it also be that your admission of error is also a way to avoid punishment for your treason?" The priest blanched and sat back in his chair. "Barak and I know of the many deals you and your Judean cousins made with our enemies, who you now call 'neighbors'." Now she leaned forward towards him, lips in a tight smile, eyes blazing. "You are cunning enough to know me both as a person and the military/political situation. Thus you know that I can not openly punish you and the other traitors here in Shiloh. But," she leaned even closer to him, "Barak and I *can* make life difficult for you and yours. And God knows a large part of me wants to do that. Yet, Barak and the greater part of me - the part connected to God - will not allow me to do so."

She leaned back in her chair, eyes never leaving his, pulling him with her so that he now leaned across the table. "We will let bygones be bygones, Malachizer. Now, together, let us usher in a new era of unity, peace and tolerance among ourselves and our neighbors." The priest sighed, his relief palpable as he nearly collapsed against the back of his chair.

"For the next year or two," Devorah continued, "Shiloh shall be the seat of the government of Israel. You and the other priests throughout the land will preach tolerance of our neighbors and," she leaned forward again, "that tolerance shall extend to my interpretation of the Covenant, our laws and teachings." The priest's eyes narrowed. "I don't expect support or even acknowledgement, just tolerance and no harassment. Agreed?" Devorah stood and extended her hand to Malachizer, who rose, clasped her hand in both of his and shook it vigorously.

"You are indeed a wise woman, Devorah; and one of the best Sars our people have ever had." He looked away from her face, then back at it. "I did mean what I said about your faith being stronger than mine and seeing the error of my ways. It will not be an overnight change, but I will strive to see God differently - perhaps, even your way."

"Thank you, Malachizer; I believe you." Devorah moved to leave; it was late and she was nearly exhausted.

"A moment, Sar; I too have visions and I have seen that our people will want a King, like Jabin, to rule over them. Our current system can no longer serve us. Do you agree?"

Devorah nodded. "I have had no visions about this, my lord. But I could not agree with you more. The power of the tribes must be transformed to the power of one nation; a King will help with that."

"True, very true," Malachizer said. "But there's another reason to move toward having a King. We need an institution that people will respect to hold things together." Devorah nodded. Malachizer continued, "You and Barak are powerful personalities, people respect and obey you; and you are motivated by the highest good for all concerned. But what will happen when you are gone?" Devorah could easily envisage the chaos of each tribe grasping for its own, and the 'neighbors' and their gods overpowering the people. She nodded again. Malachizer continued, "We need an institution, something independent of personalities that the people will respect, that will moderate their fears and petty self interest."

"But institutions can be weakened, even overthrown by personalities," Devorah observed.

*Devorah* 181

"That is so, but still our people have so little experience with institutions, the only ones we have, really, are your office and mine. Perhaps these will work for us, at least for awhile."

"They have to," Devorah said, "and they will." She stood. "We will talk more of this in the morning." The priest stood, also. "By the way," she said, staring at him with narrowed eyes, "I trust the Ark of the Covenant is safe and protected?"

Malachizer choked and the air caught in his throat. "I, I, uh, uh…" he stuttered.

Devorah smiled triumphantly. "As it turned out, priest, we didn't need the Ark. We were victorious because we had the Covenant in our hearts! Thank you for your hospitality," she said. He dipped his head, she turned and went to her quarters.

---

Six weeks later, Devorah, Lappodoth and Barak were in the large map room of the half completed Citadel in Shiloh. Malachizer had just left them. As promised, the High Priest had been cooperating fully to help limit the power of the tribes and centralize the administration of their emerging nation. He also had been tolerant of the religious schools Devorah and Lappodoth were establishing to bring their message of the inner-most God and the outer-most God being the one God of the Covenant.

Devorah suspected that Malachizer himself was moving in her direction, feeling the reality of the Covenant within his own heart and relying more on his inner-most communion with Spirit for guidance rather than the elaborate rituals of the Temple. To Devorah, the signs of the spiritual shift in the High Priest were numerous. He wasn't as formal, was warmer and more intuitive. He spent less time with the priests in the Temple inner court and more time in the outer courts mingling with the common people. He accepted Devorah's frequent invitations to meals, during which their discussions were quite open and dynamic. And, perhaps best of all to the new mother, he spent more time with his own large family: enjoying their company, growing younger and more child-like and optimistic in their presence.

The meeting just ended had focused on the difficulties of getting Judah to more actively support Devorah and Barak. Moves toward establishing a standing professional army and centralizing administrative power had been discussed. Malachizer had argued, very much in the spirit of Devorah's approach to the Covenant: that the only way to keep what power they had, was to give it away, to share it with the people of Judah.

Devorah had smiled at that; so had Lappodoth, for the idea that giving and receiving were the same was one of the foundations of the Covenant. It was rewarding to experience Malachizer taking it to heart. Paradoxical when looked at with the small, everyday mind, when practiced, the idea worked perfectly. To have a friend, be a friend; to have peace, give peace; first the inner, then the outer; seek ye first the Kingdom of Heaven and all else shall be added.

Simple to understand and say; difficult to do. That's what Devorah, Lappodoth and Barak were talking about—keeping their power by giving it away to the Judeans.

"I like the idea," Barak said, standing and walking around the long table in the center of the room. "It's the execution that concerns me. *We* don't even know what we're doing, so how can we trust *them*?"

"But that's the beauty of it, Barak," Lappodoth said, walking to him. "They are part of the solution. We don't know, they don't know, it's perfect! We will learn together."

Devorah stood, but remained next to the table. "It's the giving and receiving, again, Barak," she said. "If we were only giving to get, it wouldn't work. We and Judah want the same things. We have to help them appreciate that. We are in this together. We have only a partial understanding of what is necessary; they too, have a partial understanding. If we are able to put these partial understandings together, we will get closer to a full understanding."

Devorah folded her arms and shook her head. "No one knows better than both of you how fiercely I wanted to punish the Judeans and Malachizer for their recent treachery. But look! Now we have a changed Malachizer and have a real opening to the leaders of Judah. *We* did not make this come about; *we* did not plan it; the One Power working through us, because we opened to It and allowed It, has brought us to this - an outcome greater than any we could have manifested on our own."

She paused, thinking. "If God is good, all the time, as we say It is," she said, "then perhaps even the treachery of Judah and Malachizer was taking us where we needed to go." She closed her eyes. *Yes*, she thought, *perhaps even the great horror I have envisioned, the torment, blood, shrieks and pain are also a part of the unfoldment.* Not if you're the one shrieking and bleeding, another part of her noted. *True*, she thought, shuddering, *very true*.

But wasn't Yael an excellent example of this? She murdered the father of her child. What will come of that? *Only good*, Devorah thought. And Yael was once a slave in Charoshet, now she will be its Military Governor. Awareness of the Covenant and a connection with Its content of deep, peaceful certainty, and deep, almost irresistible intuitive desire is what's important - not the form. One could feel God and honor the Covenant, even as a slave. Even being horribly tortured as Jereboam had been. Form is often misleading, but if the content is loving and passionate it's often divine guidance. *One is truly blessed, as am I, when content and form coincide.*

"We have to commit, Barak," Devorah said. "We have to invite the leaders of Judah to take more than their rightful place in the Army and the Administration. Think of our own good Jereboam."

"Indeed!" Barak said enthusiastically. "There's a Judean who is an Israelite first!" The others nodded vigorously. "He is what is possible for the others—proud of his tribe yet prouder still of the Covenant and our rising nation. Yes," he put his hands on his hips. "I agree. We must commit. They are either part of the solution or part of the problem." He returned to his place at the table, Lappodoth trailing after him.

"Let's review our list of command positions," Lappodoth said. "We have twenty in the Army, twelve in supply, seventeen in the Military Governors detachments, and seven here in Shiloh on Devorah's staff."

Barak finished Lappodoth's thought, "When we meet with the Judeans tomorrow, we will ask their advice about who among them would be best suited to fill these positions."

"And," Devorah said, smiling and sitting down, "what contributions they can make. We are seeking men of means. It is imperative that they commit their own wealth to their assignments."

"But of course," Barak said. "It has always been thus."

"Yes, I know," Devorah responded. "But it has also always been with our neighbors - the Canaanites, Philistine, Ammonites - that leaders enrich themselves on taxes and fees. *We* will have none of that! Did we battle to free ourselves of oppression, only to become the oppressors? Those that we place in positions of power can, of course, profit a bit, but we defeat our purpose if they gorge themselves and become fat like ticks on a dog."

"Well said, Sar," Barak said, nodding in agreement. "It is in the administration of the peace that the war is truly won. It is in the administration of the peace that the Covenant is made manifest and becomes part of the people's everyday lives. If we fail to employ the Covenant in the administration of our hard-won peace, we will soon fall back on the Law and the Scrolls and lose all we have fought for."

# Part Three
# The Legacy

*And King Saul saw and understood much that he could not have seen and understood before. Now he could experience his life and times as his contemporaries experienced them. No longer bound within himself, he was not limited to his own experiences, ideas or point of view. Now he had access to the lives, hearts and minds of those who had affected him most deeply. Time was different, too; it was more fluid than it had been; he was able to move effortlessly in either direction. He smiled, remembering occasions when he couldn't do this and how desperate he'd been to know the future. No longer; the desperation was gone, he'd seen the future and it was not what he'd expected as a boy with his mother.*

# CHAPTER SEVEN

Oh, Devorah, my long ago kinswoman, Janina thought. How many years have gone by, but how little things have changed! The choice you saw between perceptions of the One God of the Covenant, one fully present and available, and the other, the God of the Scrolls—rules, rituals and regulations, mighty in battle, fierce, punishing and vengeful, is still present and with us. Will it always be so? Will we ever understand and chose aright?

Janina's eyes roamed through the oasis village. Once again she tried to imagine what this place might have been like one hundred and thirty seven years ago, in Devorah's time. She knew there were tents, not buildings, for then the people associated cities and villages with sin and the evils of idol worship - prostitution and crime. The threat of war was constant then, much as now; and though Devorah and Barak's victories had brought forty years of relative peace, paradoxically those times had also brought many of the evils of city life to the Israelites.

Now there were beggars among them and thievery. As the Israelites grew prosperous with money to spend and lived cheek by jowl with their Philistine neighbors, there was adultery, prostitution and idol worship. All of which was practiced in the open—quietly, but in the open. The priests and prophets of the God of the Scrolls grew more concerned about this, especially Samuel, and spoke more stridently about returning to the purity of the old days. Perhaps the people had become too much enamored of their neighbors' ways—the sensual delights of idol worship and the power of iron weapons.

But, really, Janina thought, going back was impossible, an illusion, and besides, when had it been different? Yes, it was more visible now; but hadn't Devorah had difficulties with the priests of Shiloh? Even the Golden Calf created by Moses' own brother, Aaron, had shown that the conflict between the Teaching and the Scrolls—the perceptions of God as beneficent, permissive and omnipresent, and God as the Law Giver, Punisher and Enforcer - would always be with us.

This was certainly the case in the years since Devorah articulated and began handing down the Teaching, the belief that God was a loving Presence, available right now, no matter what so called 'sins' had been committed. That It had both male and female aspects and was worshipped in one's heart and mind, and thus made manifest in one's daily life. This teaching was handed down matrilinealy, from mother to daughter, but freely shared with men as well. Indeed, The Teaching, as Janina had been taught to call It, was freely available to all sentient beings, whether Israelite or not.

The years immediately following Devorah and Barak's victory at Mt. Tabor, were the years The Teaching was established. Since then, without realizing or understanding what they were doing, the people lurched between Devorah's new Teaching of the Covenant and the priests' traditional God of the Scrolls. Janina and the other men and women who embraced The Teaching believed that It was responsible for the times of peace and progress in the one hundred thirty seven years since Devorah articulated It. They believed that when people, especially the leaders, came from that place within, full of joy, hope and enthusiasm, free of fear and stress, the place that has never known fear or failure, then progress, peace and prosperity flowed.

Stress and failure came from the place of fear within, the opposite of The Teaching; the belief that human beings were alone in a dog eat dog world with a God who was whimsical, pedantic, arbitrary and vengeful—the God of the Scrolls. The people of The Teaching saw everything since Devorah, and indeed, before her time as the interaction of these two beliefs.

"Did Yael have her baby, mother?" the ten year old boy asked Janina.

"Yes, Saul, she did," his beautiful, copper-skinned, twenty seven year old mother said. "She had four children."

"And how many children did Sar Devorah have?"

"She also had four children. In fact, you are a direct descendant of Devorah's first son Abimelech, and Yael's second daughter, Mari. And this place," Janina said, gesturing around the prosperous mud brick village in the cool oasis, "this beautiful place, is the very place Devorah taught her classes about the Teaching."

"Why is the Covenant so important, mother? I thought God wanted us to take care of ourselves first, and then seek His help."

Janina smiled at her bright, handsome son, leaned forward and tousled his curly reddish hair. Shouldn't he have grown out of that color by now, she wondered, bringing her hand to her side? But the older he got, the redder it became. She shook her head. It must be on her husband Kish's side; none of her relatives had red or even blond hair. Saul's size probably came from the same source. He was big, bigger than the other boys his age.

Janina was proud of his healthy size, sharp mind, and skill with weapons, but she was also concerned. He seemed too focused on what he could figure out on his own and do for himself. Eager to learn practical things like building a fire, reading and writing, he had little patience for the larger invisible aspects of life such as compassion, devotion, and faith. Saul knew the basic tenants of their faith, but these were empty of personal meaning for him, and though he asked about the Covenant, even that did not seem to guide or sustain him in difficult moments. While natural enough in a ten year old boy, Janina feared the self-reliance and rigid habits he was forming now would be difficult to change and would serve him poorly in the future.

"God *does* want us to take care of ourselves," she said, patting Saul's shoulder. "But *with* Him. The Covenant is His promise to always be there for us, to support and guide us, if we allow Him to do so, if we but ask, feeling His presence within us and in all that is, right now."

"And the Temple," Saul asked, "Isn't God in the Temple? Why do we go there?"

"He *is* there, Saul. But he is not *only* there." Janina gestured to the bubbling water, swaying palms, deep blue sky, puffy white clouds, birds, goats, dung. "Do you see all of this? Hear the sounds, smell the smells, feel the breeze? All this is God, too." She patted his chest over his heart, "And here." She placed his smaller hand on her heart, "And here." The boy looked perplexed, as he often did when she tried to explain these concepts to him. "You have only to open yourself to It, Saul, to be at peace and to experience Its guidance."

Saul nodded and looked piercingly into Janina's eyes. "I think you're right, mother. The Temple wasn't anything special to God or he wouldn't have let it and the entire city of Shiloh be destroyed by the Philistines." Janina's mouth fell open. Saul smiled; he loved to surprise her with his knowledge of adult things. "I heard some merchants from Nob talking about it. They said the old High Priest's grandson, Achituv, was upset with Samuel for not supporting them and helping make Nob a holy city."

Janina blinked at her son and brushed a lose strand of hair off her forehead. "I have heard these things, too, Saul. But controversies like this are too common, and," she looked at him with soft eyes, "add nothing to our ability to connect with Spirit. In fact, such stories anchor us deeper in the world of appearances and detract from our ability to connect with It's vision and It's will for us. Beware your penchant for getting lost in the details of the small picture, Saul. It might cost you your soul."

Saul nodded abstractedly and looked away. The boy was getting fidgety; their discussion was likely over. As Janina watched him run in a large circle around her, she momentarily envied his uncomplicated view of matters that she herself worked so diligently to understand.

Perhaps Saul was onto something when he repeated the story that God had allowed the Philistines to demolish Shiloh. As long as God was thought of as a force outside us, a literal Being active in the world, instead of a Presence in our own hearts and minds; then that long would the things of the world, the material things—wars, famines, prosperity, sensuality and fear, and their master, the God of the Scrolls—Law Giver, Punisher and Enforcer—take precedence. The spiritual experiences of peace, love, compassion and joy came from the Teaching, the experience of our Covenant and personal connection with all that is, the conception of God as a loving presence in everyone, everything and every event, no matter the appearances.

Janina stood and stretched her arms open wide, catching Saul as he ran back to her for a hug. "I think I understand all of this, mother—but how does it help me be a better swordsman or first rate athlete; what's the *value* of it?" She shook her head, sadly at the thought.

"When you believe it, Saul, when you want the connection, the Covenant, the oneness above all else, you'll feel it, and see the value."

"How do I do that mother? It's just an idea. I want to be a General above all else."

"Yes, well, my son; we will pray that *It* will find *you*. For now, give me a kiss—and go find your friends to play with!"

Abadantha, Dantha, for short, turned her big black eyes from her older brother to her mother. "Oh," Janina squealed, squeezing her daughter's plump cheeks, "you are such a good girl, Dantha! Mommy loves you so!" The five year old, with the serious mien of a high priest, smiled slightly, but kept her big eyes glued to her mother's. "Can you tell mother's worried?" Janina asked. Dantha nodded. "I wish Saul could be calmer, more like you," Janina said. "You understand so much that your brother doesn't. You listen and comprehend." Janina chucked the child under her chin. "I only wish you spoke more."

*Devorah*

I do speak, mother, Dantha's eyes said. And you're right, I do comprehend. "Saul is good," Dantha said. "He loves us."

"I know he is good, Dantha, and that he loves us. But I worry he is too..." she searched for the word, "...outward, disconnected from God."

"God loves all, doesn't He, no matter what?" Dantha said in her childish voice, face solemn. "You always say that."

"I do. And...?"

Abadantha tilted her head, eyes smiling. "God loves and protect Saul even if Saul doesn't believe in Him."

Janina smiled into her precocious daughter's eyes. How bright; what a blessing! "God's love is always within and without, Dantha. But if we do not know it, do not choose to connect with It, It cannot help us. Saul does not really know or believe It." Janina looked around her. Things were complex. More complex than she could possibly communicate to the five year old Abadantha and nine year old Saul.

She always left out the grey areas, the messy more complex stuff—the intricate, non-black and white nuances—when she told this story of Devorah, Yael and Barak to the children. Yael *did* have Sisera's daughter, Sena, and Janina and her children *were* descended from Sena and Abimelech, Devorah's first son. But that wasn't the whole story. Janina hadn't told them the messy complex stuff about what Yael had done as governor of Charoshet or about her secret worship in the Temple of Astarte, and how the peace they had all fought so hard for fell apart when Devorah and Barak died. It could not continue to flourish because the Israelites, like her own little Saul now, did not feel the Teaching and Presence of God in their hearts. With the Teaching's strongest supporters gone, the Israelites reverted to the God of the Scrolls, first looking outside themselves for validation instead of first looking within their own hearts and minds.

Janina knew the complete story; her mother had told her. At the time of Dantha's Bat Mitzvah, when her own daughter would be mature enough to fully understand it, Janina would continue The Teaching's one hundred and forty year tradition of transmission from mother to daughter by handing it down to her. Men, it seemed, were not as receptive; not that it was a secret, or women didn't share it with them. Men, like young Saul now, simply seemed to have difficulty sorting through the complexity, contradictions and paradoxes - such as how Yael was able to murder her baby's father even though she cared for him. To be a part of something greater beyond everyday understanding is a quality that Yael—and women in general—seemed to possess. Janina knew for herself that it was the Presence of God's love in her heart that allowed her to see beyond the practical appearance of events.

---

Abadantha glowed with an inner light. She looked as radiant and luminous as the sharp, crystal bright light itself - the special dazzling desert light that made everything around them - blue, cloud-flecked sky, smoky altar, well dressed, smiling people, seem realer than real. Abadantha's budding breasts thrust against the gossamer white of the ceremonial gown, graciously supporting the blood red of her cowry necklace. She was tanned, tall and healthy, with green eyes squinting for shade beneath jet black brows. A garland of blue flowers sat upon a cascade of rich auburn hair reaching beneath her shoulder blades, and which, as tradition required, had never been cut.

Janina was at Dantha's right, Saul to her left. Her older brother fidgeted, his piercing eyes looking left and right; but when they rested on Dantha, the worried, distracted look dissolved to be replaced with calm, and the hint of a smile touched his full, handsome lips. *He really does love me*, Dantha thought. 'Yes,' another part of her responded, 'then why won't he let you comfort him?' Dantha felt Saul's almost constant anxiety keenly and longed to soothe him, but up till now, had not been allowed to—even with the aid of the wonderful skill and wisdom her mother shared with her. *What he experiences is about himself; it has nothing to do with me*, Dantha thought.

Janina watched Dantha look at Saul, feeling both her daughter's pain and her own at Saul's distress. She herself had all but given up on her handsome, big, charismatic son. But Dantha was another story. Dantha was amazingly skillful, strong and loving. She had not yet given up on her brother, and Janina strove to keep her own sense of failure and regret about her son from poisoning her daughter. Dantha would soon be more powerful and skillful than her mother and in that, Janina thought, there might be hope for Saul.

Now, on the day of Dantha's thirteenth birthday, her Bat Mitzvah day, Janina debated whether to tell Dantha the entire story of Devorah,

Barak and Yael, with all the complex messy stuff—the myriad interconnected sexual, political, religious and military threads. Tradition demanded that Janina do so. No reason not to; Dantha was not really a child anymore; she was strong, resilient and bright. If the telling unbalanced her, which it might, it would only be for a little while; she'd be back on course soon enough—and the better for the knowledge. Besides, who was she to gainsay the tradition she gloried in, or to deprive her daughter of its benefits? I will tell her tonight, Janina decided.

Dantha and Janina were alone in the open air beneath a cloudless, star filled sky on the roof top of their house at the edge of the oasis, away from the tumult of the community. Janina shifted her weight in the chair of tent cloth, looked to her daughter and sighed. The day had been excellent! Dantha had done a splendid recitation of her Torah portion. The guests had had a good time at the modest reception, drinking lots of un-watered wine, consuming many barley cakes and tart fruits, dates and pomegranates and heaps of lamb kabobs and pita. Saul had gone off with three of his friends, and now, after cleaning up, she and Dantha were taking their ease and enjoying the cool evening breeze.

"You have some things to tell me, now, on my thirteenth birthday, don't you mother?" Dantha said, more as a statement of fact than a question.

"You are amazing, Dantha!" Janina exclaimed. "Just amazing, no," she said shaking her head. "Extraordinary. I am proud of you and trust you will continue to use God's gifts to you with the great wisdom and skill you have shown thus far. Yes. I do have some things to tell you. I am sure you know what about, too."

Dantha turned to look more closely at her youthful mother. *I am so blessed*, she thought. *I too, am proud of this strong knowing woman who has been both mother and father to Saul and I. I love her!* Aloud she said, "You want to tell me the entire story of Yael, Devorah, Lappodoth, Barak, Malachizer and all the rest. You want to tell me what you think is the Truth, so I may gain by it and be a better servant to our people."

"Yes!" Janina sat up, leaned to her daughter, who met her half way, and they embraced. Looking deeply, fearlessly into one another's eyes, they smiled and Janina said, "Yes. The story I told you, the one that everyone knows, is only a partial truth, almost a mythological tale. It suffices quite well for children and disinterested adults. But for one who is to become an initiate of Devorah's own Teaching and carry that tradition forward, you must have the Truth, as best as I can give it to you." Dantha nodded, her wide eyes focused on her mother's face. "As I tell you this, imagine yourself there with the people. Forget I am telling it to you. Let it be more than a story to you. Put yourself into the hearts and minds of your great, great, grand Sires. Mighty they were, but still only human as you and I are human, and full of paradox and contradiction, love and fear, hope and desire."

# CHAPTER EIGHT

Yael's child was beginning to show when she and Haber finally left Devorah's command post atop Mt Tabor to take up her duties as Military Governor of Charoshet. She rode comfortably wearing armor and helmet, at the head of a column of five hundred well fed and armed Naphtali and Ephramite warriors, Haber at her side. Haber had not only taken the news of his wife's pregnancy with aplomb, but, when she told him Sisera was the sire he'd looked unblinkingly into her eyes and smiled. Then he kissed her, deeply, soulfully and she had returned the kiss in kind.

They had been alone in Devorah's tent; finally having a few moments away from the enthusiastic crowds. Both he and Yael were regarded by one and all as heroes, his contributions of spying and iron smithing deemed equal to her military prowess. Like Yael, Haber enjoyed the adulation, recognition and appreciation, and could not imagine returning to his previous life. The fact that his beautiful warrior wife had bedded the great Canaanite war chief and conceived a child by him, yet still wanted to be married to him, Haber, made him proud. It was another feather in his cap.

A strong mounted patrol had gone ahead of Yael's occupation column. Now its lieutenant returned and reported he'd deployed his men and all was peaceful. As they entered the city, Yael was disappointed by what she saw. Haber too, seemed a bit let down. Not damaged in any way, buildings intact, roads free of debris, most of the town's windows were shuttered, doors closed and market stalls sealed shut. Few people were out, and those that were, were at the public wells.

As they rode past the still magnificent Temple of Astarte, Yael felt a stirring in her loins. So much had happened there, her meeting with Sisera, her initiation by Asmara and later her all too willing enslavement to Elkanta. What had become of the two women who had dominated her so intensely? Probably nothing. Seating herself more firmly on the saddle, Yael wondered if anything like that could happen to her now, after all she'd been through? In answer, her loins tingled and butterflies lifted off in her belly.

Haber leaned towards her. He had some idea of her experiences with Asmara, everyone did, it was common knowledge, but they'd never talked about any of it. Hakim Saul was the only person she'd ever told. "Does the place still hold strong memories for you, wife?" His tone and facial expression were quite compassionate and sympathetic.

She looked at him, felt his devotion to her, and responded honestly. "It does, husband," she said. "I have not yet made my peace with what happened here." She looked ahead, into the nearly deserted outer courtyards of the Temple. "I am both honored and afraid to be here," she said.

"Why so?" he asked.

"I am not sure what I will do," she said, shuddering.

Haber reached out and touched her shoulder. "I have faith in you and in the Haibru god that works through you," he said. "I am at your service, Yael. I will help you in any way I can."

She leaned across to him and brushed his cheek with her full lips. "Thank you, my lord!" Her tone and demeanor were brighter. "I am grateful and count you among my staunchest allies!" She raised her arm, pumped it up and down and shouted, "Make haste! To the garrison now. On me!" spurring her horse to a gallop, with Haber at her side, the column raced past the Temple.

---

After three weeks, Yael and Haber realized their official duties and workloads made in impossible to continue living in Sisera's quarters at the Citadel.

"You continue getting the troops settled in," Haber said one evening, "setting up the city administration and receiving the local leaders; I'll look for a more suitable place for us and," he patted her bulging belly, "the child."

"Thank you, my husband, you are a mind reader. I am ready for a change." Yael hugged him. "This place serves nicely as my headquarters, but," she patted her belly, "we *do* need a place to raise a child and to live properly." She kissed him, full lips enveloping his

*Devorah*

and he opened his mouth to receive her tongue. She sighed, enjoying the sensation of dominating him. No, she thought, 'dominating' was too strong a word. 'Leading' was better. He was still a very assertive, reliable and manly man; he simply allowed her to lead in a few more situations than he used to: sex was one of them.

"How quickly can that be done, husband?" She asked as they stepped apart.

"I want it quickly too, wife. But Charoshet is much in demand now. Not much is available; if I give my full effort, perhaps in three or four days."

"Good, husband. Thank you!" She glanced over her shoulder to the papyri scattered on her work table, gently dismissing him. He pecked her cheek and turned away, then turned back to her.

"I caught a glimpse of Asmara yesterday," he said, softly.

"And?" Yael's tone was stern.

"She is quite lovely, isn't she?" Yael said nothing. "Entrancing," Haber paused. "You have seen her up close, even naked."

An image of the gracious lines of Asmara's pale white buttocks as they flowed into her perfect cleft, accompanied by the deep sense of gratitude she always felt at being allowed to look at them, flashed through Yael. "She is quite wonderful," Yael said wistfully. "It is a shame she must be punished."

"Yes," Haber agreed. "A great shame." He went to the stairs, waved and said as he left, "I will soon find us a new dwelling place."

Yael blew him a kiss and as she seated herself to resume reading; Zachary, her Chief of Staff, entered. He stood respectfully before her, waiting for her to look up, which she did after making a notation on what she was reading.

"Tzevah," he said, dipping his head. "The collections of Sar Devorah's military tax are now 70% complete. All the merchants have complied and most of the landowning aristocrats have paid as well. We're having difficulties with priests and priestess and other powerful people associated with the Temple of Astarte."

Yael stood, "Well," she said, eyes on his, hands on her full hips, sunlight glinting off her shining bronze breast plate. "I have an idea of what I'd like to do, but what do you recommend?"

The experienced, bearded warrior smiled slightly. "No disrespect, Tzevah. I know our policy of strict even-handedness is for the best in the long run. But I do not see how we can let these people continue to disobey. It's been nearly a month! We're losing credibility with other segments of the city."

A month! Yael's thoughts drifted. *I've been here a whole month and have not yet laid eyes on Asmara or Elkanta.* She squeezed her legs together. *Just thinking of them...* She sighed with longing. *Just thinking of them many times a day for thirty days has been torture.* The tenor of her thoughts shifted. *They are evil though, evil personified. This is my chance to punish them for what they have done to me, as well as rid the city of the evil they embody.*

"Yes," Yael stared at him. "What do you recommend?"

"A public flogging."

"Of who, certainly not a priest or priestess? The city would rise against us!"

Zachary's smile broadened and he nodded his agreement. "True, if one of us did the flogging. But what if it was done *by* one of their own, *to* one of their own?"

Yael smiled broadly. "You have an excellent administrative mind, Zachary, for such a stalwart warrior. Once again, you show me why I am glad I chose you. Yes! Who do you recommend?"

"Thank you, Tzevah. It is a pleasure to serve you and our people. I would invite the High Priest of Baal, Kesher, to flog Asmara, the well known priestess of Astarte."

Yael's breath caught as she envisioned her former mistress' lush body naked and bound, being whipped; blood and sweat streaming down her alabaster skin. She had difficulty swallowing.

"If Asmara is too personal for you, Tzevah…" Zachary said, leaving his awareness of her relationship with the Canaanite hanging in the air between them.

"No," Yael said. "It is and it isn't. She is a fine choice. Everyone in the city knows and fears her; she has hurt and enslaved many of them. How do you propose to entice Kesher to do it?"

Zachary's smile grew even broader and Yael was intrigued. "By offering him a discount on the taxes for the Temple of Baal."

Yael wanted to hug him, but the need to maintain good discipline prevented it. "Excellent!" she said. "I think he will accept. Go to him today, and if he accepts, take Asmara into custody immediately and make arrangements for the punishment to be carried out three days hence. That should give the populace ample time to gather."

Zachary saluted, turned smartly on his heel and exited.

Yael remained where she stood, shaking slightly, her face becoming flushed, her breathing shallow. *What have I done? I still revere her. She will always be my Mistress.*

'You did what was necessary administratively.'

*But I am Her slave, how can I have her whipped?*

'*Were* her slave; *were*. You've got to stop thinking like that.'

*But I wanted to serve Her, I was willing, I enjoyed it. I could have escaped, but I chose to stay and serve as Her slave. And as Elkanta's slave. How sensual, how enchanting; how I still long to serve them. What am I to do?*

'You will not attend the punishment. You need have nothing further to do with it. Zachary will handle everything.'

*Yes.* Still shaking, Yael returned to her work table, but found it difficult to concentrate.

---

A few hours later, Elkanta stood before Yael. She wore a revealing harem girl outfit—baize halter top and diaphanous pink pantaloons, slit at the sides, a thick leather belt, dangling hoop earrings, her sacred shiny necklace and leather sandals. She stood, hands on hips, just as arrogant and voluptuously sexy as Yael remembered her.

"Who allowed you in?" Yael asked, catching a hint of the woman's powerful, earthy scent.

"Your guards. I told them I had come to plead for mercy for my Mistress - *your* Mistress."

Yael stood, trembling. "You didn't tell them *that*?"

"No," Elkanta said, swaying gently, hypnotically, from side to side. "Some know, many do not, few would believe, in any event." She stared into Yael's eyes and looked her up and down as if appraising a domestic animal. "You are quite the warrior now, My Haibru slave girl, quite the hero? Who knew?" Cruel humor glinted in Elkanta's smoldering eyes. "But you are still my Haibru slave girl, aren't you?"

'Haibru slave girl,' was the hypnotic trigger Asmara had used to condition Yael and Elkanta's voice saying it now, with that same hypnotic lilt, resonated deeply. Yael's eyes widened and dulled.

"Your armor is bright and shiny," Elkanta continued. "Like my necklace. Remember how you loved to stare at My necklace? Watch it sway and lose yourself in My voice…"

"Yes."

"You would like to do that again, now, wouldn't you, My Haibru slave girl?"

"Yes."

Yael's eyes softened further as the spell began its work, and as she drank Elkanta in: the long black hair flowing luxuriously, caressing the white flesh of her naked shoulders and coming to rest on the bare tops of her full breasts; her generous hips, creamy thighs, and red painted toenails in leather sandals. Yael remembered the smell of those sandals as she licked the red-painted toes clean, the odor of Elkanta's feet and how the smell of her saliva and Elkanta's leather mingled to dull her mind and make her even more receptive; the sensation of stiff leather on her tongue, and then how she painstakingly painted those toes the same red color they were now. Who served those feet now, she wondered?

"Yes, what?"

"Yes, Mistress," Yael said.

"Come to Me," Elkanta commanded softly, gesturing.

In a deepening trance, Yael stepped around the table, moving forward until Elkanta commanded her to stop. Eyes shut, potent memories of sensual obeisance and servitude awakening with each breath, Yael inhaled deeply of Elkanta's powerful scent - a blend of warm, heavy body odor, perfume and musk; much stronger now that she was closer to her. Every breath took Yael deeper.

"Yes," Elkanta said. "Good. I had forgotten how My scent fascinated you. Good. Breathe Me in, take deep generous breaths of My odor and open yourself further to My will.

"Now, My Haibru slave girl, open your eyes." Yael obeyed, the hint of a smile playing across her otherwise blank face. "Good, feel how easy it is to obey; remember how natural and effortless it was to obey Me; and how desperately you want to obey Me now as you stare at My necklace."

Yael obeyed. Elkanta's necklace swung effortlessly, gently before her.

"As you watch My necklace gently sway, you feel yourself effortlessly returning to the days, only a few months ago, when you were deeply entranced and enslaved."

Yael's eyes were wide and vacant; warm moisture spread through her vagina as she obeyed, watched and remembered.

"Those were deeply exciting and rewarding days, weren't they My Haibru slave girl."

Ah, that sweet, powerful trigger. "They were," Yael said tonelessly, deep in trance.

"They were, who? Who am I?"

"Mistress."

"Yes, I am your Mistress, your owner. And who are you?"

"I am your Haibru slave girl, Mistress."

Elkanta smiled. "Yes, you are My Haibru slave girl. You enjoyed your days of servitude to Me, didn't you?"

"I did, Mistress."

"Those days are here again, now." Elkanta snapped her fingers; Yael's eyes closed. "You know that all that I say is true, do you not, slave?"

"I do, Mistress."

"You want to be deeply entranced and enslaved by Me and your Mistress Asmara."

"I do."

"Open your eyes and repeat, slave," Elkanta commanded.

Yael opened her eyes. "I want to be deeply entranced and enslaved by Mistress Asmara and Her slave, Elkanta."

"Good. Now look deeply into My eyes and feel My power completely fill your mind."

Yael obeyed, feeling herself go deeper, and her desire to serve and obey grow.

"Who are you now?" Elkanta asked.

"I am Your Haibru slave girl," Yael answered.

"Good. And who am I?"

"You are Elkanta, slave of Mistress Asmara and my Mistress."

"And what do you long to do, slave?"

"To please You, Mistress; to worship, obey and serve you."

"Bow down before Me, slave."

Yael knelt before her Mistress. Elkanta turned, shifted her clothing and revealed her succulent buttocks to her slave. Yael's pulse raced with anticipation. Elkanta's firm buttocks had held special power over her; and she felt that power reawaken in her.

"I know you adore My buttocks, slave, and I remember fondly how you used to kiss, smell and lick them; and what great joy it gave you to do that and be the slave of My ass. Do you remember?"

"I do, Mistress."

"In a moment I will allow you to serve My ass again. When you have satisfied Me with your lips and mouth and tongue, you shall experience an orgasm and fall into a bottomless trance that will take you still deeper into My service. When you awaken, you shall be obedient and live in servitude to Me, Mistress Asmara and the great goddess Astarte for the rest of your days. Do you understand and accept this, Haibru slave girl—for the privilege of kissing My slave ass, you will be forever enslaved?"

"I understand and accept, Mistress."

"Then begin. First, kiss My buttocks, and then part them and inhale deeply of My rectum; I have left something there for you to smell and taste."

Slave Yael obeyed and after giving her Mistress numerous orgasms and having numerous orgasms herself, fell into a deep sleep. In her deep trance state, Elkanta instructed her thus: "You shall allow Mistress Asmara's public flogging. But, when it is done, at midnight of that night, you shall come to Her chambers in the Temple and resume your service to Her. Do you understand?"

"I do, Mistress."

"Good. You will awaken in five minutes refreshed and energized. You will not remember that I was here or that you renewed your vows to Me."

---

The days preceding Asmara's public humiliation were quite full and productive. Late in the afternoon of the first day, Chief of Staff Zachary informed Yael that many of those who hadn't paid their taxes, had done so.

"It is simply amazing, Tzevah!" he enthused. "They are coming here to the Citadel, even stopping my lieutenants on routine street patrols and offering to pay."

"Excellent, Zachary," Yael was quite pleased. "I'm glad it is working."

"I know the decision to flog Asmara was difficult for you. Perhaps now that the hold-outs are coming around you can rescind your order."

Yael's face darkened. "No!" she snapped. "The order stands. Thank you for your good work. Continue to do it. You may go."

Zachary saluted, she returned it as he exited.

Yael wondered why she'd been so abrupt with him. Something at the back of her head and deep in her chest insisted that the flogging take place as scheduled. Of herself, she no longer felt anything very strong about Asmara. It felt strange to admit that, considering how both angry and turned-on she'd been just the day before. Actually, now when she thought of Asmara and Elkanta, all she felt was a peaceful certainty.

Sighing, Yael returned to her correspondence. A few moments later, Zachary returned with a well-dressed, attractive middle aged woman. Yael looked up, "Yes?" she said.

"Tzevah," Zachary said, "this woman is from Hazor. She says she is King Jabin's half-sister, and wants to talk with you. Will you speak with her?"

Yael looked carefully at the woman. She was dressed in a pale rose colored silken shawl and the heavy white robes of a pilgrim. Since living here in Charoshet, Yael had become aware of the Canaanites various modes of dress. The woman held her head erect and stared calmly into Yael's eyes.

"Yes," Yael said, gesturing for Zachary to leave. "Thank you. I will speak with her." Zachary saluted and left.

"Please," Yael said, gesturing to the chairs in front of her work table, "sit down." The woman seated herself. "Allow me a moment," Yael said, returning to the document before her, "I must finish this."

"Not at all," the women said, "please, take the time you need."

As she worked, Yael reflected on the woman's lineage; if what she said was true, she was a royal personage. How sad, Yael thought - oh, how are the mighty fallen! A wave of compassion flowed through her. Devorah and Barak had wisely not deposed Jabin and the Canaanite royal family, but the loss of the war and death of Sisera, had effectively ended their rule. Now, they were figureheads with no real power and barely enough money.

Finished, Yael looked up at the woman. She couldn't be more than forty five, but her face, though carefully painted, revealed great sorrow. Yael felt a sisterly concern. "How may I assist you, princess?" she asked.

"My son was killed in the war. I have come in search of his body." The woman's voice was soft and tremulous, but her eyes never left Yael's. "I would bring him home for proper burial."

Yael nodded sympathetically. "And what is your name?" she asked.

"Betheena."

Yael blanched and the air caught in her chest. "You are Sisera's mother?" she asked, voice hoarse.

"Yes."

"And why do you think your son's body would be here, in Charoshet, princess?" Yael's voice was soft; she knew exactly where, not far from Mt. Tabor, his body was buried.

"A seer at the Temple of Baal in Hazor told me to attend a priestess in Charoshet, at the Temple of Astarte, and that she would tell me where what remains of Sisera could be found."

"Was this priestess Asmara?"

"Why, yes, how did you know?"

Yael dismissed the question with a wave of her hand. "And Asmara told you to see me?"

"Yes."

Yael inhaled deeply and leaned back in her chair. The glimmer of hope in Betheena's sad tired eyes, touched her heart. There had been so much horror, sorrow, death and ugliness already, Yael thought, couldn't she make this poor woman's burden a little lighter? What would be the harm? Yet she had to be cautious. She had thought only Devorah and Haber knew of her relationship with Sisera, but obviously Asmara did, as well. Yael shook her head in wonder, Asmara was powerful indeed.

Yael knew she had to be careful no matter what she told Betheena; high, complex politics were involved. But, no, she thought. She should trust her feelings and her feelings told her that this was a woman-to-woman, sister-to-sister situation and when Betheena knew the truth, she'd be quite happy and there'd be no political repercussions. Besides, Yael didn't have to tell her the whole truth, just the part that would make her happy.

But what if she misjudged the woman?

Yael leaned forward, towards Betheena, who leaned towards her. "Your gods and your priests and priestesses are indeed powerful, princess. That is one of the reasons our Sar, Devorah, wants us to live in peace and community. They have directed you to the right place. I *do* know where what remains of your son reside." Devorah stood and patted her belly. "They are here," she said.

Betheena gasped, her jaw dropped open, and her eyes widened.

"I lay with your magnificent son the day he died," Yael said.

"How can this be?" Betheena cried.

"Did not your own gods vouchsafe me?" Yael's tone was harsh. "I lay with Sisera only, and none other, for weeks before and weeks after. Here lives what remains of him. He is gone, but his seed quickens in me." Yael's voice was proud. "You have a grand child, princess. You are a grand mother."

Betheena stood, walked around the table, knelt before Yael and embraced her belly. "Oh, thank you!" she said, sobbing. "I believe you. Oh, thank you!" Betheena stood, patted her tears and resumed her seat; but the tears continued. "Oh, you have no idea what this means to me!"

"You're correct princess, I have no idea; but as this child has grown inside me, I begin to have a hint of what it would mean to give birth to new life. I am glad for your joy, and glad that I trusted you. But I'm sure you realize that we can never reveal who my child's real father is. After all, I am a married woman and the Military Governor of this city. No one can know. This must be our secret. Any scandal would ruin the child's life and many others; perhaps even renew the war."

Betheena's tears had ceased; she looked radiant, as if ten years had dropped from her. Smiling at Yael, she dipped her head in agreement. "You needn't tell me about family and politics. From the time I was twelve years old, I've lived with it and seen its effects. Your secret is safe with me. It is *our* secret, now. And I will forever be grateful that you shared it with me. I hope we can work things so that I may see my grand child occasionally?"

"It will be an honor, princess. Perhaps you can take up residence in Charoshet, possibly in the Temple of Astarte. Once you are here, we can create a program for community building, reconciliation and mutual understanding that will provide an excuse for seeing me and my child."

"Yes!" Betheena said. "I will need time to make the arrangements. When are you due - looks like four, maybe three months?"

"Yes, that would be correct."

Betheena opened her arms, Yael stepped into them and they hugged long and soulfully. Deep trust, warmth and peace suffused them, and they were strengthened in their new bond and joint purpose. Finally, Betheena stepped back. "I will send word when I have returned and together we can serve the new life within you."

"Thank you, princess. I am eager to begin!'

Betheena smiled at Yael. "Please," she said, "'Princess' in public, but Baba, 'grand mother' when we are alone."

"Yes. Thank you, Baba." Yael stepped forward and hugged Betheena again.

"You have made me very happy, Yael." Betheena said, looking deeply into Yael's eyes.

"It has been a mitzvah for me, as well Baba." Yael bowed. "I feel deeply blessed. Thank you for the opportunity! And Devorah, my Sar, will be pleased that there will be co-operation between our two peoples at the highest levels."

"Yes," Betheena said. "That will not be easy, but we shall arrange things."

Yael walked Betheena down stairs and watched her palanquin depart. Zachary stood beside her. "High level diplomacy?" he asked. Yael nodded and turned to go back to work. "A moment, Tzevah. Your husband was here while you were speaking to the Canaanite. He has found a house and wants me to bring you to see it."

Yael's initial reaction was annoyance. She had already taken too much time from her work. But, she thought - I *have* worked quite diligently. Yesterday, training with the troops and developing the new uniform, weapons and food supply paths with Barak and Devorah. We *do* need a better place to live. Getting out will do me good. She smiled at Zachary. "Good!" she said. "Take me."

---

The 'house' was more like a palace, or at least so it seemed to Yael, who looked with the eyes of a peasant girl used to living in a tent. A three minute gallop from the Citadel, it was set off by itself at the edge of the city, completely enclosed behind high, washed-out pink walls. The stout oaken gates of its arched entry way were open; and neither Yael nor Zachary had to bend in their saddles to pass beneath it.

Haber and a well dressed Canaanite were waiting, standing between the front doors and a large fountain in the palm-shaded courtyard. The Canaanite seemed familiar to Yael. As they dismounted, a servant appeared from the stables at the left of the house to take the reins.

"There is another courtyard such as this at the rear of the house, Tzevah," the Canaanite said, smiling. "I think you will enjoy living here." The man was perhaps thirty eight years old, husky, 5'7", wearing a Bedouin headdress and flowing white robes with broad pale blue stripes.

*Devorah*

Yael dipped her head in acknowledgement, still not certain of where she'd first seen the smiling man. She turned to Haber, who was also grinning ear to ear and said: "How can we afford this, husband?"

Before Haber could speak, the Canaanite spoke up. "Forgive me, Tzevah. This is my gift to you. It will cost you nothing. All you have to do is pay the servants, that is all."

"I do not think we can accept, er…?" Yael angled for the man's name.

"I am Zeber," he bowed from the waist, "the grain merchant; biggest grain merchant in this part of Canaan."

"You supply the Citadel, do you not?" Yael asked.

"I do." Zeber bowed again, this time with a flourish.

"Perhaps I have seen you there," Yael said.

"Perhaps, but I think not. This is the first time we've been introduced."

"But you do look familiar to me," Yael said.

"Possibly at the Temple of Astarte; I am a devotee and financial supporter."

"Yes, that is possible." Indeed, she'd seen a great many people there when she'd been Asmara's slave. "I think somewhere else, though; some place violent. Were you in the army?" Zeber looked down then nodded. "You served with Sisera?" Zeber nodded again. "And that butcher Sostrum," Yael looked more sharply at Zeber. "Yes! That's it! I saw you with Sostrum in the Carmel and Tivon narrows."

"I was there, Tzevah. Your Devorah is a good General. She beat us decisively."

Yael smiled. "You seem like a descent enough fellow," she said. "I'm glad you escaped, and unharmed too, it seems."

Zeber bowed, acknowledging the compliment. "Thank you, Tzevah. But not unwounded. My thigh was pierced by an arrow, and, ah, my manhood was damaged when my horse rolled over on me."

"I am sorry to hear of it, Zeber."

"Thank you, my lady. I manage, and find the best possible compensation at Astarte's Temple. The maidens and priestesses treat me well."

Yael blushed slightly. "So," she said. "You want us to live in your house. Where will you live?"

"This is but one of my houses."

"The grain business must be good," Haber observed.

"War and its aftermath always create great profits," Zeber replied. "Why not share them, is what I believe - especially with the victors."

"So you would share part with us," Yael said, "so that we do not take it all?"

"In a manner of speaking," Zeber said. "But you are people of the One God, ethical people. You would not take it all."

"But you do expect something in return, don't you?" Haber asked. "I would in your place."

"Only that you and the Tzevah think kindly of me; and remember me as a friend. I will still own the house. You will live in it rent-free so long as you remain in Charoshet. That is all."

"What became of that butcher Sostrum?" Yael stepped closer to Zeber staring intently into his eyes.

The soldier/merchant took a step back. "He left me lying there, in the narrows, and rode away. I bound my own wounds, found a horse and went on to fight with Sisera at Mt. Tabor. I have not seen Sostrum since. I do not know if he is dead or alive."

Yael continued to stare silently, as Zeber stared back. Finally, she looked away. "I believe you, Zeber. You seem to be an honorable man. But I warn you, if Sostrum appears or you have any word of his whereabouts and you do not inform me, your punishment will be severe, whether we live in your house or not."

Zeber nodded. "I have no desire to protect him, my lady. You will have my full cooperation on that, and everything." He bowed, deeply. "Now, will you accept my gift?"

"She has not yet even seen the place, Zeber," Haber said.

"Of course! Of course." Zeber spread his arms wide. "Go. Look. Talk. I will wait here."

The house was cool and spacious with eight rooms on two floors and a roof top kitchen and solarium.

"It is a palace, is it not, wife?" Haber said. "We have never lived in a house, much less anything like this. How will we ever go back to a tent?"

"We may never have to," Yael said carefully. "There is no reason we can not remain in our present capacities for many years, until we are very old, when it won't matter. We can raise our family here and be part of this place. I talked with a Canaanite royal princess, Betheena, earlier today who has reason to cooperate with us, and this man, Zeber, also has reason to cooperate with us and is well connected here."

She smiled and patted her belly, turning slowly around the biggest room on the second floor. "I see us being quite happy and productive here, husband. Devorah wants us to bring the community to our side, and she is also a friend."

"Yes," Haber said. "That is true; and it is also true that Devorah demands the highest ethical behavior from her friends, staff and Military Governors. She would not want us to be taking gifts from wealthy Canaanite merchants."

"Yes," Yael said. "That would be true if the merchant expected a favor in return. That is not the case with Zeber."

Haber looked away, then slowly wandered to the stairs that led up to the roof.

---

As she stood in the street outside the walls of Zeber's compound - *no*, she corrected her thought, *my and Haber's home* - Yael saw a man in the black robes of a physician waving at her from the gateway of a similar compound some distance away. At first, she didn't recognize the man and didn't wave back. But training herself to be more of a politician, Yael waved back anyway, then started walking to the man as he walked to her; recognizing him before she got half way to him.

"Hakim Saul," she greeted him, a bit more restrained than she wanted to be. Why? Did she fear what he might remember or say? What could he say? That she'd been Asmara's slave? That was almost common knowledge and still people respected her. Besides, that episode was over now, wasn't it? Yes; but something nagged at her. And Yael was not the only one Asmara had enslaved. The priestess was feared and hated by many in Charoshet. That was why her public flogging tomorrow would be so well attended.

Hakim Saul embraced her and she felt her concerns melt away in the warmth of his muscular body, strong masculine scent and the feel of his beard on her cheek.

"How marvelous you look, Yael!" He exclaimed. "A pregnant warrior: shiny breast plate showing off a lovely womanly belly." He took a step back and looked her up and down. "Fourteen weeks at the most," he said. "And, if you keep riding and training with your troops, as I've heard that you do, then possibly only twelve!" He smiled warmly into her eyes and embraced her again. "May I have the honor of attending you when your time comes?"

"Indeed, Hakim Saul. The honor will be all mine! It is good to be near you once again; your presence is quite soothing."

He bowed deeply from the waist. "I have been meaning to come and see you since I first heard of your arrival, but the press of serving so many kept me occupied." They began strolling down the dusty unpaved street. "I have followed your amazing career with great enthusiasm, Yael." He looked deeply into her eyes, and she felt a gentle tingle in her chest. "I am proud to have been of service to you and look forward to doing so in the future."

Yael blushed and also bowed. "I will soon need weekly visits with you, Hakim. It is convenient; your home is so close to my own."

"Yes," Hakim Saul said. "I am so pleased, Yael. You are living proof that all things are echoes of the voice for God."

Yael frowned, shuddered and blinked. It seemed that a different person, a more innocent trusting woman, had first heard that phrase ages ago at Devorah's majlise. But it had indeed been her and less than a year ago. But still, *everything*? Were *all* things, even the shameful things, really echoes of the voice for God? Even the dark place deep within that Asmara and Elkanta occupied? The part she kept locked away, fearing it would escape, swamp her, and wash the best of her away? Yael shut her eyes and swayed.

Hakim Saul noticed her frown and shudder. He reached out and touched her arm to stabilize her. "The experiences from your first time here still bother you, don't they?" he asked softly. She looked into his eyes, then quickly away and down. The doctor gently squeezed her upper arm, causing her to look up at him. "Fear makes it worse, Yael. You are a courageous women; look what you have accomplished! You have nothing to fear from your past."

"But I *do*, Hakim Saul! I do!" She shuddered. "I am still their slave; I *want* to be their slave! It is not fitting to feel as I do!"

"'Fitting,'" the doctor repeated, laughing. "It is part of you, Yael! 'Fitting' has nothing to do with it! It is a dark part of you, yes, like your shadow, but still a God-given part of you. It wants to serve you and see the light of day, too! The more you keep it locked away, the more dangerous it becomes. You must let it out and use it, Yael. I think you know that."

He stared into her face and she nodded. "Good girl! Let it flow, 'fitting' or not. Trust yourself to it as you would trust yourself to any part of God's creation." Yael took a deep breath and stood taller, a slight smile on her face. "That's the spirit!" the doctor said. "You're not alone in your feelings about your dark side, your shadow. Everyone has one, even whole cultures have shadows. In fact, your desire for passionate, sensual enslavement and worship is the shadow side of our own culture.

"Remember the golden calf that Aaron fashioned when Moses took so long to come down from the mountain?" Yael nodded. "Our present culture, the culture of the Scrolls cuts off the very natural desires for loss of self, what you experience as the desire to be a slave, and sensual adornment and worship. The result is we pay more attention to these things in other cultures like the Canaanite. In fact in your new role here in Charoshet, you might be the one to help heal our two cultures, bring the shadow into the light and make us whole." The doctor looked away and kicked at the dust. "Forgive me, Yael," he said, "for preaching to you.

"And how is Haber? I have known him for many years." The doctor's eyes sparkled with joy, and a hint of something else. "I have no doubt that he, too, is enjoying your success."

"He is," Yael said. "But he also makes a great deal of it possible. He works diligently and has the wisdom to leave me alone when I need to be alone."

"Yes; good. That is as it should be." The doctor leaned forward and kissed Yael's cheek. "Now, I must go to my workplace in the city. If there is anything in addition to medical assistance you require, please, ask me."

Yael kissed him back. "Now that you mention it, Hakim; I am going to be appointing a town council. It is part of Sar Devorah's strategy to not only hold what we have captured, but to make it a part of our new nation." Yael saw from his eyes that he understood and approved. "Would you advise me on whom, beside yourself, to appoint? You have lived here many years and are a good judge of character."

"Thank you, Tzevah! I will be honored to do so." Hakim Saul bowed again. "Now I must be off." He turned and walked quickly back to his compound.

Yael looked about her, amazed that the distance to her compound; it seemed so far away. The baby kicked, she soothed her stomach, and when her hand was chafed on the breast plate, she chuckled. How clear the contradictions were, pregnant warrior indeed! A choice had to be made and it might as well be made now. This little walk had tired her out.

Seeing Hakim Saul reminded her how much she owed Sisera; how he'd saved her, and how good their sex had been. She smiled. Too bad it had been so brief. But she really did want his child; it was a fine way to honor him.

So, no more training with the troops and no more breastplate; only non-strenuous duty from now on.

Yael turned and walked slowly back to her compound. The doctor was a good man; he'd helped her in the past, she'd allow him help her again. Recalling their first meeting, she remembered how kind he'd been and how lost and desperate *she'd* been! She smiled now to recall how she was eager to return home to her tent and her predictable life with Haber; to be free - not a slave. Free of Asmara and Elkanta... And though she felt that way still, grateful to Hakim Saul for the kind and skillful care he'd given her, a strange erotic tingle ran through her in thinking of Asmara and Elkanta.

She sighed and kicked a piece of camel dung. It was good that all the soul wrenching enchantment and slavery were over. Things were not the same, now; *she* was not the same now. Yael blinked, and her mind was swept up in an image of Elkanta's curvaceous bare buttocks just inches from her face, as the full figured woman stood, hands on hips, above her kneeling Haibru slave girl. The image was gone in an instant, but left a residue of smoldering desire.

---

Zeber and Haber were standing and talking in the front courtyard as Yael passed through the archway. "Shall we sleep here tonight or at the Citadel?" Haber asked.

Yael was annoyed. "I'd love to sleep here, husband," she said. "But tomorrow or the next day will be soon enough, don't you think? We have nothing here; no bedding, clothes, soap, utensils."

"You may use what is here already," Zeber said, bowing. "Everything you might need is here and at your disposal." Haber was beaming and nodding.

"No doubt all of the finest quality," Yael said.

Zeber bowed again. "Of course," he said.

Seeing Yael not wanting to stay, Haber said, "Return to the Citadel; work a few more hours. I will remain and get things in order here; including a fine dinner." He saw she was tempted. "Think of it Yael, something new and exquisite—fresh linen, clothes and surroundings." She dipped her head in agreement. He opened his arms and she stepped into them. After a moment, she moved towards the stables.

"A moment, Tzevah," Zeber said. Yael walked to his side as Haber went into the house. "Is the public flogging of Asmara still scheduled for tomorrow?"

"It is," Yael answered, staring into his face.

"I understand almost everyone has paid their taxes. Is it still necessary to make an example of the priestess?"

"My credibility is at stake," Yael said, icily.

Zeber looked at her with a strange mixture of compassion and pity. *What is* that *about,* Yael wondered?

"Please, Tzevah, I fear more than your credibility is at stake." She looked a question at him. The eyes that looked into her own were respectful and still compassionate. "Today is the first time we have spoken, but I know a great deal about you. And I admire you. Please accept my concern when I say that should you go forward with Asmara's public humiliation, you yourself will be in great danger."

Yael was shaken slightly, but said, "From what?"

Zeber looked levelly into her face. "Deep down, I think you know what threatens you. Believe me when I tell you that you have no idea of how powerful Asmara is and how compelling her powers."

"I have some idea," Yael said. "I was her slave."

Zeber nodded. "You are strong, Tzevah; you overcame her power with Sisera's help. But you are not as strong as you think." His eyes bore into hers. "She was playing with you then; you were merely her plaything, not a true slave to her. She has the full power of Nature and the Goddess at her disposal. She has made a covenant with them. There is no greater priestess in all of Canaan! Indeed, in all our history, there has never been one such as She. If She is to be whipped it is because She is allowing it; it is a part of some larger plan of Hers."

Yael's face was tight, her hands clenching and unclenching. "What are you saying? What do you know?"

"Your soul is in danger, Tzevah. Asmara's revenge will be full and complete. You have humiliated Her twice; first by escaping from Her, and now by having the high priest whip Her. The price will be great, if you proceed. Please, I beg you, not for your own sake, but for the sake of our community. If Asmara enslaves you again and She is able to rule through you, *all* our lives will be more difficult. Awake, Tzevah Yael! You are a Tzevah, the Military Governor of Charoshet! You are no longer a Haibru slave girl. Call upon the power of your God; do not rely only on yourself to know what to do."

"Thank you, Zeber," Yael said, patting his shoulder. "I do call upon that power. Though I am deeply responsive to the power of

Astarte through Asmara, it is the same power of the One God of my people--what I have come to understand as my greater Self. Asmara has never ruled me exclusively, though it may seem so, and at times feel so. I am always guided, guarded and protect by my Covenant with the One God."

Seeing the depth of belief shining in Devorah's eyes, Zeber smiled. "Good, Tzevah," he said. "I am reassured."

"Also," Yael continued. "You no doubt have heard that your people believe Devorah to be the incarnation of Anat, and that is why Sisera was defeated." Zeber nodded. "That means, even if I am totally enslaved to Asmara, Devorah as Anat will be a counter balance to my failure in the hearts and minds of your people."

"Let us hope so," Zeber said.

Yes, Yael thought after Zeber took his leave. Yes, let us hope so; and let us hope that I will be able to call upon my greater Self and the Covenant as Hakim Saul had explained. Let us hope the bright light of the sun will banish the darkness of my shadow. Then, blinking, Yael's mind was swept up in an image of Elkanta's curvaceous bare buttocks just inches from her face, as the full figured woman stood, hands on hips, above her kneeling Haibru slave girl. This time, Yael inhaled the scent of Elkanta's nether cheeks, warm sweat, perfume and feces. She shut her eyes and inhaled deeply.

"Yes," Yael said aloud with a twisted, sensual smile, her moist tongue slithering out along her full lips to moisten them. "I will call upon my greater Self…if I can. For now, though, I can not stop what has been set in motion."

---

The next day, Yael had all she could do keep herself from Asmara's public humiliation. Normally, she would have ridden out of the city, into the hills, or trained with the troops, but the advanced state of her pregnancy made that too risky for both herself and the child. As the time approached, she became increasingly agitated. She tried working in the tower. She couldn't *see* the Temple of Astarte from there, but as the time drew near, the noise of the crowd destroyed her concentration.

Judging from the noise, she thought 10,000 people were there already. She went down to the stables. No grooms, slaves or soldiers, were present, they'd all gone to the flogging, only the horses were there stomping, whinnying and neighing at the agitation around them. The noise level was tolerable here. She wandered around the stalls, inhaling the stink of horse sweat, shit and urine coupled with the aroma of fresh strewn hay. The contrasting odors lulled, soothed and slightly aroused her. The baby kicked twice. It didn't hurt, exactly; a strange, comforting kind of pain.

Haber could have stayed with her - would have, in the days before. But he'd changed. In the nearly two months they'd been in Charoshet, a combination of the city life and his new role of husband to the Military Governor, changed the inward-looking, quiet artisan. That person was nearly gone. Yael smiled; now he was more gregarious and self aware; more like the wife of the Military Governor instead of her husband. Still, he was bearing up well, quite well.

But now she was alone. Now, Haber wouldn't have missed the spectacle for the world. Having heard so much about Asmara and having never seen her, this was an opportunity he couldn't pass up. In fact, he was confused by Yael's insistence on not going. Actually, it confused her, too. Normally she would attend this sort of event as part of her official duties. All she knew was, she just didn't want to - indeed, *could* not go.

So here she was by herself in the stables. The noise of the mob grew louder. It must have begun, she thought. She slumped down on the clean hay stacked in a corner, holding her hands to her ears. A few moments later, the noise reached a crescendo. It was done. She sighed.

Small groups of people began to pass the stable's open doors. A groom returned, then three soldiers, then more grooms and finally the flow of people in and around and the Citadel returned to normal. Yael went back to the tower. Haber joined her, moments later.

"It was amazing, Yael," he said, enthusiasm blazing from his eyes. "I am still aroused," he touched his crotch. "You really missed something!"

She stared at him. "Tell me about it," she said.

"The woman, Asmara, is gorgeous!" he gushed. "Ah, but of course you know that," he said, in response to her stony stare. "She made a speech and made a ceremony of it. It wasn't 'punishment' at all. She turned the whole thing into a full-blown worship service to Astarte. And I have to tell you, Yael, it was one of the sexiest spectacles I have ever witnessed. If this is what they do all the time, I might just consider becoming a worshipper of Astarte."

"What did they do?"

"You have been to the Goddess' worship before, correct?"

Yael nodded.

"Well it was like that: very erotic and arousing, sensual and hypnotic." Haber squeezed his crotch again. "They had a beautifully carved table on a platform behind the whipping post, and on it sat a painted, life-like idol of the Goddess." He paused, reliving the experience. "At first the noise of the mob was deafening, until later, when she commanded them to be still.

"Ten or fifteen thousand people were jammed into the Temple area. The stink of so many unwashed bodies, the pressure of other people pushing and shoving and the noise itself, put us in a kind of altered state. I was near the front of course, as befits our status here, closer to the whipping post, so I was not as affected as the others, but still," he squeezed his crotch again, "it was intense. Perhaps because I *was* so close, that added to the intensity, I had a clear view of everything.

"The idol of the Goddess was carried out to the table by four stunning temple maidens, naked but for red loin clothes. Their youthful bodies were lush and oiled. After placing the Goddess on the table, they took a few steps back and stood facing her. A moment later, four young priests, also naked but for crimson loin cloths, took up positions behind the women, bowed down behind them and began to lick and kiss their buttocks. As the priests' penises erected, the crowd fell silent and many a man around me had his hands on his own erection, as did I, and in a few places, men had dropped to their knees and were servicing the woman in front of them."

Haber stared into Yael's serious face. "Never have I seen its like, Yael." His eyes searched her face. "But I have to tell you, I was greatly aroused, and still am. I would like to lick you that way, Yael." Her face was impassive. "Do not be offended, wife, please. It is simply one of those desires I did not know I had until I had it."

The shadow of a smile crossed Yael's face. "Yes, Haber; I will allow you to lick me that way. Now please, continue your story."

Haber dipped his head and smiled. "Thank you, Yael. I look forward to it. Then, Kesher, the High Priest of Baal, came forward, brandishing a whip. He too, was mostly naked and oiled, but wore a white loin cloth. He spoke, 'In the name of Baal, the almighty, King of the gods, I welcome you!' The crowd remained silent. They knew it was not Baal who had ordained the event, but you."

Yael smiled and stroked his cheek. "Please, continue, husband," she said.

"Before Kesher could say anymore, a draped palanquin, borne by six strapping naked male slaves, followed by a heavy-set woman in harem dress, arrived center stage. A buzz rippled through the crowd. The slaves lowered the palanquin, bowed-down, faces to the floor, while the heavy-set woman stepped forward and drew back the drapes. As she did this, the slave nearest her, laid himself flat, and the magnificent woman inside stepped out onto his back. She was truly glorious, Yael, statuesque with rich, voluptuous flesh barely concealed behind gauzy, shimmering silks.

"The buzz from the crowd grew louder. She walked to the whipping post and raised her arms above her head and turned slowly, letting the crowd admire her. Here and there, people called her name. She spoke, 'The Haibrus intend to punish me. But what have I done? Nothing, I have done nothing but serve Astarte as Her loyal handmaiden. I am the slave of the Goddess—your Goddess; by punishing me, they punish you!' A few voices called out 'No!'

"'But I do not fear punishment in Her name. I welcome it! She is almighty and cannot be harmed and I partake of Her power, thus I am almighty and cannot be harmed either. The appearance of harm is not harm. Astarte rules, the Goddess commands and all obey!' Her voice was louder now and chants of 'Asmara! Asmara!' rolled through the throng. 'Feel Her power, bow down and prostrate yourselves before Her handmaiden!' she said, and many bowed down.

"I myself even felt a tug to do so. She clapped her hands and Kesher, Priest of Baal, Father of the Gods, knelt behind her, penis erect and began to kiss her buttocks, hungrily. Inspired by the sight of Kesher and the other slaves lavishing attention on the asses of the woman before them, many men in the throng fell to the knees and serviced the buttocks of the women nearest them. The chanting of 'Asmara! Asmara! Asmara!' increased." Haber's face was red and he was almost panting.

Yael's face too, was twisted with longing, but Haber didn't notice.

"Asmara allowed Kesher to serve her for some time, until she was satisfied and had an orgasm, which Kesher licked clean. By now, more than half the throng was following their example. Then Asmara spoke, 'Hear me people of Canaan. The Haibru's intend this to be a punishment, but it is a celebration of the power of our Goddess. They wanted their One God to rule over us. But that shall never be! Astarte is almighty and cannot be resisted. Look you to the Goddess' servants on the stage. They were Haibru once, but see them now, swept up in the worship of their divine Mistress! Know too, that numerous other Haibrus amongst you, are now on their knees in adoration. And scattered across our land, are still more Haibrus who bow down before the great Goddess and serve Her. Such is the power of our Mistress.

"'Our power is great and growing greater; this so-called punishment can not diminish it, and will only increase it.' A great roar came from the multitude. 'Kesher, who has just serviced Me, will whip Me. Fear not, I cannot be harmed. The appearance of harm will cause Me no pain - no matter how hard Baal's priest whips Me - for he, as I, as all of you, are slaves of the Goddess. I shall suffer no pain. It is Baal's pleasure to bow down behind Astarte and serve Her. The great Goddess loves Her slaves and will not allow them to suffer pain.'

"Kesher, still with the juice of Asmara's vagina on his mouth and beard, bound Asmara to the post. He held the whip to her lips and she kissed it. Then he whipped her: twenty lashes strongly landed. Her flesh should have been cut to ribbons, but instead, the wounds were not deep, and glowed a dull red where the lash fell." Haber shook his head unbelievingly; Yael's eyes narrowed and she shook her head knowingly. "If I had not seen it with my own eyes…" Haber said.

"What happened next, husband?" Yael prompted.

"Kesher presented her the blood stained whip, she kissed the handle and he left the stage. The heavy-set woman came forward, rubbed ointment into Asmara's back, then cut her loose. Asmara stood, raised her arms to the crowd and as they joyously acknowledged her. She got back into her palanquin and was carried away."

"Then the throng dispersed?" Yael asked. "No further speeches?"

"No; no further speeches." Haber pulled at his face as he reflected. "You know, that was a near miss, Yael." He stared into her eyes. "Fifteen thousand people; public sex; it could have been a complete disaster. As it was, it was a minor disaster for us. Asmara turned the whole thing into a triumph! Our cause has been set back. Devorah will not be pleased."

"Yes, Haber, you are correct. Devorah will not be pleased." Yael shut her eyes, shuddered, then looked at him. "I should not have allowed this. I underestimated Asmara's power."

"You did, indeed," Haber said. "That woman is almost superhuman—she hypnotized the entire multitude, did not suffer under the lash and made a political and religious statement that will haunt us for months to come."

Yael nodded. "Shall I write to Devorah about it?"

"She will know whether you write her or not. The daily dispatch rider was in the crowd not far from where I stood. He was one of those who bowed down, and when he recovered, I saw his face and it was red with embarrassment. He left the stables as I returned and I'm sure he will tell everyone in Shiloh."

"I had better write out my side of it then," Yael said, "and send it along tomorrow."

"Good idea." He rubbed a hand across his eyes. It was getting dark. "I am exhausted," he said. "I'll see you back at the compound."

Yael seated herself at her work table. "Don't expect me anytime soon; maybe not at all. I'm going to write my report to the Sar and it may take all night."

Haber blew her a kiss from the doorway. "All will be well, wife. Please do not tax yourself needlessly."

She smiled. "I will only do what is required of me, husband. Do not wait up."

Haber dipped his head and went downstairs.

An hour later, Zachary came, lit the lamps and offered to bring Yael food and drink, but she was so intent on her writing, she barely acknowledged his presence. He departed with a sad expression on his face.

Two hours later, Yael slumped onto the scroll she was writing in. How, if she herself didn't know, could she explain her deep need to punish Asmara, other than for the taxes and to establish Israelite suzerainty? Perhaps, she should rest now and tomorrow go herself to Devorah and explain as best she could. Above all, she did not want to harm or disappoint Devorah! She and Haber would still be living in a tent if it weren't for Devorah. They shared a deeper connection too, a sisterly soul connection. Yes, she thought, slumping forward, I will rest now and go to Devorah tomorrow.

# CHAPTER NINE

At midnight, the Haibru slave girl, Yael, awoke fully alert as her Mistress Elkanta had commanded, and carefully made her way to the Temple of Astarte, being sure no one saw her. She walked zombie-like through the familiar passages to Asmara's chambers and found Mistress Elkanta waiting for her there.

Upon seeing her, Yael prostrated herself at her Mistress' dirty sandal-shod feet with a quiet cry of joy. In the dim light, the heavy-set temple maiden bent forward and patted her pregnant slave's head. "Good, Haibru slave girl. I am pleased. You have pleased your Mistress." Yael lavished kisses on her Mistress' smelly feet. "Yes, yes," Elkanta said, benevolently as if to a dog, "good girl; yes, good; enough now."

She snapped her fingers, and Yael ceased licking and knelt up. "Ah, you are so good, my Haibru slave girl," Elkanta said, hiking up her robes, turning and presenting her plump but firm buttocks to her slave's adoring gaze. "Here is your reward, slave. Sniff!" Yael obeyed. "Kiss!" Elkanta commanded. Yael obeyed. "Now," Elkanta said, leaning forward a bit, "lick between my cheeks and clean my asshole." Yael obeyed, whimpering softly.

Then, suddenly, Elkanta's body, which had grown lose and relaxed with her slave's ministrations, tensed. She took a step backwards, knocking Yael over and sending her sprawling. Elkanta's body was rigid, now. Yael crawled around in front of her and saw Elkanta's eyes sightlessly bulging and the muscles of her face straining.

A moment later, Elkanta's body returned to normal. Looking around, she saw Yael on all fours. Elkanta's eyes were more piercing than ever and Yael realized that though they were Elkanta's eyes, Elkanta was not looking out of them. Power, uncontrolled jagged energy, as if from a lightning bolt, arced from Elkanta's eyes down into her own. Yael could almost hear its crackle and smell its ozone-like scent. A clever, knowing smile twisted Elkanta's full lips and tightened the corners of her eyes.

Asmara! Yael thought, with a strange erotic mixture of awe and alarm. Instinctively, she knelt up, and assumed the Position of Adoration.

"Good, My Haibru slave girl," the harsh strained voice coming from Elkanta said.

"Mistress Asmara?" Yael asked. "Is that You?"

"It is. I am pleased with you My Haibru slave girl. You have not disappointed Me. But this," she said, thumping Elkanta's chest, "this woman who has served Me for nearly fifteen years, who has given herself to Me so completely that I may, with the Goddess' grace, inhabit her body, this woman has grievously disappointed Me. In a way it is your fault, Yael. Elkanta is so enamored of you that now—as when she first met you—she is willing to risk My wrath and abuse My power, to dominate you for her own glory, and have you serve her."

Speechless, Yael simply stared, barely comprehending the miracle she beheld—Elkanta's body inhabited by Asmara. She knew miracles were possible. A miracle in the form of a downpour had given them victory over Sisera, and her people still spoke of the miracles God had performed for Moses. Apparently Astarte performed miracles for Asmara as well.

"Elkanta was to bring you to Me in the great Presence Chamber of the Temple. I am there now awaiting you. But instead, she chose to enjoy you and use you for her pleasure. Were she anyone else, or you anyone else, the punishment for this transgression would be death. But," Elkanta yawned and stretched as Asmara continued, "she is irreplaceable, as are you. Her punishment shall simply be to be around you, the object of her passion, without power over you and unable to satisfy her desire.

"Enough of this!" Elkanta drew herself up. "Come to Me now in the great Presence Chamber. Do you remember where it is?"

"I do."

"Good. My slave, Elkanta will accompany you." Asmara shut Elkanta's eyes and fell silent. Elkanta's body shuddered violently, her eyes popped open and Asmara spoke, "I have re-adjusted her mind. Once again, she is My adoring slave and no longer your Mistress. Shut your eyes." Heart fluttering, body trembling Yael obeyed and a great wave of peace swept through her. "Arise." Yael stood. "You are now empty of all but the desire to serve and please Me. Come to

Me now and consecrate yourself to My service forever." Wordlessly, Yael and Elkanta walked side by side through the winding passages into Astarte's great Presence Chamber.

They swung the huge brass double doors open, one tugging each door, and entered the cavernous space. The aroma of incense was overwhelming and as they inhaled its hypnotic scent, they became more empty and receptive with each step. Had Asmara not been in their minds beckoning them forward, they would have dropped and slept in a hypnotic trance near the huge doors.

A hundred cubits ahead of them, illuminated by ten guttering, high-mounted torches, Asmara sat aloof and elegant upon the throne of Astarte. Two, twelve foot high statues of Astarte—one with white flesh, one with black—dressed in crimson loin cloths and halters, stood on either side of the throne. Behind it, stood a twenty foot high idol of the Goddess, legs spread so that the throne was directly beneath it, flames burning in Her outstretched hands. Asmara reclined indolently on the massive wood and leather throne dressed in crimson halter and loin cloth as was the Goddess.

When Elkanta and Yael came within twenty feet of Her, they fell to their knees and bowed down. "I speak in the Goddess' holy name," they heard Asmara's voice in their entranced minds. "You are now so open to Her power that I need not use My voice for you to hear Me. The almighty Goddess' power in you allows you to hear and obey Me." Asmara pointed to the place at Her feet. Instantly, Elkanta rose up, took two steps forward, bowed down again, crawled to Asmara's feet, and prostrated herself there to become her Mistress' foot stool.

Yael gazed up at the magnificent woman seated upon the Goddess' throne. The exquisite features in the perfect oval of Her face were warm and fleshy with life, but radiated an icy stillness, a single minded focus that was not human. It was a gorgeous, attractive face, one that opened the heart, but also froze it with the promise of soulless power and uncaring, heedless death. The contrasts enthralled and mesmerized Yael. Only hinted at months ago, when she first became enthralled by Asmara, they were now more pronounced, more captivating.

"You wonder," Asmara's voice echoed in Yael's mind, "how it is that Elkanta heard Me and you did not."

"Yes, mighty Mistress," Yael said.

"You need not speak, Yael. Your mind is open to Me. I know your thoughts. As the Goddess is within all people, so am I there, especially in those, like you, who have been made receptive to Her. Astarte's rituals implant a seed of desire and obedience to Her and therefore to Me, Her greatest adept, in all who participate in them. Even those Haibrus who attended My so called punishment, even those who were exposed to the Goddess for the first time and for just an hour, have been impregnated with Her seed.

"I can access many minds, Yael, each independently of the other. My skill and power grows by the week. Your conquest of Canaan has brought many curious people to our temples. Thanks to your victory, many who would not have been impregnated, have been. And we, I and the other priestesses of Astarte, become more potent, feeding on the energy generated as each seed takes root and grows. Our power is greatest in those such as this one," Asmara nudged Elkanta with her foot, "and you, who have been trained and consecrated." Asmara's eyes flared and Yael felt a deep desire to crawl closer to Her.

"I have not yet become powerful enough to control minds at great distances, or many minds at the same time, but within this city and in any city I visit, I can awaken and nurture Astarte's seed in those who have been impregnated." Asmara's eyes flared again and Yael felt her body, even her soul, burn with erotic, servile desire. "Are you ready to consecrate and dedicate yourself to Me and to Astarte, Haibru slave girl?" The combination of the trigger phrase and all she had experienced, overwhelmed Yael. She swooned and collapsed next to Asmara's human foot stool.

Her all-powerful Mistress smiled down upon her and Yael felt it as a lightness in her head and heart. "You would like to be a perfect slave for Me, wouldn't you Yael, an immaculate vehicle for My will?"

"I would, oh, holy Mistress!"

"You yearn to give yourself to Me."

"Yes, divine One!"

"To sanctify yourself in My service, to set yourself apart from My other servants and be My mindless slave; to offer your heart and soul and devote yourself fully and completely to My service."

"Yes, yes, yes, Great One! Please, make me into Your mindless slave.'

"I will, Yael; I will make you into My perfect mindless slave, and in so doing, help you atone for your sins. You must atone, My Haibru slave girl; mustn't you? You will expiate your many sins in devoted servitude to Me."

Yael hesitated.

"Your sins are many; your guilt is great; feel the awful weight of it." Yael moaned a withering sigh. "Did you not kill Sisera, the father of your child?" Asmara asked her.

"I did."

"That was a sin against the Goddess and your unborn child and even against your people's own one God. Feel the terrible weight of your guilt." Yael moaned. "You must atone for it."

Yael was silent.

"Did you not run away from Me?"

"Yes."

"That was a sin against Me and the Goddess. You are guilty and must atone. Give yourself in eternal servitude to the Goddess and to Me, and atone."

Yael shivered and her thoughts were muddled. An image of Devorah warmed her.

"Your thoughts are known to Me, slave," Asmara said. "Your guilt is great; you must atone; tell Me you want to atone!"

"My guilt is great, I want to atone."

"And so you shall, Haibru slave girl; so you shall. Not only shall you give yourself in eternal servitude to Me and the Goddess, but you shall give that child in your belly, and your husband into My service."

Yael shivered; oh, how delicious the degradation and humiliation. How low could she fall? Her vagina dripped copiously, her body thrilled to the shameful sacrifice.

"Kneel up!" Asmara commanded. Yael obeyed, orgasming as she did so. Asmara touched Her sandaled foot to Yael's ripe belly. "Is this not Sisera's child you carry?"

"It is, Mistress."

"Was Sisera not a Canaanite, beloved of the Goddess Astarte and Her devoted slave?"

"He was, Highness."

"Then why should his son not continue in his footsteps?" Yael hesitated. "Are you not Astarte's slave?"

"I am, Highness."

"Then your son belongs to the Goddess as Her slave also, just as you and his father belong to Her."

Yael dipped her head in acknowledgement.

"Now, your husband, Haber. Was he not present at My service this afternoon?"

"He was, Mistress."

"And did he not bow down with the others, accepting the Goddess' seed?"

Yael choked, swallowed hard, almost awoke from her trance; Haber had not told her of this.

Asmara realized the Haibru slave girl knew nothing of her husband's behavior. "He did bow down with the others when commanded to. He has accepted Astarte's seed and eagerly. You will nurture it and bring him to My service."

A lascivious grin crossed Yael's features. "I shall bring him to You, Mistress."

Pleased with Yael's progress, Asmara raised a foot to her face. "Kiss," She commanded. Yael eagerly complied. "How do you feel, slave?" Asmara asked.

"I feel deeply satisfied and passionately aroused. I feel eager to obey and serve You, Highness. I long to atone for my sins, live in eternal servitude to You, to abase myself in Your service and worship, and be Your most perfect mindless slave, a willing vehicle for Your power."

"Good, slave." Asmara arose, pushed Elkanta aside and turned Her buttocks to Yael's face. "I know you adore the beauty of My succulent ass cheeks. Contemplate them now. If you please Me, you shall be rewarded with serving them—kissing, licking and smelling them. Contemplate them now as I complete re-arranging your mind."

Yael stared at her Mistress' gorgeous ass cheeks, longing for their smell, to touch her lips and face to them and bury her head between them.

"When you leave here, you will not change in any overt way. You shall seem to yourself and all others as the same woman you were this morning."

"Yes, Mistress."

"But that person is erased. You are now My mindless slave, My vehicle, open and obedient to My will. You shall do as I command."

"I shall do as You command. You are my Mistress. I am Your mindless slave."

"You shall find ways to support the Temple of Astarte. You are now a temple slave and belong to the Temple of Astarte."

"I am a temple slave and belong to the Temple of Astarte."

"You shall come in secret to weekly private worship services here in the Presence Chamber."

"I shall come in secret each week to worship the Goddess here, in the Presence Chamber."

"You shall find ways to nurture your husband's devotion to the Goddess."

"I shall find ways to nurture my husband's devotion to the Goddess."

"When your child is born, you will bring it here, to Me, to be consecrated to the Goddess' service."

"When my child is born I shall bring it here, to You, to be consecrated to the Goddess' service."

"During your private worship of the Goddess, you shall serve as My body slave, adoring Me and tending to My most intimate needs."

"During my private worship of the Goddess, I shall serve as Your body slave, adoring You and tending to Your most intimate needs."

"You want nothing more than to obey all I have commanded you."

"I want nothing more than to obey all You have commanded me."

"You are a slave, dirt beneath My feet, living only to serve, worship and obey Me."

"I am a slave, dirt beneath Your feet, living only to serve, worship and obey You." Yael felt the words deep in her heart and soul. She wanted only that they be true, that she be allowed to smell and serve her Mistress' ass and feet and body forever. Once a week was not enough! She hoped that if she was good and obedient, Mistress might grant her more.

Asmara smiled, hearing the slave's thoughts. "If you are pleasing to Me and your Goddess, slave, it may come to pass that you shall be rewarded more often. For now, once a week will be all." She bent forward slightly, opening wider the sacred valley between Her ass cheeks. "You *have* pleased Me, My Haibru slave girl. Your reward awaits. Bury your face between My buttocks and serve My ass." Yael obeyed.

Asmara also allowed Her new body slave to tend to Her warm, dripping vagina. As the slave girl tended Her in a trance of ecstatic adoration, Asmara implanted additional instructions. "Because I can read your mind, you can also pray to Me." Yael paused in her lapping. "Continue, Yael. I am pleased with your service." Yael resumed.

"Yes, what I'm telling you *is* important—you can pray to Me; you can, in a state of deep reverence, call upon Me and I will hear and answer you. Such is Astarte's power, that we may use it in Her name to honor Her. When you have need, pray to Me and I shall hear you and direct you in the Goddess' will. No need is too small My darling slave girl," Asmara gently stroked Yael's hair. "For I accept your devotion to Me and would honor it by being devoted to you, in turn. Pray to Me, Yael. You need not ask for anything or call upon Me, but let your thoughts turn often to how you feel now and offer up a prayer of gratitude and thanksgiving. Will you do that?" Yael grunted and continued her adorations.

Asmara orgasmed again and again, and soon sent Her slave girl away. Yael was saddened by their parting but knew she would soon return to her blissful servitude. As she left the Temple, her Mistress' words returned to her: *When you leave here, you will not change in any overt way. You shall seem to yourself and all others in your life as the same woman you were this morning.* Yael shook herself, like a dog shaking off water, and felt her normal, everyday persona slide over her. Now she was all business and authority, walking through the deserted streets to her new home.

---

Haber was awake, pacing the floor of the great room, waiting for her.

"You have been gone a long time, wife." His eyes searched hers.

"I was working on my report to Devorah."

"I found Zachary. He said you were gone from the Citadel. Where did you go?"

She returned his searching look. "You did not tell me that you bowed down before Asmara."

Haber blushed and looked away. "I did not want to upset you. I was carried away. I told you how moving it was. I have never experienced anything like it."

"Would you like to experience it again, but stronger and better?"

Haber's expression was a mixture of fear and eagerness. "What do you mean?" he stammered.

"You have found favor in Astarte's eyes. Asmara would like to take you deeper into the Goddess' service and her own."

In spite of himself, Haber erected; Yael noticed and smiled. "She is amazing, is She not?"

"What do you mean?" Haber said. Yael stared steadily into his eyes. Then he understood. "Is that where you've been?" Yael nodded, a strange smile pulling at her mouth. "How do you know I have found favor in Her eyes? Did She tell you?"

"She did," Yael answered. "Would you like to go to Her now, husband?"

The fear was fading from Haber's face, giving way to hope and eagerness. "Now?" he said. "It's so late."

Yael stepped closer to him, kissed him, her tongue probing his mouth; she took his hand. "Let us kneel and pray to Her, husband. Perhaps She will accept you now."

Haber was trembling as he knelt with her.

Yael shut her eyes and allowed herself to return to the unearthly blissful state she had just left. "Almighty Mistress," she intoned. "Your Haibru slave girl begs You to hear her plea. My husband, Haber, who bowed down before You this afternoon, is most willing to come to You now, and enter more fully into Your service. Is it Your will that I bring him to You now?" Yael fell silent; Haber's trembling increased.

Within three minutes, Yael heard her Mistress' voice, "I am pleased, slave; you have made Me proud to own you, it is a pleasure to rule over you. Yes, bring him to Me now, in the great Presence Chamber."

They made their way through the deserted streets, seeing no one. At the Temple gates, two guards who had not been there when Yael left an hour ago, stood, entranced, staring straight ahead, unseeing, shields and spears gripped firmly. Yael thought of the guards she should have posted at their new home, now the official residence of the Military Governor. She smiled and thought, 'what a funny thing to think about now, as I am about to sacrifice my husband to this foreign deity.'

As she led Haber deeper into the depths of the temple and the incense filled her nostrils and numbed her mind, Yael grew more aroused and empty of thought. Feeling her flesh grow warm and the juices begin to flow from her vagina, Yael looked at her husband. He, too, was showing the effects of anxious sexual anticipation coupled with the experience of the dark, winding path filled with heavy, hypnotic incense. He followed almost blindly as she led him forward, holding his moist hand. By the time they reached the Great Presence Chamber, they were exhausted and could barely stand. The huge doors were already open and Yael led her husband down the central aisle. As they came nearer to the Goddess' throne, Yael saw Asmara seated there with Elkanta still prostrate as Her footstool.

Haber had never seen a human being used as furniture before and the idea of it, the casual, indolent way Asmara used the other woman and the other woman's sighs of contentment to be so used, aroused him. Asmara read his mind and spoke to him, "That is My slave Elkanta. She is totally dedicated to My service and is in ecstasy now as I use her as My furniture. She has no higher purpose than to be My footstool. Would you like to be as she is, Haber the Kenite, beneath My feet, serving as My footstool?"

Haber stammered incomprehensibly, eyes darting between the Mistress seated elegantly on Her throne, and the slave woman on her knees before it. Yael watched him, mouth hanging open, eyes wide, vagina moist. How powerful her Mistress was! Haber's fully engorged penis stuck straight out in front of him.

"I think your desire is clear, Haber," Asmara said. "You salute Me with your manhood. Now it is time to offer all of yourself to Me. I do not take all men as My slaves, Kenite. Willingness to serve is but the first step. Now I would inspect you, to see if your body pleases Me. Remove your clothes!" Dazed, Haber hesitated. "Obey your Mistress, Haber, My slave," Asmara said coaxingly as if to a puppy. "I know you have much to learn and want to learn it. Obey Me now; show Me your body! I would inspect My property."

Haber obeyed quickly, but his nervousness was apparent in his fidgeting attempts to hide his nakedness with his hands. "A slave must be relaxed and eager in his Mistress' presence, Haber. You want to be My slave, do you not?" He dipped his head in agreement. "Breath deeply of the sacred incense, it will steady you." He obeyed and grew steady for Her. "Good boy," She said. "Now speak to your Mistress, slave. Tell Me your desire to give yourself to Me, to please and serve Me."

"From the first moment I laid eyes on You, oh, magnificent Asmara, I was moved by Your beauty and power. Since that time, I have thought constantly of You and yearned to be near You." Haber's eyes shown with true devotion. "But I did not know until yesterday, when You commanded us to bow down, that I wanted to be Your slave. Here in Your presence, in Your sacred temple, I understand that my place is at Your feet. Please take me as Your slave and allow me to be Your footstool."

"Come nearer," Asmara said. Haber walked to the throne. Asmara extended Her sandal shod foot and nudged his erection. He orgasmed instantly and copiously, his semen touching Her foot and the naked rump of Elkanta, the footstool.

"You have much training to endure, slave," Asmara said.

"Forgive me, Mistress! I had no idea that would happen. Forgive, please; do not send me away."

"Fear not, slave; you have found favor in My eyes. You shall serve Me for the rest of your life."

Haber sighed and smiled. "Thank You, Mistress," he said.

Asmara held Her foot out to him. "Kneel now and use your tongue to clean your seed from My foot and shoe." Haber knelt, cradled Her ankle in his hands and began licking. "When you have finished, lick your seed from My slave's buttocks."

Haber obeyed and Asmara sat back and watched Her new slave for awhile, then spoke into Yael's mind. "I am most pleased with you, My Haibru slave girl!"

"Thank you, Highness," Yael respond without speaking, unearthly bliss, and a deep sense of inspiration and purpose, the realization that all things especially this thing, are echoes of the voice for god, throbbed in her chest. "Your power is irresistible and it is a privilege to be in Your presence and witness as You use it." She nodded to Haber busily tonguing Elkanta's gently rocking ass cheeks. "His bliss is as mine," Yael said mentally, "as is hers," she gestured to Elkanta. "You are an inspiration, a joy and a blessing to all who serve You. Please, may I bow down and worship You?" Asmara gestured Her approval and Yael bowed down before her Mistress.

---

The next day, only a few hours after Yael and Haber had returned to their new home, a crowd, even bigger than the previous day's, overflowed the courtyard of Astarte's Temple. On his own authority, Zachary deployed the entire garrison to surround and contain it. As the multitude continued to swell and demands for retribution for Asmara's punishment became louder and more frequent, Zachary sent a messenger for Yael.

He needn't have bothered, Asmara was already communicating telepathically with Her slave. "I will appear before them and pacify them," she said.

"Thank You, Mistress," Yael responded.

"But you will come to the Temple, bow down before Me, kiss My feet and make a public apology to Me, and Astarte."

"Mistress, I am not sure that would be a good idea. My authority as Military Governor would be seriously undermined."

"You are My willing, mindless slave and will obey."

"I *am* Your willing, mindless slave, Mistress; and will obey You. But in a deep trance my apology will not appear natural. Should it not be done in such a way that Devorah will not remove me as Military Governor. What shall I tell Devorah, Highness?"

"The truth, Yael: you shall tell Devorah the truth."

"Tell her I am Your slave and worshiper?" Yael's inner voice was filled with disbelief.

"Yes, Yael," Asmara's voice was calm; and she was not calling Yael, 'slave.' "What you feel for Me, was in you before you met Me, Yael. I did not put it there, the life force did—what I call Astarte and what you Haibrus call the One God. I merely drew it forth and amplified it. That is true for Haber, also, and for all human beings. From what I have heard of your Sar Devorah, she understands the life force as I do."

"Yes, Mistress," Yael responded, "she does; in fact Devorah calls it, 'It,' neither male nor female, but both; and she says all things are echoes of the voice for God."

"Excellent. Thank you, Yael. That is as I thought. So, when you tell Devorah you have given yourself to Me, but also wish to remain as Tzevah and continue to serve her and the new Haibru empire, she will understand and see that there need not be a conflict between your worship of Me and your duty as Military Governor."

"Perhaps, Highness."

Asmara's tone became haughty. "Questioning Me is foolish, My Haibru slave girl. I have powers beyond yours and know what you must do and how it will turn out. You have but to obey. You will attend Me in one hour at the Temple courtyard to make your public apology."

Asmara's tone softened. "Hear Me and understand, My beloved slave girl. I am your shadow, the deep, dark powerful passion you have not allowed to see the light, until now. You are My slave because

I own that part of you; accept it completely; witness its power, value, honor it, and use it, allowing it to express itself, unshackled and free in the light. You adore Me and belong to Me because I value the darkness within you, allow you to use it in My service, to offer it up to Me for My approval and appreciation. And I do appreciate it, deeply."

In her mind, Yael saw Asmara hold out Her hand; and she took it gently, covering it with passionate kisses. "In your ecstatic service to Me," Asmara continued, "you embrace your shadow and become complete. I am the dark; Devorah is the light. You need both of us to be whole and fulfilled. I believe Devorah understands this as I do."

"But," she said, "If I apologize, I do not know what to say or how to behave."

"You have but to obey and have faith. You will be guided in what to say and do. Go; prepare yourself; wear something befitting your status as Military Governor. Bring your husband and your bodyguard."

Yael obeyed. An hour later, she and Haber walked between two columns of her body guard through the raucous throng. Silence punctuated by "Oos," and "Ahs," rippled ahead of the column as they neared the high dais. Asmara was nowhere in sight. Yael prayed from the depths of her soul and her Mistress answered her. "Wait at the stairs at the base of the dais. I will appear shortly. Cease your whining. I will not speak to you again, until the ceremony is completed."

As they neared their destination, Yael saw Hakim Saul not far off. For a second, their eyes touched; his shining softly into hers. Yael felt again the doctor's faith in her and her connection to the Covenant. He smiled, Yael returned his smile, then Yael turned away to wait patiently with Haber, looking up at the dais.

A moment later, they joined the cheering as Asmara took her position at the center of the platform. She looked magnificent, hair piled on top of her head, face exquisitely painted to accentuate her piercing eyes and full mouth; lush body barely covered by a thin maroon halter top and thong overlaid by a nearly transparent silken robe.

Asmara raised her arms to the sky and the multitude bowed down before her.

---

Devorah, Lappodoth and five of the Sar's elite body guard stood heavily cloaked at the edge of the throng, near enough to the dais to hear everything. Upon learning of Asmara's public punishment-turned-triumph from the post rider ten hours earlier, Devorah consulted with Barak and Lappodoth and they agreed that only she, Devorah the Sar of Israel, was capable of dealing with the potential danger in Charoshet.

For her part, Devorah thought it an opportunity, a chance to begin uniting the two cultures, not a threat. Nonetheless, they had ridden hard all night and in spite of the physical strain, Devorah felt invigorated by the exertion, the challenge and the prospect of seeing Yael again. This was the first genuine exercise and authentic challenge she'd faced since the battles against Sisera. I know who Yael is, she thought, that's why I appointed her. She's deeply passionate, ardent and intelligent; uninhibited by rigorous traditional moral codes; and totally committed to finding the best, most effective and innovative ways to achieve our goals and shared vision for their new state.

They'd been in the Temple fore-court for an hour before Yael and Haber arrived, and Devorah used the time to study her surroundings and the people around her. This was the biggest city she'd ever been in; probably three or four times the size of Shiloh. There was so much to take in: the color of the clothing; the diversity of the people—size, shape, skin color and race; and the grace and magnitude of the buildings and gardens pleased her and inspired visions of what her own people might one day be a part of. But as the square filled and the tumult grew, she became agitated and distracted by the smells, noise and press of bodies.

Yael and Haber arrived moments before Asmara appeared, almost, Devorah thought, as if their actions were coordinated. As impressed with everything she'd seen thus far, Asmara's dress, bearing and demeanor impressed Devorah more. Asmara looked like a goddess come to earth! Not that Devorah, had any idea of what a goddess was supposed to look like, never having been in a pagan temple, nor seen any idols or images, but she did have an idea.

Asmara was voluptuous, graceful, aloof and looked six feet tall. But, Devorah reasoned, that last was due to having to look up at her. She looked to Lappodoth to see what effect the priestess was having on him, and saw the same slack jawed look of wonder that was probably on her own face. The multitude was very quiet now; she felt the thrill of anticipation racing through them and her. Asmara raised her arms, and as one with a great sigh, the people bowed down before her. Devorah felt Her own knees tremble, but did not kneel; none of the Israelites did.

*Devorah*

"Look," Lappodoth said, gesturing, "Haber and Yael are bowing down as the priestess commanded!"

"Yes," Devorah said, "I wish she hadn't done that."

Asmara stretched out her arms to embrace the crowd. "Oh, mighty Astarte, hear me! I have come in Your most holy name and in the name of Your worshippers to rededicate myself and them to Your divine service." Asmara lifted her arms, lowered them to her sides and the multitude knelt up, gazing upon her.

"All power and glory is Yours oh, sacred One, and we gather here to offer thanks for Your almighty favor. There is one amongst us, a Haibru woman, a high government official, who is most grateful for Your benevolent rule and wishes to apologize and beg forgiveness for having offended You. She wishes to atone and re-assure Your worshippers that she means them, and You, no ill will. She is aware of Your power, but does not know the full extent of it. She comes in the name of peace and community to unite her people, the Israelites, with Your people, the Canaanites. A good and worthy purpose that I know You and we," she gestured to include the multitude, "support. Yet, when she sees the full extent of Your power, Your ability to work miracles, I think her plea to You will be more heartfelt."

With this, Asmara pulled the gauzy shimmering fabric from her body and stood before them in her bright red halter and thong. Raising her hands above her head as she had when she first came forth, she turned, showing the crowd her back. "Behold the miracle wrought by Astarte," she said, turning slowly. A great "Ohh!" and "Ahh!" arose from the crowd as she slowly turned allowing them all to see that the wounds inflicted on her back from the whipping of yesterday were entirely healed. Only slight pinkish tracings were visible.

Cries and cheers and praise for Astarte erupted throughout the crowd.

Haber looked at Yael, his eyes full of wonder. "She was well and truly beaten," he said, "I saw the wounds with my own eyes."

Yael said nothing. Her breathing was slowing, her eyes grew wide and vacant as she slipped into a trance. Hakim Saul saw her transformation.

As she quieted the multitude, Asmara noticed the shift in Yael but did not know from whence it came. "It is now time for Yael, wife of Haber the Kenite, Tzevah of Charoshet to beg the Goddess to forgive her for punishing me, the Goddess' devoted slave."

Whispers ran through the crowd as Yael ascended the stairs. The electric tingle of anticipation was palpable. It was obvious to all close enough to see that the Tzevah was in an altered state. She bowed stiffly, respectfully, formally, from the waist, to Asmara, then more deeply to the idol of the goddess, but did not kneel nor prostrate herself.

"People of Charoshet," her voice was thin and soft, "the ways of gods and goddesses are a mystery to me." Many in the crowd dipped their heads in agreement. Yael shook her head as if to clear it, inhaled deeply and her eyes cleared and her posture became more fluid. "As you know, I was not present yesterday when the public punishment of Asmara, priestess of Astarte, was carried out." Yael's voice was gaining in volume and resonance. "But my husband," she gestured to him, "was; and he tells me your priestess was well and truly whipped." Angry grumbling rippled through the throng. "This then," she gestured to Asmara's back, "is indeed a miracle.

"As I said, I know very little of the ways of gods and goddesses, be they yours or the One God of my people. Yet here," she gestured to Asmara's back, "do I see a power beyond human at work, a divine power." The crowd was warming to her and there were more nods and whispers of approval. "I am heartily sorry if I have offended a power such as this. I beg its forgiveness and now do solemnly promise that I will not knowingly offend it in the future.

"I also honor the power that manifests in Asmara as the same power that manifests in the One God of my people—one, invisible God, with many manifestations. In the name of the One God as It manifests in Astarte and Asmara, I further promise to serve and attend to Her until she is satisfied that I have atoned sufficiently. I want to serve Her, am deeply drawn to do so, and desire to do it. Asmara brings honor and glory to Astarte and the people of Charoshet." Applause and soft cheers arose from the throng.

"All of this I do promise in the name of peace and harmony between our two peoples and in the name of Devorah, my leader and the Sar of our previously two nations that are now one. I said I know nothing of gods and goddess; that was not the whole truth. I do not know a lot, but what I do know I would share with you now." A hush enveloped the multitude and they leaned forward expectantly.

"The power that Asmara uses to enslave; the power Astarte used to heal Asmara's wounds; the power the Children of Israel used to overcome the great and powerful army of Sisera," moans from the crowd, "is one power. We, you and I, have this power within us, now, this moment. As we honor our gods and goddesses and live in peace and prosperity with one another, we are using that power. It is my purpose and intention and that of my Sar, your Sar, Devorah, to use that one power to bring forth an era of peace and prosperity unknown until now. I beg you to join with me in this endeavor. Long live Astarte, long live the One God and long live Asmara, priestess of Astarte!" As the crowd roared its approval, Yael knelt and kissed Asmara's sandal-shod feet.

---

"Then what did Devorah do, Mother?" Abadantha asked, her face flushed with excitement.

"She waited a moment and when Asmara commanded Yael to rise, Devorah went onto the dais and embraced her. Yael returned the embrace with deep heartfelt gratitude. Asmara, who was reading Yael's thoughts and knew who Devorah was, joined in their embrace. The crowd, not sure what was going on, was eerily silent.

"When the three beautiful women stepped back from their embrace, Yael stood between her Sar and her Mistress and raised their arms with hers. 'This is Devorah, Sar of Israel, your Sar and my leader and commander.'

"A strange, disconcerting hush hung over the multitude. Then, as a few people began to talk to one another, someone shouted out: 'Anat! Anat! It is the Goddess Anat!' Others repeated: 'Anat! Anat!' and soon it became a chant, then a roar: 'Anat! Anat!'

"Asmara seemed confused. She looked from Yael to Devorah. Of course she knew who Anat was, but until that moment, she hadn't fully understood how deeply the people believed the rumor that their war goddess Anat, had incarnated in Devorah. As Devorah/Anat waved to the crowd and gestured for them to be still, Asmara shuddered as she clearly understood the strange power of the One God and the need to cooperate with it."

Janina saw recognition in Dantha's eyes, and she continued, "When the crowd quieted, Yael spoke again: 'As you see, Sar Devorah accepts your priestess and accepts my dedication to your priestess. Today, the promise of our new nation, yours and ours, is fulfilled. Peace, power and prosperity are ours through the one power that rules us all. Welcome her; welcome Devorah, Sar of Israel and Canaan, daughter of the Covenant!'"

Tears of joy and passion ran down Janina's cheeks as she said the stirring words and completed Yael and Devorah's story.

"Why do you cry, mother?" Dantha asked.

Janina sniffled and wiped her eyes and nose with a cloth. "I cry, darling, because it is such a wonderful ending; and because I am so very sad that the promise of those words and those lives eludes us still. While Devorah, Yael, Lappodoth, Barak and the others lived, our ancestors enjoyed peace, harmony, mutual understanding and prosperity through the wisdom of the One power in its many forms, including Astarte. But after they died, their children and their children's children drifted from the spirit of the Covenant.

"They lost themselves in the material world and the appearances of an existence separate from Spirit. And the very things that were a cause of hope for Devorah, Yael, Lappodoth and Barak—the tolerance of other religions and the worship of Astarte, the movement into cities, the integration of the two peoples—Canaanite and Israelite, and the slow development of the new centralized state of Israel and the gradual weakening of the tribes - has all led to the unsettled conditions we experience now.

"The work they began is incomplete. There is much left to do." Janina looked deeply into Abadantha's clear green eyes. "And I think, daughter, you and your brother Saul will have great parts to play in that work. It is in your blood and genes."

Dantha looked down. "Mother," she said shyly, after a long pause, "when you told about Yael's worship of Elkanta and Asmara I felt something here...." She touched her groin. Then, looking into Janina's warm brown eyes, she asked, "Does that kind of worship still go on?"

"First, there is nothing wrong about what you felt. It is natural and very powerful. As you heard, even a great warrior like Yael succumbed to it. You, too, may feel its pull and passionate heat, perhaps even to dominate another, as Asmara dominated Yael, or to *be* dominated as Yael was. But that power is a part of the One God and our covenant with It. We seek not to use that power as the Canaanites did, and as they have grown closer to us, they too, have ceased using it in those ways. But the Philistines still use it in those ways—to dominate and be dominated, and to worship as the Canaanites did."

"I would like to experience it," Abadantha said simply, eyes sparkling.

Janina swallowed her fear, remembering that she herself had had a similar reaction when her mother told her the story of Yael and Devorah. She reached out and stroked her daughter's cheek. "One day you shall, Dantha; when you do, remember that all things are echoes of the voice for God."

"Yes, mother," Dantha said, gazing up at the heavens. "I always try to remember that. Even now, even while I'm looking at the stars, I'm remembering it."

"Yes, my heart. I know." Janina reached out and embraced her daughter; happy, yet remembering Saul's voice as he played, sad, too. Swallowing hard, Janina held Dantha at arm's length and stared into her clear green eyes. "The desire to feel things here," she patted Dantha's heart, "and here," she patted Dantha's groin, "and to do things in the world, as your brother wants to do, is a physical link to the mystery of devotion and the ecstasy that our embodiment of the Covenant and the One God brings forth.

"We women inherently have what men do not, daughter, a deeper sense of how to receive and use love, the true power of the Covenant here in the world—whether it is the communion of one body with another in sexual surrender or in the welcoming of the Covenant into our thoughts and deeds." Dantha nodded solemnly.

"Your brother will need your help to understand this. He will feel both the Covenant and the Scrolls; he will act, torn by his conflicting feelings, but he will not understand what is happening to him without your help."

Janina sighed, smiled and patted Dantha's cheek. "Your desire to experience what Yael experienced in her worship of Astarte and her servitude to Asmara is a great gift, my daughter!"

"Truly, mother?" Dantha asked, face long and serious. "It feels awkward, almost wrong."

"It is wrong, if you examine it from the perspective of Yahweh and the Scrolls. Instead, see it from the perspective of the Covenant and the knowledge that there is only One God, one force in and behind all things: male and female, human and animal, Israelite and Canaanite. You already do understand this, my darling girl, and as you grow, you will not fear your deepest sexual and spiritual desires, but will bless and honor them - and in so doing, bless and honor the mystery of life and your devotion to the Covenant."

"Saul is almost incapable of this, isn't he, mother?" Janina nodded. "Then," Dantha said as she stood, opening her arms wide to embrace everything and nothing, "I will share my gift with him!"

# Saul

# The Covenant and the Scrolls
## Book Two

## Preview

*Book Two aims to render Saul, first King of Israel, a human being while addressing a number of intriguing contradictions in the Bible's telling of his life.*

*First, the Bible depicts Saul as hero, sinner, and tragic tormented figure, chosen by God as the savior of Israel, then condemned by Him. Given that both he and David were sinners, why was Saul singled out to be utterly rejected by God, while David is given a divine promise of eternal rule? One explanation might be that history is written by the victors and—given the titanic struggle between David and Saul—David's victorious partisans made Saul worse than he was to make their man look better.*

*Second, King Saul is not mentioned in any source outside the Bible. Although there are archaeological and historical data paralleling the high points in Saul's story,* is *he a real person or a mythological one?*

*Third, the Bible is not clear on* when *Saul was King. The book contains a single, garbled verse describing Saul's age at the time of anointment and the length of his reign:* "Saul was...years old when he began to reign; and he reigned...and two years over Israel" *(I Samuel 13:1). Contemporary scholars believe that the text is defective on these points and given the long sequence of events attributed to King Saul, twenty two years is more likely than two. Some scholars have even speculated that perhaps the reigns of Saul and David overlapped.*

*Fourth, though the Bible says that Saul was King over "all of Israel," most of the activity it describes happens in Saul's home territory of Benjamin, immediately to the north of Jerusalem, extending further north to the land of Zulph, in Devorah's beloved hill country of Ephraim, with occasional forays across the Jordan to Gilead in the east. All the detailed descriptions of activity south and southwest of Jerusalem are only contained in Saul's pursuits of David or in the stories of David alone. Perhaps Saul was not King over "all of Israel" but only over the north, while David was King in the south.*

*These are just a few of the intriguing contradictions in the Bible's descriptions of the first and second Kings of Israel. They might be forgiven, considering that the best evidence suggests that Saul and David lived around 1030-1010 BC - well over three thousand years ago, and that their stories were incorporated into the Bible two hundred years after that.*

*But who were Saul and David, really? The Bible offers only a framework, a starting point for understanding them. Of what were their hopes, dreams, fears, lusts, loves and everyday lives composed? This story is an attempt to resolve the biblical contradictions and answer those questions. If only a portion of the Bible stories about Saul and David are true, their lives are worth knowing, the contradictions worth resolving, and the answers worth having.*

# About the Author
# Steven Liebowitz, Ed.D.

Dr. Steve has been married to his first wife, Tanya, for 42 years. They live in South Florida with their two dogs Zachery and Zoe.

He began his career as an educator in 1966 when he completed his training to be an English teacher with the Peace Corps in Ethiopia. Now with forty-one years of experience as an author, public speaker, coach and consultant, Dr. Steve specializes in building individual and organizational strength from within.

Dr. Liebowitz received his Doctorate in Human Resource Development from Florida International University in 1991. He also holds Masters Degrees in Health Care Management (Florida International University, 1977), and Public Administrations (Florida Atlantic University, 1974). For the senior year of his undergraduate degree, a dual Economics/Political Science major from Drew University in Madison, NJ, Steve studied in Europe at the London School of Economics and the Free University of Brussels.

Throughout his 27 year career with Miami-Dade County, Dr. Liebowitz kept active in the South Florida Community. He was one of the founders of the Miami Chapter of the American Society for Training and Development in 1970; served as its President in 1974. He also helped found Hospice, Inc., now known as Vitas, and served as President of its Board of Directors. He served two terms as President of the Board for the F.I.U. Alumni Association; as Board member of the International Coaching Federation, South Florida Chapter; two terms as President of the National Writers Association South Florida Writers

Chapter, now South Florida Writers Association; and was active in the South Florida Chapter of the American Society for Public Administration, and the Florida Speakers Association.

Along with teaching at F.I.U., St. Thomas, U. of M. and Miami Dade College as an adjunct professor, Dr. Liebowitz served as an educational innovator on the faculties of the University Without Walls successor, the Union Institute in Cincinnati, and on the National Faculty of Pepperdine University in California. Dr. Liebowitz has also pioneered programs in computer assisted instruction and distance learning.

Among those to have recognized Dr. Liebowitz for excellence are Junior Achievement Inc., International Society for General Semantics, Leadership South Dade, the M.E.E.D. Program, the National Association of Counties, the Bass Museum of Art and the Children's Museum of South Florida. His non-fiction book, *The New Professionalism: Connecting Science and Spirit*, was published by Harmony-Quest Publications in 1998.

Dr Liebowitz served in the US Army from 1966 to 1969. Serving with the Strategic Communication Command at Ft. Ritchie, MD; the First Logistical Command, Saigon Support Command, Viet Nam, where he was in country for the first Tet Offensive; and the European Electronic Intelligence Command, Weisbaden, Germany, where he arrived just in time for the Soviet invasion of Checkoslavakia.